Antiques To Die For

Antiques To Die For

To Fran –
Who loves a
mystery
Enjoy!
PL Hartman

by

P. L. Hartman

Strategic Book Publishing and Rights Co.

Strategic Book Publishing and Rights Co.
12620 FM 1960, Suite A4-507
Houston TX 77065
www.sbpra.com

ISBN: 978-1-62516-746-0

For my fellow antiques dealers, past and present, who unwittingly aided and abetted.

And for Bill, my fellow conspirator.

The past is always present: yet it is not what was, but whatever seems to have been.

G. K. Chesterton

The past is always there, lurking around. If it were a snake, it would bite you.

M. Yeager

CIDER RUN ANTIQUES

Partners

Marv and Helen Yeager
Hal and Sylvie Thompson
Jake Gennari and Annette Durand

Dealers

Ruth Arden
Sally Ann O'Neill
Laurel Fisher (Joe)
Owen Griffith (Lynn)
Cora Lehman (Bob)
Grace Dutton (Frank)
Emmy Greene (Charles)
Richard Keating
Keith Mackinnon (June)
Elaine Barr (Kurt)
Andy King (Mable)
Clair Somers

Chapter 1

The body was found at 10:15 on a May morning, a fine, fair morning as unsuitable to the horror of murder as anything could be.

A blue untroubled sky, soft and subtle, spanned from ridge to ridge. Across the valley on the hillside, the sun was picking out and intensifying the bright yellow greens of new leaves. Beside the shop where remnants of an old orchard stood, apple trees, long-forgotten varieties from another era, basked in the morning light, while their pink blossoms, sparkling from last night's rain, presented an aroma sweet and ancient. Cardinals and finches trilled non-stop and blue jays darted between branches. Even the stone building, a leftover from past centuries, took on a warm hue, the way stone can absorb and make itself comfortable in any season.

Comfort, longevity, birdsong, light and warmth, color and fragrance: into this abundance of reflective and sensory pleasures, murder intruded itself, cruelly, irrevocably. It rearranged things, thrust away complacent, familiar assumptions of the past and caused a shifting and heightening of perception. The past, the far past, the hidden world in which the hills were shaped and the trees planted, and the combination of all the other events that went into the creation of this morning's incomparable setting, receded in importance. Taking its place was a sharp awareness of the last two years and of the very recent past, as recently as last night.

But for forty-five minutes, from the time the first person came driving up until the discovery of murder was made, all was tranquil, all was serene, except for the birds' exuberant singing. All was as it should be, and the normalcy of those forty-five minutes gave the people there time to appreciate the day, go about a morning routine, socialize briefly—in short, brace themselves, although they didn't know it, for what was to come.

At 9:30 Ruth pulled into the gravel parking lot in front of the shop and backed her car close to the door. It was loaded, the result of a week's antiques buying in New England. Boxes of ironstone china, a pair of pine chairs painted a dark green and decorated with a stenciled flower design, and a walnut demi-lune table were wedged in the back. More boxes held glassware, including a berry bowl set in pattern glass, and resting on the passenger seat, carefully wrapped in pale blue padding, was a beveled-glass mirror framed in oak. She could take some items in now, she thought, looking around the car's packed interior, but Marv had been adamant about her not unloading the heavier items by herself, and everything was heavy. No sense injuring her shoulder again as she'd done before, hauling furniture and boxes of crockery. Ruth was just as glad to wait until he got there and, anyway, last night when they talked, Marv had said he'd be in early.

"I need to shift things in my area so I can get the corner cupboard in tomorrow. I did tell you about the corner cupboard, didn't I? Poplar, the original red paint, from a farm in Bucks County. I saw it last fall and was all set to buy, but the people weren't sure they really wanted to sell. So this past week I went back to see them just, mind you, to make sure it was as stunning as I remembered and, amazingly, they offered it to me."

"But only after you played on their sympathy," she had replied with a laugh. "Let me guess: did you possibly tell them it was a twin of the one that belonged to your old Granny and you had to have it?"

"Ruth! Would I do that?"

"Without a qualm." What delightful bit of fabrication had he used this time? When it came to acquiring antiques, Ruth knew that his inventiveness could be almost inspired.

"You're right. But, actually, I only had to convince them it was going to a good home. They capitulated when I described Cider Run in all its 200-year-old limestone perfection. Of course, I didn't let on it was a shop. But wait till you see it, Ruth. You'll love it."

And that's another thing about Marv, she thought. His enthusiasm for antiques is unquenchable and infectious.

Ruth got out of her car and walked to the edge of the parking lot where she could feast her eyes on the hillside. It was almost a ritual, looking at the hills, and the other dealers as well as many customers were also drawn to look out across the valley. Here was one of the most glorious views imaginable, Ruth thought, come upon inadvertently, as a bonus to people going to Cider Run. Even though the shop was perched only a few blocks up from a busy thoroughfare, it gave the impression of being far removed from the traffic. By holding her arm just so, she could completely block out the road below and let her eyes rest on the hillside, wander to fields and farms on the lower slopes and to woods climbing the ridge on up to the ridgeline.

Retired school principal, former teacher and life-long antiques collector, Ruth had thought she'd never again move away from her native New England, from being near the coast with its stiff sea breeze, the kind that cleared the head and blew away illusions. She had felt compatible with that environment. Yet here she was, land-locked between long, graceful ridges of the Appalachians, most elderly of mountain ranges, worn down through eons and ice ages, but still formidable. And beautiful, mantled in hardwoods and mountain laurel and ever changing with the seasons.

Ruth gazed appreciatively, not only taking in the beauty of the hills in their present spring green, but thinking how daunting the mountains must have seemed, how impenetrable, when viewed by settlers making their way westward in covered wagons. From where she stood she could imagine the whole panorama, mountains rolling away, ridge upon ridge, concealing the gaps which made passage possible. But the gaps were there, and the pioneers found them. For Ruth, it was a liberating thought; things only seemed insurmountable. She felt a resonance with the courage of the settlers, to pick up and move, with all their belongings, and make their way across the mountains. And then, antiques dealer that she was, her thoughts turned to those belongings and, mainly, the white ironstone china which would have been stowed inside the covered wagons, the china that went west with the pioneers and hardly sustained a chip because it was so strong. The same kind as the century-old ironstone packed in boxes in Ruth's car, waiting to be taken into the shop. There was resonance in the ironstone too, and to handle it and use it was like being part of another time.

Familiar thoughts, pleasant thoughts, as she stood in the sunlight of a May morning.

It had been two years since Ruth's brother had convinced
her to move down to the Pennsylvania town where he and his
family lived. She'd had difficulty making the decision, and
in the end it was antiques that tipped the scales. For several
summers she and a couple of friends ran a small, briskly busy
antiques shop in Maine. Busy in the summer; it was not the
place for a year-round enterprise. When, as yet undecided,
she first visited Cider Run, workmen were still finishing the
interior renovations, but she could see how well-configured
the shop was, how it would suit her. And Marv, the day she
came in, let her know he wanted her to be part of it.

Now she was attuned to this environment and, standing
there admiring the view, musing on the past, car stuffed with
antiques, she felt very much at home. She had, she thought,
at last let go of the reserve that had marked her personality,
the holding back, as if something were ever ready to throw
in a note of caution, telling her to suspend belief. It was
true she'd had a few heartbreaks, but the basis of her self-
image had been formed early and without her consent:
some Viking ancestor's carelessly bestowed genes had
blessed her, or in Ruth's opinion cursed her, with red hair.
Being the only one so inflicted in her family and among her
friends, Ruth thought herself an ugly duckling. She spent
her childhood under the shadow of freckles, pale skin and
bright copper curls, having to endure the nicknames and
taunts that are the lot of the redhead, not able to have the
golden suntans other girls had or wear the luscious colors
they wore. For a child it was something almost shameful,
as if it were her fault. To compensate for this disastrous
flaw, she developed kindness and humor, and the backbone
required to withstand her affliction. That people thought
her lovely as she grew older was lost on her. And, as a result,

after she was grown up, she had been genuinely surprised when men sought her out.

But now, in her late fifties, as the red in her hair began to fade, or maybe partly because of it, she had laid much of her former ways of thinking aside. She had a new life in a new location and the location itself, today in particular, was splendid. With a final deep breath of the morning mountain air, Ruth turned and walked back to the shop, thinking to herself, it's a perfect morning; it is going to be a perfect day. Had Marv come in last night as he said he might? She noticed that the gravel had plenty of tire marks, some ruts still holding water. Busy place, Ruth mused, as she unlocked the door.

Inside the old stone building the dampness from last night's downpour lingered, bringing out even more the shop's characteristic mixture of aromas. Ruth sniffed appreciatively. Eau de antiques shop, she called it: mustiness combined with the acrid smell of oak, furniture polish and an occasional sharp tang of mildew—individual accents, blending harmoniously with each other. All in all, thought Ruth, very satisfying, very complementary, and without which it would be like a winery when there is no scent of the crush.

Another odor joined in, the fresh air Ruth had brought in with her. But the shop didn't open until 10:00 and they were not ready for business yet, so she locked the door behind her and set about turning on the overhead lights, the computer and printer, the surveillance monitor. Then, stashing her bag behind the front counter, she began to go around the shop, switching on lamps in dealers' areas and lights in their display cases.

The entrance to the shop was by way of the original door location in the south-facing wall. When the owners remodeled, an entrance foyer had been created, delineated by one arm of an L-shaped front counter on its left and an old church pew, some ten feet in length, on its right. The main part of the shop was laid out with fourteen separate dealers' areas. These were located along the front, south-facing wall to the right of the church pew, and along the west and north walls, with several placed back to back in the center of the room. Along the east side were the doors to the two restrooms, and also the swinging door that went in to the kitchen, and from there to the office, storage room and the back door. The shop layout made for good circulation and also gave it the feeling of wholeness. The areas seemed to flow into each other, marked off only by often-changing pieces of furniture or the display cabinets of individual dealers.

Not being at the shop for over a week, Ruth enjoyed seeing what was new, what had been brought in lately. She'd check on her own sales when she got back to the computer at the front counter, but in the meantime, she was interested in catching up on what other dealers had done while she was away. As she went from one area to the next, she was aware once again of the pleasure, the privilege, of being among such a variety and abundance of antiques and, in this brief, quiet moment in the morning, having it all to herself.

Clair had put in a whole new display of 1920s and earlier spring garden party hats in straw and fabric, adorned with leaves and flowers, ribbons and lace, and had them hanging on pegs on a white lattice rack. Nearby, head-high, was a white wicker framed mirror. A very tempting invitation, Ruth thought. Clair certainly knew her clientele.

In the Thompsons' area there was a white painted Hoosier kitchen cabinet she had not seen before. Sylvie had put green Depression glass plates, cups and saucers on the shelves and placed green wood-handled mixing spoons and forks in the open drawer. And, nice touch, thought Ruth, she even had a couple of green McCoy bowls on the top.

Cora and Grace had a combined area. Like Ruth, they were retired from public school teaching careers; Cora had taught art, Grace first grade. In their area a dozen children's books had been placed on a maple school desk, over which was propped a sign that said *SPRING READING* with a watercolor of a boy and girl in old-fashioned dress reading books under a pink blossoming tree. This would be Cora's doing. Ruth saw another new item, a walnut Eastlake-style washstand holding a set of green transferware china pieces, not just the ewer and basin, but toothbrush holder, soap dish with lid, shaving mug, drinking cup and, sitting on the shelf below, yes, the chamber pot. What a find, thought Ruth. All that was missing was the footbath, but they were almost impossible to come by. This was Grace's contribution to the green-for-spring theme that several of the dealers had featured.

Ruth continued on, passing Sally Ann's area, reminding herself that she was working with her today. Sally Ann specialized in the Thirties, Forties and Fifties, a time which yielded objects in some of the brightest and most cheery colors. Her area was a mish-mash of white painted furniture, Fiesta plates and cups, floral and fruit patterned tablecloths, Bakelite and other costume jewelry, Life magazines, chenille bedspreads, clothing from the era and anything else she could get in. She also had baskets full of gaily printed hankies, which were replaced as the season suggested. Now they were all flowered, but in February there had been ones with hearts and cupids. Sally Ann's collection as a whole gave the impression of a kaleidoscope, but Ruth was not surprised that her things sold and sold well.

Richard showed more restraint. In his area there was an early pine blanket chest, Amish probably, the top thrown back, displaying a quilted coverlet of blues and greens. So seasonal. So Richard.

An oak bookcase with a carved design caught Ruth's eye as she came to Elaine's area. The shelves held Elaine's collection of dolls ranging from the late 1800s through the 1950s. Dolls, Ruth had often thought, seemed incongruous for Elaine, with her sophisticated style and her cigarettes-and-whiskey voice. Richard had once said to her, "Dolls, Elaine? You?"

"Don't look so incredulous, Richard. I've been collecting dolls since my first Madame Alexander."

"When was that, back in the 19th century?"

"I will ignore that remark, Richard, because I have sold more dolls in one month than you have sold quilts all year."

"I'm always rather sad when I sell a quilt; a little part of me is gone. I relinquish them with a sigh and a heavy heart," Richard said with a suitably mournful expression.

"Pah!" scoffed Elaine.

But Elaine had knowledge and savvy about the dolls, and also about the rest of the antiques she sold, and her customers trusted her expertise. Ruth, however, was more interested in the bookcase. I hope she has a NOT FOR SALE tag on it, Ruth thought, if she wants to use it for display. Bookcases just flew out the door in a college town like this.

In Marv's area Ruth noticed that the big mahogany four-poster bed was gone, the one that had taken up so much room and caused Helen such consternation. Still, there didn't seem to be space for the corner cupboard. He'd have to do quite a bit of reshuffling.

There was a blanket chest in Jake's area that must have just been brought in, this one a large oak Mission style, the lid closed. Ruth had to admit that Jake had excellent, understated taste. Also, he had the choice area around the hearth, for which there had been some vying among the partners. Early in the history of the building, a stone fireplace had been built into the north wall. It was still a functioning fireplace, a real link to the past. Ruth thought how it lent an authentic touch with its heavy oak mantelpiece. Now, through the chimney, she could hear birds singing in the orchard. As she bent to move a piece of furniture that was pushed too close to another, Ruth saw a museum guidebook lying on the floor and retrieved it. There was always a little tidying to do first thing in the morning, she thought. Whoever had worked the day before had also forgotten to turn off several of the lamps, but that happened frequently, dealers being in a hurry to close up after a long day.

Ruth moved on, appreciating what she saw, until she came to her own area where she stood, hands on hips, surveying her domain and planning how she'd rearrange things.

At 9:45 the white Mercedes sedan belonging to Sally Ann turned into the parking lot and crunched its way along the gravel to park, slightly at an angle, next to Ruth's car. Not a terribly good driver, not a car conducive to antiques drayage, not a pair of shoes to stand around in all day, but that was Sally Ann. "Honey, I was all set to live happily ever after with Fred, but he had to go and have that heart attack and die on me!" And leave her very well-off, so that she could travel about on buying trips, enjoy her antiques business and keep an eye out for husband number four.

To do her credit, she picked up interesting things and her colorful area was matched by the clothes she wore, her vibrant makeup, her ever-changing blonde hairdos and her outlook on life. This morning, in honor of spring and sunshine, she wore a primrose-yellow skirt with a fluttery gathered flounce at the hem and a vivid pink blouse with ruffles at the deep V-neck. There was motion in this outfit, although sometimes the motion occurred independently of the wearer.

Sally Ann backed herself awkwardly out of the car, almost spilling a large box of doughnuts and jiggling some of her coffee down the side of the cup. Then, like Ruth, as if pulled by an irresistible urge, she walked gingerly in her fuchsia pumps, carefully avoiding the puddles, over to the edge of the parking lot to look at the hills beyond.

She stood for a minute or two, thinking about her wardrobe and the infinite possibilities the day held. Would it be today that he walked through the door, altering her life forever? Would she change her style of dress as a result? It didn't seem likely, but if so, she felt up to the challenge. Then, having recognized Ruth's car and eager to find out about her trip, she turned and walked back to the shop. She fumbled in her matching fuchsia bag, found her key, unlocked the door, got herself in, relocked it, and announced, "Ruth, I'm here!"

Ruth glanced up and, catching sight of the brilliance that had just appeared in the doorway, burst into a smile and exclaimed with genuine appreciation, "Sally Ann! Springtime personified!" and saw the happy look it brought to Sally Ann's rose-blushed face.

Sally Ann had taken note of what Ruth was wearing too, and thought she was dressing much more becomingly of late. She was intrigued. Was there some new love in Ruth's life? It looked that way. Sally Ann was convinced exciting things were happening to Ruth and was ready to share in any romantic emanations that might be in the vicinity. It would be an interesting day, she was sure.

Ruth went back to work and Sally Ann chattered away as she fussed about the front counter getting things ready for the day. "Oh, you got the lights already. Thanks, Ruth. I brought doughnuts. Did you see the Thompsons' Hoosier? That won't be here long! I'll count out the change in the drawer. When are you going to tell me about your trip? I can't wait to see what you bought! Who left this CD with the really sad music on the player? How about if I put on Hits of the Forties and Fifties and the one of Big Bands? Don't you think it smells musty in here? It always does after a rain storm." And so on, as she went about the shop routine.

Ruth, listening to her, called out, "Great! Whatever! Thanks, Sally Ann," as appropriate, and resumed moving things to clear a space for the table and chairs waiting in her car. The teapot and almost-matching cups and saucers she had brought in shortly before she left were gone and she moved the square oak fern stand that had held them to one side, regrouping some small pots on it which had previously been sitting on the floor. And then, she thought, she could arrange some of the ironstone on the half-round table when it was brought in. White ironstone would look nice against the dark wood, and maybe she could borrow some English silver from Emmy's area to add to the effect. Emmy—husband a professor but, unlike Marv, not retired yet and always taking Emmy off to Europe, where she buys antiques, particularly silver. In fact, aren't they there now?

Rousing herself to wonder if Sally Ann needed her help at the front, she headed that way and saw Sally Ann go to the door and unlock it, just as some of the repeater clocks that had been wound and actually kept time started chiming the hour. At the same moment, Laurel could be seen outside the glass door, baby straddling her right hip, diaper bag slung over her shoulder, left arm encased in a truly ugly faded red velvet lampshade and left hand holding the rest of the lamp. She had partly turned, preparing to push the door open with her backside, but was spared the indignity by Sally Ann coming to the rescue and holding the door for her.

Laurel said with an apologetic smile, "Thanks, Sally Ann. I could have gotten it. This big rear end of mine should be useful for something."

Big rear end? Nothing, thought Sally Ann, could be farther from the truth. Laurel is so slim and elegant in those silk shirts and designer jeans, and she's married to a doctor at the hospital and what does she sell? Shabby chic! Sally Ann's thinking was linear, albeit with breaks in the line.

But aloud she exclaimed, "Laurel, that baby has got to be the most adorable thing I have ever seen! What is Ben now, six months old? The miracle baby! Do you want me to watch him while you're busy? He isn't crawling yet, is he?"

Laurel laughed and set the baby down on a small Persian prayer rug in the middle of her area. "Any day now he will and then I won't be able to trust him to stay put anymore. I've just got a few things to do and then we're off, but thank you for offering."

Ruth joined them to express her admiration for the baby. Then, since Sally Ann had already dealt with the cash drawer, she decided to return to her work while she could. With a "Call me if anyone comes in," she went back to her area.

"Call me if you need a doughnut," was Sally Ann's reply, as she opened the cardboard container and put it out on the front counter.

Normal conversations, friendly conversations, a little socializing, a little busy work.

Ten minutes past ten o'clock. I'm glad there are no customers yet, thought Sally Ann, as she toddled around the shop in her high heels, sipping coffee and munching a sour cream doughnut.

"Ruth, did you see this blanket chest in Jake's area? He shouldn't have it closed. I'll bet there's that little box with the hidden compartment inside."

Not one to let her curiosity go unsatisfied for long, Sally Ann drained her cup and put it down on the floor. She attempted to lift the lid but it seemed to be stuck. She got onto her knees and tried pushing it up. "Ooof! It isn't locked is it? It's hard to open. Ruth," she called, "come and help me."

As Ruth left her area, Sally Ann tried one more heroic tug at the lid and raised it, swiveling around as she did to beam "I got it!" at Ruth.

Sally Ann turned back to the chest, immediately let out a piercing scream and, starting to gag, scrambled to her feet and rushed for the front door. Laurel snatched up the baby and hurried to the chest, clapped her hand over her mouth and tore after Sally Ann. Ruth, thoroughly alarmed, stood frozen for an instant, then, reaching the chest, felt her stomach lurch violently. Swiftly, automatically, she picked up the overturned coffee cup and the half-eaten doughnut and fled outside to where Laurel was holding the baby so tightly he had begun to wail, and Sally Ann was retching into the shrubbery beneath the sign embellished with a picture of an old-fashioned cider press, gold letters spelling out *Cider Run Antiques.*

And that was when Marv drove up. He parked his truck, got out and came towards them, silver hair shining in the sunlight. He cast a sympathetic smile at Sally Ann being sick and went on to Ruth and Laurel.

Looking up into the lovely clear sky, he exclaimed, "What a perfect morning!"

Chapter 2

There really had been a press in operation and cider produced on Cider Run Road. According to Colonel Marcus Parmalee Tyler, in his celebrated work of 1888, *The History of Cross & Marten Counties, Pennsylvania*, one Jacob Schmidt, later changed to Smith, former captain in General Washington's Continental Army, was given a land grant in Marten County in 1789 "in lieu of payment for his soldierly service." Jacob quickly discovered, while the land was too steep for farming, the south-facing slope was perfect for an orchard and less prone to both early and late frosts, as was the case in the lower lying regions. There was a small stream that ran through his property and, with the limestone soil, the drainage was good.

Jacob built himself a cabin out of the material at hand, the ubiquitous limestone, which also had the benefit of clearing the land for planting his orchard. He weathered the first winter and by the next fall had planted a large orchard of apple, pear and peach trees, intending to sell the fruit in the area, which was rapidly being settled. While his trees matured, he supported himself by working at the new iron furnace recently established nearby.

Iron forges were operating in many of the Appalachian valleys, the ore occurring in drifts close to the surface and not necessitating deep mine shafts. Farmers, while plowing their fields, had turned up rich deposits of iron ore, and often this land would be subsequently purchased by iron companies. The region's heavily wooded hillsides yielded the fuel needed for the smelting process, charcoal, which was produced by slowly smoldering wood in small batches. Limestone furnace stacks soon dotted the county.

Besides providing employment, the ironworks brought about the development of the area. Transportation systems needed to be developed to move the finished product to its market. Old cart roads were in use until the canals were dug in the 1830s, and later these in turn were made obsolete by the railroad. Another outgrowth of the forges was the establishment of supporting businesses. Where the iron was worked, there were also gristmills and sawmills, boarding houses, barber shops and stores, the latter an outlet for farmers' products, including cider.

One more result of the iron business was the rise of the ironmaster and the owners of the enterprise. Much money was made, and the influence of these entrepreneurs spanned many generations. Sons and grandsons became Pennsylvania governors, elaborate Federal style and Victorian mansions were built in the larger towns, and wealth used for numerous philanthropic and civic improvements, including the endowment of libraries and institutions of higher education. But at the present time Marv, doing research in the library of one such institution, was more interested in the history of Cider Run.

Col. Tyler does not say exactly when, but at some point Jacob installed a cider press, as he had much success with the apples, although apparently not with the pears and peaches. The demand for cider exceeded his hopes and he was turning it out in great quantities, as well as doing a business pressing the apples of his neighbors. He built a separate small stone building for the press, put in a spring house, raised a barn and made the first expansion of his own humble cabin.

He now decided he could afford to marry and did so, but not to the daughter of one of the established settlers. He had found his wife among the tribe of native peoples—Col. Tyler does not scruple to say Red Indians—who made their home on the fringes of the settlement. This action must have caused severe indignation because, after a few years, a fire of suspicious origin took place at Jacob Smith's cabin. While the Smiths escaped unhurt and the stone building itself was not seriously damaged in the blaze, Jacob soon moved his family west to the Alleghenies. Here he disappears from the record since, being in neither Marten nor Cross counties, he was no longer of interest to Col. Tyler.

Although Col. Tyler fails to enlarge upon 18th and early 19th century cider, Marv did some reading on this interesting subject. Cider back in Jacob Smith's era was not the cider sold at farm stands and in grocery stores today. Cider then was a potent alcoholic beverage, put down to age and, when deemed ready, brought in to be drunk by all members of the family. It was believed to strengthen the body, numb the pain, steel the nerves and harden the resolve. Clearly, it had an important function in dealing with the rigors of frontier life.

The cider press was reinstated after the fire and continued to be operated by various owners. New varieties of apples were planted in the orchard. Later, there was some speculation as to whether some of the apple trees had been planted by Johnny Appleseed himself, but Col. Tyler lays the notion to rest by stating emphatically that this fabled personage never set foot in Marten County. In spite of Col. Tyler's assertion, however, Marv was repeatedly reminded of the durability of an appealing myth, a phenomenon so galling to historians. It set him to wondering for a moment. Had he ever, as a historical researcher, inadvertently rearranged facts? Was he guilty of having tinkered with the past? Well, no matter now, and he read on.

By about 1840, roads had been improved to such a degree that stagecoach runs were frequent and more and more people were traveling the valleys of the Appalachians. Needed now were places where travelers could eat, drink and stop for the night. Jacob Smith's stone house was sold again and reincarnated as an inn.

Another extension of the stone building was made and a second story and front porch, both constructed of wood, were added which, according to Col. Tyler, "provided an exceptional view across the valley to Marten's Mountain. This handsome structure afforded to the weary traveler not only a much appreciated bed for the night, but also the finest of food and spirits, including cider pressed from apples on the premises." The enterprise was called Cider Run Hotel, after the popular name for the stream that watered Jacob Smith's orchard.

In the mid-1800s the railroads were starting to come in and the small, mostly contiguous, settlements decided that consolidation would be beneficial. By becoming one political entity, they would have more of a presence and be in a better position to attract train service to their community. Also, a female seminary had been proposed by the state legislature and only larger towns could compete for this highly desirable institution. The governing bodies, such as they were, of the several villages appointed a committee of six to come up with a name for the new town.

This was not as easy a task as might be supposed. The original settlers had descended from English, German and Scots-Irish backgrounds, and the names of towns up and down the region were reflective of this, ending in "town or ton" or "burg or berg" depending upon the ethnicity of the population. Also, right after the Revolutionary War when many settlements were being established, there was a newly-found appreciation of France, owing to the gratitude of the nation toward General Lafayette, resulting in a large number of "villes."

Complicating this was the fact that the to-be-consolidated villages, ranging from Struthers' Mills to Bog Hollow to Heliopolis, population 35, to Johnsville, Eisenburg, and Foleystown had sent their delegates off with instructions to make sure their village name was the one chosen.

The committee wrestled for days with this knotty problem. Finally, deciding that no one existing town name would be fair to all, they decided to use the county name, Marten, and add a suitable suffix. "City" seemed a little ambitious, but whether Marten should end in "town" or "burg" or "ville" caused even more wrangling and contention. As Col. Tyler describes it, in this deliberation process "the proprietor of the Cider Run Hotel was so frustrated at the delays and wanting to get back to the running of his business, declared he would propose the town be named Horatio, after his dog, which was so many breeds no one could figure it out."

In the end, someone came up with the suffix "dale," although they weren't sure exactly what it meant and "were without a dictionary being to hand, but all had heard of hills and dales, and were confident it likely meant valley." Marten's Dale or Martensdale was given the nod by five of those present, with one vote going for the dog.

Martensdale, now named, went on to win not only two railroad lines and the women's college, but to become the biggest town around, eclipsing the county seat. The small college became co-ed, and then grew into a large and prestigious university. As the years went by, the town prospered to such an extent that the Great Depression of the 1930s had far less of an impact in Martensdale as elsewhere, and dozens of homes, many of them Sears, Roebuck & Co. mail order houses, "Sold by Mail, Shipped by Rail," were built on neighborhood streets bordered by newly planted elms, maples and oaks.

After the entry on town naming, Marv was sorry to see that Cider Run did not make another appearance in Col. Tyler's tome. However, going into the archives, he found an advertisement in the long-defunct *Marten County Reporter* for June 10, 1895, which invited the populace to come out and enjoy the fine food at Schmidt's Tavern. There was a rendering of the stone building, now with second floor and porch removed, probably victims of another fire. The picture showed it flanked by apple trees, complete with apples on the branches. The copy went on to extol the virtues of the menu, in which the enterprising restauranteur had capitalized on the history of the place and its German heritage and featured everything *apfel,* including *strudel, kuchen,* and *sosse* for the potato pancakes.

With the beginning of World War I and the sinking of the *Lusitania* in 1915, a wave of anti-German sentiment took hold. Schmidt's Tavern quietly became Smith's Tavern, carrying on as before, but with the substitution of Homemade Apple Pie, Brown Betty, and Potato Pancakes with Fresh Apple Sauce.

Prohibition meant the end of the "tavern" part of its name, but Smith's Restaurant continued. At that time in the Twenties it was, most likely, a speakeasy, with its location away from the center of town and convenient outbuildings for the storage and concealment of various products. After the repeal of Prohibition the building was modified again. The name Cider Run Inn was reinstated, a wooden dance floor was installed over a portion of the stone floor, and a tap room was added. A roadhouse now, it was a popular place where people could motor out for dinner and dancing and a little smooching in the orchard under the stars. It soon became a favorite spot for the college crowd, as several photos in the collegiate yearbooks for that era attested.

Marv was delighted when he saw that the Marten County Historical Society in its publication, *On the Back Roads of Marten County: Treasures from the Past*, had two photographs of the building. One was from about 1870, judging by the fashions worn by the women, when it was still a hotel with its second floor and porch intact. A group of well-dressed guests stand on the porch in front, with men unloading a wagon off to the side.

The second picture was taken in the 1940s, an interior, which shows men in uniform and women with rolled hair. Couples are on the dance floor and people are sitting at tables with cocktail glasses and cigarettes. Marv had copies made of both pictures to hang in Cider Run Antiques.

A third photo was also put up. In it, seated on long benches under blossoming apple trees, are women in leg-o-mutton sleeved dresses and girls with huge hair bows, men with stiff collars and slicked-down hair, and uncomfortable looking knickerbocker-clad boys. By the expressions on their faces—earnest, but weary—and the books on laps and in hands, Marv judged it must have been a revival or prayer meeting, circa 1900, held in the orchard at Cider Run. Just a portion of the building was in the picture, but it was unmistakable. Marv had discovered this gem purely by accident when he bought a small walnut pump organ at an estate sale. As he went through the hymnals in the bench, there it was. He was ecstatic. Amazing, unexpected finds like this brought it all together: the past joined by an antique item to the present.

During the 1950s fraternities held affairs at Cider Run and notices in the newspaper advertised the bands and vocalists who entertained there. Such favorites as "Dutch" Groshoft and "Hoots" Hansen played gigs at Cider Run Inn. Food was definitely not the big draw anymore.

The decades went on. By the pretentious 1980s the barn and other outbuildings had either fallen down or been removed and the stone building housed The Inn at Cider Run. The emphasis was on "superb dining" and "gourmet cuisine" and the finest imported wines, an "excellent cellar," according to the *Martensdale Times*.

Cider Run Road eventually became a through street. It went to a new housing development and then connected with another road. This brought about the installation of a traffic light down on Martensdale Pike, the main road, making the turn up the hill less difficult.

Cider Run, the little stream itself, was no longer allowed to run free. It was channeled into a culvert, but farther down the valley it emerged again, to join forces with Martens Creek and, ultimately, after many more unions and name changes, to flow into the Susquehanna River from whence, a hundred meandering miles later, it emptied into and became one with the waters of the Chesapeake Bay.

In the research he did, Marv was aware that Pennsylvania geography had played a large role in the history of the region and was responsible for much of its subsequent character.

The Appalachians, cutting diagonally across the state from northeast to southwest, kept the area relatively isolated and, besides saving local speech patterns, regional foods and crafts, and granges and tenting fairs, had the effect of encouraging people to hang on to things because replacements were not to be readily had. The result was that, even though ranging far and wide for antiques was the recreational activity of choice for the dealers, the local area was a prime source, many antiques still found in the homes and farms of descendants of original owners.

Geography, Marv knew, also had a hand in the county's name. According to Col. Tyler, one Tobias Marten had left his home in Philadelphia, intending to join up with the young George Washington during the French and Indian Wars. He was headed toward Fort Duquesne, near present-day Pittsburgh, but got himself lost in the mountains. He wandered around for months, winter came, and still he was lost. Homesteaders' diaries from the period tell of a strange, wild-looking man, a hunter or trapper, who would descend on a settlement from time to time, partake of any hospitality that was offered, and then disappear again. Settlers assumed he was the first to reside in the area and, when needing a name for a geographical feature, be it mountain, valley, creek or river, simply referred to it as "Marten's." The name stuck. What became of Tobias is anyone's guess.

By the end of the 1990s a kitchen fire, to which restaurants seem particularly susceptible, closed the Inn. The building was being used to store air conditioning equipment by a firm located down the road when it was once again put on the market and bought by Marv and Helen, Hal and Sylvie, and Jake and Annette, doing business as Cider Run Antiques, Inc.

Chapter 3

All of his friends knew exactly what Marv would do the minute he retired, and he did not disappoint them. In fact, he exceeded their expectations, not only by going into the antiques business fulltime, but also by becoming a part owner of one of the most historic properties in the county.

Marv and Helen had always dabbled in antiques. From the first years when they were newly married, Marv had been fixing and refinishing the old, out-of-style furniture that people had discarded or disdained. Whenever they could, he and Helen went looking for things at estate sales, auctions and junk shops, flea markets and yard sales. And, leaving no stone unturned, at the curbside where, on trash night, there were interesting castoffs to be found before the garbage truck came in the morning. This was especially true in a college town, as students moved frequently and were constantly getting rid of all manner of things. Desks, chairs, tables, dressers and wardrobes, many of which were old pieces and therefore of little interest or value to younger, more modern tastes, were left behind on the parking strip.

In all this enjoyable acquisition process Marv and Helen learned a great deal: what to look for, what was authentic, what would gain in value over the years. Two or three reference books on antiques soon became a whole bookcase full. After a while, the garage and basement held dozens of projects for Marv to work on, as well as pieces of furniture to be kept in their original condition, not to be redone. Begun as a necessity and reinforced by appreciation, antiques had become a part of their life.

Before recycling came into the vocabulary as an environmentally conscious virtue, Marv and Helen were practitioners. Before attics and basements were being scoured to find "vintage" items that might be worth hundreds of dollars, Marv and Helen bought the old things that nobody had any use for anymore—kitchen utensils, tin ware, lamps, baskets and artwork. They began a collection of Flow Blue ironstone china; they filled their house with pewter and primitives. They slept in, sat on, ate off of, decorated with and stored things in the products of past centuries' craftsmanship.

Although there was interest in antiques on both their parts, it was Marv who became more involved. There were two reasons for this. One was that he liked the intellectual component of antiques collecting, hence the shelves of books. He wanted to find out what an item was, what it was used for, what it was made of. Old things were not always self-evident. He wanted to know when and where it was made and everything else he could learn about it. He wanted to put it into a historical context, into an era, and relate it to other objects, trends and practices of the time. And then go on to the questions: Why do things change? Why do some things never change? For Marv, as much fun as finding wonderful old things was the fun of finding out about them. Like Ruth's musing about the ironstone china that had been taken west in covered wagons, it was this aspect of antiques that captivated many dealers and collectors.

The second reason Marv threw himself so wholeheartedly into antiques was that it compensated for another part of his life that was missing, missing not right away, but gradually and, eventually, inexorably. Their first child, a son, was born with serious birth defects, and the baby only lived for a few days. Marv was able to recover and accept their loss, but Helen was not. At first they shared their grief and found an outlet together in antiques collecting. Finally, after several more years, Helen got pregnant again. This time they had a girl and Helen seemed to have fully recovered. She became an extremely devoted and protective mother, and she and Shirley had what could be called an exclusive relationship. Marv thought this understandable after their first loss. He didn't question it, although the exclusive relationship pretty much excluded him. But he was busy with his own career and did not want to start examining his feelings. Awareness comes slowly when changes are subtle and happen little by little over thirty years, subtler still when never discussed.

Dr. Marvin Yeager, professor emeritus, had been Chair of the History Department at the university, specializing in, but not limited to, rural and small town America during the 19th century. By the time he retired, he had a number of well-known publications, including the highly respected *Arts and Artifacts of Rural Pennsylvania: An Appreciation of Antiques*, tying the history of the central Appalachian area with the useful, decorative products, the blanket chests, coverlets, cupboards, for example, made by the settlers of the region. Another critically acclaimed book, *Antiques as Clues to the Past: Revealing Hidden Patterns of Living*, which he co-authored with a colleague in anthropology, brought together the culture and lifestyles of the past as manifested by the folk art, furniture and objects from the era. And, most popular, was the profusely illustrated, often cited, *Articles of History: What We Can Learn from Antiques*, his culminating opus, applying scholarly perspectives to the relationship between rural Appalachian Pennsylvania antiques and their context. All three were hailed as making significant contributions to the field. Of course, to Marv it was all fun and games; antiques were not work.

Besides teaching, writing, doing research, advising, being on committees and the other usual academic activities, Marv gave classes on antiques for the community education program. After their daughter was older, he and Helen took students on tours of historic sites and museums and they volunteered their time and expertise at the Marten County Historical Society, where Marv was on the Board. They had both become serious about historic preservation and lived it, having as their own home one of the Sears houses from the Thirties.

It was during some renovations at the Historical Society, which had as its headquarters an old ironmaster's mansion, that the Yeagers got to know the Thompsons. Hal, who was part of a local firm of consulting engineers, was supervising the work in progress and Marv was fascinated by the way he kept insisting on doing things that were in keeping with the time period, down to hand finishing with antique tools.

"The only way to get the shape of this molding correct is with the kind of plane that was used in the 19th century," Hal confided to Marv the first day. "Materials, finishes, even nails, are all important to maintaining the integrity of the building. I don't want to be quoted," he said, looking furtively over his shoulder, "but they don't build buildings like they used to."

Marv wondered, is this an engineer? But when Hal later confessed to having what was probably close to the world's largest collection of antique woodworking tools, Marv knew he had found a kindred soul.

Hal, big, strong, with hands and feet to match, had also been buying old furniture. As his wife Sylvie once put it, "Nature has specifically designed Hal to move furniture." Sylvie was the one who became the furniture refinisher in the family after their two children were in school. She had long ago stopped fretting over her stained fingers and nails, and could be found in the workroom Hal built for her listening to music, getting just the right color for the wood, rubbing it down, reapplying: hair limp, drenched in sweat, happily engrossed.

The Thompsons, like the Yeagers, had the habit, and soon had the storage problems associated with it. They had even thought about a shop, but until the children were launched, that would have to wait. Meanwhile they joined in with Marv and Helen and the couples together started to do a little selling at antiques shows. They had enormous success, especially with their beautifully refinished furniture, and this only encouraged more buying. Weekends would find them at public sales out in the country or in the small Appalachian towns.

Perhaps it was the place, rural central Pennsylvania. Perhaps it was the time, the old farms and homesteads beginning to change hands. But it was definitely a chance to be seized. Every week there were public sales, and antiques were being auctioned off at almost all of them.

Down a country road, over the next hill, up a winding and rutted lane: then they would come upon the cars and trucks parked in a field, hear the auctioneer's voice in rapid staccato over the loudspeaker, and the excitement would build. There would be an old farmhouse, a wooden barn, weather-worn red, some stone outbuildings and a grassy yard, bordered by bushes of lilac and rose-of-Sharon. The aroma of grilled sausages would be coming from the lunch stand provided by the Ladies' Guild of the local Methodist church, always a line waiting patiently outside of the porta-potty, and then there were the antiques. Laid out on tables, piled in boxes on the ground near the auctioneer or stacked in a wagon pulled up to the back porch, the contents of the house and barn were all on offer. And out in the side yard, where people could have a good look, was the furniture. It was irresistible.

Marv often wondered why it was that the old oak dressers, beds, tables and chairs looked so appealing on grass. Perhaps it was green setting off golden brown oak, a return of the wood to its original habitat, outside. Actually, he thought, to the auction goer, everything looks good in the out-of-doors on a mellow day in autumn or under large-leafed trees in the summer, and the pies baked by the church ladies taste delicious, people around you are all interesting characters, and the game is nothing if not stimulating. It starts out as a spectator sport, he mused, when you are passively watching who is buying what for how much, but it quickly becomes a participatory sport, as you leap in and make the next bid.

Marv felt the thrill of anticipation as the bidding went up, got a jolt of excitement each time he bid, felt exhilaration when he was the successful bidder and disappointment when he decided to drop out of the bidding. There were many dimensions to the wonderful world of antiques and an emotional component was another facet to be enjoyed. Sometimes it was enough. But not always.

Helen liked antiquing with the Thompsons and Marv was glad of that, since Shirley married and moved east to Bucks County. There was some talk about Helen resuming her own career. She had been a bookkeeper and helped support them when Marv was working on his Ph.D. But an opportunity to work had not materialized and then she became a grandmother. Their daughter's family, with first one grandson and then another, increasingly absorbed Helen's time, interest and energies, and she was often away. Shirley was used to depending on her mother and Helen was only too happy to oblige.

It could have been predicted. Marv, cut out of much of Helen's life, strayed. He became involved with a younger woman, a junior faculty member from another department. It didn't last long and after it was over he owned up to it, although he was not proud of it and felt terribly guilty. However, he learned from it that even though he had been desperate, having casual affairs was not the way he wanted to live his life.

He and Helen agreed to stay together and try to put their relationship on a better plane, but it stayed at a superficial level. From his defection on, Helen kept him at arm's length. Nor would she talk about it and let it be worked through, and rigidly refused any kind of counseling. So it remained, always there, in the background.

It was also that, in spite of the interests they had in common, there was and probably had always been a substantial difference in their outlooks, in their attitudes towards just about everything, even, to some extent, antiques, and which was manifested in their personalities. Marv had a youthful enthusiasm that went with his boyish good looks, and he was quick to find the humor in things. Helen, on the other hand, gave a literal interpretation to most everything and she tended to concentrate on details rather than the larger picture.

That the tendencies were there to develop different, incompatible views of the world was becoming evident.

Marv hadn't looked at his marriage from that angle yet, at least not closely, and figured as long as he was busy, he'd be all right. But Helen was after him to take early retirement, ostensibly so they could spend time together. More likely, Marv guessed, to remove him from temptations. He was not convinced this would help the situation and he was not eager to leave the academic milieu. Then the chance to buy the Cider Run property came up.

Hal had advance knowledge about the property becoming available, as his engineering firm had dealings with the company that handled the air conditioning equipment being stored there. On a cold, wintry day which would normally discourage anyone from anything, the Thompsons and the Yeagers waited in the Cider Run parking lot in their cars, engines idling and heaters on, to meet the real estate agent. She failed to show up at the appointed time, failed to show up at all, and just as the two couples were deciding to leave, a shiny red truck came roaring up, slid to a snowy stop and Jake emerged into their lives.

Tall, blond, strikingly handsome, apologetic for his missing colleague and completely disarming, he had the front door open in an instant and ushered everyone inside. As they toured the building and chatted about possibilities, Jake entered into the discussion, becoming more and more interested in the use they were planning for it.

"The fireplace over there, for example, could be a centerpiece for displaying antiques. I can see it hung with wrought iron utensils, a copper boiler holding kindling on the apron, maybe a stoneware jug on the side, pewter candlesticks on the mantel." He held his hands up in the shape of a spyglass, as if peering through the lens of a magic device that could look into the future.

Helen was absolutely charmed. She realized she had seen Jake before. "You've been at auctions and antiques shows, haven't you?" she asked.

"Been and bought," replied Jake, with an intimate co-conspirator's smile.

The next hour was spent talking antiques with Jake and learning as much about him and his wife, Annette, as about the property. She was a lawyer, had recently passed the bar exam and was working for the university. Jake had met her when they were both in law school. "But I didn't take the exam," he confessed, "I figured one lawyer in the family was enough."

He had instead gotten his broker's license, a more logical thing for him, since he had been managing property for years. Most of the property was his family's, located in the western part of the state, inherited from parents and grandparents who had made wise choices in real estate. Their investments had paid off and Jake, still in his thirties, was in very good financial shape. He could afford to indulge in antiques and he did.

"Jake Gennari," said Helen. "Your father was Italian, yes? But where did the 'Jake' come from?"

Jake, who was used to this question, answered, "From Pittsburgh," then went on to explain that while his father's side of the family was Italian and came to this country shortly before World War I, his mother's side was Irish and had been here since the mid-1800s. "My great-grandmother was a maid and worked for the family of one of the Pittsburgh steel company owners. That's what Irish girls did then."

There was more to the story of the young Irish girl. In May of 1889 she was working at the family's summer home, which was part of an enclave of houses built by wealthy iron and coal executives, their summer camp, as they called it. A lake had even been constructed for their pleasure by damming the creek at South Fork, a tributary to the Conemaugh River which, downstream, ran through the city of Johnstown.

It had been a rainy spring and the water level in the lake had already risen so high that it was spilling over the top of the dam. On May 31, as the downpour continued, the dam slowly gave way and at 3:00 in the afternoon, with a rush, a flood of backed-up water slammed down the valley, taking everything in its path. When it hit Johnstown, it was a 20 million-ton wall of water a half a mile wide and 40 feet high, containing all that had been carried away from upstream—houses, barns, livestock, uprooted trees, bridges, railroad cars. Little warning had been given, and Johnstown was decimated. Over two thousand lives were lost, 25,000 people were made homeless. The responsibility was put squarely on the Pittsburgh moguls, who quietly folded their tents and stole away.

"It's not something our family exactly brags about, but the newspapers were so avid to get the story and place the blame that some of the wealthy owners paid their servants not to talk to the reporters, who were coming around in droves. Great-Grandmother Sadie played both ends against the middle and came out with a pretty penny."

With the proceeds, Great-Grandma opened her own dress-making business and, later, a hat shop and did exceedingly well. Her descendants, instead of working in the steel mills and for the railroad, bought up land. That was their history, a legacy from a tragedy, almost as if it were retaliation.

But now, for Jake, history obviously meant antiques. Among other things, he collected furniture and decorative objects from the Craftsman period—the clean-lined, elegant,

Art Nouveau-inspired style associated with the Arts and Crafts movement—which flowered in America at the start of the 20th century, incorporating Mission influences from California.

It was clear Jake had plenty of disposable income and he was disposed to become part of Cider Run. As Helen put it later, "His tongue was just hanging out; he was so excited by the prospect of being one of the partners of the shop. It was so sweet." Helen had definitely taken to Jake.

All along the Yeagers and the Thompsons knew they needed to pull in more cash to make the deal. Jake and Annette provided the perfect third and the deal went through. Cider Run Antiques, Inc. was a reality.

Through the rest of the winter and spring, the stone building underwent the renovations necessary to transform it into a shop. Marv and Helen had the idea that it should be more like a gallery, with a movable back partition in each area where artwork and other items could be displayed. Jake visualized the layout so that one could wander freely from area to area, dissipating some of the claustrophobia often felt in a relatively low-ceilinged 18th century space. The individual areas were designed to be flexible, able to be enlarged or decreased depending on need. Hal made it happen, installed a new heating and air-conditioning system and saw to anything structural. Annette handled legal matters, and all six of them scrubbed, painted, cleaned up after workmen and put in plantings by the outside entrance.

With most of the work completed and at least twelve areas roughly blocked out, it was time to recruit more dealers. They would pay rent based on the size of their space, work at the shop four to five days a month, also depending on area size, and bring additional expertise and a wider variety of antiques to the enterprise.

Both the Yeagers and the Thompsons knew many of the antiques people in the county and when the remodeling got underway, word got around. Jake had contacts as well, and by the time the shop was finished and ready to open in June, there were fifteen dealers in Cider Run, with three more joining by the next summer. Each of them was hand-picked, Marv liked to think, chosen with care and consideration.

Later, he hoped they had chosen wisely.

Chapter 4

For twenty-four years the chief charity fund raising event in Martensdale was the Fall Antiques Show and Sale. This two-day extravaganza attracted antiques dealers from all over Pennsylvania and many from out of state. Close to a hundred dealers could be counted on to set up booths, and they bought as well as sold. Customers flocked to the show—dedicated antiques collectors, Christmas shoppers, decorators, home furnishers and people who just liked to buy what appealed to them. It annually raised many thousands of dollars for various charities and had become an autumn pilgrimage for antiques lovers.

The show was also an opportunity for the Yeagers and the Thompsons and those like them to sell antiques, their own as well as others'. One part of the high school gym where the show was held had an area set aside for things brought in by the Antiques Committee. This committee solicited donations and consignments to be sold at the show, a role that involved running all over town, picking up genuine antiques and questionable items from charitably-minded donors and consignors. It also meant that committee members could sell the antiques they had acquired themselves, minus the percentage taken for the charities. Even better, they had first chance to buy others' things. These advantages offset the many hours of sorting, cleaning, listing, pricing, tagging and, sometimes, rejecting of items, the set-up the night before the show opened, helping customers on the days of the show, packing up afterwards, returning unsold consignments and storing donations. Being on the committee required time and effort, but there was much fellowship and high spirits. The Yeagers and the Thompsons were members of this committee and, among the rest of the twenty or so others, there were several like-minded, true antiques people.

The true antiques people, as Marv dubbed them, were genuinely interested in "old stuff" to the point where they wanted to know more. For them, an antique item brought to the show needed explanation, be it a porcelain teacup or a roll-top desk. As they readied things for the show, conversations buzzed about the items being hauled in and taken out of boxes. Marv, with his long-standing experience in antiques, got most of the questions.

"Marv, what is this? There's a doo-hinky here and a thing that goes around, and a plug here."

"How old do you think this platter is? There's no mark on the bottom."

"OK, I know the top of this table is oak, but how about the legs?"

"If a glass vase has three mold marks, it's old, right? But what about four?"

"Can I borrow your book on Depression glass? All these patterns are starting to look alike."

"Do you think this is the original paint? If it is, I know it's worth more."

"Look, folks! The note from the consignor on this says it's a genuine 1948 Roy Rogers lunch box. So how come there's a zip code on the side?"

They were ready to admit it when they didn't know what the whatchamacallit was, or its age, or the host of other questions surrounding an item from the past. They wanted to find out as much as they could, so they invested in reference books on antiques they were particularly fond of and shared information. There grew a mutual appreciation and reliance on each other's respective areas of expertise. After many years, this group of friends looked forward to the fall show, spending a good part of the summer at auctions and sales buying antiques to sell.

But theirs was not the only committee. The show had an executive committee with overall control representing the different charities, and this group held the purse strings. Turf fights, quarrels about advertising, personality conflicts and power struggles had always been present over the years, but finally got the upper hand. In the spring when Cider Run was being renovated for the shop, it was also time for planning the 25th Anniversary Gala of the show. Instead, it was canceled with no explanation, just like that.

"Just like that," said Marv disgustedly on hearing the news. And from the ashes of the defunct show, Marv could see his opportunity. He and Helen proceeded to call friends on their committee, hoping they would like to be part of Cider Run.

Owen Griffith, a teacher at the high school, had been on the committee for five years. His involvement came about by accident. One evening, on the day before a show, he was finishing up some work in his classroom when Helen blundered in by mistake, looking for extra tables. Earlier in the evening he had watched some of the items being unloaded and set up, and the antique toys had him transfixed. He had been given tin plate and other trains from his father, gone so far as to join the Train Collectors Association, and had been buying old Lionel and Marx sets. When he confessed his interest in what he'd seen, Helen simply asked if he'd like to be on the committee. He pitched in then and there, and was hooked.

Over the next few years, Owen and his wife, Lynn, became enthusiastic sale and auction attendees, going after the scenery and little buildings of the old train layouts, all sorts of toys, models, games, and holiday memorabilia. Like the other true antiques people on the committee, they built up a collection of reference materials to learn more. They had fun buying and fun selling, particularly when serious collectors who came to the show appreciated their things.

Helen, having such good luck with Owen in the past, gave him a call. The rumors had gotten around already, so Owen and Lynn had heard that the old Cider Run place had been sold and to whom and for what purpose. The idea of being part of the shop was stimulating to both of them and, as before, Owen did not hesitate.

Cora Lehman and Grace Dutton, long-time committee members, were a package deal. They had just retired from elementary school teaching careers and were ready to find an outlet for their talents and energy, of which both had plenty. They decided to take a fairly large space at the shop and share it, dragooning their husbands into the heavy lifting. Not only were they antiques-smart, they had their own special strengths: Cora was the Yard Sale Queen, and Grace's husband was a fearless, if sometimes reckless, bidder at auctions. Marv, after he had spoken with them, was glad that the dealers' areas could be flexible. He could see that the ability to adapt to different needs was a good decision.

Emmy Greene was landed by Jake. Even though she had been on the committee, loved buying antiques and working at the shows, she was worried that her "very busy schedule, with all the traveling and everything" along with the social commitments she and her husband had, and then her own piano teaching, would give her little time to spare.

"Leave her to me," said Jake, when Marv confessed failure.

Jake had known Emmy originally through Annette. She and Emmy had taken golf lessons together as part of a university women's group. Emmy and her husband Charles played golf, and Jake and Annette had made up a foursome with them occasionally.

Jake called Emmy back, as Marv stood by listening to Jake and becoming more impressed by the minute with his persuasive abilities. "Emmy," he began, "your taste is so absolutely flawless. And you know how to treat customers. Don't you remember when you used to sell me things at the show? Those Steiff animals? You made them talk to me. What a sales job! Listen, we need you. Do you think you could handle a smaller area, only work three days a month? You could get Charles to help. He needs to get out of the office more. Don't tell him I said that." And Emmy was on board.

Some of the committee members Marv talked to didn't think they could afford the time commitment that being a dealer entailed. However, they were all looking forward to being customers, which is not a bad thing, Marv thought.

Recruiting dealers is only the first step. Where will the customers come from? But one thing at a time.

Jake also brought in Richard Keating. He had met him the previous year when Richard, thinking he might be selling his mother's house, needed a realtor. Richard had been working for an insurance company in Baltimore and had come back to Martensdale to be with his mother for a few months before she died. The insurance company had an office in town, and he was offered a similar position should he decide to stay which, ultimately, he did. While Jake didn't sell the house for him, as Richard opted to keep it after all, he did spend some time talking with Richard about antiques. Richard's parents had collected and furnished their home with antiques and he had grown up with them. He was quite knowledgeable in an offhand manner, the way people are who have always been around them. Being back in Pennsylvania, however, gave him a renewed interest and he took one of the classes in antiques that Marv taught. Jake saw him at auctions, and noted that he bought only the best things. Richard was funny, outspoken and unabashedly gay. He was also Jake's insurance agent.

Laurel Fisher came from the show too, but from the other committee. Some years before, her husband, newly hired at the hospital, asked her if she would represent the hospital's fund raising. At that time she was just getting started in her decorating business and needed to make all the contacts she could. Three years of shows got her absolutely enamored of antiques. She bought antiques voraciously and changed her whole decorating approach to include them. Disgusted with the infighting of the committee, she had resigned before the final breakdown. However, she kept in contact with Marv and his committee people, often buying antiques from them.

When asked if she would like to be part of the shop, she told Marv, "I can be there this afternoon."

Keith Mackinnon was brought in by the Thompsons through one of the oldest social networks going: he went to their church. The Presbyterians had a large and active congregation and after Keith and his wife June had children, they decided that perhaps they should be churchgoers. Keith had grown up Presbyterian, but had not attended church for years. June, who had Anglicized her name from Jun-Yun, was born in China and, more than happy to start afresh in a new country, eagerly embraced Keith's culture. What with youth groups for their children and social events, it wasn't long before the Thompsons and the Mackinnons were having evenings in each other's homes.

Hal liked the sandy-haired Keith, a serious, intelligent veteran of the Gulf War with a slight limp, a leftover from being wounded. Keith had just started back at the university, working on a graduate degree in business administration and had an assistantship which gave him free time. He also had, to Hal's interest, Civil War and other military antiques, old hunting and fishing gear, and antique sports equipment of all sorts, some of which he'd restored. Sylvie particularly admired the refinished wooden skis and wooden-shafted golf clubs.

Keith had once confessed to Hal that he wasn't sure why he first started collecting, although he knew at one time it filled a need. But he had books and references and knew the history that went along with much of his collection, and that was the fascinating part for him. Holding a Civil War cavalry rifle was a thrill, he said, but learning about its place in history was even more of a thrill.

As for making the leap from collector to dealer, Keith said simply, "I'm ready."

Elaine Barr didn't have to be recruited. She had been popping up every few days to check on the progress of the remodeling. Cigarette in hand, she'd walk through, chat with the workmen, and make suggestions to Marv about what should go where.

"You know, Elaine, when we're open there's not going to be any smoking inside," Marv warned. Did he want Elaine? He wasn't sure, but it looked like they were going to have her anyway.

"Come on, Marv!" Elaine protested indignantly in her slightly husky voice. "I never smoked inside at the other shop. Anyway, I'm quitting." She had been a partner in a nice little antiques shop in town, but during the past year the borough council decided that a parking garage should go on the site, and the landlord of the building which housed the shop had no choice but to agree.

Marv thought, "Hah! Elaine will never quit!" But in spite of his misgivings, he knew Elaine was an asset. She had been dealing in antiques longer than he, seemed to know everyone in the business and had a huge following of loyal customers. True, her area in the former shop could be described at best as scattered or, perhaps more accurately, as a fire hazard. On the other hand, she knew her antiques and they were all quality. And she was utterly indefatigable when it came to helping customers find what they wanted, whether it was her own or others' merchandise. In a co-op setting, she definitely cooperated.

Marv had no idea how old she was—she had college-aged grandchildren. Helen thought Elaine was the epitome of sophistication, with her upswept ash blonde hairdo and her wardrobe of linen and pearls in the summer, cashmere and pearls in the winter. That the sophistication was early 1960s was even better, giving Elaine an aura of credibility and class which, like a halo effect, extended to the antiques she sold. Elaine was in.

In his efforts to convince his sister to move down to Pennsylvania, Ruth Arden's brother threw out a temptation he knew would arouse her interest.

"And," he had said, "there's a new antiques shop opening. They've taken an old stone building that used to be a restaurant. It's on a hill overlooking the valley and has an orchard on the property. The place reminds me so much of Vermont. Anyhow, I hear they're looking for dealers."

When Ruth came for a visit, Marv was there overseeing some of the last remodeling, and he took her around. He enlarged on the history of the place, talked about his hopes for the shop, and drew Ruth out, learning about her background and antiques expertise. He remembered having met her bother, Eric Arden, who taught in the College of Education.

"There are three other public school people here. You'd feel right at home," he told Ruth.

I think I just might, thought Ruth.

By the time Cider Run Antiques was ready to get started, there were eleven dealer areas. As the dealers began to bring in their wares and set up their displays, dimensions got modified and there turned out to be more room than initially thought. Some dealers only had small pieces of furniture or didn't deal in furniture at all, but used display cabinets and shelving for their items. However, over the first year of operation, this extra space was used to create three new dealer areas, thus bringing in more people to staff the shop, more revenue in the form of rent and more variety in the antiques offered.

Sally Ann O'Neill came to the shop in the fall to buy. Her husband had recently passed away and she had money to spend. She had always loved the color and brave hopefulness of the Thirties, and had put her life back together by buying and embellishing her home with Fiestaware, pink Depression glass and bright flower and fruit themed linens. She put herself back together in a similar fashion, as a walking testament to the era of "Cheap and Cheery."

Richard, who was working the day she came in, adored her at once. He could see what a breath of fresh air she would be, and the kinds of antiques she had were not represented in the shop. He convinced her to stay the whole afternoon, he let her help customers, and she decided she was in her element.

Andy King wandered in one winter day to sell, or at least to find out what he had. The Kings were a local farming family who went back almost as far as Jacob Smith in Marten County, close to the beginning of the 19th century. Andy had some of the original stone buildings on his property, along with a later, circa 1870, brick house and a handsome bank barn. He also had the clutter of two centuries of homesteading; the Kings apparently never threw anything away.

Sylvie, who was there when he came in, was happy to help. What Andy had brought in was an early form of the washing machine: a long shaft with a cone-shaped tin piece on the end. This implement was used to manually agitate the laundry while it was immersed in soapy water in a tin or wooden washtub. They were probably not that unusual, Sylvie told him, but the only one she could remember seeing was in a museum of antique farm equipment run by the agriculture department of the university.

This information, when given to Andy, while not quite an epiphany, was nonetheless a transforming moment for him. These objects were museum pieces!

"I, we, have a whole lot more things like this," he said with wonder in his voice. "Are they worth anything?"

Sylvie assured him that they were, but did he want to sell off his family heirlooms?

"These are heirlooms?" Andy asked incredulously. "I thought heirlooms were, like, silverware and such."

Sylvie suggested he have a look around the shop, as they had a few farm-related antiques and he could get an idea of what things sold for and also what the dealers had written about the items on their price tags.

Andy had a long, slow ramble around the entire shop, then found Sylvie again. He told her about a number of items which had been misidentified: "That pitch fork someone has? It isn't," he said. "No, that's a manure fork. Have a real close smell of it sometime."

He also expressed amazement at the prices of other items.

Two days later he was back, having gone to the museum Sylvie had mentioned. He talked with Marv for a long time, and both decided that he would be a happy addition to Cider Run.

And last of all was Clair, who came towards the end of the second summer. Clair Somers had been one of Marv's students. After she graduated, she went on to study for her master's degree in art history and design in New York. With an MFA, she landed a job at the Metropolitan Museum of Art. This had been her goal in life ever since she was a teenager and had gone to see the Costume Institute's exhibition of Victorian dress. But cataloging and making notations in the back rooms of the museum was not what she had in mind. She wanted to be designing exhibits and mounting shows.

And then there was her on-again, off-again boyfriend who, after causing her many tearful nights, went on to Chicago without her. She decided to go back home and think things over.

Clair's interest in antiques had always been strong and was due in large part to Marv and Helen. She spent summers and holidays in Martensdale with her parents, and had visited the shop several times during its first year. When she could, she bought antiques, small watercolors and a piece of estate jewelry now and then, but mostly she had been buying period clothing. She had found that the secondhand shops in New York were a treasure trove of dresses, hats, silk flowers, gloves, bags, menswear, as well as linens and lace. With her love of costumes and fabrics, it was impossible for her not to take advantage of this bonanza. When she came back to Pennsylvania, her car was loaded with boxes, old suitcases and even two steamer trunks full of vintage articles. Not sure of what to do, she went to see Marv and Helen at Cider Run.

Jake was at the shop that day. He was at his gracious, charming best and told Clair that her clothing and accessories collection would add a desirable, unique dimension to the shop. He proposed an area for her near the front. He offered her some of his own furniture pieces to use for display. He swept her off her feet.

Chapter 5

The shop's renovations were nearly complete when Marv arrived with the crowning touch: an old wooden cider press, circa 1880, which he had bought at a farm sale. A cylinder twelve inches in diameter and 24 inches high, it was made of oak slats held in place by circular metal bands. It had a wooden-handled crank to press down on the apples. Several of the dealers were readying their areas and the new acquisition sparked a lively discussion.

"It's pretty small, isn't it, for a cider press?"

"It could be a vinegar press."

"Or maybe it's a grape press."

"Oh, no, a grape press is much bigger! When we were in the Napa Valley for our wine tour..." This last was from Emmy.

"Maybe they came in different sizes."

"Shouldn't we be looking for one from about 1810?"

"Wasn't there a separate outbuilding here for the cider press? Then this one is much too small."

"I still think it could be a vinegar press."

"Cider, vinegar; they're both made from apples," Marv stated definitively, and the press became the shop's symbol. The *Cider Run Antiques* signs down on the main road, at the entrance to the parking lot and by the door of the shop were duly designed with a cider press logo on them. The cider press itself was put in a place of honor on a stand near the front counter.

In late spring most everything was in place. The entranceway had been made wide enough so that pieces of furniture could be brought in and taken out without catastrophe, and a new front door, glass, heavy and secure, was put in. A soft gray carpet had been laid down on top of the stone floor, over which several dealers had put braided rugs or Oriental rugs in colorful hues in their areas. Jake donated a Mission oak hall tree and it stood near the front door for use by customers. An old church pew was brought in to help define an entrance foyer, as well as providing a place for those who wanted to have a sit-down while others browsed. The restrooms were enhanced with nicely framed Victorian prints and small pieces of period furniture, most of which had price tags.

In the kitchen, long devoid of restaurant appliances, a new refrigerator was installed, along with a microwave oven and a coffee maker. The cabinets and counters were still in place and they soon held a supply of cups, plates, mugs, glasses, bowls, vases, trays and anything else thought important by the dealers. Most of the tableware was from the Thirties and Forties, but there were a few older ironstone pieces with only a small chip or two. Marv brought in a chestnut farmhouse table, nearly twelve feet long, which had been languishing in his garage and annoying Helen for a long time, as it took up a lot of room and was too large to go anywhere in their house. A dozen chairs were assembled from various dealers who were going to refinish them but never got around to it, a common circumstance among antiques people.

There was an office which opened off of the kitchen. It was furnished by Jake with an oak filing cabinet, a barrister's bookcase and an oak partners' desk, pieces which had already seen a hundred years of duty in a law firm. The former pantry became the supply and box room; it also had hooks for hanging jackets and coats. Somewhere Marv had found an old wooden mailbox case and this was put up in the kitchen. Each dealer had a box, where the monthly checks for sales went, as well as nametags and whatever else would fit in the pigeonholes.

The basic shop operations were learned by everyone: opening and closing procedures, the computer program to handle sales transactions, where to find things, where to put things, and the many other details that went with operating a business. The partners had written a policy manual and each dealer had a copy.

Since all dealers had days on which they worked, each one also had a key to the shop. This was necessary, not only for opening up the shop in the morning and locking the door at closing time, but for after hours, a better time for bringing in furniture and other large items and doing rearranging without getting in the way of customers.

A meeting was called in early June to go over questions and for dealers to choose days to work for the next three months. At least two people were always on and at least one of the partners arranged to be there daily. A sense of optimism and comradeship prevailed. The evening was warm, people helped themselves to beer and soft drinks from the refrigerator, and everyone trooped out to the orchard where a couple of picnic tables had been set out under the trees. It was the beginning of the social club aspect of Cider Run Antiques.

"Hal, why do you make Sylvie do all the work? Is that fair?"

"Cora keeps her husband chained in the basement and won't let him out until he gets the refinishing done. Isn't that so, Cora? I haven't seen Bob for months."

"Oh, go on, Marv!"

"Richard, I've been meaning to ask you: how much did you end up paying for that hap you were bidding on last weekend? I had to leave and missed it. OK, it isn't any of my business, but I just wondered."

"I didn't get it. I dropped out at $45."

"I was sure you'd gotten it. I thought she was wavering."

"And then someone else got in the bidding and it just kept going up and up."

"Who needs another beer?"

"I've got a few more things to unload and that's it!"

"Is it always this warm at night in early June?" Ruth asked.

"This ain't warm. Wait till it gets *warm.*"

"I will never complain again about how hot it gets in Pennsylvania after that one summer Charles and I spent in Eastern Europe. Nothing, absolutely nothing, was air-conditioned and..."

"I can't wait till summer. No school and two or three auctions every week." Owen was planning ahead.

"I can't wait until we open! What do you suppose is going to be the first thing sold? I mean officially. I'm already buying one of Marv's stands," Laurel confessed.

"I wish it would be my van. It's on its last legs," Ruth said, more to herself than anyone in particular.

"Well, I'm on my last legs, folks, if I don't stop drinking beer," Grace announced. "See you tomorrow!"

"What do you say, Marv?" asked Jake. "Can the little lady sell her van? Out in the parking lot, of course. Or are we sticking to the fifty-years-old rule?"

"Cider Run Antiques and Used Vehicles."

"Keith, another beer?"

"Where's Annette, Jake?"

"Doing lawyer stuff. Hey! What do you have when you see a lawyer buried up to her neck in sand?"

"Jake!" exclaimed Helen, horrified.

"Not enough sand."

"You're mean," she said, but smiling at him.

They had planned to have a grand opening complete with mailed announcements and advertising and refreshments, but on a morning a few days later with some of the dealers still moving things in, the front door had been left open and in walked the first customer. Granted, the first customer was one of the old show committee people but, nevertheless, she bought a small walnut candle box and the shop was now a going concern.

Since the shop's opening seemed to have already happened, the partners decided they didn't need a splashy event. A few days later, the *Martensdale Times* ran an announcement that the partners had carefully composed.

Cider Run Antiques
Open for Business in the old stone Cider Run Inn
Fifteen Dealers specializing in fine antiques
From the 18th, 19th and first half of the 20th centuries
Open daily, 10:00 to 6:00, Sundays, Noon to 5:00

There was an address, a telephone number and the cider press logo. Marv thought the understated manner in which the opening was announced lent an air of quality and excellence, as if it said, "We are really something, folks. We don't need to enthuse."

In the spring Marv had briefly worried whether customers would find them. But the first weekend they were open, it seemed as if all of Marv's and Helen's friends showed up and the entire congregation from the Thompsons' church. The sign down on Martensdale Pike pulled in June travelers and when a flyer, complete with sketch done by Cora of the cider press, was distributed by the Marten County Visitors Bureau, more people drove up the hill and filled the gravel parking lot of Cider Run.

The dealers found that waiting on customers who shared their interest in antiques was not only rewarding but downright fun. There was the cookie cutter lady who was always searching for the odd piece she didn't have. There was the guy in overalls who looked as though he never left his backhoe, but who was after first editions, preferably with dust jacket, from the Twenties. A young man came in hoping to find just the right piece of antique jewelry for his girlfriend and did. A young lady asked for help to buy "some fishing thing" for her boyfriend and left happy when she was able to purchase a lure and know how old it was too.

Oak highchairs were sold to first-time grandparents, pattern glass celery holders and water pitchers were sold for wedding gifts. There were milk bottle collectors, postcard collectors and button collectors shopping. People came needing to furnish homes. It was soon clear that the new, large houses being built were perfect for the old, large pieces of furniture from the Victorian and Edwardian eras—the armoires, dining tables, sideboards, and high-backed beds. Likewise, the relatively smaller pieces from the Twenties through the Forties went nicely in the older, smaller homes in town. Furniture was selling fast.

Maybe there had been a pent-up demand for antiques. There were no other shops in town, and it was common knowledge that the show had been cancelled. And also it was summer, the time when dealers from other areas make buying trips, looking to purchase stock for their own businesses. The partners had announcements placed in the *Antiques Weekly* and the *New England Antiques Journal* and several other periodicals of the trade and the response was gratifying.

Sometimes people came in who just wanted to pass the time of day. There were those who brought in elderly parents, to escort them about and hear them exclaim over the present-day prices for things that they themselves once had, and threw away. When it was very warm, some came in for the air conditioning, but they often found something they wanted. Summer thunderstorms kept others inside longer than they had planned, giving them enough time to find and buy just the item they'd been searching for. Every day brought interesting people into the shop. Conversations were convivial and stimulating, the day went by quickly and the Cider Run dealers were enjoying themselves tremendously.

Part of the success of the shop had to do with the rapport that existed between dealers and customers. Each and every dealer was also a collector. They had all been, and still were, looking for things, buying things, collecting things. Customers could sense this easily in the dealers' understanding of their searches, quests really, for antiques.

It didn't matter whether the item simply went in a drawer or was displayed on a shelf or was used at the dinner table. Antiques were wanted for the warmth and beauty they added to a home or the aura of history they imparted, and also as an investment since, unlike most new things, their value appreciated over time. Dealers knew and understood the thrill of the chase, and it was obvious that they were happy to encourage others.

A library of antiques reference books was kept near the front counter, and dealers helped by looking up specifics for customers, suggesting other sources for information, and recommending different places to try. A Wish Book was put out so customers could write in what they hoped to find.

Need pieces for repairing cast iron wood stove.

Looking for anything in Oneida silverplate "Friendship" pattern.

Wanted: small drop-leaf table, 24" x 36" max.

Have just bought windup Victrola. Looking for 78RPM records, Swing, Big Band era. Also where can I find a cactus needle?

Customers were enthusiastic about the shop, the quality and authenticity of the antiques and the helpfulness of the dealers. They hung around and chatted, they came in frequently to see what was new. In a month the shop was doing so well that everyone was kept busy trying to restock, and more people were needed to work than had been anticipated. The partners took up the slack. It was all rather exhilarating even if exhausting.

Owen, with the summer off from teaching, had time to go to a lot of sales and brought in collections of toys that had lain long in attics and closets: windups, mechanical banks, cast iron cars and trucks, even riding animals.

Keith had a display case in his area full of military paraphernalia. Not too unexpectedly, his merchandise had an electrifying effect on buyers. World War I and II rifles, bayonets, helmets, knives, pistols and other items in such variety and condition were immediately sought after. Civil War items, scarcer and more expensive, were grabbed up by collectors. Another case held Keith's hunting and fishing gear, and then there was his sports equipment: wooden tennis rackets strung with catgut, leather baseball gloves. Keith's stock became alarmingly low and he, too, needed to keep up with the demand.

Keith and Owen quickly found that they enjoyed each other's company when they worked together, and soon started going to many of the same auction sales. Since they bought different things, there was no competition between them and they became good companions.

Sylvie, those first few months, was in her workshop past midnight almost every night, frantically readying furniture for Hal to take out the next day and which was usually sold by the weekend.

Laurel's clients from her decorating business came in to pick out antiques for their homes, buying from other dealers as well as from Laurel, which had been Laurel's strategy all along. Being part of a shop full of antiques enlarged her business, and gave it prestige and a new dimension.

Ruth was surprised at the satisfaction being at Cider Run brought. It was so different from the shop she'd had in Maine, where it had been only herself and another couple. Here there were always interesting people around, happy to help out and give their opinions on antiques, or anything else for that matter. Mostly, though, everyone seemed simply pleased to be there. For them, being an antiques dealer was an avocation, something done for its own sake and the pleasure it brought. They vied in being amusing or clever or sociable, but not in sales. Ruth thought that not only had she landed on her feet and found herself many new friends, she had entered into an atmosphere. Was the rest of Pennsylvania like this?

She felt an immediate kinship with Cora and Grace. They shared elementary education anecdotes and, since released from actually having to be in a classroom, could tell impolite tales out of school. It was plain to see that Cora and Grace were thriving in this phase of their lives.

Emmy and her husband put off their trip to Spain so she could be in on the shop's first few months. Emmy thought Charles would not be too happy about this, but he spent the summer writing a book on economic theory instead, another book, for which he already had a publisher panting.

Richard and Elaine, with thirty years of age difference between them, had taken to each other, much in the way of Owen and Keith, except that they expressed their friendship by sparring incessantly, trading insults and witty, if nasty, remarks. Richard, who had been concerned about small-town homophobia, felt comfortable at the shop and was glad he had decided to stay in Pennsylvania.

Elaine, in her trademark rumpled linen jacket and skirt, greeted all her old customers and was helpfulness personified, even if she did disappear periodically to have a quick smoke. The first set of china she sold at the shop—sets of china being notoriously hard to sell, so many dishes at once—was an occasion that sent her out for a bottle of champagne, which was opened right after closing and shared by all the dealers who were there.

With all the things to do and think about, with all the decisions and busyness, plus the fun of the enterprise, Marv and Helen had reached a state of, if not rapprochement, at least working together smoothly to make the shop successful. Their outward appearance as a couple looked stronger than it had in years, although it was not matched by a change in their personal relationship. When Marv had needed someone to confide in about his marital problems, someone not connected with the university, he had turned to Hal. Now, Hal thought, perhaps things were finally resolving for Marv and Helen, and noted that Marv was certainly too happily involved in the shop to look elsewhere. Helen had taken on the job of keeping the Cider Run books, so she was feeling more confident, and also could not run over to Bucks County quite so frequently.

It was true that Marv had his hands full with the business and it dominated his thoughts. He knew things would slow down eventually and he would miss the academic life, but he was happy with the present, with the people they had brought together and with the place. After a busy day, when they had locked up and everyone else had left, he would go around the shop, thinking about the history of the stone building and about the use it now had. Sometimes he wondered what Jacob Smith and the other former owners of the place would have thought; sometimes he imagined himself in conversation with them.

"Jacob, we have an antiques shop here now. How does that sit with you?"

"Well, Marv, I think it looks right nice the way you have fitted it up. But those ain't antiques, not really, you know. Some of those things look awful new to me."

"Now, Jacob, you have to remember you've been dead for almost two centuries. In the intervening time a lot got made. It's plenty old now."

"If you say so. But who'd want to buy that stuff?"

Marv, unable to answer this, would go on to another former owner.

"Sorry we had to modernize a bit. Hope you won't be offended," he might say to the proprietor of the first Cider Run Inn.

"Don't make no difference to me. Place was always catching fire. You keep an eye on them stoves, though, and mind you don't let the gentlemen lay their cigars on the furniture."

Marv often found himself ending up in Ruth's area after the day was over. There was something about Ruth that interested him and, looking at her things, he would wonder about her. Her antiques were unquestionably superior; that was important to Marv. And Ruth herself? She was bright, good humored and nice, very nice, to have around. But there was a reserve about her that Marv couldn't understand. Maybe it came from being a school principal. Did she know how attractive she was? She didn't act that way, the way a woman does when she knows she's attractive. Would he be able to tell her someday? These were thoughts he knew he'd better put aside, so he did, but they kept coming back.

In August the Yeagers left town to be with their daughter, who was about to bless them with another grandchild. Jake volunteered to fill in for them, which meant he spent considerably more hours at the shop. He also had his work with the real estate agency, and so he had very little time for restocking his area. And even less time for Annette.

Some things occurred which probably could have been anticipated. In the melee of customers, several items went missing and unaccounted for. It was brought home that Cider Run was not immune to shoplifters. The police department sent an officer to give the dealers a talk on what they could do to help prevent thefts. As a result, surveillance cameras were installed which fed into a video monitor at the front counter and a system was devised for securing the back door which opened off the kitchen. There was a light near the front counter that went on when the door was unlocked, and an alarm which would sound if the door was opened without deactivating it first.

So Jake was particularly upset when he arrived early one morning to find the front door unlocked. No one was there and, as it turned out, nothing was missing. Still, he was quite irritated about it and posted a strongly-worded notice in the kitchen. At least it raised everyone's consciousness about security, and there were no more instances of an unlocked door.

These occurrences were minor set-backs. They showed where adjustments needed to be made and, as in any business, where there were vulnerabilities.

When Marv got back from the week in Bucks County, Hal and Jake filled him in on everything that had happened in his absence. "Looks like you have taken care of things beautifully, partners," he observed. He realized again how glad he was to have good people to help solve problems which would, inevitably, come up.

Chapter 6

The Cider Run dealers found their customers varied and interesting, but there was another group who aroused even more interest. These were the people who came in to sell.

The shop had a clear policy on this kind of buying—dealers working that day had right of first refusal on anything offered, unless another dealer had specifically arranged for something to be brought in. If no one on duty was interested, the sellers were told when people who dealt in such items were going to be in, or they might even give them a call. The Wish Book was again put to use.

For sale: Fireplace surround, solid marble, U haul.
Twin rocking chairs for sale, his & hers, circa 1885.
Large walnut dresser, tilt mirror. (Photo included)
Selling old Kentucky rifle, made in Pennsylvania. Works.

Generally, there were three types of sellers who came into Cider Run: those who were desperate, those who were downsizing, and those who were other antiques dealers.

The first type, the dealers agreed, made them uneasy. Sometimes they drove up in a car or truck so covered with rust that it looked as if it had spent the winter in a ditch and had just been hauled out. They carried their offerings in plastic grocery bags or torn cardboard boxes and laid them on the counter for inspection with an apologetic air. The main dilemma for the dealers, outside of maintaining common courtesy to people who were often alarmingly disreputable looking, was the worry that what was being offered had not been obtained legitimately.

When the shoplifting incidents had occurred, the police officer had given pointers on avoiding this problem and dealing with it, should someone be acting suspiciously. Along with this he cautioned about accepting merchandise that was "hot." It was a known fact that antiques lifted from shops in one area were taken to another locale and offered for sale. Notices circulated to antiques shops listed "lost" items, often with photos of the piece, and sometimes there were even larger items, such as a wall clock or a pieced coverlet or an early camera. Be on the lookout, the officer had warned.

So the first question usually was, "Where did you get this?" The answers ranged from plausible to creative.

"It was in the house when we moved in."

"It was in my grandmother's attic/basement/garage."

"My mother/mother-in-law wants me to sell it for her."

"Got it at a flea market/yard sale/ thrift shop. One of those places."

"I don't know. I can't remember."

"Found it by the side of the road. Must have fallen out of the back of a truck."

Sometimes dealers didn't care how questionable the origin of the merchandise was. If they wanted it, they could offer what they were willing to pay and it was usually accepted. Sales were almost always made in cash, names were rarely given. Some sellers of this type returned regularly, getting an idea of what dealers were looking for and catering to their tastes. Most of the time it was all above board, at least insofar as the dealers were concerned, and some didn't concern themselves too much. This is not to say that they would knowingly buy questionably-obtained goods. They discussed things with other dealers, seeking a second opinion on the goods offered if something didn't seem right. But they were in the business to buy and sell antiques, and it was the genuineness of the article that was uppermost in their mind. The seller's integrity was of lesser importance.

The second type of sellers was what the dealers called part of the "little old lady network," although they were by no means all small, elderly or female. These were people who were downsizing and didn't mind making a little profit, while stressing that they just wanted to see their things go to people who appreciated antiques. Someone was going to a nursing home, someone else's parents were leaving their large house and moving into a condo, the children did not like the furniture they'd inherited, someone else just wanted to clear the clutter. Often these were local people, known to one or more of the dealers. They had whole sets of china and silverware or nice pieces of furniture to sell. They took checks and everyone was scrupulous about giving fair price.

Dealers were much more at ease with these sellers, consulting reference books, identifying items when necessary, and informing them if they could only offer a fraction of book price. It was much more an exchange between peers, in which dealers would honestly tell sellers if they would be better off putting an ad in the classified section of the newspaper, or if they even ought to sell at all. Children who are not interested in heirlooms now often change their minds when they have grandchildren themselves.

These sellers did not always come in. They or a relative would call the shop and explain that they had antiques to sell, and would anyone be interested?

Given the nature of the items, several dealers regularly bought from the little old lady network. Emmy who dealt in linens, silver and china, Marv with his eye for furniture, Ruth with her ironstone and glassware expertise, Richard who understood little old ladies, and Elaine with her knowledge of everything. They made house calls and bought on site. Sometimes it was heartbreaking.

Ruth one day, having come into the shop with a set of etched stemware in every size from cordial to goblet, put her boxes down near the front with a sigh.

"Ruth! What you got? Can't I help you carry those? Is there more?" asked Hal, who was staffing the front counter.

Ruth smiled weakly at this big, healthy engineer and then, unable to help herself, her eyes filled with tears. This was not like Ruth, crying in public, but the sadness she felt at the plight of her client, the octogenarian whose glassware she now had—this sweet, frail lady who was so distressed at having to leave her home, the pathos of her situation, the way her life was being removed from her piece by piece—the sadness Ruth felt was overwhelming.

Sylvie, who had been nearby, came running and put her arm around Ruth. She knew what was going on. "Even Emmy," she told Ruth, "even Emmy says that when there's a box of linens at an estate sale, beautiful linens that were put away so carefully to be saved for some special occasion but then never, ever used, even Emmy says she feels like crying."

Ruth smiled gratefully through her tears at Sylvie, glad that she had friends who understood the sadder side to antiques.

There was one more type of seller: other dealers. This could be the dealer from across the aisle or across the country. Across the aisle was pretty cut and dried; dealers bought from fellow dealers all the time. Sometimes they even made swaps.

Out of town was another matter. One met dealers at sales, on buying trips, at shows and in other antiques shops. Their names were known and more or less where they came from. They were invited to stop by Cider Run if they ever came to town and it was hoped that they would. Many came and bought. Some came with things to sell, knowing what the dealer had been interested in when they met previously. There was a slight feeling of obligation to buy, but bargaining was always a possibility, so this was considered a practical and acceptable means of obtaining antiques.

It didn't mean that dealers didn't have to be careful with this kind of seller. Could they be sure of their reliability? Not always. There were reproductions out there and some of them were very genuine looking. The Cider Run dealers usually consulted with each other if there were any questions, but not always.

Not always, because when someone came up to the front counter with a box or asked if anyone wanted to come out to the parking lot to have a look at things in the trunk of a car, it was an exciting moment. Caution might not be entirely thrown to the winds, but the antiques hunter in every dealer was immediately activated. It was a moment to subdue all outward signs of eagerness and say, casually, "What do you have?" And once in a while, Bingo!

Summer wound down, new working schedules were begun and fall slipped in with its hold-your-breath beauty. Whatever might be said about the Appalachian spring, autumn is the triumph.

By late September yellow leaves began to fall quietly in the orchard and crickets chirped in the dry grass in the daytime. It was still warm, but the shadows were earlier and longer. Then came October, the driest month, living up to its golden, blue-skied promise, with valley fog in the morning, bright days, and cold, clear nights. Gradually, the hills started turning gold and red, first the lower slopes and then on to the ridge tops, until every hillside blazed with color up and down the length and breadth of the mountains.

As in response at Cider Run Antiques, corn shocks, with pumpkins nestling underneath, were arranged outside flanking the door. On the front counter there was a big pot of chrysanthemums and a pressed glass compote filled with candy corn. The cider press was decked with dried flowers of autumnal hues. In the dealers' areas the harvest theme manifested itself with vintage papier-mâché jack-o-lanterns and cardboard black cats. There were candles from the Forties in pilgrim and turkey shapes, and Indian corn in yellowware bowls.

The outdoor auction sales took on a kind of urgency. Like the crickets, their time was almost over. Keith and Owen, standing well in back of the rows of chairs, viewed the action one Saturday afternoon.

"See that old guy over there?" said Owen, nodding discreetly toward a portly, unkempt-looking, sixtyish man wearing dirty jeans and a soiled corduroy jacket.

"What, him?" asked Keith.

"He's a millionaire. Used to be a farmer, used to own all the land the new shopping mall is built on. He just buys whatever he wants, for the hell of it. Doesn't even care. I hear he just piles the stuff on the floor of his basement."

"You're kidding," Keith replied.

"I've seen him in action at auctions. It's a damn pity."

Observing people at the sales and commenting on them was one of the pleasures of the day. Depending on the location or the type of goods on offer, different people showed up. A farm sale might bring country people, one in a small town could have half the town turning out. In the larger towns, neighbors were drawn by the sound of the auctioneer's amplified voice and also drawn by a general curiosity—the house at last open, its contents revealed. But at most advertised auctions, many of the same people showed up, collectors, dealers and entertainment seekers. And an auction could be good entertainment. There weren't always bargains, though. People who really wanted something, and often this was family when an estate was being auctioned off, would go much higher than a dealer who needed stock. Also, of course, there were newer household items mixed in with the older things. Still, even if the goods were uninteresting, there was a lot going on. When the bid went back and forth between two parties, it was like watching a tennis match.

On that October day, as people sat or stood chatting, eating, bidding, watching the drama of the auction, most were oblivious to the other drama: the hills rising up behind in an achingly lovely crewel-work tapestry of crimson, copper, bronze, amber, and deep evergreen against an azure sky. It was almost too beautiful to deal with, to view without emotion, without a silent response deep inside that acknowledged the end of summer, the coming of winter.

"You gonna bid on that fly rod?" Owen asked Keith.

"And on the box of lures. I'd like to bid on the creel if he ever brings it up. It's just been sitting there on the table; they keep ignoring it. Think I'll move in a little closer."

"I'll get us some coffee," Owen offered.

"Wait. They're bringing out that treadle sewing machine you said Lynn wanted."

"I'll stick around. But that's just the sort of thing that greedy bastard likes to get. At least I can bid him up." Even though it's dangerous, thought Owen, it can be fun.

The sun was settling lower over the hills, casting a diffused, golden haze. A chill pervaded the air, rising from the ground. The auctioneer's sing-song continued, like a siren call, mesmerizing its listeners.

Owen started collecting his purchases. "I need to pay up and go. We're having Lynn's parents over for dinner tonight," he said with a grimace.

"Want me to bid on the Matchbox sets for you? I'll be here a little longer."

"Thanks, Keith, if you wouldn't mind. Stay under, oh, $25. No, that's wishful thinking. Stay under $40."

As Keith headed to his car later, he heard the auctioneer saying, "Folks, we're losing the light. I want to thank you all for coming and remember we'll be finishing up next week, so I expect to see everyone back here then."

You can be pretty optimistic about that, thought Keith, because you never brought up a whole bunch of the good stuff. Oh, well, it's a game and by now everyone knows the rules. But he had gotten the fishing equipment he wanted and Owen's Matchbox sets for less than $30, and he was quite pleased.

The partners decided that since there had been no grand opening party, they'd have an "Off to a Great Start" party for dealers and their guests.

Helen proposed that it be a little more than casual, perhaps a chance to dress up a bit. They decided that holding it in the shop would be the most atmospheric, with candles and, wait! Could a fire be lighted in the fireplace too? Wine and beer, cheese and French bread. How about pate? Yes, at least two kinds. Cider, without question. A few desserts. Something in dark chocolate. It was going to be a swell sort of affair because Cider Run was definitely a swell sort of place.

A notice was posted by the mailboxes and murmurs of approval were heard. "It's a dealer appreciation party. We couldn't have done it without you," Marv told every dealer he saw.

"Aren't you afraid we'll burn the place down?" asked Elaine, when she learned of the plans to have a fire in the fireplace.

"You? Worried about smoke and flames?" taunted Richard.

"Off to a Great Start," said Grace, reading the notice. "Doesn't that remind you of school, Ruth, when the principal always began the September letter to parents with 'We're off to a great start!'"

"They could hardly say, 'We're off to a rocky start,' though we sometimes were," Cora rejoined. "Remember those awful portable classrooms in the playground? The ones they brought in when the overcrowding got too bad. Stifling and then the rain so loud on the metal roof. Great start, ha!"

"Oh, dear," laughed Ruth, "I'm afraid I always said 'great start' in my new-school-year letters."

"So it isn't any different in New England. Well, that's a comfort. When it comes to public schools, you can depend on things to be the same everywhere," Grace affirmed.

"Although," Ruth allowed, "the six years I was in Maine were very different than being in a suburb of Boston."

"Maine? That was plucky of you. Boston is as far north as I'd want to go," Cora stated. "What made you want to live in Maine?"

Ruth hesitated and Grace realized it was an awkward moment. She said quickly, "You haven't lived until you've wintered in Maine, I'll bet, huh, Ruth?"

Ruth, not wanting to appear cagey, responded, "I needed a change of scene and they offered me a very good position."

Marv, hanging around the sidelines of this conversation, entered in. "I didn't realize you'd lived in Maine, Ruth. Massachusetts I can understand. It's pretty much gotten civilized over the years. Well, in some aspects anyway, as long as they're not behind the wheel. But Maine? I thought it was turned over to the moose and bears in the winter."

"It does test one, but you get used to it," admitted Ruth with a smile.

"You're going to have to tell us about it sometime," Marv urged. "You'll be able to keep us entertained for hours with tales of large, hungry animals. It will be just the thing on long, slow afternoons in January when the customers have forgotten we're here." And I might not mind a long, slow afternoon like that, he thought to himself.

The party was held on an evening that promised frost. The fireplace had been seen to by a chimney cleaner and a fire was burning cheerily. The food had been put out on one of Sylvie's beautifully refinished tables. Since she had applied two coats of polyurethane varnish to protect the top, she was not worried about damaging the finish. White English ironstone plates and brown patterned transferware held the various goodies. Emmy had brought in French wine glasses and the drinks were put on one of her large silver serving trays. Only a few lamps in the background were on.

Candles in candlesticks of pewter, silver, brass, china and crystal provided the lighting. The silver gleamed and the wine sparkled. It was definitely swell, as had been hoped. It was, one could even say, romantic.

The partners greeted everyone and introduced any heretofore unmet spouses. Sylvie had a new, svelte hairdo and Hal wore his tie with the antique tools print. The tie was a sensation and everyone asked where Sylvie had found it.

Marv was wearing a coat and tie, even though he had vowed never to be seen in them again once he retired. He looked impressively professorial and took a lot of ribbing. Helen was quite radiant, or maybe it was the lighting, but she was too busy right now to brood on past betrayals.

Elaine was wearing her first cashmere twin set of the season, although with a linen skirt. She had brought her husband, the normally monosyllabic Kurt ("Hello, I'm calling from Cider Run. Is Elaine there?" "Yep," or "Nope, not here."), who turned out to be quite chatty, no doubt warmed by the fire, the drink and the food.

Laurel, elegant as always, had Joe with her, at least for part of the evening, until he got a call and had to go to the hospital.

Emmy and Charles came but said they could only stay "for a minute," as they had another party to go to. The minute ended up being closer to two hours.

Bob had been let out of the basement and was there with Cora. Grace and Frank, Owen and Lynn, Keith and June, people all commenting on the transformation of the place. Who knew it could be such a perfect setting for a sophisticated affair like this? And the antiques looked so right in candlelight.

Sally Ann had recently joined Cider Run and arrived at the party wearing one of her vintage Thirties dresses, a splashy print of giant cream-colored magnolia blossoms on a purple background, the rayon fabric draped over one hip, with purple toeless high heels. Sally Ann's outfit was, as Richard said, "absolutely magnificent." Sally Ann was overjoyed at being part of this marvelous group. Would there be parties all the time?

Ruth, in a decision she could not have explained to herself then, had chosen a very flattering little black dress and black sling-back heels. She had on a gold necklace and earrings, which caught the firelight and set off the dark of her dress and the paleness of her skin. To see Ruth in this extremely becoming mode was startling; at the shop she always wore slacks and shirts or sweaters. The effect she had on Marv was arresting. He found himself stealing glances at her whenever he could. Ruth, on her part, had never seen Marv in business attire, and while the conventional side of her mind registered this as, "Oh, and doesn't Marv look nice too," something deeper gave her a rush of excitement and made her ache a little when she looked at him, and of this she was very conscious.

Jake was there alone with apologies from Annette, who was called out of town. He was cordial to everyone and the candlelight only made him more handsome. He kept the fire going, and since the fireplace was in his area, it seemed as if he were presiding over the event.

In this pleasant ambience of friends and shared interests, good food, drink and soft lighting, the evening flowed in a relaxed swirl of happy talk and laughter. Most of what was said was soon forgotten, but the basic impression of ease and fellowship was a lasting memory.

Except, there were two conversations that were not forgotten.

Marv, after refilling Ruth's glass with wine, finally decided to say what he had been wanting to. "You look lovely tonight, Ruth," he said sincerely, his eyes expressive.

And Ruth, flustered by his attention after experiencing a new and unmistakably emotional response to him, reverted to old habits of deflecting compliments and replied, "Everyone does. And the shop looks lovely too."

"That's not what I meant," Marv said quietly.

And,

"Laurel, do you need a ride home?"

"Thanks, Jake, but I'm sure someone can take me home. Aren't you supposed to stay around and help clean up?"

"Not necessarily. I'll take you home."

Chapter 7

November came in with a dry scuttle of leaves. On a Saturday morning during the first week of the month, Ruth and Sally Ann, working the day together, had just arrived at the shop and were considering the box of doughnuts Sally Ann had brought. Jake was already there, busy in his area and had made a pot of coffee.

"They cheated me on the chocolate filled. I said I wanted two of those," Sally Ann observed with a pout.

"I'm happy to have a plain one," Ruth offered. "Jake!" she called. "Would you like a doughnut with your coffee?"

The front door opened with a whoosh of air and a few leaves blew in, accompanied by Emmy carrying a large open box from which protruded all manner of silver items. She set the box down on the front counter and began the chant, "Remember, remember, the fifth of November, gunpowder, treason and plot." Having got the attention of her fellows, she continued, "Did I ever tell you about the time we were in Lewes on Bonfire Night?"

On cue, Sally Ann asked, "What's Bonfire Night?"

"In England they celebrate Guy Fawkes Day," Ruth started to explain, as she had lived there one year and spent much of her time in Sussex.

"It's the day they burn all the Catholics. They throw 'em on the bonfire," Jake said with relish, coming up behind Emmy.

"Ooh, then you'd get burned to death, wouldn't you, Jake?" asked Sally Ann, big blue eyes open wide.

"Not me. I quit all that years ago. Annette would, though. She never misses Mass."

With doughnuts and coffee and no customers yet, a sense of companionship prevailed, heightened by the recognition that this lull was temporary.

"Is Annette coming in to work sometime? I haven't seen since summer," Ruth said to Jake.

"As a matter of fact, we're going off next week. Annette has a conference in Holland and wants me to go with her."

"How nice, Jake!" exclaimed Ruth.

"Where in Holland are you going?" asked Emmy, England and bonfires immediately dismissed. "Amsterdam? Have you been there? So many things to see! The canal house museums: they're just fantastic. When we were there..."

One had to interrupt Emmy sometimes. "Amsterdam, yes, and Annette wants to go where they grow the tulips. I can't see why, as it's November and there won't be any tulips, but we've got a rental car lined up anyway."

"Then you must," Emmy commanded, "you absolutely must, go to Maastricht. It's near the German border, only about two hours from Amsterdam. Maastricht, on the Maas, you know, was a center of the porcelain and pottery industry."

"I've sold Maastricht china," Ruth put in, "bowls, plates. They're beautiful."

Emmy nodded, adding, "Maastricht didn't get bombed during the war and the main ceramics factory is still there. In the downstairs showroom they have a special separate exhibit of Maastricht china, starting from the early 1800's and going straight through to Art Deco. It's out of this world. I just stood there entranced."

Not having been interrupted, she continued, "The factory doesn't make china anymore. That part of the industry ended with the war, but they're one of the leading producers of bathroom fixtures in Europe. You should see their showroom, the sinks and tubs and toilets and all, Euro-modern but just gorgeous. We are so behind the times here compared to their styles. I simply couldn't resist using the restroom, to see if they had installed fixtures with as much class as the showroom and they had. It was completely luxurious!"

Jake took a deep breath. "Emmy," he said, "I will go to Maastricht and visit the factory with only one goal in mind, and that will be to go into the restroom and sit on the same seat and think about your plump little bottom having been on the very spot."

Emmy's eyebrows shot up. "You'd use the *Ladies*?!" she gasped.

It was all Ruth could do not to laugh out loud. Jake fixed a stern look at her.

"Listen, Jake," Emmy went on, quite seriously, "if it says 'Damen' on the door, you don't want to go in there."

One more auction, Keith decided, and that was it for him for the season. His knee ached in the cold and even with Owen's diverting company it could be a tiring day. Sometimes it took forever for what he wanted to be brought up by the auctioneer and then the bidding might go much too high for him. When you're a collector, it's different, Keith reflected.

You don't mind paying for things you want for yourself. But buying to resell means you have to figure out what price you can put on something and then try not to pay more than about half of that. And this is what made auction sales so interesting, he thought, never knowing who would be there and what they'd want and what you might get or, on a good day, get away with.

Owen picked Keith up Saturday morning and they drove to a farm where the auction was to be held, but for some reason, either they had the wrong day or it had been cancelled, there was wasn't anything going on.

"Do you want to go back home?" asked Owen. "Lynn is taking the kids to her parents and then she's going shopping with a friend, so we could do something else. Did you happen to check if there are any more sales around here?"

"I did, and there aren't. But there is something up this way I wouldn't mind seeing. It's a hunting camp for sale. I think you can buy an individual cabin. When I was looking through the paper this morning I saw it in the real estate section and I thought maybe it could be interesting." Keith had brought the paper with him, tossing it onto the floor of Owen's van when they first started out, and he reached for it now.

Owen wasn't a hunter, but he enjoyed being with Keith and knew how much Keith appreciated antiques having to do with the sport. He might learn something and the day, although chill, was bright.

They headed up one of the ridges. By the side of the road oaks grew thickly, their burnished copper leaves standing out in the sunshine. Last of the trees to lose their leaves, the oaks still hung onto autumn, while others had long since spilled their color on the forest floor.

For a while the road went beside a tumbling creek that Keith looked at with interest. "You fish, don't you, Owen?" he asked.

"Yes. But now?"

"No, no. Next spring. I have a boat, well, an aluminum thing, but it's fine for the purpose. We can go out to one of the lakes."

Nice, thought Owen. He'd look forward to that. He decided to get a rise out of Keith. "Do we get to use your antique fly rods?"

Keith grinned. There was nothing like a bamboo rod. "Sure, as long as you don't get the price tag wet."

They found the camp turnoff, a dirt lane with a chain across it barring the way. "Shall we try anyway?" suggested Keith.

Owen parked the van, and they stepped over the chain and began to walk down the lane. Pale yellow and brown leaves covered the ground beneath them. Overhead, bare branches intertwined like a trellis, letting the autumn sunlight through and casting a network of shadows. The narrow lane and the woods drew them in, and Owen was conscious of a lump in his throat from the quiet beauty of it all. He wondered if Keith felt the same way, then noticed Keith was walking with difficulty. Would it be appropriate to say something? Darn, thought Owen, I'd like to find out more about him but I don't want to pry.

About a quarter mile from the main road, the lane ended in a clearing. There, in a circle, stood half a dozen stone cabins and a larger stone building. Stone fireplaces and wooden picnic tables were grouped in the center.

"I'll be damned." Keith whistled softly.

"What is it?" asked Owen.

"Do you know what this is?" Keith said, sweeping his arm around the compound. "This is CCC work."

"Civilian Conservation Corps? You mean from the Thirties?"

"They built camps just like this. Look at the stonework. It's master stonemason quality. I can't believe it. We've just walked into an old CCC project."

In the distance they could hear the splash of water and they followed the sound to where a little stream, doubtless the same one that had been heading down the mountain, flowed into a pool. A stonework ledge ran around the sides of the pool and formed a dam at one end. A stone bridge arched prettily across the run-off downstream.

"I'll be damned," said Keith again.

They went back to the clearing, peered into cabin windows and tried locked doors. Then Keith asked, "Do you mind if we sit down for a bit? My knee is giving out."

The sun had warmed the weathered wood of the picnic tables, and they sat on the top of one, their feet resting on the bench. It was very still, only the sound of the stream in the background and an occasional bird calling somewhere in the woods. The place, the moment, gave the hushed sensation of enchantment, and both of them felt it.

"You know," Keith began after a while, "I had an uncle who spent summers when he was a teenager working in CCC camps. Not around here, down in Cross County. He was my father's older brother, and after my dad died we spent a lot of time with him. He took us kids to a CCC project once. It had a big stone lodge and a whole lake they'd made. This is like a miniature version."

Owen had picked up on the "us kids." He asked Keith, "How old were you when your father died?"

The morning drew on. Keith talked about his father, his own time overseas in the army, his injury, and his rehab experiences. His voice got softer when he spoke about June and his two children. He wasn't sure what he'd do with the business degree once he got it, but things were looking quite promising.

Then Keith turned to Owen. "Griffith. That's Welsh, isn't it? You're not from Marten County, are you?"

"Well, not that far. My great-grandfather came over from Wales to work in the coal mines. They settled in Hazleton, Shamokin, around there. The company owned them. A hard life. Black lung, the whole bit."

"Those were tough times," agreed Keith. "Your father, though. He didn't work in the mines too, did he?"

"He was smart. Or maybe just lucky," Owen replied. "He married someone whose parents had a store, and then he and my mom took it over." Owen smiled. "Maybe that's why I like working my days at Cider Run. I have retail sales in my blood." Owen went on, "When I was in college, I had a professor who was putting together a book of photographs taken in Pennsylvania during the Depression. I got to help him sort the pictures. One was of the same slag heap that was practically right outside the door of my grandparents' house. You look at those old black and white pictures of the miners, their faces smeared with coal dust and the dismal landscape, just the whole grimness of their lives..." Owen looked away, then said, more decisively, "Well, the mines shut down and that was that, but they still haven't put out the fires that have been smoldering for decades underground."

The two were quiet for a moment, then Keith broke the silence and brought them back to the present. "I'm starving! Let's get out of here and find some lunch."

That evening, after their two boys had been put to bed, Owen told Lynn about Keith. His father had been killed in Vietnam when Keith was eight. Naturally, his dad was his hero and all Keith wanted was to emulate him. Keith's mother was bitter; what she wanted was to have nothing to do with anything military. Keith, to please his mother, hid his feelings. When he graduated from high school, she remarried and he joined the army. The Gulf War started and he got shipped to Kuwait along with others from Pennsylvania. There he took a hit, his knee got smashed up pretty badly. Friendly fire, the same kind of action that killed his father. That was the changing point. Out of the army, with his benefits, Keith went to Vietnam to try to put things into perspective. It wasn't a success.

"What happened?" asked Lynn.

"He said he really didn't know what to do or how to go about it, whatever 'it' was. He thought he could come to terms with his father's death if he went to Vietnam, but as he was standing there looking at rice paddies he realized he was just sorry, just so damned sorry about everything, that's all. So he left."

Keith decided to spend a few days in Taiwan on his way home. His knee had been swelling and he needed a break before the long plane trip. He met a young woman named Jun-Yun in a bicycle rental shop, bike riding being good exercise for his knee. He ended up spending almost a month there, getting to know her. She spoke excellent English and they rode their bikes all over and talked about everything. She had lost her father when she was young too. He was shot, in Beijing, for his political views. It was incredible to find someone who had so many of the same feelings about things. They got married there and came back to Pennsylvania and began the long road of college for Keith, jobs, children and, most remarkably, happiness.

"And his antique stuff? The guns and all?" asked Lynn.

"Keith said he was seeing a psychiatrist for a while. The doc told him to just collect things, instead of trying to live it."

"The therapeutic side to antiques."

"I always thought so," Owen agreed. "But, you know," he added, "Keith is the kind of guy you wouldn't want to have for an enemy."

Lynn asked, "What makes you say that?"

"Well, for one thing, he's so calm, unlike me. He's been through hell and he's calm. You have the feeling that he has strength, conviction. If he were convinced that something needed to be done, he would just do it. He's also self-assured, unlike me. Calm. Strong. Self-assured. Like you."

The conversation he'd had with Keith had got Owen thinking about the past, a subject which had always interested him, even though he had opted for teaching science, not history. It wasn't about his own past. His thoughts were tied up more with antiques. Why do we feel so strongly about antiques, he wondered? Was it a way to experience the past? Or maybe, as in Keith's case, a way to settle some score with the past? You couldn't relive it, you couldn't bring the past back, but you could have some of the things from that time. He was not, he felt, a deep thinker, and this was about as deep as he could go, but it intrigued him and, like many of the other dealers at Cider Run, he was glad he had a hand in preserving some parts of the past.

Keith was thinking about today's conversation too. He hadn't talked much about himself before, hadn't opened up to anyone except June, but today had been different. Partly it was Owen, with whom he felt comfortable and compatible, but it had also been the place, the secluded, sturdy beauty of it. It was a step back to the past that had affected them, beckoned and charmed them both. He felt liberated by today, and he was determined to pursue buying the property.

Ruth had gone through the rest of Saturday still amused over the comedy scene that had taken place that morning between Emmy and Jake. It turned out to be a busy day, as Saturdays were, with at least eight to ten customers in the shop most of the time. Hal had come in, Emmy had stayed, and the five of them were needed. At 6:30 with everyone gone, she and Sally Ann had closed up and settled the day's business, and Ruth sent Sally Ann home. As she locked the door, she was aware for the first time of a thought hanging around in the back of her mind, but which had not yet made itself manifest.

She went back to the kitchen with the coffee cups, washed them and the coffee pot. The insistent little nagging thought was still there and as Ruth came back into the shop area, it began to fall into place. She stopped in the middle of the floor.

England. They had been talking about England to start with this morning. That was what it was. It had brought back the year she had spent there on a Fulbright. How long had it been since she'd thought of him?

"Brad," said Ruth out loud.

"Excuse me? Did you just say 'Brad?'" asked Richard, putting his head around the corner of his area.

"Oh, Richard! I didn't know anybody was here!"

"Well, I may not be anybody, but I am here and I distinctly heard you say 'Brad.' Who or what is 'Brad?'"

"My husband," said Ruth.

84

"Great God Almighty, Ms. Ruth!" Richard exclaimed with genuine astonishment. "I didn't know you had a husband! And why have we not met the fortunate Mr. Arden?"

"No, Arden is my family name. Brad and I were divorced years ago."

"And where is this Mr. Brad now? Not at the bottom of the sea, I trust?"

Ruth smiled, "He's probably right where I left him, in Florida, with his wife of," Ruth reckoned, "nearly thirty years."

"Ruth, you absolutely take my breath away! Do you want to tell Richard about it, or will I be left dying of curiosity? I cannot imagine you ever having set foot in Florida."

"And I probably shouldn't have. But I didn't meet Brad there. I met him when we were both in England on an exchange program, school teachers from the U.S. on the loose." And it was grey and I was homesick. Then it was romantic and exciting, thought Ruth. Aloud she said, "Girl meets boy, boy and girl hit it off, girl marries boy and goes home with him. Then, well, complications set in."

"Although I wouldn't know about the boy and girl part from personal experience, I can extrapolate. But do go on. I must know how it ends."

Oh, Richard, thought Ruth, you are such a delight! She went on with her explanation. "How it ended was that when he took me home to Gainesville, his Mama and his sisters and his cousins and all his friends wasted no time in showing their extreme disapproval of this outlander. In the South, this is done by heaping the despised object with sugary sweet talk until you are dazed and can't tell they are actually insulting you. After that they ignore you."

"I thought Gainesville was enlightened. They have the university there and all, don't they?"

"I guess that aspect hadn't rubbed off on Brad's people. When they found out I was from New England, I must have heard the 'Yankee' joke a hundred times. They acted as if I should just love the cuteness of it every time they told it."

"Wait," interjected Richard, "don't tell me. Is that the one that goes 'Until I turned eighteen, I always thought damn Yankee was one word?'"

"Or the one that goes, 'What does Yankee mean anyway? Oh, that's just an abbreviation. For what? For damn Yankee.' And Brad would laugh along with them."

"So, what did you do? Agitate to emigrate?"

"It was taken out of my hands by Brad's womenfolk. Within a few weeks the old girlfriend was back on the scene and after some more unpleasant months, Brad and I agreed to an amicable parting. Story over," Ruth finished, not without a smile at Richard.

"Whew! I am relieved you are out of there. We shall not speak of the contemptible Brad again."

"Brad wasn't so bad, when he was away from home. But it was obvious no one was going to let him leave home again. One of life's lessons, I guess, that you learn the hard way." Well, thought Ruth, better to have loved and lost, etc. Although, at the last, it had been painful.

"Ruth," Richard proposed, "what say you and I blow this place and get some chow. I don't know about you, but I'm frazzled just hearing your tale, and I could not get one more thing done after such a revelation. Let's go. God knows you've earned dinner."

As they were leaving, Richard turned to Ruth, "What about antiques hunting when you were in Florida? Anything interesting?"

Ruth, laughing, said, "No luck there either."

Chapter 8

A few weeks before Thanksgiving, Helen and Cora got together and came up with the Cider Run Christmas card. Cora took the fireplace as the subject and, with Helen's suggestions, did a watercolor which had all the elements Jake envisioned the day they first saw Cider Run. It must have made quite an impression on Helen, because she remembered everything he had mentioned. The pewter candlesticks, the crock and jug, the copper boiler holding logs, the wrought iron utensils hanging from hooks: it was all there. Cora added some greens on the mantel and a wreath hanging above and had a fire burning brightly in the hearth.

The card went out to customers and other dealers who had come in and left an address, and everyone else they could think of. Cora framed and presented the original painting to the shop and it was put up near the fireplace.

If Jake felt a glow of personal satisfaction in his prescience, he did not mention it. He plunged himself in backed-up work at the real estate agency after he and Annette returned from their trip to Europe. This had the effect of curtailing his time at the shop, at least up until the day after Thanksgiving. Then, as everyone in the world of retail sales knows, things get interesting.

On Thanksgiving evening all the dealers who had stayed in town for the holiday came into the shop to remove autumn and install winter. The cider press was decked with holly, the chrysanthemums taken away and a big pot of evergreens put on the counter. A wreath went up over the mantel, as well as outside by the front door. In the dealers' individual areas, tempting items for gift giving were laid out, suitably embellished with Christmas cards, tinsel, ribbons and glass ornaments from the past. It was busy and sociable. Excited chit-chat flowed between dealers.

"Do you have any space in your area for this market basket? I'm clean out of room. You can put decorations in it or anything else you want."

"Market basket? I need a place to put this dresser!"

"I've got a whole bunch of holly here if anyone wants it."

Grace was putting up a paper chain made by the grandchildren. Frank had come in to help, his function being to hold the chair she was standing on, a chair that Bob had labored over for hours in the basement, getting the finish to the exact degree of smoothness, before bringing it in to their combined area. Grace instructed Frank, "If Cora and Bob come in, distract them."

Elaine showed up and explained, "I only came to see what everyone was doing," a patent lie, as she was carrying a Minton cachepot, two dolls and a box of embroidered linen guest towels. "Then I saw all the cars in the parking lot and decided it must be a party."

"Slightly different from the last one, more's the pity," Marv commented, thinking not only of the food and wine.

Sylvie asked, "Richard, where in the world did you find the red and green quilt, with *stars*? It's just perfect!"

"I hope it doesn't sell until Christmas is over. It would absolutely ruin my whole décor if someone bought it. Pay attention, everybody! The quilt stays!"

Emmy set a table with a white damask linen cloth and matching napkins, gold-rimmed Haviland dessert plates, and beautifully polished silver spoons, forks, knives and seldom-seen serving pieces. She had at least four pairs of silver candlesticks and several singles in which she placed red candles and had them surrounding a silver coffee urn filled with holly. A little table-tent sign which said *Entertaining Ideas* was the final touch. Emmy stepped back to judge the effect and smacked into Laurel, who was carrying an armful of velvet throw pillows in various states of faded glory.

"Oh, Laurel, I'm sorry!" Emmy apologized, stooping to pick them up.

"That must be why they're called throw pillows," Laurel gaily answered back.

Sally Ann had also set a table, her tablecloth brightly printed with poinsettias and pine boughs. On it she had stacked red and green Fiesta plates, cups and saucers. Even though it was slapdash, it had a haphazard charm and was eye-catching and colorful. Having finished with the table, Sally Ann was concentrating on placing Forties and Fifties plastic icicles, Santas and snowmen on a white painted stand covered by a fluffy "snow" tree-skirt. It was instant nostalgia.

Keith came in followed by Lee, his eight year old son, who was proudly carrying a fishing creel.

"Lee!" called Grace, stepping down from the chair. "Have you brought that for me?"

"Tell Mrs. Dutton she'll have to buy it," said his father, and to Grace, with a grin, "Of course there is a buyer's premium."

Frank snorted. "We've stopped going to those auctions where they have a 'buyer's premium.' So annoying!"

"What Frank will not tell you," explained Grace, "is he bid much too high for the settee he bought and when I said, 'Frank, don't forget there's a buyer's premium,' he made a scene with the auctioneer."

Lee nudged his dad excitedly, as Helen came by carrying pumpkin pies. "Pie and coffee in the kitchen!" she called out. "Then we have a surprise!"

Everyone gathered around the table in the kitchen where the coffee was ready and there were four pies being cut and served, two apple and two pumpkin, along with huge dollops of sweetened whipped cream from a big yellowware mixing bowl. When there was a lull in the chatter and compliments, Marv made his announcement: the owners' Christmas present to the shop was a CD player. Applause and cheers went up from the group. The unit, which also had AM-FM, was going to be fully installed and operational this very evening, hooked up to the three speakers so kindly left by the former restaurant. There were more cheers. Then, as might be expected, talk turned to the kind of music that would be played.

"Marv wants opera," Helen declared. "And classical."

"Second," said Emmy.

"Double second," Ruth put in hastily, thereby forestalling Emmy's inevitable "When we were at La Scala" or "Last season at the Met."

"Why do you want to drive customers away?" asked Elaine. "I mean, I like opera. But would you want to buy antiques while you're crying over poor Violetta in *La Traviata?*"

"Whatever, we are an antiques shop, so the music should have been composed at least fifty years ago, don't you think?" Laurel remarked.

"Cole Porter would be nice," suggested Richard.

"Dave Brubeck, too," added Ruth.

Marv said, "I brought a few CDs along, some Mozart, some jazz."

"Anything, just as long as we don't have to listen to Christmas music for the next month straight. It's all they've been playing everywhere, and it's been going on since Halloween. No, *before*," Frank complained. Not that he worked days at the shop, but Frank did have opinions.

"What's wrong with Christmas music?" Sally Ann truly wanted to know.

"There's nothing wrong with the *Messiah*," Emmy pointed out.

"Oh, come on, and do we stand at attention and suspend sales during the *Alleluia* chorus?" asked Elaine.

Owen and Lynn came through the kitchen door. "We wondered where everyone was. We saw all the cars," said Owen.

"Did you have a nice Thanksgiving?" asked Helen.

"Thanksgiving!" exclaimed Richard, slapping his forehead. "When was Thanksgiving? I thought this was Christmas! I must have missed it completely."

"Isn't it astounding how you can be so full that you think you'll never want to eat again and then three hours later you're pigging pie?"

"Three hours later? We just got up from the table!"

The music question finally got decided. Dealers could play whatever they wished on the days they worked, as long as their fellow workers did not object. The only stipulation was that it be pre-Beatles, so there would be at least some old-timey feel to the music being played. "This means we can go through the Fifties," stated Marv, "and maybe a little ways into the Sixties."

"Vic Damone is in, then?"

"Yes, and we get Doris Day too."

"I thought the Beatles *were* old timey," Sally Ann protested.

Jake got to the shop after almost everyone had left. He and Annette had gone to Philadelphia to spend Thanksgiving with her parents and he had come back, without Annette. He had obviously felt an obligation to be at the shop on Black Friday; Annette had not. Jake had brought in some beautiful crèches and other antiques of a religious nature which he'd gotten in Europe. Hal was still at the shop, installing the music system.

"Jake! There's pie and coffee in the kitchen. We've been having quite a party here."

"What did everyone think of the CD player?" asked Jake.

"They were very pleased, but as you could have guessed, a heated discussion took place about types of music. We managed to settle on the Sixties as a cut-off. Or was it the Seventies?"

Hal finished hooking up the system. He put on a CD, one that Marv had brought in. Jazz, smooth and warm. George Shearing. Maybe not before the cut-off, but close enough.

"Well, that sure dates us," Hal observed.

The Christmas shopping season was good for Cider Run. On weekends, Helen and Sylvie made sure there were plates of cookies and a pitcher of cider for the customers. Dealers volunteered to come in and work extra hours and the shop stayed open until 8:00 several evenings. No one seemed to object to holiday music being played after all, maybe because the songs were ones originally recorded before 1970, and although they did without the *Messiah*, there was plenty of

Mendelssohn, Tchaikovsky and Bach to satisfy Marv and the other classical music fans.

Right before Christmas one afternoon, when darkness came before 5:00 and a light snowfall had begun, only a few customers were in the shop. Marv was helping someone who was trying to decide about a small cherry-wood framed dresser mirror with turned stanchions, the kind that sat atop a chest of drawers and tilted to the desired angle. Elaine had just brought it in that morning. The wood was beautifully finished, the piece itself was nicely proportioned, and there was a little drawer with a brass pull in its base, but the mirror itself was murky. Finally the customer, who was buying it for his wife, explained, "She's going to be using it, I hope, and even though I know she'd love it, the mirror is, well, it's so *old*, I mean, it's all cloudy."

Marv, who could see what the problem was, proposed the solution at once. "There's no rule that says an antique has to be left exactly as it is. You're planning to use it? Get a new mirror put in. Martensdale Glass does them all the time."

"Oh! You mean I can do that?"

"You can do anything you like," Marv affirmed, and the sale was made.

Helen was at the front counter, taking off a tag prior to ringing up the sale of a white ironstone serving dish embossed with a wheat and berry motif. The customer asked, "Can I keep the tag? It has so much information on it and I want my daughter to know how old it is and everything. I think she'll appreciate it more."

Helen looked at the tag, on which Ruth had put not only the date of the item, but the maker's name, place of manufacture, pattern name and the name used in the 19th century: nappy. Everything but a bibliography! Wait. Helen turned the tag over. There it was: "See Wetherbee, *White Ironstone.*"

"Certainly you may keep the tag, or would you rather I copied the information for you? We have Cider Run holiday cards."

Grace was helping another customer who was peering intently into Keith's "huntin'-fishin' case," as Richard called it. "Would you like me to open it for you?" she asked.

"I don't know. I think my dad had a bobber like that one once, years ago. Yes. I would like to see it, thanks."

Cora was on the phone with Bob. Since it was snowing, she would catch a ride home with Grace.

Jake was in the office checking sales, which he did from time to time. He had been in the shop to help out, but when it had slowed down, he went in to have a look at the books. Marv, whose customer had made his purchase and left, came in the office and slid into the chair on the other side of the partners' desk.

"So, what do you think, partner? Are we in the right business or what?" Marv asked brightly. To his surprise, Jake's answer was not as expected.

"You are. I am. I'm afraid Annette is not."

"But, man, she's our legal eagle!"

"Not for much longer. She's had a job offer in Washington. D.C. She's seriously considering it."

"Washington? She wouldn't leave us? Wait – you'd leave us too?" Marv was clearly distressed.

"Hey, Marv, I'm a part owner. I love this stuff. I go nowhere!" He seemed thoughtful for a second, then said, "Look, better not tell the others yet, but she's already made up her mind. You must have noticed, she really isn't all that wild about antiques. I used to buy her things and she'd be polite, but she isn't even polite about antiques anymore, not to me anyway. The shop was interesting to her at first. That's all." He didn't exactly sound hurt, mostly resigned.

Marv ventured, "When did things fall apart, or is it none of my business?"

"Things fell apart before we got married, if you want the truth. Catholic girls have different ideas on love and marriage, or some of them do. We never should have gotten married. *I* never should have gotten married."

Marv felt a twinge of empathy, more than a twinge. He thought, Jake's situation surely couldn't be similar to his own, could it? Some marriages are just a mistake. He said, "You're going to try to work it out though, aren't you?"

"Frankly, I don't want to, nor does Annette. No, I paid my dues long ago. I'm here to enjoy things," he said, "and I intend to."

Paid his dues? Marv wondered at that, but before he could ask, the door opened. "So this is where you two are!" exclaimed Helen. "Jake, someone has come in asking for you. I think he's got something to sell. Marv, Grace is going to take Cora home before the snow gets heavier, so could you come out because there are still one or two customers."

Between Christmas and New Year's the shop continued to bustle and, in addition to selling, the dealers were kept busy restocking, especially with things for dinners and parties. Emmy's *Entertaining Ideas* sign must have hit a resonant chord, as she had sold much of her silver, dinnerware, and several damask tablecloths and sets of napkins. Sally Ann's Fiesta sold quickly and also the gaily-printed holiday tablecloth, and in its place she had put out a tablecloth printed with sleighing scenes, which sold too, and she now had one in a bells and evergreens print. Pink and green Depression glass took the place of the Fiesta. Ruth, to her great relief, sold several sets of etched wine glasses, a relief because she had begun to despair of ever selling them. Richard was also relieved because he was able to convince a buyer to let the star pattern quilt stay where it was until New Year's, taking a markdown for the courtesy.

While some dealers went out of town for the holiday, others had guests and they were brought in to the shop. The cookie plates were kept full, the plates being some of Sally Ann's green Depression, and this led to several more sales. The cider, which was served from a pattern glass pitcher, also reinforced the idea that antiques should be used. The shop was bright and cheery in contrast to the grey of the winter landscape outside and merely being there lightened the spirits.

Ruth, with her brother and his family in Martensdale, did not go out of town and worked extra days for people who were gone. She felt happy being at the shop. If she'd had to explain it, she would have said it was because she enjoyed the people, her fellow dealers as well as those who came in. If she'd had to go a little farther, she would have admitted that it was stimulating. Which it was, all of those things. And more. But there was no need to explain or examine anything, and the holidays were better for her than they had been for years.

Marv and Helen did not go to Bucks County. Instead, Bucks County came to them, so while Helen was occupied with the family, Marv slipped away and came into the shop. Since it was usually busy he stayed to help. He was aware of Ruth being there, very aware, and glad of her presence, even though they didn't talk together about anything except the business at hand. But she smiled at him and that was enough. She warms the place up; all right, her smile warms me up, he thought happily. If he'd had to describe why her smile was so warm to him, well, he'd just keep that to himself.

During the first part of January the weather remained cold but dry, although earlier snowfalls still covered the ground. On the ridge, the dark trees stood out against the white background, like an old-fashioned photographic negative, thought Marv, as he stood looking across the valley at the hills. He had come out of the shop to ponder an increasingly annoying phenomenon: snow accumulation on gravel.

The snow removal service had suggested that they merely plow it high, which they had done, but this left more snow in the parking lot than what Marv considered safe. Not being satisfied, he called the service back and they came and sprinkled salt. That took care of most of the snow, but the melt-off made the gravel messy and muddy and salt was being tracked into the shop. Marv did not want to think about what the parking lot would look like come spring. Or the rugs. They would have to come up with a solution eventually.

Not to anyone's surprise, January was a slow month and seemed more so when compared to the wild activity of December. One morning, with no customers and Sylvie at the counter and Emmy staring intently at the diminished display in her area, Jake came through the front door. He stopped abruptly when he caught sight of Sylvie and, with no preamble, burst into song: *"Who is Sylvia, What is she? That all our swains commend her."*

Sylvie exclaimed, "Heavens, Jake! What a beautiful voice you have! I didn't know you sang! Better watch out, though, we'll get you for our choir and turn you into a Presbyterian.

Now tell me, is that the Irish tenor part of you or the Italian tenor?"

Emmy had come up, roused by Jake's rendering of Shakespeare's lines from *The Two Gentlemen of Verona*, and pronounced, "German, actually. Lieder. Well, you know, the music's by Schubert."

Emmy is so dependable, thought Sylvie. She commented, "It's terribly Victorian, isn't it? The kind of after-dinner entertainment that made the ladies swoon."

"Victorian, romantic and absolutely essential on a freezing winter day when one is surrounded by such loveliness." He kissed his fingers, wafted the kiss at Sylvie and Emmy, and went back to his area.

"Could be the entertainment," said the ever-pragmatic Emmy, when Jake had left, "but more likely too tight corsets after a heavy meal."

This was the day when Andy King came in with his washing machine. Sylvie thought he was quite nice and, particularly after Jake, very sensible and sincere, a farm boy grown up.

Keith came to tidy his area and put in a few new things, among them a genuine Flexible Flyer sled that he'd cleaned and repaired and meant to get in before Christmas. He saw Jake across the room and, when he finished in his area, went over.

"Jake, I need to talk to you about some property I saw last fall," he began.

"Come back to the office," said Jake, the realtor.

At 5:00 Annette came in the door. Sylvie looked up and exclaimed, "Annette! Where have you been keeping yourself?"

"Between the pages of legal documents, it seems," answered Annette, "and I'm only here to take Jake out to pick up his truck after it was serviced."

"We haven't seen you for ages. How was your conference in Amsterdam last fall?"

"It was good, very good. I made a number of contacts," Annette murmured, somewhat vaguely.

"Jake enjoyed the conference too, I take it?"

"Jake spent all his time hanging around antiques shops," answered Annette. "Sylvie, I may as well tell you, I've taken a job with a Washington D.C. law firm."

"Annette! How..." Sylvie started, then looked stricken. "Will you be moving down there then?"

"I will. Jake won't," Annette said with emphasis, and went to find Jake.

Chapter 9

The snows which held off the first half of January made their appearance in the second half. The shop opened despite the weather, opening time depending on when the snow plow came. Customer activity was at an all-time low. However, some of the out-of-town dealers showed up, hoping to bargain during this period of otherwise slow sales. Sellers came in, the little old lady network had not entirely shut down, nor had the desperate sellers faded out completely.

Still, it was often a long, uneventful day for those working at the shop, as Marv had predicted, and particularly so on weekdays. One couldn't tidy or sit and read forever; any distraction was welcome. Since someone always stayed at the front counter, this was a gathering place for dealers to pass the time.

It started out innocently enough. Maybe with Marv, certainly Jake was an active participant, Sally Ann got caught up in it and eventually almost everyone was roped in. It was the Best, Worst and Most Obscure contest and it got more competitive the more dealers it involved.

"Best" was the Best Buy You Ever Made or, alternatively, the Best Deal You Ever Got. Marv had begun by telling about the prices he and Helen had paid for furniture back when he was a graduate student.

Jake topped him by his story of how he got the partners' desk from a former law professor who knew nothing about antiques and just wanted new furnishings. "And he threw in the oak filing cabinet," Jake added smugly.

Elaine snorted. "I wouldn't be proud of taking advantage of someone."

"Now, Elaine," Jake retorted, "you know you've done it countless times."

Sally Ann entered in with, "My first husband's mother gave me her old set of Blue Willow china because she was sick and tired of it. I wasn't too crazy about it either, but I put it away, and you all know how much I got for it last fall!"

They had to agree that Sally Ann had a solid contribution for a Best on that one.

Helen looked up from the *Antiques & Auction News*, peered over her reading glasses and asked, "Did Marv tell you how we used to go out on trash night and get walnut dressers off the curb?"

"Did Helen mention that I still do?"

"But there are no more walnut dressers out there now," Jake amended, "although I did find a solid oak door with leaded glass panes last summer."

Elaine said contemptuously, "Bottom feeders."

The "Worst" referred not to the worst deal you ever made, as mistakes are less of a laughing matter. All dealers remember their chagrin at finding an overlooked "Made in China" sticker on what they thought was a piece of 19th century American art pottery, or thinking they were bidding on the whole lot, when it turned out the auctioneer was selling "by the piece." No, "worst" was the Worst Sale You Ever Went To.

By the rules of the contest, Marv reminded them, this had to be strictly the truth, no fabrications. But the quest for antiques can bring strange experiences and there were quite a few stories.

"The worst sale we went to was that one, you remember, Marv, where the woman whose things were being sold stood around and got so upset that she wasn't getting the prices she wanted..." Helen began.

Marv finished, "...that she made the auctioneer stop the sale. He forgot to turn off the loudspeaker and they got into a really nasty argument, not a word of which was lost on the hushed crowd. He finally realized we could all hear and told everyone the sale was over and to pay up and go home."

Jake said, "That wasn't so bad. Not at all a Worst. Sounds like it was good entertainment."

"It was," Marv granted, "except that the things I really wanted hadn't come up yet."

"That does put a different complexion on it, you must admit, Jake," said Elaine.

Helen asked, "Do you recall, Jake, that auctioneer who always used to berate his helpers? They never moved fast enough to suit him and if they brought the wrong thing up at the wrong time, he snarled at them. I felt so sorry for them."

Jake added, "And if he didn't think the crowd was bidding high enough, he would berate us too. It really put you off going to his sales, in spite of what was on offer."

"I dunno," countered Marv. "A little berating is a small price to pay for an excellent and inexpensive Marten County hutch."

"Oh, dream on," Elaine challenged him. "The last Marten County hutch disappeared in 1980, sold to some big dealer from Philadelphia."

"One can always hope," said Marv wistfully.

Sylvie was the next entrant. "This might not have been the worst sale ever, but it is one that had Hal absolutely incensed. The auctioneer was taking bids off the wall. I'm serious. Hal would bid and then the auctioneer would look somewhere behind him and nod and up the bid. And he had the gall to say "Thank you" each time. I looked around and I know for a fact no one else was making bids. Later, someone told us he was famous for that trick. The thing that made it so bad was that we really wanted the dining table we were bidding on, so we kept going. We must have paid twice as much for it."

"I remember that auctioneer," Marv commented. "I heard they shut him down finally, got his license."

"Serves him right," said Sylvie.

Richard weighed in. "Absolutely the worst sale I ever went to was once when it was raining and the auctioneer had not provided a tent. It was out in the country and everyone was standing under any shelter they could find. There were trees dripping on everything. The auctioneer couldn't see people holding up their numbers, but he would not quit, and people would dash out to make a bid and dash back to cover. You couldn't be sure when the bids were all in or even what it was you were bidding on half the time. And the quilts all got soaking wet."

"The worst sale for me was the one where they ran out of food and all they had left were hot dog buns," proffered Sally Ann. "And I'd gone early and hadn't had breakfast."

"These are all good," Marv nodded. "Worthy of Worsts."

"My worst sale," began Elaine with a disgruntled look on her face, "was when there was no porta-potty or privy or anything. And I'd had several cups of coffee before I realized it, and after a while I really had to go."

"What did you do?" asked Sally Ann

"Well, I couldn't leave because something I really wanted, and I cannot even remember what it was now, was going to be coming up to bid on, so I couldn't just get in my car and drive to find the nearest restroom. I mean, why did I come clear out there, anyway? So, I had no choice; I had to use the bushes. Just about the time I was done, I looked up and these guys..."

"Do we really want to hear the rest?" asked Richard.

"Oh, but we must!" protested Sally Ann.

"This does not speak well for human nature," Richard said gravely.

"I'll tell Sally Ann later, in private. But you're right, Richard. Men are pigs. Except for you," she added.

"I'm overwhelmed by your generosity, Elaine," said Richard.

"Don't get too overwhelmed. You can stand improvement."

"Sometimes it's no good even when there is a porta-potty. I remember one day the line was so long ..." Marv began.

"I am about to win the contest," announced Jake, effectively silencing Marv. "There was a farm sale I went to once in early spring, a warm day after the snow had melted. It was solid mud from the road in. People who had parked where they told you in a field had to be pulled out by a tractor by the time the sale was over."

"That ain't much," scoffed Marv.

"No, wait, there's more." Jake continued, "The place was falling down. A guy got hit on the head by a porch roof support that gave way and had to be carried out. Some of the stuff was in a chicken coop and the auctioneer decided to sell from there, so we had to go inside. It was airless and there was dried chicken poop all over and a woman fainted. I am not making this up," Jake vowed when Marv started hooting. He went on, "There was an outhouse which I tried to use, but it was so foul, I decided to go out behind it. The smell got worse as I went around to the back. The ground behind sloped off into a little gully and when I looked down, there was a dead cow lying there. It must have died over the winter and nobody had bothered to remove it."

Everyone was silent in awe and admiration. Then Marv declared soberly, "Hands down. Jake wins."

By the time the Most Obscure Source for Antiques contest got underway a week later, the Dead Cow Auction, as it was referred to, had become legend among the dealers at Cider Run. Being patently unsurpassable, it had a slightly dampening effect on the lengths to which dealers would go to win the next segment of the contest. However, long, boring periods of time, a fresh pot of coffee and few customers brought them back around the front counter. It began slowly and built up momentum.

"I stopped at a yard sale and there wasn't anything interesting. But when I was leaving, I saw these tablecloths out drying on the line in the back yard. I bought them right off the clothes line," Sally Ann said proudly.

"Good one!" Richard complimented her.

Laurel, rather sheepishly contributed, "I bought a handbag off of someone on the street once."

"Nice going," Richard interjected. "What did you do, leave her with a plastic shopping bag for her things?"

"More or less. But it was a real carpet bag. It was made of tapestry. It was definitely over a hundred years old."

"OK, you're in the running," Marv agreed.

105

Keith weighed in, "I was at this marina and they had some old metal signs on the wall for Coca-Cola and Camels. Asked the guy how much he wanted for them."

"That counts. Next!"

Elaine said, "I got a call from someone in Cross County. She said she had a bunch of things to sell and did I want to come and see? The place was down near a creek and you could tell it had flooded over the winter. I rang the doorbell and she answered the door. The mildew smell in the house was something fierce. I asked where the stuff was and she said, 'Oh, not here, out back' and led me out the back door. I saw a garage and figured that was where we were going but, no, we went on past it and there was this old school bus, broken down, weeds growing through the wheels."

"You bought out of a *school bus?*" said Richard in a shocked voice.

"She buys out of cars all the time, in the parking lot, from her cadre of little old ladies," Marv pointed out.

"That's different," insisted Elaine. "Those are operating vehicles."

"So what did you get?" asked Sally Ann.

"Surprisingly, a whole bunch of very decent McCoy planters plus several boxes of Lu-Ray china, and all in good condition."

Richard, looking out the door, said, "OK, folks, hang on for a moment. Here come some customers."

An hour later the group reconvened bolstered by more dealers, Andy among them. Marv asked, "Andy, what is the oddest place you've found to buy antiques?"

"Gosh," replied Andy, "I don't really need to buy antiques. They're just lying around in the barn. All I do is load them up."

"Some people have all the luck," Elaine commented.

"But I did get some things the other day, to sell at the shop. Do you mean that kind of buying?"

"Right. Where did you get them?" asked Marv.

"Which? The gate or the tombstone?"

"This is getting better and better," remarked Richard.

Andy explained, "The gate is that fancy wrought iron one I brought in last week. I got it from a neighbor down the road. He said he needed a new one anyway."

"Soliciting the neighbors. I like that. It has possibilities," Marv observed. "And the tombstone? I don't believe we've had the pleasure yet."

"Grace suggested I wait till next October."

"And quite properly, too," agreed Richard.

"You didn't buy it from a ghost by any chance?" Marv wondered.

Jake said, "Think before you answer, Andy. The contest could be won right here."

"What contest?"

"Most Obscure Source for Antiques contest, part three of three. I'm out of the running, having won segment two, Worst Sale."

"The suspense is getting to me. Where did the tombstone come from?" begged Richard.

"A cemetery."

"Yes, of course. A cemetery. Yes. Go on."

"This guy from the monument company was putting in a new marker for some family, and I asked what was he going to do with the old one and he said did I want it, so I said yes, how much, and he said, oh, $25, so I said, fine."

"Contest over!" Marv announced. "We have a winner!"

The contests served to spawn more stories, tales of the Antiques that Got Away and the Antiques that Never Were, the latter being fakes, particularly in china and glassware. Since there wasn't a clear winner in the Best Buy segment, dealers continued to swap experiences. Cora, the Yard Sale Queen, told of getting to a sale early one morning before it started and convincing the seller to let her have a Roseville jardinière for a fraction of its worth. Emmy, as it turned out, drove up just in time to see Cora walking off with the prize.

Helen told about a cross-country antiques buying trip she and Marv made when their daughter was young. "Shirley simply shudders when we remind her of it," said Helen. "We took back roads and Marv insisted on stopping at every little dump that sold anything. His favorite places were the ones with the sign painted on the side of the barn, *ANTIQUES 4 SALE.*"

"Yes," Marv rejoined, "with the 'N' backwards."

Elaine said, "Everyone knows that's where the real finds are. If you have to grub around underneath stuff to come up with the little finger-lamp or the unmarked Weller pottery piece, you really feel you've gotten a gem."

"Is that why your area is always in complete disarray" asked Richard, "to make the customers think that by working hard to find something it's going to be better?"

"And how are your sales this month?" Elaine fired back.

"No one's sales are great this month," Helen sighed.

"There's nothing like junk yards," said Keith. "You get dirty, but you find some really good things, and if you can fix them and clean them up, it's a very good deal."

Andy, by now a fully functioning member of Cider Run, had been taken under the combined wing of Cora and Grace.

He had been bringing in all sorts of interesting tools and farm items, a barn lantern, tin advertising pieces, old seed catalogs, and enamelware. Cora had arranged them into a series of groupings where they were displayed effectively. She and Grace also helped Andy to price things, as they had found guides that had illustrations and prices for many of the type of items Andy had. Then they made a list of other needs, like old crates and boxes to serve for shelving, which Andy promised to find and bring in.

Cora said, "I've been meaning to ask, Andy, what does your wife think of you selling all your things?"

"She's been after me for years to get rid of this stuff. If someone wants these old flour bags and scythes, that's better than tripping over them on the barn floor."

"But now you're even buying," said Grace.

"It doesn't take long to get the bug," Cora said encouragingly.

"Well, it is fun. Andy goes along with me sometimes."

"Andy is your son?"

"Our daughter. It's Andrea."

"And you are really Andrew, I take it."

"No, I'm Andreas. There's always been an Andreas in the family somewhere in each generation. When our daughter was born, we didn't know if we'd have another, so she got the name."

"What if you'd then had a son?" Grace wanted to know.

"Oh, we did. His name is Michael."

Toward the end of the day Marv found him staring fixedly at the fireplace.

"Nice, isn't it?" said Marv. "We all wanted our areas around it, but Jake won the toss."

Andy said, "That wasn't what I was thinking, although it is nice. No, I was just wondering about it. How old did you say this place was?"

"As far as we've been able to find out, the area where we're standing right now was built in 1790 or thereabouts," Marv explained. "It was added onto many times, but most of the shop part dates from the early 1800s."

"Then the original fireplace would have been different," Andy said stoutly, adding, "I'll bet," as fit his modest nature.

"No kidding?" said Marv, the historian in him saying he should have known this.

Andy went on to explain that the original fireplace was most likely quite large, made for cooking, and might have had an oven built in on the side. It would probably have extended halfway across the back wall. Obviously, a huge, gaping hearth would not have done for a fine restaurant and so it was modified.

The two immediately did some wall tapping in time-honored history sleuth fashion and found that Andy was indeed correct. Hollow sounds emanated from all around the fireplace. "And I'll also bet," Andy continued, "that there was a summer kitchen out back where they did their cooking when it was hot."

This news intrigued Marv and added even more to his high regard of Cider Run, gravel parking lot notwithstanding.

As Andy stopped by the front counter on his way out, Elaine asked, "How are things going?"

"Well, I'm learning a lot, and everyone is really helpful." Then he added, "Now that my wife has taken a job, it's nice to be here while the kids are in school."

Emmy was also getting ready to go and had just come up to say goodbye.

Elaine asked Andy, "What's your wife's name, so we can call her something other than Mrs. King?"

"Mable," said Andy.

"Mable! *Pirates of Penzance!*" Emmy snapped her fingers. "I've been meaning to bring in some Gilbert and Sullivan CDs."

"Who's Gilbert and Sullivan?" asked Andy.

"Your education is just beginning," Elaine declared.

Winter, a time when the outside world is a risky place and social interaction becomes necessary. Cider Run provided a palliative to the rigors of the season, an atmosphere clubby and communal, people on good behavior turning to each other for entertainment, people sometimes stuck together for a long time, too cold and snowy to go anywhere else.

Hal had a load of wood delivered and the fireplace was often used. Grace and Frank brought in the over-priced settee and Jake produced a Victorian fainting couch for sitting by the fire. Jake also brought in a very handsome oak Morris chair, one of the early recliners from the Arts and Crafts era, with black leather cushions. These items were not for sale, but were to be used to create a cozy place where people could relax and chat when business was slow.

An unmistakable sense of well-being pervaded when music was softly playing, overhead lights were dimmed a bit and a fire was burning. In the early darkness of a winter afternoon, the fire cast a glow on the pine and oak and cherry furniture, twinkled on brass, reflected on glassware, and bathed the faces of those around the hearth in a soft warmth. When customers came into this setting, they had the distinct urge to buy antiques.

Marv was appreciating Cider Run more than ever. What a wonderful, unanticipated bonus, the way the people and the shop went together, he reflected. Why would anyone dread winter if it could be spent like this? He thought it would be fun to write a *Guide to Survival in Winter in the Mountains of Central Pennsylvania*, with entries such as: 1. Start a business of something you find fascinating. 2. House it in surroundings that have history and charm. 3. Bring together people who are knowledgeable, lively, harmonious and endlessly interesting. 4. Have one person whom you want to get to know better.

Here his mind turned to thoughts of Ruth. Not that he'd had any chances so far to break through what he perceived to be her reserve, never being alone with her long enough to talk about anything much. How could he get to know her better, he wondered? And just what were his motives in wanting to know her better? Friendship, but maybe more? Was that fair? Wouldn't someone get hurt? He didn't want to face those considerations yet. Take it slow, he told himself. For the time being, Ruth seemed to enjoy his company and that was important. He could amuse her and make her laugh. It was refreshing and welcome.

To Ruth, the winter seemed much milder and brighter than the New England winters she was used to. Further, with her brother's family here, she had her nieces to enjoy, and she truly liked her sister-in-law, who was more like a sister to her. Ruth had joined a book review group and the Friends of the Art Museum. There were musical events on campus and foreign films. And she was comfortably settled. She had bought a very nice 1940s Cape Cod when she moved to Martensdale, a small, two-bedroom in a quiet neighborhood. Someone had added a large double garage in the Eighties, and although it was woefully out of scale with the rest of the house, it was useful for her antiques storage. But the best part of her home, she thought, was the backyard with a patio off the kitchen, mature trees and perennials and room for a good-sized garden.

Now in winter she could gaze out her kitchen window while sitting at the breakfast table and plan for spring. Spring wasn't something she pined for, the way she had in New England. She was finding the winter here to be quite bearable, more than bearable. She acknowledged that it could be because everything was new, the honeymoon effect coloring her perceptions. But she looked forward to being with her friends at Cider Run and in those afternoons when there was a fire crackling in the old stone fireplace, the whole shop reflected a feeling of warmth and congeniality. And if Marv were there, everything took on another dimension, a dimension not without excitement. He would smile at her, make her laugh, and she would think about him, think how companionable he seemed to her. And then she would sigh, and tell herself not to dwell on this last thought, because what did it lead to? Only frustration. And what could she do about it? Nothing.

But most susceptible of all that winter was Laurel.

Chapter 10

Winter wrapped around Cider Run and made it an outpost, so that once the road up from the pike had been traveled, the shop had the feel of a welcome safe harbor. Customers, having gotten this far in chancy weather, prolonged their stays to chat as well as browse. Friends dropped in, often bearing a treat: brownies, a coffee cake using the leftover cranberries from the holidays. The cookie cutter lady came with treats she'd baked using antique cookie molds. Coffee was available and lots of talk about antiques. People made it a social call.

Dealers felt the same as customers. It was hard to leave the cheering atmosphere of the shop, and after having arranged the items they had brought or getting their areas in order, they wanted to linger. There were goodies and coffee, the conversations were interesting and enlivening. Winter increased the appetite for both, food and talk.

Even the out-of-town dealers stayed around after their business had been completed. Elaine's parking lot sales moved indoors, so other dealers got a chance to look over the things offered. Jake had some foreign gentleman from whom he bought, and who kissed Elaine's hand upon being introduced. He seemed particularly fond of the cranberry cake, which was new to him. Laurel, with time on her hands, found Cider Run more enjoyable than her empty house, empty because Joe was at the hospital so much. She ran her decorating business using her mobile phone, so it didn't matter where she was, as long as she got to her appointments. She and Joe had winter-worthy vehicles, his for getting to the hospital in bad weather and hers for getting to clients who lived in remote places. Both had accepted the fact that this winter, with the hospital short-handed for doctors, would mean more hours on duty for Joe. That is, Laurel had accepted it, but was not prepared for its effect on her life.

It wasn't that she was restless, not more than anyone else in the semi-confinement of winter with its short days and long nights. The condition that Laurel was experiencing went deeper than that, right past the normal, rational functioning of Laurel's very rational and intelligent brain. It was buried in some unexamined substrata, a part that had lain dormant and unconscious. That it was unexamined was not too surprising. There had been no reason for her to delve into anything. She and Joe were busy, social and happy together.

If she had been conscious of any ruffles on the waters, she would have taken a look at them, had a nice heart-to-heart talk with Joe, felt better and gone on. But as long as it stayed unconscious, nothing could be done about it, and her behavior was able to be motivated and her thoughts directed by this force.

Being so much at Cider Run was one symptom. Wanting to be there so much was another. Her reasons were easily justifiable: loneliness, need for friends. But those weren't the only reasons. There was another reason and, because it had been so deeply buried, when she finally became aware of it, she was completely unprepared.

The first outward sign of the inward state came at the end of the summer, when Helen and Marv had returned from visiting their daughter. Helen had photos of the new baby, which she showed to everyone. Not awfully appealing to most people, a newborn, but Laurel inexplicably found herself crying. She would be thirty-five her next birthday, she and Joe had talked about having a family, had not been actively preventing it, but had agreed that there was plenty of time and they were both involved in other things. So why the tears?

The second sign was a sense of excitement about Cider Run. Driving up the hill, turning into the parking lot, she felt nervous, a little thrill. More than that: a surge of anticipation. Why? The thought of having made a big sale? The thought of those lively and provocative conversations? Whatever it was, she didn't question it. She enjoyed the feeling of excitement, which should have tipped her off and started her on the process of inner examination, but didn't.

The tip-off came eventually, though, and when it did, it came with the force of a thunderbolt during, of all unlikely places, an auction.

In winter the public sales went indoors. Unlike the year-round activity of auction houses in urban locations, indoor auctions in the rural Appalachians did not attract many buyers until the weather prohibited outdoor sales. Then the indoor venue came into its own, drawing collectors and dealers from the immediate area and beyond. But while there might be four or five outdoor auctions every weekend to choose from in the summer, there would be only one or at most two indoor auctions on winter weekends and these were crowded. There could easily be over two hundred people packed inside, all after antiques.

The places themselves were whatever the auctioneers had been able to obtain in which to conduct their business. A converted barn, an old church, a former auto body shop, one of the buildings at the fairgrounds, the fire hall: they were all the same. Uncomfortable, poorly heated, poorly ventilated, poorly illuminated, barely tolerable in terms of restrooms and serving appallingly bad food, if any. The outdoor lunch setup with its homemade pies, barbecue sandwiches and hearty soups had vanished with the season, and in its place was the too-salty wiener buried in commercial kraut. The ladies of the church guilds were sorely missed.

After the hiatus of the holidays, auctioneers began holding sales on Saturdays again. There was an auction in Marten County most weekends at different locations by different auctioneers, and the dealers of Cider Run often saw each other there. A kind of tacit agreement seemed to have been made in regard to bidding. They did not bid against each other, knowing each other's preferences. Anyway, there was plenty of competition from other sources. They also continued their tendency to sociability, comments centering on the quality of the goods, the excessive amounts bid, and the terrible food.

Laurel usually didn't go to auctions; she did her buying on trips and online. But as Joe began a Saturday schedule at the hospital, she decided it would be to her advantage to get out of the house for the day and restock her antiques inventory. So in January she became part of a group of Cider Run dealers who sat together at the auctions, varying with the goods advertised. One that had primitive furniture would bring Marv. One with toys would bring Owen. Elaine would come for most anything. Richard came if he felt like it. Laurel came for the company and also for small pieces of furniture and interesting one-of-a-kind decorating items.

"Laurel, wait! Don't bid yet!" Richard warned the first time she joined them, seeing her lift the card with her bidding number when the auctioneer asked for the first bid. "Let the starting amount drop down a bit."

"Richard, don't coach! Laurel knows the drill," Elaine chimed in.

The auctioneer's patter made an agreeable backdrop. "Ladies and Gentlemen, we have a very nice set of porcelain figurines here. We got 'R S Prussia,' something else I can't read, uh, 'Germany,' and, oh, this here one must be, what does it say, excuse me, folks, my reading glasses aren't as good as the doc said. 'Czechoslovakia,' it says here. And, what else we got? Well, I dunno. But you've all had a chance to look at them. Folks, they're in perfect condition. OK. By the piece, with the privilege. Who's gonna start me off at fifty dollars apiece? Fifty dollars. They're worth at least that much, folks. Fifty dollars, fifty dollars. Forty dollars? Look at this here one. Isn't she a sweetheart? She's worth at least a hundred dollars, I kid you not. Forty dollars, forty dollars. Thirty-five. You're breaking my heart, folks! Thirty-five dollars. Twenty-five. Twenty-five dollars for genuine porcelain, hand-painted—did I mention that, folks? Hand-painted. They don't make 'em like this anymore. Twenty-five dollars. Twenty-five. Twenty dollars, twenty dollars. Thank you, sir! I've got twenty, do I hear twenty-five? Twenty-five, twenty-five, twenty-five? Thank you, ma'am! Twenty-five. Do I hear thirty? Thirty-thirty-thirty. Thirty? Twenty-seven fifty? Twenty-seven fifty? Twenty-seven fifty? All in? All done?"

"I'm going to get a cup of coffee. Want some, Laurel?" Richard offered.

"That coffee is rotgut. Don't drink it," Elaine warned.

"Laurel drinks tea anyway. Haven't you noticed?" Jake had just materialized and sat down next to her.

"Thanks, Richard," said Laurel, "but Jake's right. The tea here won't be any better than the coffee, will it?"

"Worse. They only have one tea bag. They use it over and over."

"Look. Here comes Ruth. Ruth! Over here. Oh, damn it, he thinks I just bid on those ugly figurines!" Elaine shook her head, mouthed "no," and made a negative face at the auctioneer.

Laurel found herself looking forward to the weekend auctions. She bought well and built up her inventory. At the shop the following week she joined in the postmortems of the latest auction: who was there, the exorbitant bids some people made, how low other things went for, what, if anything, was edible at the lunch counter and what was up next week.

The first auction in February had advertised some things Laurel was interested in, although she admitted to herself that she would want to go no matter what was advertised. Before the bidding started, she was having a look at the antiques located on tables behind the auctioneer's podium. Jake was also checking the offerings. He smiled at Laurel from a few tables away, shook his head over the piled-up furniture off to the side, and came over to where Laurel had found what she wanted.

"Piano babies? Is that what you're going to bid on?" he asked.

"I have a client who wants some. The real ones, like these, are getting harder to find," Laurel said, turning over one of the pair of seated bisque dolls to look at its mark.

"Does your client have an upright piano, suitably draped with a Spanish shawl, and will perch them upon it to watch over her musical evenings in the parlor?"

119

Laurel laughed. "No, seriously, Jake. People put them on their cabinets and bookcases now."

"You're going to bid? How high will you go?"

"I'll try to stay under $100," Laurel said, "if I can."

They wandered off in opposite directions and Laurel went back to the seat where she had put her coat. She saw Grace and Frank in a row closer to the front, but there was no space near them, so she decided to stay put. All of a sudden she felt cold, unsure of herself. She turned up the collar of her tweed jacket and wondered what was eating her. The bidding started.

As was often the case, it was fast and furious at the start of an auction. Laurel was outbid on several things, managed to get a box of leather-bound books for a good price, and concentrated on the bidding until the auctioneer moved on to larger pieces of furniture. Here she let her mind wander. Then she noticed Jake, standing by the side where the furniture was, giving just the slightest nod as the bid went up.

As the bidding continued back and forth between him and another bidder, Laurel could not take her eyes off Jake. Was it something about the way he was standing there, arms crossed casually but with his attention fully engaged, oblivious to everything else for this brief period of time, while hundreds of dollars swung in the balance? He was hers to stare at and it was as if she had never seen him before. The auctioneer looked towards him for the bid; it was Jake's turn to up it or not. Jake shook his head "no," breaking the tension, then turned away and caught Laurel's eye. He smiled at her, gave a little "That's the breaks" shrug, and turned back to see the next thing coming up.

In that moment, Laurel's throat constricted. The electrical circuitry of her brain suddenly went to work. All the stops were pulled out and the doors leading to the depths of her inner state, so long tightly shut and blocked, flew open and cleared the way. Up bubbled a consciousness, a realization. Her eyes still fixed on Jake, it took over her mind and expressed itself to her succinctly and unequivocally: *I want him.*

Laurel shuddered violently. She plunged her hands into the pockets of her jacket and squeezed them into fists. She shut her eyes tightly and her whole body stiffened. Good God, she thought, what has happened to me?

Lovely Laurel, with her long, shining dark hair and violet eyes. Always the object of desire, sought after, wanted, the pursued, never the pursuer. She was used to the techniques that boys, and later men, had used. The looks and posturing, the seduction strategies of words playful or pleading. Sometimes it had pleased her, sometimes not, but never was it her initiative; it was always theirs. They had the needs and expressed them. It had been no different with Joe, but he was strong and confident, gentle and easy-going. Being with him was a comfort and a pleasure. It was a good life. It was, Laurel thought, catching her breath, totally unlike this, this absolutely overpowering feeling of desire. And Jake had not done anything at all to encourage her!

"Excuse me, madam, but are these your children?" Jake had seated himself behind her and had the piano babies, one in each hand. "I looked over at you when the bidding started and you seemed to be off in a fog somewhere, so I went ahead and bid."

"Oh, Jake, I am so sorry! How high did you have to go? Let me pay you right now." Laurel realized her hands were trembling too much for that and just tried for a bright and normal looking smile.

"They went terribly high. You will have to go without for a long, long time." He paused. "$35.00"

"Apiece? That's wonderful!"

"For both. You *were* out of it, Laurel!" Jake exclaimed. He handed her the dolls and went back to his place near the furniture.

For Laurel the rest of the day took on the aspect of an altered state. It was true: her mind had altered, had rearranged itself, the top was at the bottom, the bottom was at the top. She drove home, trying to be calm, but everything had changed.

How long, she wondered, how long has this been going on? Since last fall? Since he took me home from the party? They had talked about the shop and their fellow dealers. He stopped in her driveway. She said, "Thanks, Jake." He said, "You're welcome. See you on the hill. Good night, Laurel." And he had driven off. What had she felt then? Disappointment? Maybe.

She had, of course, seen plenty of him since that night, saw and was amused by his outrageous remarks and shameless flirting, but it wasn't directed at her. She would see him, he might notice her and smile, and continue whatever he was doing or saying. Now she realized why she liked being at the shop so much. Now she realized what it was like for all those boys, all those men, who had wanted her. Now she knew how they must have felt. Had she been unconscious all her life, not to have felt this way before? Not to have been, out of the blue, hit with this overwhelming desire for someone?

It was an irrational situation, to be conscious of such feelings for a man who had not done anything to warrant them. That she was married and knew she loved Joe had less to do with it, although that was upsetting enough. Nor were Jake's good looks and dazzling smile the reason for her confusing emotion. Other men had been good-looking in her past. It was that *she* wanted *him*, not the other way around. It was simply not rational.

However, irrational or not, the next week Laurel was scheduled to work at the shop and could not, nor would she, make some excuse to avoid it. Was she hopeful that she would see Jake? Yes, she admitted, but wouldn't it be better if he weren't there? And yes, it would be better. But she couldn't help being aware of that familiar excitement as she drove up the hill and pulled into the parking lot at Cider Run, and now she knew why.

Not unexpectedly, Jake's truck was not there, only Helen's car. She gave herself a little pep talk. Try, she told herself, try to put those thoughts of him out of your head. You've been around him for months and been fine. But it's all different now, she couldn't help thinking, and the part I can't get over is that it's all in my mind. Oh, damn!

Helen greeted her with "Laurel! Do you think it's really going to be as bad as they say?"

"What is, Helen? Or isn't going to be?"

"The storm! Didn't you hear? They're predicting up to ten inches of snow, starting this afternoon!"

Laurel had noticed it was snowing lightly on the drive in, but there had been snow on and off for a month. And she thought, it's a wonder I notice anything. I am the most hopelessly preoccupied, pathetic idiot there ever was.

Helen went on, "If it's coming down hard after lunch, we should probably close for the afternoon."

"That's fine," agreed Laurel. "We wouldn't get customers anyway."

By late afternoon the snow had begun in earnest and was piling up. Marv had called at 4:30, suggesting they leave and Helen got ready to go. Laurel said she would total up the few sales they had, turn off the lights and close up.

"Don't stay too long, Laurel!" Helen called on her way out.

"My car is fine in snow. Don't worry." Laurel locked the door behind her.

She had turned off the lights in the back of the shop and was coming up to the midsection when she heard the front door being unlocked, and in walked Jake.

Chapter 11

Jake stamped the snow from his shoes and took off and shook out his snow-covered parka. He looked up at Laurel as she approached and his face registered concern. "What in the world are you doing here?" he asked her. "I saw your car. You should be on your way. It's a real mess out there."

"I'm just about to leave," Laurel replied. "Helen left and I was closing down."

"Don't worry about that. I'll take care of it," Jake offered, as he hung his parka on the customers' hall tree next to Laurel's coat.

He must have come from his real estate office, Laurel guessed, as he had on a jacket and tie. She had seen him in coat and tie before, at the party in the fall, but now his professional attire made him all the more appealing. It had the effect of enhancing his masculinity, of giving him a more formal hence more remote, and more desirable, aspect, and only serving to further fuel Laurel's already impressionable state of mind.

Jake said absently, "It's cold in here. When the wind blows, it comes in somewhere. I've told Hal we have to find the leaks." Then he noticed Laurel, still standing there, arms wrapped around herself to keep from shaking, to keep from falling apart, she thought to herself. Jake frowned. "You look like you're freezing. I'll make a fire. I have to be here for a while anyway. At least you can get warm before you go outside."

Laurel went back to her self-appointed task of turning out lights. Everyone had lamps and display lights in their areas. It could take a long time. Oh, damn, oh, damn, what am I doing, thought Laurel. Prolonging the agony?

Click! Another lamp off.

Is it hormones? Is that it? Is this nature's way of telling me to get on with it?

Click!

I don't love him. I am not in love with him.

Click!

I just want him.

Click! Click!

I love Joe.

Click!

Joe has nothing to do with this.

Click! *Crash!!*

Laurel stood horrified as the lamp hit the floor. Jake came quickly, righted it and said, laughing, "Granted it's a sorry-looking specimen, but there's no need to kill it."

Laurel managed a smile, murmured an apology.

Jake continued, "Now, Laurel, the fire is going, so if you would care to stop punishing the merchandise and come this way, I am sure the other dealers would be grateful."

He had loosened his tie and now had that uniquely approachable look men had at this stage. The tie loose, the top button undone. This was the prelude, the first step in the series of easing and letting go and discarding the trappings of the outer world that led ultimately to... I must not go on with these thoughts, she told herself.

"Laurel, you're shivering. Will you just sit down?" Jake took off his jacket and put it around her shoulders. "Look, I'll make you a cup of tea if you'll just sit here and see that the fire doesn't go out."

"Thanks, Jake," said Laurel, taking the closest seat to the fire, the settee. She had a few minutes to think. His jacket felt warm, still holding his body heat, the thought of which was almost overpowering. She buried her head in her hands. Like a wire stretched taut, that's how I feel. If he does one thing, Laurel thought, just one thing, make a clumsy move, cheapen the moment, just one thing and I can walk right out of here.

But what if he doesn't? What if he goes on spinning this out in his pleasant, slightly distracted way? How long can I last? Will I say something, do something? Perhaps, she told herself, Jake might not even be interested. That was a possibility, certainly, and also he had met Joe. Maybe he was not the kind to seduce another man's wife. These thoughts calmed her somewhat. Jake was really a decent person. She must be decent too. Then to her chagrin, her eyes rested on the fainting couch and into her mind came the thought, blanking out all others: *Where will he take me?* She closed her eyes and fought off the image.

Jake came back with two mugs of tea and set them down on an oak stand. "Oh, darn, I forgot!" he exclaimed, hastily removing them again. "This stand is Marv's. He won't appreciate ring marks on the finish."

Laurel laughed and with a steadier hand than she'd thought, took her tea. Jake sat down in the Morris chair and stared into the fire.

It had grown very dark outside and the wind was moaning in the chimney. Laurel realized she had forgotten to turn off the CD player and the disc now playing, competing with the wind but still discernible, was the kind of jazz that Marv liked.

Jake must have noticed it too, because he said with a laugh, "Hal says that music dates us." He got up to go to the front of the shop.

Say something, you dolt, Laurel thought to herself. "Oh, don't turn it off. I like it." She realized as she said it that Jake would immediately know she didn't want to leave, didn't want to leave him.

Jake stopped and looked at her. He said, as pleasantly and evenly as ever, "No, I'm just going to check the door."

The fire crackled. The tea was finished. Laurel knew she should go now, but she couldn't bring herself to and, besides, she had relaxed to the point where she was able to converse. We will just sit here and talk a bit more, she told herself, and then I'll say goodnight. I can do it. I can have a conversation with him without his knowing how I feel. They had been talking about connections to the past and how antiques can bring the past to life, a subject fitting and suitable for the atmosphere.

"How do you view the connection?" Laurel was saying. "For instance, when I pick up an object and hold it in my hand, I sometimes think of who else might have had it, what their life was like."

"Or," he replied, "about what use was made of the object. Think of Keith's weapons, for example. Were they the instruments of someone's death?"

"Jake, what an idea! But, you know, you're right. I won't be able to look in Keith's case again without..." Without thinking of you and tonight, she thought, of your face in the firelight, a distant look in your eyes, of how I yearned for you.

He seemed to brood for a minute, staring into the fire. "The thing about the antiques business," he began, and swept his hand in the direction of the rest of the shop, "is that it can be so all-consuming. Once you start searching for things, you get single-minded and go after them with a sense of disregard."

"Disregard? Of what?" she asked, and thought, of my marriage, of tomorrow when I will hate myself even more.

"Depends on the things you want," Jake answered. "Disregard for the conventions, for the price, for the consequences even."

Surely the double meaning must be evident to him, thought Laurel. She could feel the tightening of the wire. Where have I been all my life that I know so little? What must I do, what must I say, to have him? She was past fighting with herself. The firelight, the night, their closeness was in control of her. She must simply go along with it. Very quietly and with an emotion in her voice that she couldn't disguise, Laurel said, "And is it worth it?"

At that Jake turned and looked at her steadily and got up slowly, gave the fire a poke, put the poker back in its stand. He looked at her again, went over to where she sat on the settee and slipped the jacket off from around her shoulders. He put his hands on her arms and gently lifted her to her feet, gently, ever so gently, cupped one hand under her chin...

A voice in her mind cried, *Run, Laurel, run!*

I can't, she answered it. I am lost.

...and drew her face towards his. His lips barely brushed hers, as if it were he who was hesitating and then surrendering, giving up the struggle. He put his arms around her and his kiss was no longer tentative but warm and strong, and she felt herself soften, respond, caring about nothing else.

And at that moment someone opened the front door and walked in. A shadow at first, then a shape coming into the light, and a man's voice said, "Mr. Gennari! There you are! I hope you are still here even in such weather and then I see your truck, so I come in and have found you!"

And Laurel fled.

She drove home on the deserted streets, her eyes mesmerized by the near-horizontal snow throwing itself against the windshield. But her mind had cleared and the feeling she had was one of astounding relief. Relief that they had not, after all, gone ahead. Relief that she had been miraculously rescued at the last moment. Did she feel remorseful? Yes, because she had led Jake on and it was unfair of her. He had, she sensed, been reluctant. He had given her no cause to doubt his integrity. When she saw him next, she prayed he would have written it off.

Laurel pulled into the garage, surprised to see Joe's snow-laden car there, and came into the kitchen to find him stirring up a pot of chili, concentrating seriously on getting it simmering at just the right heat. She felt almost giddy with happiness at seeing him home early, and when Joe turned and said to her, "Well, it's just you and me tonight, Babe," and went back to his cooking, Laurel knew what she wanted. Her mind, chastened and wiser, had accommodated itself to what she had learned, what she had experienced, and after supper, she told herself, she would make it up to Joe, even though he didn't know what had been happening in her head and never would.

"I wish," remarked Emmy one day toward the end of the month, "that Charles would change his teaching schedule so we could go away in winter, but it just can't be done."

Icicles dripped steadily under the eaves in the south facing front of the sun-warmed stone building. The parking lot was a quagmire of melting snow, pot holes and gravel piles, worrying Marv more.

Helen nodded at Emmy in agreement. "When Marv was teaching we said, 'The minute we retire, we're spending our winters somewhere in the south.' And look where we are!"

"I've loved this winter," Ruth said, almost in protest. "I mean, compared with Maine. And today is so bright. It's almost warm."

"Ruth, don't be led down the primrose path," Marv advised. "This is only a February thaw. Mark my words, winter will be back, although it won't include the predatory animals you had to deal with in a former life."

Emmy's initial remark had been precipitated by a postcard just received from Cora and Bob, who were on a Caribbean cruise with their bridge group. "Not that Charles would ever go on a cruise," Emmy had added.

"Well, there are no antiques to be had on a cruise," said Helen with finality, and she headed back to the kitchen, while Emmy wandered off to her area.

For a few minutes, Marv and Ruth were alone. He wanted to talk with her, had been wanting to talk with her for months, but felt the constraint of the situation. What could they talk about? Something neutral, not about how much he'd like to get to know her. They could talk about predatory animals. That would be safe, except that when it came to her, he felt not too unlike a predatory animal himself. She had put a pressed glass cake stand with an intricate sunburst and palm design on the counter next to her and was checking through some reference books, looking up glass patterns. Antiques, what else?

"I thought you knew every pattern there was," he said by way of beginning. Probably not too brilliant a comment, but at least a start, he thought to himself.

Ruth was aware that they were alone the minute Helen and Emmy left, and felt Marv's presence keenly. He was so close, if she moved only slightly, she'd brush against his arm. It was tempting, but that would be like playing games. Then he said something to her, something ordinary, and she responded, "Far from it. I rarely saw these Pennsylvania and Ohio patterns in New England. McKee seems to have cornered the market down here."

She had mentioned New England. He could take it from there. "You were going to tell me why you went to Maine and what the winters were like," he said, in spite of the fact that he had perceived her discomfort with the subject the first time it came up.

Ruth looked up at Marv, so close to her. How could she tell him she had run away from the ending of a long-term love affair? But she smiled and said, "What, and bore you to death?"

"You could never bore me," he replied, and saw the softening in her eyes for the fraction of a second before she hastily looked down again. He decided it was time to go outside and check the condition of the gravel in the parking lot.

Laurel had another day scheduled to work in February and she felt some trepidation at the prospect. The agitation and self-loathing had abated, but she was still worried she had not been discreet enough, that Jake had known her feelings. Why else had he looked at her that way, almost with curiosity, before he decided to kiss her? She didn't want to think about that kiss, didn't want to remember how it had made her feel, how close she had come. She had been studiously avoiding thinking about that one moment and had been fairly successful. But it had happened, although she was sure it wasn't intended on his part. Whether he had meant to go on—that was something else. She was just grateful, grateful to Jake for not taking advantage of her distraught state, even though she was sure he must have guessed, grateful to the person who blundered into the shop. More so for the latter. If he had not come in then... She had, however, convinced herself that she would have come to her senses in time.

Jake was not at the shop when she was next working. Of course, everyone knew the work schedules. Laurel wondered if he'd stayed away to avoid seeing her. If so, she was grateful to him for that as well. She felt she was still on shaky ground as far as he was concerned, and wanted to put some time and distance between herself and that night. Soon enough, however, they were at the shop on the same day surrounded, fortunately, by others.

"Laurel!" Jake exclaimed, as she walked in. "Where have you been? I was afraid you'd gone off in the snow the other night, gotten disoriented and disappeared forever!"

Marv, not taking his eyes off the computer screen, said, "And ended up in Rio at Carnival. Not a bad idea, that."

Thank heavens for Marv, thought Laurel. "Well, I tried, but I'd forgotten my passport," she was able to say, and things passed off smoothly.

In March, as Marv had predicted, a few more snowstorms blew in, having been fed by moisture coming up from the Gulf of Mexico and chilled by the Canadian air aloft. But, being March, the sun was stronger and the snow melted faster. The hours of daylight were increasing and customers were becoming more numerous.

Mid-March was spring break for the schools and the university. Owen and Lynn packed up their two little ones and went to see Owen's parents in the eastern part of the state. Keith and June, June's mother and their two children went to Washington D.C. Grace and Frank took the grandchildren to Disney World.

Emmy and Charles went to Italy, where Charles had a paper to give. Emmy left the shop with a cheery, "Well, I'm off to Rome in the morning!"

Ruth, hearing this, remembered she had volunteered to take one of Emmy's work days, but that was all right, as Emmy would pay her back. Ruth was already filling in for Laurel, who had called in sick several times, then showed up in the afternoon feeling better. No one had any question as to the reason, but forbore to say anything.

Marv, Hal and Jake got together at the end of the week to go through business matters, sitting over coffee around the kitchen table. Jake's separation was one of the topics, as he had to buy out Annette's one-sixth share.

The physical state of the building was then brought up. Jake said, "The wind just whistles through the cracks. One night, during that snowstorm in early February when Laurel and I were here..."

Marv's eyebrows went up.

"...she was so cold. This place was like an ice box. I had to make a fire to thaw her out."

Hal said, "We'll probably need to repoint the stonework. I can call a mason for an estimate, but it's going to be expensive."

The point, thought Marv, is not the stonework. The point is Jake's too-casual "admission."

The last item on the agenda was the gravel parking lot, such an annoyance to Marv. They decided to open it up for general discussion among everyone who was there, so adjourned to the front counter where several other dealers had gathered.

Hal introduced the topic. "Do you want the parking lot paved or what, Marv? You've been obsessed with it all winter long."

"Paving is not the answer," Helen stated.

"Why not?" Marv asked his wife.

"It doesn't make good ecological sense to pave large areas."

"Helen is right," Andy put in, then realizing how forward he had been, added, "I think."

"Because?" asked Marv.

Andy counted on his fingers, "Because, one, there wouldn't be as good drainage as there is with gravel. We're on a hill here and the water on the paved surface would run off onto the road. And, two, because we're on a hill we'd have to do a lot of grading before we could pave. Isn't that right, Hal?"

Hal nodded.

"And, three, the process of grading and paving would probably mess up part of the orchard. When you get those big trucks in, they cause all sorts of damage. One of our neighbors decided to get his driveway paved and some of his trees got destroyed."

"Is there a 'four' as well?" asked Marv in a resigned manner, when Andy paused.

"Well, yes," Ruth allowed, gently, as she knew this was a sensitive issue for Marv. "Paved surfaces heat up in the summer and, with the orientation to the south, it could be baking out there."

"Uncle! I give in!" exclaimed Marv. "Even Ruth says we shouldn't pave! All right then, can anyone suggest an alternative to tracking in salt in the winter and mud and gravel all year round?"

Hal looked thoughtful. "If we bring the front walk out a bit more, increase its width, and extend the existing sidewalks on either side, it might be enough paved area to walk off the salt and gravel," he said.

"And why not put an awning and marquee up," suggested Sylvie later, "and roll out a red carpet."

"And have a doorman, in uniform," was Richard's addition, after this discussion had expanded to include even more dealers.

"Or a concierge," said Emmy, who was back from Italy by then.

"What a good idea, Emmy!" Elaine interjected. "And I'd like some little café tables and chairs."

"Then we'd need a waiter, to serve the wine," said Jake.

"Oh, you could do that, Jake. You could be a singing waiter," Sally Ann proposed.

Jake cleared his throat: *"If her eyes are blue as skies, That's Sally O'Neill"*

Sylvie commented, "Now, that certainly is the Irish tenor side of Jake."

"But I'm not Irish," Sally Ann said sadly. "I'm one hundred percent Dutch. Fred was Irish." But she did have very nice blue eyes under all the mascara, and even Mr. O'Neill was part "Dutch," as people of German descent are called Pennsylvania.

"Then it's all settled," Marv affirmed, returning to the subject. "We don't pave the parking lot. We reopen the restaurant."

"Or the hotel," said Jake.

Chapter 12

Late in April when the threat of snow was over, Marv had a truckload of gravel delivered. He watched as it was smoothed expertly over the winter-ravaged parking lot, he winced when he was handed the bill.

"That should do it for you, Dr. Yeager, until, oh, I should think, depending on how much rain we get, probably you'll want another load at the end of the summer. Yep. Definitely by then. If not before," the truck driver stated confidently.

Right, thought Marv, or after the next time the garbage truck comes and gouges out yet another six inches.

The sidewalk expansion had been managed with little trouble. However, it had turned out to be more costly than expected. Also some of the landscaping would have to be replaced. Ruth had stepped into the breach.

"I'm going to be planting my garden any day now. I'll be happy to pick up some things when I go to the nursery," she offered.

"That would be awfully nice of you, Ruth," Helen said. "Last year Annette took the responsibility for the landscaping choices, although we all helped plant."

Annette was gone. She had moved to Washington before the end of January, having taken not even one antique. Jake seemed cheerful and acted vastly relieved. Whether it was because she was gone or because his antiques were not, Marv couldn't say; probably it was both. He and Helen now, if they ever parted, thought Marv, they'd have the devil of a time dividing up the Flow Blue china. And what about the furniture and all the other things? It just couldn't be done. They would have to stay together, if only for the sake of the antiques. It was something he hadn't really considered before. Was his future to be dictated by the possessions they'd acquired together in the past?

He gladly came back to the present, as Ruth was suggesting several types of bushes she might get for the landscaping. "Rhododendron grows all right here. Does azalea thrive in this climate? How about bayberry?"

"Bayberry? Uh, oh!" Marv rolled his eyes. "Ruth is still living in New England."

"You'd better go with her, Marv," suggested Helen, "otherwise, she might forget where she is and get lobster pots to decorate the walkway."

A day later Ruth met Marv in the Cider Run parking lot, ready to follow him to a Mennonite nursery Helen had recommended. Marv cast a disapproving eye at Ruth's van. "Is this the vehicle that was on its last legs not too long ago?" he asked her.

"Afraid so, Marv," she admitted. "But my brother found a good mechanic for her, so I've been told we have a few more miles left."

Marv knew he'd have to be more direct. "Let's go in my truck. That way we have plenty of room for the plants, we save gas and avoid the risk to your vehicle, miracle mechanic or not." And we will be alone together for a little while.

Ruth thought, we will be alone together, something she hadn't ever believed possible. She wondered if she should demure, insist on taking her van. Why should she? She should, she told herself, be able simply to enjoy the day with Marv. There was no reason to hold back because, just because, she liked him. "If you don't mind," she asked, "transferring plants to my van when we get back?"

"I would be honored," he replied.

Ruth locked her car and climbed into Marv's truck. She was wearing jeans for this outing, and Marv thought she looked splendid in them. Marv was wearing jeans as well. Ruth thought, we seem almost a pair, the two of us, how I wish...but, no, I will keep myself from futile wishes today.

As they pulled out of the parking lot, Ruth at his side, Marv thought how being with someone you like in a closed vehicle lends a distinct sense of intimacy. Henry Ford must have known what he was doing. Not only could people motor to remote places, they could feel remote from the rest of the world. In spite of the fact that Marv had wanted a chance to talk with Ruth, this feeling of intimacy was so sweet to him, he almost didn't want to disrupt it by conversation.

Ruth was silent too, silent because she also felt she had entered into an atmosphere of closeness with Marv, and if she started a discussion she would lose this delicious feeling. Not that he felt the same way, she told herself, but she would savor it for a bit before the silence became awkward.

When Marv finally broke the silence, it did not really break the spell. With the confidence born of their shared interests and experiences, they began talking about the shop, the idiosyncrasies of various auctioneers, the customers they'd liked, the ones who had been a real trial, sharing thoughts they hadn't shared before. Even though Marv didn't ask questions about Ruth's past, in which, he realized, he was becoming more and more interested, he was getting to know aspects of her better. How she laughed, how her eyes shone, how she looked in profile beside him. The historian would have to take a back seat to the lover, he thought, and then caught himself up sharply at the last word. Was that his goal?

Ruth was thinking, I could drive forever with him, just talking. I wish this never had to end. When the nursery came into sight, she fought a tendency to sigh. She consoled herself with the thought that they had a few more hours together.

The nursery, deep in the farm country of Marten County, was vast and Marv and Ruth attended to their tasks of picking out plants for Ruth's summer garden and shrubbery for the shop's landscaping. They were easy in each other's company, having fun. Ruth confessed she didn't know what to grow in this new climate of Pennsylvania; her brother hadn't a garden. Marv did his best to be helpful.

"What about these cherry tomatoes, Ruth? Sweet 100's. Can't beat 'em."

"I've never heard of Sweet 100's."

"Where have you been, girl? Summer ain't summer without these,"

"By all means then! Put them in the cart."

They got bedding plants and vegetables for Ruth and handsome bushes for Cider Run, some flowering, like spirea and rhododendron, and some evergreen shrubs to decorate with lights at Christmas. They discussed every item and Marv was glad to see Ruth taking such an interest in Pennsylvania horticulture. She was so perfectly delightful to be with, he thought and wondered, not for the first time, why had Ruth never married? Did she have high standards that no one had ever lived up to? Was there something that happened in her past? How could he ever find out?

Ruth, intent on doing a credible job choosing plants and realizing she wanted desperately not to disappoint Marv, felt restrained at first from enjoying the day as much as she would have liked. But the greenhouse—close, hot, damp—reinforced the feeling of intimacy begun in the car. She started to loosen the hold she had on herself. They were having such a good time, immersed in what they were doing together, careless of anything else. It was the sort of day to be gone over in her mind again later, at leisure, relived and relished.

And the day was not yet done. Under the guise of showing Ruth more of the countryside, but mainly to prolong their time together, Marv took a different way back on a country road. It was then that an opportunity so irresistible to antiques collectors presented itself. They spotted a hand-lettered sign on a cardboard box placed by the side of a gravel road:

SALE!
HOUSEHOLD
GOODS

For Marv this was the equivalent of a sign reading Entrance to Heaven This Way. He came quickly to a stop, turned in and they bounced up the rutted lane.

"This looks promising," he said with barely subdued excitement.

At the end of the road they saw an old white farmhouse with paint peeling off, a deteriorating barn, several outbuildings in various stages of disrepair, and abandoned vehicles.

"Even more promising!" he exclaimed, the excitement unconcealed.

Ruth saw his reaction and laughed. What did he think might be here?

Marv stopped the truck and turned off the motor. They waited for the barking of farm dogs to begin, but it was quiet. A few chickens were pecking in the yard. Marv and Ruth got out of the truck and climbed rotting steps up to the front porch.

"Do we knock?" asked Ruth.

"We saunter slowly to the door, stand there for a while so they can get a good look at us, and..."

A voice from behind startled them. "You-uns come for the dry sink? The missus said she thought you'd be stopping up. Well, better come in have a look, then."

Their greeter was an overall-clad man of close to eighty, wiry and powerfully built, face lined from a life lived outdoors. Ruth started to say, "We saw..."

"No, no, missus, you come this way. Don't matter if she's to market. You just step in." He held the door open and motioned them through.

The front parlor, into which they were ushered, held the accumulation of what appeared to be over a century's worth of furniture and bric-a-brac. Two or three stiff, horsehair-stuffed sofas, several stands and tables, mostly oak, and more pieces spanning the Victorian era through the Forties filled the space. There was picture molding an inch down from the ceiling running around the whole room and from it, suspended on hooks, hung oil paintings, prints, and photographs. Even the frames were exceptional: carved, gilded, embellished with fruit and flowers. A china cabinet with curved glass held, Ruth looked in to see, a white ironstone sugar bowl with a fig finial on the lid, more and more ironstone and mulberry transferware on the shelves.

Marv saw Ruth's attention riveted on the china and it pleased him greatly. Just an old farmhouse. Entrance to heaven it was.

"Better come through, then. It's back here," their host insisted.

The back parlor, through which they now walked, held anything that might have been missing in the front parlor, including two pianos, a square Knabe and an upright player piano. Marv stopped, absolutely enthralled. Ruth was as fascinated watching Marv as she was in the treasure trove of a place they had stumbled on.

"No, no, mister, back *here*," and another door, this time to a pantry, was held open for them.

The dry sink, tin-lined, was sitting off to the side. Marv felt his heart beating faster. He looked it over, saw where a pump had been attached once, squatted down to see the bottom, got up. "How much did I say I'd give for it?"

"Missus said $150. I said, that can't be right. No-uns going to pay that much. She told me, 'Samuel, he said $150, so that's what it is,' and you don't argue with the missus."

Marv reached in his pocket for his billfold and took out a check. "Is this all right?" he asked.

"Since I already writ down your truck license, I reckon so."

"Marv, you can't!" Ruth protested, but her eyes were filled with laughter.

"One fifty, you say?"

"Yup, and my apologies, mister, but when she makes up her mind, that's it. I'll help you load up. No, ain't no trouble."

They got the plants in the back of the truck moved over and the dry sink loaded and secured, and then Marv turned to his host and asked what Ruth knew would be next, "Now, is there anything else for sale?"

"Well, mister, there might be, but you got to talk to the missus about that. She don't let me sell anything without her making up her mind. You know," he winked in the direction of Ruth, "your little missus there is just the same, I bet."

Marv nodded his head. "Aren't they all?" he agreed.

Ruth made a spluttering sound trying to keep from laughing out loud.

As they drove back down the lane, Marv said, "Now, Ruth, don't say it! Don't say what you're thinking!"

Ruth could not imagine anyone so completely enjoyable and uninhibited. "OK, Marv," she answered. "It's not that you blatantly bought a dry sink promised to someone else. When fate throws a dry sink your way, how can you be expected to pass it up? The problem is, what if the person who was supposed to buy it comes into the shop and sees it?"

"There are lots of dry sinks with tin linings. Don't worry. If it had been zinc, it might be more unusual. The problem isn't that. The problem is how can I go back there to buy more things? If the missus isn't home, he won't sell me anything. And if the missus is home, she'll know I'm an imposter."

"And if you show up with Helen, they'll think you're even worse!"

Marv and Ruth agreed that the less said about this, the better. Ruth, because she didn't want Marv's character compromised, and Marv, because he didn't want anyone else to find out where the place was.

When Helen was told about the dry sink, she shook her head. "Typical Marv," said Helen. "He once was able to buy a photograph album for half the price asked because he convinced the seller that it contained pictures of his great-grandparents. A complete fabrication, of course."

"Well, they did look a little bit like Abe and Fanny," said Marv.

"All the men had whiskers in those days and all the women parted their hair in the center," Helen stated firmly. "Everyone wanted to look like Victoria and Albert."

"One or the other, depending," Marv clarified.

A week later, as she was working at the front counter, Ruth heard a commotion at the door and saw Marv and Hal bringing in the player piano she had last seen in the back parlor of the farmhouse. They set it down near the front of the shop and went back out, returning with the matching bench and at least two dozen piano rolls. When they had things in place, they put on "Beer Barrel Polka" and it brought everyone around. Marv decided not to put the piano up for sale. It made a nice addition to the ambiance of the shop.

As soon as she could speak to him in private, Ruth asked Marv, "How did you do it?"

"Ruth, such skepticism!" he exclaimed, giving her an arch look. "I went out there, explained to the mister that I would be pleased to buy more things. He said he'd ask the missus what she wanted to sell. When she appeared, she had a good look at me and proceeded to show me what was on offer. As we were loading up, the mister said that she could 'abide' my having bought the dry sink, as the other gentleman never came back anyway. So, all's well that ends...Oh! I forgot! I told him that my missus was interested in the ironstone and he told me to send her right over. That's you, Ruth." Marv made a little bow.

Ruth realized that the highly questionable position Marv had put her in was much to her liking, and with the possibility of ironstone china too. She would just have to remember to pay in cash.

As a result of the day in the country, Marv and Ruth entered a new phase in their relationship. It wasn't dramatic and it wasn't noticeable to anyone else, but they knew each other better and felt a sense of affinity. They now shared a secret and a source of amusement. It was easier to talk and less constrained. Ruth was learning to accept her feelings for him and enjoy him. Marv was becoming infatuated with her.

The dry sink, meanwhile, had been put in Marv's and Helen's area with a price tag of $500. "And a good deal for someone at that," Marv had said.

Andy came by and looked at it. "I have one or two of those in my barn. Are they really worth that much?"

"And more. Andy, when are we going to get to see your barn and all the other wonderful things at your place?"

"You can come out anytime, but I really don't have anything."

Spring farm work was keeping Andy away, so he was not there the following week when the curator of the university's agricultural museum came to Cider Run. The museum had a healthy budget to purchase items used on the farm and in rural homes before the advent of electricity and motor power. Marv took the curator around the shop and they discussed effective display of items and gathered those that were of museum quality for him to purchase. The curator even bought from Sally Ann: a cup and saucer, cereal bowl and plate with Currier and Ives-type early farm scenes, premiums in oatmeal boxes from the Forties and Fifties.

At Andy's area the curator stopped in disbelief and bought up all he could: a wood and leather apple corer and peeler, farm sieves and a handsome flat basket for winnowing grain, a barn lantern, a square standing butter churn with three gears and a handle on the side, a triple tiered egg basket and the egg sorter to go with it. And he asked where he could find more.

When Andy came in again, Marv told him about the curator's excitement over his things. "He said what he really appreciated was the Marten County connection, that they were used right here during the 19th and early 20th centuries. Not only are they perfect examples of the era, they tell of local history."

"Heck," said Andy, "I would have given them to the museum."

"Andy! Let us not hear you talk like that! The museum has money to spend. You are a professional antiques dealer now," Marv remonstrated.

"Naw," Andy demurred, "I'm only a farmer."

"Only a farmer, who buys a tombstone fresh off a grave? Who talks his neighbor out of an ornate Victorian wrought iron gate? How much did that last go for? I notice it got sold almost immediately."

Andy smiled a slow smile. "Well, I guess I am in the business now." He looked over his area. "I guess I better bring in some more things in to sell."

"Atta boy, Andy. Don't let the side down."

This interchange with the curator had stirred up the historian in Marv and his awareness of the need to get back to a little research and writing. With Andy's input and the venerable Col. Tyler's invaluable tome, as well as other local sources, Marv wrote a history of the King family farm, going back to when the first German immigrants, Koenig being the name then, had arrived in Pennsylvania. It included copies of old photos of the farm and portraits of Andy's ancestors, paintings which were in the family home. Andy assuaged his conscience at not making his antiques a donation by presenting this document to the museum, where it was placed on display with much ceremony, and a copy was given to the Historical Society, as well as the university library. It could be said that Marv assuaged his own conscience in the process also, having a little uneasiness about some of his acquisition tactics.

The fullness of spring had now arrived in Marten County. At Cider Run the orchard was a glory of pink blossom and birds returned to sing their hearts out. The hills were the softest green anyone could remember. Even the gravel parking lot behaved and did not get itself into ruts.

At the end of business on a warm day in May, as the sun still cast its afternoon light, several of the dealers had gathered at one of the picnic tables which had again been set out under the apple trees. Paper cups were being refilled from a jug of California Colombard, the wine of sunshine and fresh air.

"And to think," Sally Ann was saying, "these apple trees were planted by Johnny Appleseed."

Marv harrumphed. "I hate to be the one to burst your bubble, but good authority places Johnny Appleseed well to the north and west of Marten County."

"How cruel you are, Marv!" Richard protested. "We all live on the stuff of legends. I, for one, will continue to believe that Johnny Appleseed planted the orchard."

"And maybe George Washington slept here too, huh, Richard?" Sally Ann pursued, getting into the spirit of his remark.

148

Elaine who, after finishing her cigarette away from the group, had been allowed back, added, "Perhaps Edgar Allen Poe came by to quaff cider in the tap room."

"Oh, why not," Marv sighed with resignation. "Keep drinking this California wine and you can believe anything." He poured himself another cupful.

"I lived in California once," Sally Ann said mournfully.

"Why so glum about it?" asked Richard.

"It was with my second husband," she took another drink of wine, "who will forever be known as 'The Creep.'"

"Being in California should have compensated though," suggested Elaine.

"Oh, no, it was awful! There was no proper winter and when spring came, you didn't even know it. Fall was a matter of a weekend, and then only if you knew where to go to see it. No, I was so happy to get back to Pennsylvania." There was silence all around while this fundamental truth was digested.

Sally Ann went on, "And what antiques there were cost an arm and a leg."

Marv reflected, "That's enough to make anyone glum." More silence followed this baleful observation.

Elaine, in an effort to inject some lightness, ventured, "Well, Sally Ann, if hubby number two was a disaster, one assumes hubby number one was all right. At least you got Blue Willow out of it."

"And, of course, Rosie," said Sally Ann in a much more cheerful voice. "But after she was born, her daddy decided he had better things to do and lit out. Honey, that marriage was so short I had to stay with his parents just to remind myself what Rosie's last name was."

Rosie, the daughter of this ill-fated union, was now a competent young woman, a secretary in one of the state government offices, and an enthusiastic partner in her mother's business, eagerly scouring the thrift shops, garage sales and flea markets of the Harrisburg area.

"'Tis a lesson best learned, um, I forget how the rest goes," Marv started to say, then poured another round. He took up the theme again. "We do have a spectrum here, Sally Ann on one end and our spinster Ruth on the other."

"Except that Ruth, our ravishing redhead, isn't a spinster," said Richard. "Our Ruth is a gay divorcee. Well, not gay in the contemporary sense. More along the lines of the smart set who dined at the Ritz."

"Ruth at the Ritz?" wondered Sally Ann.

Marv looked dumbfounded. He'd had no idea. He'd just assumed. "Richard, how do you know this?"

He must have sounded incredulous, because Richard answered slightly on the defensive. "She told me. That's how I know. Look, she didn't mind talking about it. You can ask her about What's-his-face."

"No, I couldn't," Marv stated flatly.

"Hah!" exclaimed Elaine. "I'm not at all surprised. I never saw our Ruth as the spinsterly type."

Marv was quiet for a second, taking in this astonishing revelation. Then he raised his cup in a toast. "*In vino veritas,*" he proposed. "We should do this more often."

Chapter 13

It was mid-May and Cider Run Antiques had been in operation for nearly a year, a year in which things had run overwhelmingly smoothly, better than smoothly. The shop was flourishing, business doing well, morale high. Even though the deep winter months had been slow and sales off, the camaraderie and good times enjoyed by the dealers compensated for it. Everything was encouraging and, as the shop's reputation spread, more and more customers were driving up Cider Run Road to park by the orchard, perhaps stroll over to take in the lovely view of the hills, and then spend an interesting time browsing among a wide variety of antiques. And buying.

"Good Morning, Cider Run Antiques. Yes, from 10:00 to 6:00, Noon to 5:00 on Sundays. Straight out Martensdale Pike. No, two more lights. Then a left on Cider Run Road. You're welcome."

There was a rhythm in the day-to-day business of running the shop. Dealers took turns at the front counter, greeting people who came in, answering the phone, entering sales. Each day was similar and each day was different, depending on who was working, who came in, what was sold, bought and sought after.

"Cider Run. What pattern was that? Cherry Blossom? I think one of our dealers has Cherry Blossom. The pink or the green?"

"Cider Run Antiques. You have a hold on the stepback cupboard? Yes, I can get someone to measure it for you. Hang on a moment."

The first year had gone by and some things had changed. Dealers were gaining in expertise from each other, they knew more about the merchandise and felt a greater confidence in their knowledge of antiques. They knew more about each other too, having spent hours chatting, gossiping and sharing stories. There had been some subtle changes as well, like the growing regard of Marv and Ruth for each other, although it wasn't obvious, and there had been some less subtle changes, like the breakup of Jake's marriage.

"Cider Run Antiques. Hi, Richard. Yes, the washstand sold! But now you need to bring in something to fill the empty space."

"Emmy? It's Cora at the shop. Someone came in and bought that table cover you had hanging up in your area. Yes, the one with the crochet border. She was planning to use it as a curtain. Well, now she's called back to say she forgot to get the plastic hooks you used to hang it onto the rod. I know. I told her the hooks were not antiques and we couldn't sell them to her. She sounded so absolutely distraught, I said I'd call you and see if you could tell her where you got them. Right. Supermarket. That's where I said you'd probably gotten them. Do you want to call her? I'll give you her number. Thanks, Emmy. Yes, pretty busy!"

A year of operation and there would be a second year and then, out of the blue on a May morning: murder. Shocking, appalling, tragic. Something had gone terribly wrong, something that must have been brewing over the last two years.

Surely during that first year someone might have begun to see, to have an inkling of trouble ahead, or if not trouble, at least the start of a veering-off that, if unchecked, could set in motion what would culminate in tragedy. But who could have foreseen? Everyone was happily caught up in making the shop go. And after all the socializing, the schmoozing and lively interplay, it came back to antiques, the love of antiques, dominating everything.

Antiques. That was what it was all about, talking with customers, being helpful, explaining, sharing the passion.

"This jelly cupboard? It's poplar and it has the candle shelf here on top. The trim on the drawer fronts is called 'railroad tracking.' Let me open a drawer so you can have a look at the inside. See? The drawers are all hand dovetailed. Those could be the original porcelain pulls, but even if not, I'm pretty sure they're close to a hundred years old. The key is most likely not original, but it fits and works."

"Four spindle back chairs; no, wait, there are two more over here. A set of six. They've been refinished and the seats have been re-caned. Probably chestnut, sometimes they mixed oak and chestnut. They'll go great with almost any table. Not that old, maybe from the early Twenties."

"Limoges, France. The underglaze mark is the factory. This one is Theodor Haviland. The mark on top of the glaze— run your finger over it and you can tell which is which—that's the studio where it was decorated. Oh, hand-painted, for sure."

"They just brought in this blanket chest. That's the original ocher paint, rather rare. Well, the yellow is not found that often here in central Pennsylvania. Blue? Blue painted furniture is usually from farther west, Ohio. This box inside is a candle till or safe. There's a sort of secret compartment, here, where this board slides down. Somewhere between 1850 and 1875."

"With much of the older English ironstone, you can date it and not only to the year, but to the exact day of the month that it was made. There's a code they used and you look up the marks. If it doesn't say England, it could be before 1891, when our McKinley Tariff Act required imported goods to be labeled by country of origin. That is, unless someone bought it when they were abroad. That happened a lot, since you went by ocean liner and could bring back a ton of things."

"It's called a 'kick toaster,' and it's made of wrought iron. You set it down by the fire and put the bread slices in so they can be held in place here. To brown the other side of the toast, you only have to give it a nudge with your foot and it spins! Ingenious, isn't it?"

"Yes, it does have a crack in it. That's why it's marked 'as is' and is priced so low, but with that beautiful embossed grape and vine pattern, you can't bear to think of it being tossed in a landfill. I use my damaged ironstone pitchers to hold dried flowers, and just turn the cracked side to the wall."

"A much smaller blanket chest. All dovetailed construction. The surfaces are hand planed. Feel the unevenness? And, look, it has square nails. Around 1840 most likely."

"So much furniture from the rural areas of central Pennsylvania is one-of-a-kind. People made what they needed. I like this pie safe with the punched tin doors. I think the pattern of pierced stars is just inspired. And there is this drawer at the bottom."

"A cottage dresser, oak, with the little dresser boxes on top. The drawer pulls are carved oak leaves, nice touch! Marble topped too. Marble was usually reserved for pieces made of walnut, the more elegant wood."

"It's a grain box. It came out of a barn here in Marten County. Go ahead and lift the lid. Well, yes, the mice did get into it, didn't they?"

"I'm sorry, honey, but I can't run the electric train around the shop. If you come back at Christmastime, though, he'll have it set up."

If there were one person who should have been paying attention, it would be Marv. He was more involved in the shop than anyone else, certainly more than Helen. She was still dividing her time between Martensdale and Bucks County, the balance favoring Bucks County. But Marv's own busyness at the shop, along with his antiques buying, and his pleasure at the success of the venture kept him from feeling any vibrations of a negative sort. It also kept him from dwelling on his empty marriage. And then there was the distraction of Ruth, who had captured his imagination and was beginning to figure in his dreams. So he was not attuned, if there had been anything to be attuned to, and there didn't seem to be, really, that first year anyway.

"Good Afternoon, Cider Run."

"Cora, what would you say if I told you I am looking at an eight foot high solid walnut wardrobe?"

"Oh, go on, Marv! Eight feet? Are you serious?"

"Which I just bought."

"Where?"

"At an estate sale you wouldn't believe. If you could get Helen to find Hal, we might be able to figure out a way to get it back to the shop."

"OK, Marv, I'll go get Helen but you know she won't like it. Eight feet high!"

And Ruth, who was a sensitive and observant person, was equally unaware of whatever clouds may have been building. That Helen sometimes acted disparaging toward and dissatisfied with Marv she was aware of, though, and it saddened her. He didn't deserve that kind of treatment. But Helen's behavior toward Marv was erratic, and when Helen was uncomplaining, Ruth felt guilty for her former thoughts. Ruth—caring, good spirited, enjoying her new surroundings: how would she notice anything in her state of mind, Marv beginning to dominate her thoughts so much? If, indeed, there had been anything to notice.

"Helen, I think Marv wants you."

"Where is he, Cora?"

"He and Hal just got back with 'it', the eight-foot-high wonder of the world. They're in the parking lot, trying to unload it. He asked if you could find any customers in the shop who might be willing to lend a hand. I had a look. The thing is a monster! It must be four feet wide and almost three feet deep."

"Oh, Lord, how's our liability if Marv drops it on someone's foot?"

"More likely it would drop on Marv's foot, I'm afraid, Helen."

"It might teach him a lesson. Oh, well, could you look around for some helpers while I go out and talk to Marv?"

"Do I give them 20% off their purchases if they help move furniture?"

"Marv, this is ridiculous. We can't ask customers to cart furniture for us."

"Isn't this the most beautiful wardrobe you've ever seen, Helen? Look at the trim. Carved flowers, birds. It must have come out of some Philadelphia mansion originally. I can't imagine how it got up here in the mountains."

"Marv, you aren't listening to me."

"He got a really good deal on it, Helen. He only paid $200."

"I don't care how cheap it was, Hal. They should have paid him to take it."

"You guys need some help? Me and my brother-in-law can help you. What end do you want us to take?"

"Sent from the gods! Here, just help lift this down and... Helen, hold the door open, will you?"

"Hell's bells. It won't fit in the door, Marv."

"I believe you're right, Hal. OK, crew, no problem, we'll go around to the back. They made deliveries there when this place was a restaurant. The doorway is much wider."

"And just how do you think you are going to negotiate through the kitchen, not to mention the kitchen door, Marv? I can't believe you've done this!"

"Maybe, Marv, if we turn it on its side, it could get through the door."

"Good idea, Hal. On three, everyone."

"And even if you do get it through the door, it will never be able to stand upright inside. The ceiling beams are lower than it is."

"Hal, do you see how the top could be removed? It might come apart somehow. I looked once but may have missed it."

"Watch out, someone is trying to get out of the door."

"Oh, my God, what a magnificent armoire! Did someone just buy it? I wish I'd seen it first!"

"Are you looking for a walnut wardrobe?"

"Is it walnut? I have nothing but walnut! Do you have any more of those? We're trying to furnish our new house. It has cathedral ceilings and we just got a walnut Victorian bed with one of those really high headboards. But this is even better. I need it for the foyer, when you first walk in the door. What a statement it would make!"

"I was taking it in to give it a coat of wax. But it will be for sale."

"If you would like to buy it 'as is,' I'm sure we could arrange that. Marv, what do you say?"

"Well, if she thinks it's all right the way it is. It would have to be cleaned up, so I would lower the price to $1200. We could deliver it for another $50."

"It's sold! Stay there! I'll go pay and be right back! And don't worry. Our entrance has double doors."

"Hey, guys, want to go along and deliver this baby with us? There's fifty dollars in it for you."

Perhaps, out of all of them, it was Emmy who might have perceived something which, sorted out later, could make sense. Her brain, so adept at storing information, vast quantities of information, and retrieving it at a moment's notice, enlightening anyone within hearing range, then going on to something entirely different, was busy as usual, filing everything away that first year. But, whatever the information was that she had taken in, it wasn't useful yet. So it remained in storage, to be added to as time went by, and used when prompted later.

"Who brought in that CD?"

"I thought it was yours, Emmy."

"*Boheme?* No, it wasn't me. I love it, but it's so *tragic*. When you get to the last act, you're ready to die yourself. Puccini is almost more than you can bear. Things pale by comparison to a Puccini opera, even selling antiques."

"It's probably Jake's then. He's been singing along with the tenor all afternoon. He must know Italian. Was he an opera singer or something? You'd think so to hear him."

"He's had serious musical training and he's talented. I've always wished he'd kept up with it."

A year for the shop and its people to establish themselves as an entity and another year to reaffirm, reinforce and deepen the ties even more. Then, the totally unexpected, the utterly incomprehensible, coming so suddenly and decisively into their midst.

Or were the ties deepened? Not between everyone they weren't. Some had slipped and some were strained, strained to the breaking point.

But *murder?*

"Cider Run. No, you have another, um, forty-five minutes before we close. Sure. See you in a few minutes."

"Cider Run. Oak dresser? Several of them. Do you remember which dealer you talked to? No? Do you remember where you saw it? In which area? OK, walking in the door, was it to the right or to the left? Straight back? I'm sorry, but I think you'll have to come in. Well, we're about to close for the day."

In any event, the first year of Cider Run Antiques, all would have agreed, was exciting and eventful, positive and profitable for the individual dealers. There was only optimism for the second year and why not? Everyone was working together to make it a success.

"Owen, you're trying to teach an old dog new tricks. It can't be done! I just keep making mistakes."

"Now, Grace, there's nothing to it. You can learn to use the computer. Kids in second grade are using computers."

"You forget, I taught first grade."

"Here, the program tells you what to do. Punch in what it asks for. Dealer code, stock code, item description, price. There, that wasn't so bad. You got it right."

"I'm hopeless!"

"Not at all. Want to check your sales? Just put in... That's right! You got it!"

"What I'd really like to do is change the thing that floats across the screen when you haven't used it for a while."

"The screen saver?"

"Yes, the one that says, '*Cider Run, Antiques for All Occasions*. It's been on there forever."

"OK, let's change it. We'll get into it here, and put another background color up, and what shall we say?"

"Something snappier. How about: '*Cider Run, Antiques To Die For*.'"

Chapter 14

"We need," said Marv one day toward the end of May, "a gimmick."

"A gimmick?" Helen asked. "Why? Don't we have enough customers? You mean we need extra publicity?"

"It's more a case of people having gotten to know what to expect when they come here. We could give them a different exhibit every now and then, a new treat. I was thinking that if we featured something or other, we could have them do a story about it in the *Martensdale Times*, get some free advertising that way."

When Hal and Jake came in, Marv consulted with them to get their views on his idea. They were standing to the left of the Thompsons' area, which was in the line of sight of the entrance. "I'm thinking," he mused, "that if we do a bit of shifting around, we could create a space here for a special display."

"That might work," Hal agreed. "We could move the player piano over to the wall by the restroom doors and Sylvie and I could squeeze our stuff together. We're sort of spread out right now and we really don't need to take up so much room. What kind of display did you have in mind?"

"It should probably involve several dealers," Marv continued thoughtfully.

"It could be seasonal," Helen put in.

Andy, just coming in the door with a few things, was startled to see Marv looking at him with studied concentration.

Marv's face lighted up. "A summer kitchen!" he exclaimed.

The summer kitchen was set up in the newly created space. A placard labeled *The Summer Kitchen*, with a watercolor painting done by Cora of a cooking fireplace, was put on an easel in front of the display. Below the picture there was a description of this practice.

When the weather got warm, meal preparation was moved into a separate building or semi-attached room, so that the fire or the cook stove did not contribute to additional heating in the house, and cooking odors were kept away.

An old cast iron stove brought in by Andy, crocks and bowls, iron pots and pans, cooking utensils, flour sack aprons, granite ware, a pie-safe: almost every dealer contributed something and the display was arranged. Marv had a reporter and a photographer out, and the weekend special features section of the *Martensdale Times* ran a story.

Cider Run Antiques, which opened a year ago in the 18th century stone building on Cider Run Road (formerly housing a restaurant), has put together an interesting and appealing display.

Called "The Summer Kitchen," it showcases cooking paraphernalia from Grandmother's day when making the meals was hard work. Full of nostalgia, it will recall times past for those of us who remember Grandma in her apron slaving over a hot stove. All of the items in the display, from the cookstove to the stirring spoons, are available for purchase.

Cider Run, which boasts an orchard planted by Johnny Appleseed, is open every day and has a variety of unusual and one-of-a-kind antiques.

"That myth will just not go away!" fumed Marv when he read the article. "Now that it said so in the paper, Richard will never let me forget it."

The story and photo of the display had the desired effect and, over the next two months, antiques in the summer kitchen were constantly being sold and replaced by other appropriate items. Even the cookstove sold, although no dealer was eager to find one to replace it, the delivery to its new owner taking its toll, at least temporarily, on the backs of Hal, Jake, Keith and Owen.

Before school was out Owen proposed a Saturday outing to Keith. In early April, on his way back from the annual train collectors meet and sale in York, Owen had taken an alternate route and found something that excited his imagination. He thought Keith would be interested and wanted to get his opinion of what it was he had discovered. Also, he was looking forward to being able to have a slice of history to show Keith after their mutually rewarding experience together in the fall.

Now on a morning in late May, Owen picked up Keith and they drove over several ridges until they came to one of the tributaries of the Susquehanna. For a while the road followed alongside railroad tracks paralleling the riverbank, and then it began to climb. After a few more miles, Owen pulled off, parking on the roadside, and they walked down a slope in the direction of the river. It was a mild, overcast day, fine for being in the woods, when the leaves were still young and small, and the smells sharp with river dampness. Down in the distance, they could see a glint of the river through the trees and hear the rushing sound of water.

Halfway to the river, about a hundred yards from the road, they stopped. There before them was a sunken oval, about 50 feet deep, maybe 150 feet long and 75 feet across, with a handsome stonework wall built up all around its sides. There were several tall trees growing within, but the bottom was mostly free of brush. Attached to one side of the oval was a square projection, slightly higher than the wall, built with the same limestone masonry.

Keith gave a short whistle of delight.

"I thought you might like this," said Owen, pleased at Keith's reaction. "I recognized the stonework. Am I right? It's CCC, isn't it?"

"Even better," Keith judged. "Have you guessed what it is?"

As if in answer, farther on below them in the area near the riverbank, half hidden in the trees and bushes, a freight train thundered by.

Owen said excitedly, "Tell me what you think."

Keith replied, "A reservoir. Yes. OK. And there," he pointed to the stone projection, "I think..."

They walked over to the square stone edifice. It was hollow and they peered down into the blackness. Keith dropped a stone in. It hit some metal rungs on the side and ended with a *plop*.

"There would be valves, a mechanism to control the water leaving the reservoir, or pump it into the reservoir, from the river. It looks like a ladder going down, maybe to check water level." Keith was visibly excited by Owen's find.

"That's what I was thinking," said Owen.

"While, down on the tracks..."

They looked at each other and then, like two little kids, and in spite of Keith's knee, they went running and sliding down the slope the rest of the way, until they got to the track, now empty of the passing freight.

"And the big steam engines would lower a scoop and take up the water, which had been released from the reservoir into a pan between the tracks..."

"On the fly!" Owen finished the sentence.

The two began to grin in the perfect meeting of minds, in the midst of an adventure, in the woods at that. Not entirely comfortable with the emotions they had stirred up in themselves, they ended with a nervous laugh, and trekked back up the hill. A little winded from the climb and the excitement, they perched on the stone wall of the reservoir.

"You know," Keith began, "we seem to gravitate to places like this. Although, I think this was Pennsy built, not CCC. The Pennsylvania Railroad did its own construction. You know the bridge at Rockville?"

Owen nodded. The handsome stone span that crossed the Susquehanna just north of Harrisburg, once having the distinction of being the longest stone railroad bridge in the world, was an icon to train guys like him.

Keith went on, "Look at those trees growing inside down there. They must be sixty years old."

"The last time the reservoir was used, before the steam locomotives all disappeared," Owen said pensively.

The two sat silent for a while, almost, as Owen said later to Lynn, as if listening for the steam engine's long-gone, long drawn-out whistle.

"God, I love history," Keith broke the reverie. "When you can sit in the middle of it, like this, you feel you've captured time You want to just pick it up and hold it, or at least save it."

"This stuff, yes, but not all history is what you want to embrace. I mean, the terribly sad histories, like what happened to your father and June's father."

"Well, we saved June's mother, anyhow. We brought her over here. She's been living with us since we came. I have so much respect for that lady. She's been a godsend, taught the kids Mandarin, takes care of them so June can work. I feel honored to know her."

Owen reflected that he did rather take his own in-laws for granted, decided he'd do better in the future, and then remembered, "What about that place we looked at last fall? Did you ever learn how much it was going for?"

Keith frowned. "I've run into a problem with that."

Keith had found out that the whole camp was for sale, not just one unit. It was at a price that he might possibly be able to swing, with GI benefits from his father and from his own service, and with money they'd saved, as June had always worked.

"Did I tell you she was a dentist in China? Her mother was very ambitious for her, and June went to dental school. Here, though, she's been working as a dental assistant. But she'll get started on her American DDS after I graduate. No, money isn't the issue. I talked to Jake about the property initially. But he didn't get back to me on it, so I learned what I could, and then when I knew more, I went back to him, to put a deal together." Keith paused.

"What happened?" Owen asked.

"That's just it. I'm not sure. I went to his real estate office. The secretary said he was in, he was with someone and could I wait. Jake came out of his office about five minutes later, looking like he'd just had a dip in the pond, if you know what I mean. A few minutes after that a young woman, appearing more than a little disheveled, came out and headed straight for the ladies' room. Now, it's none of my business. After all, the guy's wife left him."

"And probably took half his assets, don't forget," Owen said thoughtfully.

"That's right, I hadn't considered that," Keith admitted. "Anyhow, Jake told me he was looking into it, but I could tell he was stalling. I haven't an idea in hell what is going on."

"Do you think there's another buyer in the picture?"

"I came out and asked him that. He said there are always other buyers interested, but he'd do what he could. That was weeks ago. I'd really like to go ahead with the property. I have some ideas about it, making it into a summer camp for kids."

"I'd be interested in that if you ever need a partner," Owen offered at once.

Keith looked at him in appreciation. "Seriously? I'll be happy to take you up on that," he said.

"You know," Owen observed as they walked back to the car, "we seem to do all our serious talking in the woods."

"But not just any woods," Keith added. "Places like these—nature and history rolled into one."

Later, after Owen had told Lynn about his day, he thought for a moment and then said, "There's another thing about Keith. He has passion."

It was Lynn's turn to say, "Like you."

"No," Owen demurred, "I'm just excitable."

The warm green days of June came in and with them began the high buying season for antiques dealers. There were dozens of yard sales every Saturday. Cora told Bob she didn't see how they could go away this summer. Bob knew, however, that she'd find yard sales wherever they went.

Regular Wednesday, Saturday and Sunday flea markets in several of the towns around started up again, bringing flocks of buyers who combed the stalls and makeshift stands looking for overlooked treasures. There was some gold among the dross, but much more dross than gold. None of the Cider Run dealers sold at the flea markets, but a few of them made an early morning round, occasionally bringing back a find: a cottage table, only small repairs necessary, or a bunch of very grimy silver, with three or four sterling pieces mixed in with the silverplate, or a box of linens, most stained, but some redeemable. Emmy, Sally Ann, and Richard were not above going to flea markets, although they regularly swore off the practice, as the rewards were so few and far between for the effort involved.

The public sales at country auctions were a better source of good quality antiques, but sales could be very time-consuming. Quite frequently the whole day had to be dedicated to one auction. Nonetheless, the Cider Run dealers were ready to make this sacrifice, and willingly, with gusto.

Andy had his hands full with work on the farm at the beginning of summer, although he found it hard to resist a sale held at another farm. He often knew more than the auctioneer about the items being sold and, now that he also knew their value, bought and brought home, much to Mable's alarm, more things. "But they're to sell at the shop," he explained. "They count on me there." Mable was from the country, but she was not a farm girl. She could understand sales, so tolerated his new-found hobby, particularly as it was becoming profitable.

Grace and Frank had a summer home, so Frank was prevented from going to as many local auctions as he would have liked, but kept his skills honed on the sales around the Finger Lakes region, complaining bitterly about the higher prices things went for in New York.

Ruth was still happily exploring Pennsylvania, and the auction sales out on back roads were a good way to see the countryside. Her route often took her over some of the same paths the settlers did, the road following a creek or river through the mountains, and on the other side she would find herself in another wide green valley, Amish farms with dark-colored laundry hanging out to dry, a buggy trotting by. Then there would be the sign *Auction Today* beckoning, cars parked all over the place, buggies parked up near the barn.

Arriving at an auction, Ruth would plunk her folding chair down, quite frequently next to another Cider Run dealer, then go to a shed or up on the porch of the house to sign in and get her bidding number. If she were early enough, she might be able to go in the house to preview what was on offer, trying to see everything before the bidding started.

The thrill of the chase—this was where it began. There would be tables laid out with a century or more of household goods. Ruth would sift through, look swiftly, check for damage if something caught her eye, all the while trying not to think about the lives lived there, in most cases, the lives that were over. It was a bittersweet endeavor for Ruth, but it was a totally involving activity. It was like gardening, Ruth reflected. You had no guarantee of success, but it was rewarding just to get in there and be part of it, mess around, do something.

Elaine went to auctions religiously. Her folding chair was equipped with a seat cushion and drink holder, and she always managed to establish herself in the front row. Drink in hand, wearing her floppy, wide-brimmed hat, she would soon be surrounded by boxes of what she had successfully bid on—books, sheet music, china, lamps, glassware, framed pictures. To Elaine, everything was fair game and sitting in the front row, she seldom took notice of who might be bidding against her. If you wanted something you thought she might bid on, Ruth decided, your best bet was to sit next to her or at her feet on the ground in front of her, after letting her know your plans. Elaine was fine with that.

At one auction held on the front lawn of a home in a nearby town, it was Jake, casually leaning against a tree off to the side, halfway back, who bid against Elaine. It might have been that he was too far away to see whom he was bidding against, but with that signature hat, it would be hard not to identify her. Several times they bid against each other. Both wanted the set of Audubon prints, the maple humidor, the oak and brass smoking stand and the small tea chest. Elaine had to go much higher than she wanted on the smoking stand. She got outbid on the rest.

It would not have mattered; these things happen at every auction. But when she finally turned to see who the successful bidder was and realized it was Jake, and he smiled ever so slightly condescendingly at her, she had a strange feeling that there was a change in the weather, that some small midcourse alteration had taken place in the smooth sailing of Cider Run.

Hal and Sylvie took their vacation as an extensive buying trip. With their older daughter attending summer session at the university, and their younger one at a college-based summer program, they got themselves a rental truck and headed north, determined not to come back until it was filled. Their route was carefully planned to stop in the small towns and country villages where, by buying furniture that needed repairs and refinishing, they could pay a pittance. Their strategy worked, as it had other summers, and Sylvie had projects for the entire winter.

Helen and Marv still had a basement and part of a garage full of antiques. Marv, while relishing any opportunity to seek out and buy more, was somewhat chastened by the eight-foot-high wardrobe near-fiasco. Anyway, sellers came by the shop more frequently in summer, particularly on Wednesdays after a buying spree at the flea market, hoping to double what they paid by selling their buys to Cider Run dealers. And sometimes they had gold, not dross. Walk-ins, Marv called them.

"The best walk-in I ever had was the guy who came in with the Hudson River School oil painting," said Marv one afternoon at the shop, "in the original frame."

"Why am I never here when there's good stuff?" Richard complained. "But I hope you took down his license plate number, or did you merely assume the car was hot too?"

"I haven't heard of any art heists involving the Hudson River painters, although if it had been Rembrandt now: I'm not sure if the Gardner Museum in Boston has ever recovered any of their stolen paintings."

"Nor the museum in Oslo, or the one in Florence, or in St. Petersburg at the Hermitage," Richard added. "You asked, no doubt, where he acquired the prize?"

"No, Richard," Helen put in, "Marv did not ask any questions, did you, Marv? He just took out his wallet."

"Doing what comes naturally," Marv replied.

And pilgrimages. Summer was a time for pilgrimages. These were trips not so much to buy antiques, as to be among them.

Because so much glassware manufacturing had taken place in Ohio, West Virginia and western Pennsylvania, there were museums around the region full of beautiful pieces, ranging from the earliest tumblers through the cut glass brilliance of the Victorian era to the last of the dime store Depression glass pieces. There was a museum in Newark, Ohio, where Heisey was once made, and at the Fenton factory, on the banks of the Ohio River, and one in Wheeling, West Virginia, with big, stunning exhibits, and even in little Washington, Pennsylvania, where Duncan-Miller had its heyday. A road trip to these places was an inspiration, and with it came new respect and appreciation for glassware.

It was Emmy who told Ruth about this wealth at their doorstep, getting a map and marking a route for her. Ruth, who knew Sandwich and the New England glass makers, was eager to learn more about the glassware she was now buying in this area.

"And, of course, you've been to Corning," Emmy had said.

No, Ruth admitted, she hadn't. Wasn't that Pyrex? Emmy's face registered disbelief that Ruth would not know about Corning. What was at Corning?

"The premier glass museum in America, maybe the world," Emmy proclaimed.

High praise, thought Ruth, coming from the globe-trotting Emmy.

Emmy looked at the map she had been marking for Ruth. "You can't do them all in one trip. But you've definitely got to go to Corning. Wear comfortable shoes. Prepare to be totally overwhelmed. They have a very decent restaurant, too."

And where else must she go?

"Winterthur, in Delaware, although it's way beyond our hopes and dreams. Mr. Du Pont was able to buy anything and everything, and the gardens are stunning. No, Ruth, I don't know where you should go first. I would be paralyzed with indecision."

"Well, I know where I'm going," said Richard, coming into the conversation, partly to rescue Ruth from Emmy's directives and partly to hear what Emmy would have to say. "I'm going to Cincinnati to see Art Deco. Expect a transformation on my return."

Once again, Emmy came through. "Richard! Cincinnati! Where will you stay? At the Netherland? You must! It's out of this world. The Palm Court, oh, good heavens, Richard! Union Terminal. Rookwood pottery. When we were there last..." and here Emmy broke off, expecting to be interrupted as usual. Then she turned to Ruth. "You'd love it, Ruth. You need to go there too."

As for Laurel, she and Joe went to visit Joe's parents where they were summering in the Catskills and shared their happy news, then spent a few weeks in Maine at Acadia and drove home by way of the antiques shops, filling the back of the car with baby-themed antiques.

Chapter 15

Ruth's garden was doing nicely. Her lettuces were flourishing, the parsley and basil were coming along, the tomato plants had all flowered and some little green tomatoes were already set, and even the bush cucumbers were up. Moreover, everything had been chosen with Marv when they went to the nursery together. It made it special, personal, and reinforced the feeling of closeness that had begun that day.

She looked with satisfaction at the garden as she sat, book on her lap, in a lawn chair on her patio, shaded by one of her backyard maple trees. It was all one big adventure, gardening in this climate. There were many adventures here, she reflected. It's an adventure leaving the part of the world where you've lived all your life. And one should, she said to herself. Depending on where you went, she amended.

She had gone back to that improbable farmhouse, as his "missus," as Marv had arranged, and gotten the pieces of fig patterned ironstone she had seen and some of the mulberry transferware. They were now in her own china cabinet; they would not be resold at the shop. Meanwhile, her auction-going had resulted in much new inventory. Ruth let her mind drift with the drowsiness of the warm afternoon.

Ironstone china, plain white or embellished, was hidden in farmhouses and barns all over the county. All she had to do was go out and find it. Pressed glass pieces in sunbursts, diamonds, shooting stars, comets, flowers, fruits and a hundred other patterns were tucked away in cupboards out there too, waiting for her. The little towns with old houses lining narrow streets, front porches almost touching each other side by side, the poorer towns up in the hills, whispered softly, "Depression glass," to Ruth as she drove through them. Emmy said there was much to see. Ruth was ready for that road trip.

"Darn!" Ruth jumped up from her chair as a cottontail bounded away from the lettuces, leaving several chewed-off stumps. "Darn!" said Ruth. She thought, there always has to be an annoyance, a fly in the ointment and, with that thought, Helen's face popped into her mind. "Stop this at once!" she commanded herself out loud.

She had been trying not to let her thoughts continually center on Marv. He was married, he was someone else's husband. Long ago, well, not really that long ago, Ruth realized, she was asked, begged even, not to end an affair because her lover was going to get married. It was not a marriage of his desire, he had assured her. It was something he had to do if he wanted the prestigious position he had been offered as the superintendent of a wealthy school district. Incredible, Ruth had thought, that this woman had so much power in the community, and money, as it turned out, to essentially buy a husband. Incredible too, that he could actually believe Ruth would agree to stay under such unacceptable terms. Don't leave me, Ruth, he had implored her, but she did, she had to, and to make the break she moved to Maine. That had been, she thought now, a relatively clear-cut decision for her. The tremendous complications of continuing with him had been obvious, the eroding of his commitment to her explicit but, above all, there was Ruth's sheer distaste at his expecting her to share him with someone else. The arrogance! And yet, it had hurt, hurt terribly, to have given all that love and have it end up that way.

But now? Marv was certainly not her lover and wouldn't be. If she wanted to think of him, fine, she told herself. It wasn't going to lead anywhere. She could just enjoy being around him.

She got back to the planned trip. It's too soon to leave the garden now, she thought. It might be a better idea to wait until later in the summer. As things turned out, Ruth had no choice.

June hummed along and the bright skies of spring slowly took on the hazy pale blue of summer. No longer were the trees on the ridge across from Cider Run standing out clear and crisp; they had become blurred in a mist of humidity. In the heat of the afternoon, cumulus clouds billowed up, then slowly disappeared, leaving without a breath. The late afternoon sun suffused the sky with a rosy hue that lingered long past sunset and, as it grew dark, the warm aromas of grass and earth and foliage came out to merge with one another. The stars looked dulled; at night it did not always cool off. In the morning there was often fog on the fields.

One afternoon in early July, after several hot and humid days of building and then dissipating clouds on the western horizon, the unmistakable rumble of the first thunderstorm could be heard. Still far off, there was no telling when it would hit, if at all. The air was unnaturally calm and oppressive. If rain came, it would be welcome.

Ruth had a number of things to take to the shop. There was a mahogany lady's writing desk she had wrestled into her van, and several boxes of assorted china, glassware and yellowware, some of it destined for the summer kitchen. She hadn't been in for over a week and needed to restock.

She was hurrying getting the van loaded, as she wanted to beat the storm. One of the boxes got out of her grasp and she grabbed it awkwardly before it could fall. Heat, thought Ruth, makes me clumsy.

The coolness of the shop was welcome after her trek across the parking lot. "Ruth!" Laurel, sitting at the computer, greeted her. "You look very fit! What have you been up to?"

"Gardening and gathering, mostly. I'm like a hunter-gatherer, without the hunting part."

"Except hunting for ironstone, I bet," Laurel suggested. "Or can you just gather it too, like Andy does his farm things?"

Ruth responded, "Wouldn't that be fun? But you're the one who looks fit, Laurel. Absolutely terrific. How are you feeling?"

"Now, I'm feeling marvelously healthy. More healthy than I've ever felt in my life. Of course, I take all sorts of vitamins and my appetite is ravenous. Thank you for filling in for me during those first miserable months."

Cora, who was herself filling in for the vacationing Grace, came up to the front with a small group of Victorian tintype photographs that a customer had picked out. "She is still looking and doesn't need me," she explained, setting the pictures down on the counter. Then she said, "Ruth! You look very fit!"

Laurel said, "I've just told her that. She won't admit to fitness, however."

Ruth laughed, "It's only the weather and I've got a bunch to unload. Summer was a bit cooler up in Maine. Will the storm break, do you think?"

"I hope so," said Cora. "But, come on, I'll help you unload. Marv went to pick up something and you know how easily he's sidetracked. It could be pouring before he gets back."

Marv must have been chasing down elusive antiques, because Ruth and Cora brought everything in, and Ruth did her dispersing and arranging and was getting ready to leave. As she stood near the front counter, Cora suddenly said, "By the way, Ruth...Oh, Laurel, can I tell?"

"Certainly. Go right ahead."

"It's a boy!" Cora stated proudly, as if she were the grandmother.

"Oh, Laurel, how exciting! You can start choosing names."

"Thanks, Ruth. We just found out, so it's still a little unreal."

Cora said, "Did you hear how they named Andy's first born? They had a girl, but since there was always an Andreas in the family, they named her Andrea. Then when a boy came along, the name was already taken, so they named him Michael."

"Like our family," said Ruth. "My brother's name is Eric, and they named their first Erica."

"Did they have another?" asked Laurel.

"Yes, she was named Eleanor, after her grandmother."

"And then they had a boy?" Cora ventured.

"No, another girl, last one."

"And what did they name her?"

"Ruth," said Ruth, with a shy smile.

Ruth had errands to run and left soon afterwards, the storm still threatening, the thunder getting closer. She was sorry she didn't see Marv, but that would have kept her around the shop even longer and would have resulted in, she knew, that feeling of happiness-tinged-with-sadness, that sense of longing. Things to do, Ruth, she told herself.

The thunder rumbled. Marv came back to the shop, toting a Marten County split-wood basket, the kind they made back in the cider press days, quite rare and very sought after.

"Marv, where in the world?"

"Don't ask, Cora. It's better not to ask about these things."

"You can tell me. My lips are sealed."

"I stole it off an Amishman. It fell out of the back of a buggy. It was a prize in a pretzel box."

Cora put her hands up in protest. "Marv, stop that!" She glanced obviously in the direction of the entrance. "Oh, look, here comes a really angry-looking Amishman up to the door now!"

"You can't get to me, Cora," Marv said, shaking his head. "I will not reveal my sources."

Laurel had gone into the kitchen to have her midafternoon fortified orange juice and half a bagel. She thought how much she would love to take a nap. Maybe she could just stretch out for a moment on the table. She felt she could sleep literally anywhere. Really, this was ridiculous. It was as if she were back in kindergarten. She took off her sandals and climbed up on the table, cradled her head in her arms. She could not keep her eyes open.

She awoke to find Jake standing by her side, looking down at her with an amused smile.

"Oh!" exclaimed Laurel, struggling to get up halfway gracefully. Jake held out his hand and she took it, and got herself into a sitting position.

He had come in the back door to unload boxes—computer paper, office supplies, restroom and kitchen supplies. He must have been watching her sleep for quite a while, because the boxes were piled neatly on the floor.

The wind, so calm all day, suddenly started gusting. Jake quickly closed and locked the back door. A bolt of lightning flashed a second later and a clap of thunder followed right on its heels. With that, the rain came.

"It seems as if the weather likes to conspire for us," Jake observed, seating himself next to her on the table top. "Here we are again. We could take up where we left off last time."

Laurel, in her great happiness and sense of fulfillment, could afford to be offhand, could afford to laugh. "I'm afraid our time has passed. That is, if we had a time."

Jake gave her an earnest look. "But you know we did, Laurel. We got cheated out of it. You got cheated out of it. That should, by all rights, be my child." He put his hand on her stomach.

Laurel gave a start. "Don't be despicable, Jake. I wanted... I want to remember that night as it was, warm, congenial; that's all."

Another flash of lightning, another clap of thunder. The rain increased in intensity.

"You wanted me. That was plain to see. And you had me seduced, until Sergi walked in."

"I?" asked Laurel. He read me like a book! But thank heavens for this Sergi.

"Ah, but it was a sweet seduction," Jake went on. "Or could have been. You look lovely, Laurel. You're blooming. It's too bad I can't lock the kitchen door."

Laurel thought of something then, something she hadn't thought of before. "You didn't go to make sure the door was locked that night, did you? You went to make sure it was unlocked. You were expecting Sergi." Then he had no intention of carrying through!

"My appointment with Sergi was arranged before I ran into you. But I really didn't think he'd show up in all that snow."

There was more lightning, more thunder, and the rain drummed hard on the roof. The ferocity of the storm served to heighten the tension in the room, almost, it seemed to Laurel, to give things a malevolent aspect. She wanted to close the chapter, get back to reality.

Jake leaned close to her ear and said very quietly, "It could have been mine, Laurel."

Yes, it could have been. And he had known, very clearly, how she felt about him that night. She said only, "Jake, how unkind of you."

"Oh, I would have been very, very kind. You don't know how kind." He stood up, gave her a beautiful smile, a little shrug, and walked out into the shop.

Ruth woke up the next morning, tried to turn over, and felt a searing pain shoot through her right shoulder. It got no better with a shower and, holding her arm to keep the shoulder from movement, she called her sister-in-law.

After a trip to her doctor's office they ended up at the hospital, where Ruth had the shoulder examined and learned that she had, indeed, torn some ligaments. She was checked in and scheduled for arthroscopic surgery. They'd keep her overnight and she'd be home the next day.

Joe Fisher, on duty in the emergency room, came up to see Ruth later. "Don't worry about the shop. Laurel says she'll be happy to take over for you."

Ruth said she would be grateful, "But please don't let them make a fuss over me. My niece is going to come and stay with me, so I'll be fine."

Back home, stiff, still with pain, Ruth was slowly getting better. The hard things were the simple ones taken for granted: shampooing, brushing her teeth with her left hand, cutting food. Ruthie, her youngest niece, had been more than willing to move in with her Aunt Ruth and was a thoroughly enjoyable companion. Like her aunt, Ruthie had an observant and practical-minded nature, this twenty-year-old, but it was combined with the vitality of youth. She was exactly what was needed: helpful and energetic. She did the driving and they went to the farmers' markets and came back with fresh produce. They fixed meals and Ruthie did the paring and chopping. Their time together was an unlooked-for benefit coming out of misfortune and, while the two of them had always been close, this opportunity gave them an even firmer relationship. It made Ruth doubly glad she had moved to Martensdale.

Helen, Cora and several other dealers from the shop called to inquire how she was doing, and Ruth was glad to hear what was happening, what was sold, what someone had brought in and all the other news. Laurel came to see her and was assured that Ruth was in good hands when she met Ruthie.

A few days later, arm still in a sling, she was sitting on the patio reading, when Ruthie came out with Marv.

"Marv! How nice! Come to see the invalid."

"You don't look a bit in valid to me. You're as valid as ever."

"Ruthie, this is Marvin Yeager. I guess I should have said Dr. Yeager. College students need to keep the proper respect."

"I've already introduced myself," said Marv. "She is to refer to me as 'Marv' or whatever she wants. 'You there' is perfectly acceptable."

"Aunt Ruth, I told Marv I just made some iced tea. Would you like some?" asked Ruthie.

"That would be wonderful. Here, I can get it," said Ruth, half rising. "No," said Marv firmly, "you stay put. I'll get it for us."

Marv brought out the tray, and he and Ruth sat at the patio table drinking iced tea in a harmonious silence. A cardinal was singing tirelessly in the maple. Sparrows chirped in the annual beds. Like the first time they had been in Marv's truck together, they both felt an intimacy that neither wished to lose by immediately engaging in conventional conversation. Again, when they began to talk, the sense of closeness remained, but this time Ruth knew it was a feeling they both shared, while Marv only hoped she felt as he did.

Marv told Ruth he had been anxious about her and had wanted to see her and put his mind at ease about her. He said it lightly, but Ruth was aware of his underlying concern. She smiled at him. "As you can see," she said, indicating her incarcerated arm and matching his lightness, "I'm out of commission, but other than that, I can't complain." And if this is what it took to bring you here, she thought, I do believe it is worth it.

Relieved, and to keep himself from gazing too fondly at her, Marv let his attention focus on the back yard, lush with viburnum, forsythia, and lilac bushes. He had not been to Ruth's home before, and since it was an older house, it had the advantage of mature landscaping. Marv voiced his approval, especially of the vegetable garden, jointly planned, as it had been. "Hey, your Sweet 100's are almost ripe! Have you had any yet? Was I right or was I right about them?"

"Ruthie put the very first of them in a salad last night. You were absolutely right. They are superb."

"By the way, coming through the dining room I noticed some familiar looking pieces in your china cabinet. The 'missus' did well, then?"

Ruth laughed. "Marv, one of these days, someone will catch on to your ways. Cora says you showed up with a museum piece the other day."

"The Marten County basket? Well, seek and ye shall find. Cora tried to wrest it away from me, but I stood my ground."

Suddenly Ruth jumped to her feet. "Oh, no!" she exclaimed. "There's that rabbit again in the lettuces! He'll decimate them!"

"I'll get him," said Marv, racing out to the garden. "Stop, you Wascally Wabbit! Leave the lady's lettuces alone!" he called.

Startled, the rabbit did what rabbits do when chased; it ran in a circle. The rabbit tore around the backyard in ever-widening circles, Marv running behind it, shouting and shaking his fist at it, until it finally saw an exit under a bush and scooted out of sight.

Ruth, in fits of uncontrollable laughter, collapsed into a lawn chair, laughing so hard her shoulder began to throb.

Marv came back to her. "Well, we showed that old rabbit, didn't we? He's not going to darken our garden door again anytime soon."

"Oh, Marv," gasped Ruth, tears in her eyes from laughing so hard. "Oh, Marv, all you needed was a rake in your hand and you could have been Mr. McGregor after Peter!"

"I think that old gent had a white beard too. I could grow one for the next time."

They looked at each other in the most exquisite rapport.

Ruthie said later to her aunt, "He's very charming, Aunt Ruth. I can see why you like him so much."

Ruth said with a sigh she couldn't suppress, "Charming and taken, Ruthie."

When Ruth came to the shop the next time, she went into Cora's area and found what she remembered having seen there: the little Fredrick Warne & Co. edition of Beatrix Potter's *The Tale of Peter Rabbit*. She bought it and went into the kitchen, where she read the story with its beautiful illustrations over again. She took out a pen and inscribed on the flyleaf: *To Marv, with Appreciation* and then, after a pause, added, *and Affection, Ruth.* She slipped it into an envelope she had brought, wrote his name on the front, and put it into his mailbox.

Chapter 16

Emmy and Elaine were discussing how to get stains out of antique linen tablecloths. They were sitting at one of the picnic tables in the orchard. Elaine was having a smoke and Emmy, used to smokers from being in Europe so often, was tolerating it.

"It's enough to make you weep," Elaine was saying. "They didn't have the laundry products we have, and they couldn't whisk the thing off the table after a meal and dump it in the washer. So it could sit with the stain in it for weeks or months."

"Until wash day, whenever that was, or a good drying day, which in winter meant in front of the furnace." Emmy went on, "When we lived in England," waited to be interrupted, but Elaine was taking a long drag off her cigarette, so continued, "I couldn't understand why they didn't have clothes dryers. I mean, it's the worst climate in the world for drying things outside, but they insist on hanging their laundry on the line, where half the time it gets rained on, and they have to rush out and take it off wet and hang it up on folding racks in their teensy little kitchens."

"They think it's more sanitary that way. You know, sunlight killing germs," Elaine suggested.

"On the rare days when there is sunlight. I suppose they're trying to save money. Electricity is so expensive over there."

"Is your boy back at Cambridge now? Or is he on holiday?" Elaine asked.

The Greenes' son, the equally well-traveled Noel, fluent in six languages and working on his doctorate in England, was not a subject to be asked about lightly. Elaine knew she might be in for a long litany of Noel's latest achievements, but since Emmy was tolerant about her smoking, she would hear patiently about Noel.

Emmy looked at her watch. "2:15," she announced. "I imagine he's somewhere over the North Atlantic right now. He's coming into Philadelphia this afternoon and spending a few weeks with us. So, I must get home soon and put his room in order."

Emmy and Charles, like Marv and Helen, also had a pattern book home, theirs built in 1925. For all his Euro-centered orientation, Noel liked coming home to the big, comfortable, brick Dutch colonial, visiting friends, riding his bike out on country roads and catching up with his parents. The rest of the time his parents had to catch up with him somewhere in Europe, a not-at-all unpleasant endeavor for the Greenes.

Elaine, having gotten off easy this time, expressed the expected, "How nice for you," with genuineness. They rose to go in, Elaine stubbing her cigarette out in a heavy glass ashtray from the 1939 New York World's Fair. It would normally be for sale, but had a small nick in the rim.

As they started back to the shop, Emmy picked up on the original topic again. "I used to use lemon juice. Then I tried an oxalic acid powder mixture for rust stains. It worked pretty well, although the solution would never stay in suspension, so you had to be continually stirring. You'd spread the tablecloths out on the lawn in the sunshine and paint the solution on, but you had to do it right at midday and very close to the summer solstice, and then be quick about it or the grass would be suffocated underneath. I've found a new stain treatment now. It works all right on white damask but not on natural linen colored things." As a dispenser of information, of which most was usually relevant, Emmy had few peers.

The shop was not busy. It was the slower part of the summer. Business would pick up again toward the end of August, so dealers took the opportunity now to rethink their merchandise and change things around.

Richard had come back from Cincinnati, inspired as predicted, and headed out on a buying trip to find Art Deco. It was not that easy to find. The Art Deco period lasted less than a decade, but he had bought as much as he could of the jazzy, stark lines and bold colors of the Twenties and early Thirties, rounding it out with "moderne" pre-WW II styles. Richard was working in his area, putting the finishing touches on his arrangement. Gone were the quilts and country furniture. In their place was urbane sophistication.

Emmy and Elaine looked with interest and approval at the collection of Deco-themed picture frames, movie posters and sheet music laid out on a chaise lounge that had been designed with futuristic, fluid lines. Richard had a number of ceramic pieces from the period, decorative tiles with geometric, stylized flowers, vases in squared-off shapes and a figurine of a nude and faun in an intertwined pose. A Heywood-Wakefield curvy-legged glass-topped table held a gleaming chrome cocktail shaker, a few pieces of Clarice Cliff's exuberantly colorful pottery, and an enameled cigarette case.

"It's breathtaking, Richard," Emmy told him.

"I can let you have my Manhattan pattern Depression glass to put in if you'd like, Richard," Elaine offered.

"That would be ideal. May I have that ashtray you're holding, disgusting as it is?"

"What you really ought to do," Elaine suggested, "is team up with Sally Ann. She could wear one of her Thirties dresses and drape herself over the chaise and lend the perfect authentic touch."

"And you should wear evening clothes, Richard," said Emmy. "You would look divine."

Richard would look divine. In a tuxedo with his dark wavy hair and his piercing blue eyes, Richard could be a model on a Twenties poster himself. His good looks had gotten him into more than a few uncomfortable situations, but from those experiences he had decided, early on, to be honest with people and make it clear that he was gay.

On this particular day, Richard had been summoned by Jake and in the afternoon met with him on an insurance matter. Jake wanted to transfer his life insurance to a new policy, one that paid benefits into the partnership, a "business continuation" policy, so that if one partner died, the others would be able to carry on.

"A change in the beneficiary? We can do that, but why do you want to?" Richard asked.

"Until this marriage thing gets straightened out, I don't want to crash in the truck some night and have Annette get all the money," Jake said bluntly. "Hell, I've even changed my will."

"When is the divorce final?"

"That's the issue. There can't be a divorce. Annette wants an annulment. If we get a divorce, she can't remarry. She's just so, so Catholic. Annulments are a lot more difficult; it could take years and it might not ever be granted. I don't care whether I'm married or not. Never did."

And that attitude, thought Richard, was doubtless one of the reasons why Jake and Annette had split, one among many, probably. Jake was so very attractive—people who were that attractive could cause all sorts of damage. Richard knew this first hand, and that was why he did not want to be the kind of person who hurt people indiscriminately, by deceit. He felt that Jake, on the other hand, did not have such scruples.

Richard tried to keep his own feelings strictly out of any dealings he had with Jake. Jake had attracted him when he first met him. But now, Richard thought, if I were to let him get to me, it would be so uncomfortable around here. No, better to keep Jake at a distance emotionally, if I can.

On the slope behind the barn the fields stretched upward, spotted with limestone outcroppings, all the way to where the woods began. Owen and Keith and Keith's son, Lee, had climbed the hill a little ways and now looked down on the activity below. The auctioneer's voice, chattering on over the loudspeaker, could be heard wafting on the breeze. People were milling around furniture set out in rows on the grass, cars were parked helter-skelter on the road leading to the farm.

"Dad?" asked Lee. "Are there pumas and foxes up here, do you think?"

"Lee," Owen answered for Keith, "the only fox around here is you." Lee had inherited Keith's sandy hair, June's golden brown eyes. The analogy was apt.

Keith said, "Mr. Griffith is right. You sneaked up into the attic just like a sly fox and we were worried sick when we couldn't find you anywhere."

While they had been previewing the auction in the old farmhouse, Lee had wandered off. At eight years old, it was not something to be immediately concerned about, but when they didn't see him back at their chairs after the bidding started, they had begun to worry. But Lee had them in his view. He was upstairs in the attic, looking out the windows, seeing them and everything that was going on. An old house where no one lived anymore, strange and musty smells, hallways and staircases: how could he resist exploring? And then to stand at the very top and weave a story about what he saw. This was like being in a story himself. When he decided to leave his watching post and re-enter the adult world, Keith was close to being more than a little upset. They decided to take a walk to cool off a bit.

"I found this secret staircase. I had to go up it."

"And what did you find up there? A lot of dust and cobwebs, by the looks of you," said his father.

"I can't tell you what I saw." Lee looked down at the ground. His voice got very quiet. "I saw the end of everything," he said dramatically.

Keith sighed. All those mysteries the boy liked to read, started, no doubt, by his older sister reading him Nancy Drew when he was only five. Keith winked at Owen and shook his head.

"Hey, look, Dad. There's someone from the shop!" Lee pointed excitedly, glad of the opportunity to shift the center of attention elsewhere.

Keith and Owen saw Jake, sun glinting off his blond hair, arm around a woman who was looking up at him and laughing.

Keith frowned a little and said to Owen, "I was thinking I'd give him one more chance, about the property. But I don't know. Maybe I should start all over again with a new realtor."

Owen looked thoughtful. "I guess I feel a little sorry for him and I can't really say why. You know there are plenty of women and he's got money and looks but still, sometimes, if you catch him off-guard, there's a sort of haunted look in his eyes." Owen added, "Lynn says he's terribly attractive."

"OK, one more chance. Maybe I can talk to him today, if he's not too busy bidding or," Keith looked down at Lee, "whatever."

August with its hot, smiling, expansive plenteousness was full upon the hills and valleys. The nights were warm and filled with the scent of dry grass and, though the fireflies of July were nearly gone, the crickets were coming into their own. August days were brimming with piles of sweet corn and tomatoes at the farmers' markets. As always, there were too many tomatoes, too much squash. The first apples ripened and fell in the orchard. Marv had to rake the fallen apples away from the picnic table, as the bees had found them very inviting and swarmed alarmingly. At one point in his raking he stopped, rake poised. Then he held it aloft in an attitude of brandishing it like Farmer McGregor after Peter Rabbit, and he laughed out loud, the happiness of that afternoon at Ruth's coming back to him in a rush.

Ruth had more than enough vegetables from her garden, along with the other gardeners at Cider Run: Helen, Owen and Lynn, June's mother, Sylvie. Baskets holding the extra produce appeared on the counter at the shop with HELP YOURSELF signs attached.

Ruth and her niece decided that a trip to Corning would be a good way to celebrate Ruth's full recovery from her shoulder mishap and, since it wasn't that far, they could take the back roads through the wilder, scenic stretches of northern Pennsylvania in a leisurely fashion.

The afternoon before they left, Ruth went into the shop to leave a few things. In her mailbox was a note from Marv: *Thanks, Ruth. Shall I start growing that beard for our next garden romp?* M. She smiled as she read it, then put the note in her pocket and, for the rest of the day, found her hand closing around it frequently, each time aware of a warm, half-expectant feeling. Silly, she told herself, like a teenager. After all, she had been the one to initiate it by giving him the book. But now this little tangible bit of him was precious, she admitted, like the memory of their afternoon in her backyard.

Marv and Helen, meanwhile, went to the Maryland shore with their grandchildren for a week. Hal and Sylvie spent a few days with her parents in Iowa. With the other partners gone, Jake took over at the shop. It was during this time that Clair Somers came back to Martensdale from New York and went to Cider Run hoping to find Marv and Helen.

"Clair!" Jake, at the front counter, greeted her. "All grown up and fresh from the Big Apple! Sophistication and polish emanating like an aura! Have you come to remind us country bumpkins of what we've missed by eschewing life in the big city?"

Sophistication and polish not really. Clair was wearing a pair of denim Capri pants, sandals and a T-shirt that had "MMA" emblazoned on the front. True, the T-shirt was black, but 50ish Emmy wore black all the time, so that hardly counted. All grown up was closer to the mark. Her light brown hair was no longer pulled back in a ponytail, but had been cut at the chin line. It gave her the look of a soft and comely young woman rather than the unkempt student who had hung around the place last summer. Her unaffected manner was still there, though; the ingénue about her had not disappeared.

She remembered Jake. He was that very nice-looking older man who was one of the partners in the business. She went over and shook hands, a grown-up thing to do, and her clear hazel eyes looked straight and unfalteringly into his.

"It's Jake, yes? You had those beautiful Arts and Crafts pieces. Do you still?"

Jake looked heavenward. "Lord, where have I gone wrong? I am only thought of in connection with my antiques."

Clair also remembered that being around the shop and its people was fun. "It looks so good in here now. I love what you've done outside too. Did Annette do more landscaping?"

"Times change, Clair. Annette has gone on to better things in Washington. I have been left behind in the dust."

"You didn't go with her?"

"She wouldn't have me. Let's not talk about Annette. Let's talk about you. Are you here to brag about your conquests? Share urban legends? Revel in our rural ways?"

"Well, I've really come to see Dr. Yeager. Is he or Mrs. Yeager here?"

"That's Marv and Helen to you now. Someone who has sampled the highest expression of urbanity this country has to offer should have lost that college-town attitude, that awe of the professoriate. No, they're off for the week. But I'm here."

Jake is a great guy, thought Clair, even if he is older. "I guess I've left the city behind in the dust myself," she admitted.

What had transpired was that Clair had come home to stay, at least until she found what she wanted to do. Her parents were glad she was home, relieved would be more accurate, and she had found a job with a local theatre group doing set and costume design. She was also doing consulting and display production with the historical museum, and had some prospects teaching costume design at the university. None of these jobs were fulltime, and with her interest in antiques and the haul of goods she'd accumulated in New York, she had hoped to go into Cider Run as a dealer, if they'd have her.

Jake went out to her car with her. As he told Marv later, he realized at once that Clair had the makings of a unique and complementary collection of antiques in her vintage clothing and accessories. The softness of the fabrics set off the harder surfaces of the furniture and made a good counterpoint. He offered her space, and she accepted gladly.

The rest of the day Jake, Clair and Sally Ann cleaned out the summer kitchen and installed Clair in the space. Sally Ann, who had not met Clair previously, was happy to have a comrade who was interested in clothing, and since hers was so vastly different than Clair's, she did not feel in the least competitive. Not that Sally Ann ever did anyway; she had the most generous of natures. Also Clair, at twenty-five, was only a year older than her Rosie. And, similarly, only a year younger than Emmy's Noel.

They returned the remaining summer kitchen items to their various dealers' areas and Jake added a small table and two chairs from his area to put some of Clair's things on. The whole display went together very nicely. Customers who came in admired it and were told that the items would be for sale in a day or so. Pricing, tagging, and other technicalities were gone over, Clair sent off for her dealer's tax number, got a taste of the computer program, and went home tired but happy. Jake had been so very kind.

Marv, with a big box of salt water taffy for everyone, came back to town a few days later and walked into the shop before opening time to find dresses and parasols, a steamer trunk set open with a dressing gown laid across, sun bonnets and a dozen more objects of this type where the summer kitchen had been. He waited impatiently for Jake to show up. Instead, after the shop opened, Clair Somers came in.

"Clair! How nice to see you! How's life in the big city?" asked Marv of his former student and protégée.

"All over for me, Dr. Yeager," said Clair. "I'm starting a new life. How do you like my display?"

"That's yours?" Marv replied, taken aback. "When I left it was a kitchen. Now it's a bedroom or maybe a first class cabin on the Cunard Line. It's very nicely done, but I don't understand."

Clair explained that Jake had offered her a place and had been "truly wonderful," and that he and Sally Ann had helped her set up and learn about things. Over the weekend Mrs. Greene was here and someone named Andy, and they were very helpful too.

"Does this mean you have decided to become one of us? Clair, it's a hard life, fraught with danger, self-sacrifice and long periods of boredom. But I'm pleased you've come aboard. I'm sure Helen will be delighted. I only wish Jake had checked with me first, because this space had been, oh, well, it doesn't matter. Your things look very good. Tell me about them."

Marv was proud of Clair. She had been one of his best students, had gone on to get her graduate degree, but he knew her heart and her roots were back here. He was not surprised that she had been disillusioned by New York and, although he was sorry she had given it up after only one year at the Metropolitan, he was glad she wanted to be part of Cider Run. Here was another enthusiastic antiques seeker, like all of them. He could tell by her eager talk about the things she'd amassed.

"And this trunk has all the old hotel stickers on it. I couldn't believe it only cost $20. It did smell of mildew pretty badly at first, but I wiped it out with a baking soda solution and set it in the fresh air..."

Within another week, Clair had started getting her own customers and was doing quite well. It seemed to be a very good fit.

The partners had agreed at the start of the business that there would not be any unilateral decision-making, but by the time he saw Jake again, Marv was reconciled to the new dealer area. Jake told him how impressed he had been when he first saw Clair's inventory. "I didn't want to discourage her," Jake said.

"I wish you had called me or Hal, just to keep us informed. The other dealers were counting on having seasonal displays there. But it's done now, and I wouldn't displace Clair."

"Look, Marv," Jake countered, "we get rent this way."

Chapter 17

Besides Ruth's shoulder injury, only one other summer mishap occurred. Keith and Owen, with Lee and Rob, Owen's five-year-old son, had taken Keith's boat out to Martens Lake. Fishing was the ostensible reason, but other things became more attractive to the boys. An area thickly choked with water lilies was found to harbor frogs and Rob, almost beside himself with excitement, was determined to come back with one.

Keith cut the motor and they floated slowly in the tangled shallows, everyone trying to keep very quiet. Rob had the net, ready the moment they came upon an unsuspecting frog. Owen could see that Rob's arm would never reach far enough and to prevent disappointment, when a frog was spotted, Owen whispered, "Rob, there's one now. Hand me the net."

As the boat floated near, Owen stood up to make the grab. He began leaning out, leaned out farther, the boat still moving, then leaned out too far. In another second, he had lost his balance and fell headlong into the lake with a giant splash. His keys, which were in a pocket of his vest, got dumped out in the process. The laugh they all had as Owen emerged dripping with tendrils more than compensated for the loss of the frog.

Since they had brought Keith's car, there wasn't immediate concern. Keith gave Owen his Cider Run key to get a duplicate and the next day Owen went to have a key made at the local hardware store. There he was told, in no uncertain terms, that it was not a duplicable key. He'd have to go back to Cider Run if he wanted to get another key.

Hal, who was at the shop when Owen came in, tried not to laugh when he was told about the frog incident. He explained to Owen: all the keys were registered and each one had to be accounted for. Clair had gotten Annette's old key. Hal had three more and he signed one out to Owen.

"What would happen if you need more keys?" Owen wanted to know.

"We can get new keys made if necessary, but I'm the only one authorized to have them made. Marv said he didn't want to be bothered, and Jake didn't seem to care either. It's not a problem and I don't mind. By the way, did you ever catch your frog?"

Keith also had a question for Hal. Perplexed by Jake's strange behavior regarding the real estate transaction, he decided to see if Hal could shed any light on the situation. He took the opportunity on the following Sunday after church services at the coffee hour in the social room. "Hal, a question," Keith began.

"I heard about the frog escapade," said Hal with a knowing wink.

Keith grinned. "Everyone's probably heard by now. You can't keep things quiet for long at Cider Run." Keith took a more serious tone, "But what I wanted to ask you about was Jake, how long you've known him."

Hal had to think about that for a moment. "Not very long at all. We met him when we first looked at Cider Run a year and a half ago. Marv and Helen remembered that he'd bought at the charity antiques show and at some auctions, but they didn't know him then. Richard takes care of his insurance business, but I guess Emmy has known him the longest. Why, or should I not ask?"

"It's just that I've been trying to buy a piece of property with him and he keeps dragging his feet. I can't figure it out."

"That doesn't make any sense. You'd think a realtor would jump at the chance to put through a deal."

"I wondered if maybe he was bailing out, leaving the area or something, since Annette left."

"I don't think so. He told Marv he was here to stay. He is an independent cuss, though. I'm sure you've heard Elaine's complaint about his bidding against her at an auction, and there's also the fact that he made the decision to bring Clair in without our knowledge although, of course, we're glad to have her."

"That's gotten about, yes. Well, thanks, Hal. I'll talk to Emmy."

Emmy, with their son in town for a few weeks, was spending less time at the shop. Keith called her at home and when he got her on the phone, heard the sound of a piano in the background. "I have a pupil right now, Keith. Hang on. Don't stop! Keep practicing those scales! Sorry. Can I call you back?"

Keith wasn't sure what to ask Emmy. How do you go about seeking clues to someone else's personality? How close were they, the Greenes and Jake? He didn't want to be regarded as snooping.

"Keith, sorry," Emmy apologized when she returned the call, and went right on without pause, "If you want Lee to start piano with me, I will have an opening in the fall. Just let me know."

Good way to begin this conversation, thought Keith, and since it wasn't so far from the truth, he said, "I do, Emmy. Lee has been asking us to let him take lessons. You know he loves that player piano in the shop." Keith continued on this subject for a while, got the shop as the main topic and then moved into talking about Jake. "How long have you known him, by the way?"

"Long enough to know he's only really interested in antiques and money," replied Emmy in her forthright way. "OK, and women. But other than that, and the fact that I wasn't a bit surprised at Annette's leaving, I don't know a whole lot." Emmy, who did know quite a bit about Jake and for whom giving information was second nature, went on, "I wish he'd get back to his music; he should be singing professionally. He told me he was a choir boy in the church growing up. You wouldn't think it, would you? I can't imagine him so cherubic. He and Annette were such a striking couple. But she wanted to start a family and he definitely did not. I think it was an acrimonious parting; suddenly she wouldn't talk to me. But actually, I didn't really know her all that well, just through golf. She was never at the shop that much. And she and Jake weren't even matched on the course. She was an awful golfer."

Emmy, you're amazing, thought Keith. Lee, my boy, you are going to be taking piano lessons. He thanked Emmy for putting Lee on her schedule, and they said goodbye.

Out of the array of facts Emmy had produced, Keith was able to extract the few which had a bearing on Jake's recent behavior. He and Annette had had a serious falling out and she may well have been vengeful. Owen had suggested that Jake might be strapped for cash, since Annette was entitled to half his assets. Someone must have offered to pay a higher price on the property. Keith decided he had better find himself another realtor.

Meanwhile, summer was coming to an end and Labor Day was on the horizon. Since school started the day after and all the dealers were back from their various travels, Marv thought it might be time for one last fling, a potluck picnic for dealers and their families on Labor Day when the shop would be closed. It would also be a way to celebrate the first successful year of operation. The partners agreed.

The question was where it could be held. Marv and Helen did not have room enough inside, in case it rained. Anyway, a picnic with children shouldn't have to move inside a house even if it did rain. If it had to move inside, the place to go was a...barn. "Andy," said Marv.

"It's fine with Mable and me, Marv," Andy had said when asked, "and our kids will love showing everyone around. We have plenty of tables and benches and a couple of grills. There's even a fire pit if we need it. Yep, that'll be real nice."

A notice and sign-up sheet were posted. Cider Run would provide drinks, table settings and barbecue offerings, plus a special treat to be revealed later. Directions to the King farm were given. Dealers were asked to indicate how many people would be in their group and what kind of dish they would bring for the potluck.

"I like the 'special treat' part.   What's it going to be, Marv?" asked Grace. "Are you going to raffle off your Flow Blue china?"

"Can't tell."

"Oh, good," remarked Elaine, reading the notice. "Something to do on Labor Day besides waiting for it to be done with."

"What an attitude, Elaine," protested Richard. "You mean that you and Kurt don't host the neighborhood for a softball game and sausage fest like one is expected to do?"

"I know how Elaine feels," Clair said sympathetically. "Labor Day always gave me a double bad case of the Sunday Night Blues. The weekend is over, the summer is over, vacation's over, and dread for the morrow."

"It's worse in England," said Emmy, to no one's surprise. "Bank Holiday is always such a downer. There isn't any theme, like a real holiday. At least Labor Day stands for something. We always called it Bloody Bank Holiday. Long tailbacks on the motorways, everyone trying to enjoy themselves in that particularly grim English way. Even the Brits don't like bank holidays anymore. Noel sent us a clipping last year from *The Guardian* which said..."

Grace asked Cora, "Are you going to bring an appetizer, salad, main dish, or dessert?"

"She'll bring her tamale pie, if she knows what's good for her," Marv instructed, remembering the potlucks the old committee used to have during the antiques shows.

"Oh, Marv," said Cora.

Keith said he was bringing Chinese food.

"I'll be happy to eat anything," declared Laurel. "Do I put down two people or two and a half?"

Sally Ann announced that she was bringing Rosie.

Jake remarked it was about time they met Rosie.

Sylvie said she was sorry their older daughter had already left for college.

Ruth said she would have loved to bring her niece if Ruthie hadn't left for college as well, and she would think about bringing a main dish.

Jake said very quietly, "Will that be a rabbit entrée, Ruth?"

Ruth wondered if she had heard him correctly, but when she looked away from the sign-up sheet, he had disappeared. She decided she must have been mistaken in what she heard.

Marv had been to Andy's place in the spring, when they were working on the King family history document for the museum. Spread out between rolling hills, the farm covered well over a hundred acres, with corn being the main crop now. In the old days, he had learned, the farm had a dairy herd and grew everything a homestead needed to be self-sufficient. Later, there had been wheat, barley, and rye, the grain taken to nearby mills to be ground into flour. During Prohibition, some of the grain and cornmeal went in another direction, to the moonshiner, whose movable stills were hidden away in the hills around.

"That's why we didn't lose the farm in the Depression," Andy told Marv. "I don't drink hard liquor, but I have great respect for whiskey."

The farm had also been a way station on the Underground Railroad in the 1850s, and during the Civil War, two King brothers had left to fight for the Union, not to return. One fell at Gettysburg, one at Antietam. Marv had wandered around the property with Andy, feeling a strong sense of place. The barn, the stone outbuildings, the fields themselves: they all held their share of history.

The house, a much newer replacement of the original stone home, was a brick Victorian Gothic built in the 1870s. It seemed as if it belonged more in a town setting, except that a white-painted wood extension had been added, and with so much space available, added to again. The house had a screened-in sleeping porch on the second floor, overlooking the garden, with views to the hills beyond. The whole farm was a perfect setting for a picnic, and fortunate were the people who could be there to enjoy it.

The Yeagers first, with the ice and the drinks, and then the Thompsons, with their younger daughter and the special treat components, drove up the long lane from the main road early in the afternoon on Labor Day. Pleasant in the spring, now in late summer with the flower beds in full bloom and under a canopy of leafy trees, the farm was idyllic.

"Andy, I don't see how can you stand to leave all this and come into the shop" said Helen.

Mable seconded the observation. "That's why we got married. It was fall when I first came out here and it was so beautiful with the hills and everything, I didn't want to leave."

Jake arrived, his truck loaded with the rest of the picnic and barbecue supplies. Tables and benches were set out under the trees in the side yard leading to the barn, drinks were put in tubs filled with ice, and the grills started. Andy and his two children had picked several dozen ears of corn and were readying a pot of boiling water on another grill. People began arriving, the food was organized and set out on two more tables, and drinks were poured. If you had to define Labor Day, thought Marv, this pretty well summed it up.

Ruth came out with Richard, as her van was being uncooperative. They had brought a windup gramophone and a box of 78 RPM records that were earmarked for Richard's area in the shop. The sound of the old bands and crooners warbled out from under the trees. "Oh, darn," exclaimed Richard. "I should have worn my boater."

"Speaking of boats," Marv raised his voice, "Owen would like to say a few words."

Owen, who was heading off to the barn with Rob, waved his hand in a deprecatory salute in Marv's direction without turning around.

Sally Ann introduced everyone to her Rosie, a less blonde and more conventionally-dressed version of her mother. When Sally Ann got to Ruth, she said to Rosie, by way of introduction, "And this is Ruth. She's not from Pennsylvania but you'd never know it."

And that, thought Ruth, is undoubtedly the highest of compliments.

Lee came panting up to Keith. "Dad, you should see what's in the barn. It's a machine where you put an ear of corn in and turn a handle and all the kernels come off."

"Is that where you've been?" Lee would always be off somewhere, Keith said to himself, an adventurous child.

"Michael showed me. We're going up to his attic after we eat."

Cora brought tamale pies, as requested. Grace had platters of end-of-summer fruits. They and their husbands took over the job of husking the corn.

Laurel strolled with Lynn and the Griffiths' three-year-old Gil. The afternoon shadows were long in the hollows.

Until called to eat, Andy was kept in the barn satisfying the insatiable curiosity of Marv and Hal about the old farm equipment. One wooden contraption in particular Marv could not get over admiring.

"It's a treadmill," Andy explained, "for a horse or mule. You hitch him up and he powers the threshing machine. There's this drive belt that goes around this outer wheel, here, and you attach the thresher."

"Andy," said Marv, "this thing is fantastic. If you would agree to bring it to the shop, we could build an annex for it."

"No, I'm giving it to the museum."

"Andy! I protest! It must be worth thousands of dollars!"

Keith and June had brought June's mother, who spoke near-flawless English, and she and Ruth were having an animated discussion about gardens, Chinese cooking, New England and China. Elaine got into the conversation and for the second time her husband Kurt was heard to speak in full sentences, quite enlightening too, as they had lived for a while in Hong Kong. June was talking with Joe Fisher about medical schools in China. They had found many experiences in common.

Last to arrive was Noel, who had cycled out. He hoisted his bike onto the rack on his parents' car and took off his helmet. Hmm, Clair thought with approval as she watched him, the Tour de France has come to Marten County.

The promised "special treat" was prematurely revealed: hand-cranked ice cream in an old-fashioned ice cream maker, supervised by Alice, the Thompsons' fifteen-year-old, assisted by fourteen-year-old Andrea, the Kings' daughter, and helped out by the Mackinnons' Kristine, age thirteen. The girls took their responsibility seriously, but the secret was out when Rob came upon them cranking studiously on the side porch and went shouting, "Ice cream! There's gonna be ice cream!" all the way back to his parents. Excitability, Owen reflected not for the first time, must be a hereditary trait.

Jake had volunteered to barbecue the hot dogs and hamburgers, explaining that he'd learned the trade grilling at family gatherings with his "brother Brian's ever-burgeoning brood." The children were rounded up and Jake served them first, then the adults, with the fare that, as Marv described, "No Labor Day picnic worthy of the name should be without. Or without which."

It was an afternoon of supreme ease and enjoyment and it left a glow that would stay on in everyone's memory. Fragments of conversations, like bubbles, formed and filled the air and disappeared. What was lost over time of the particulars remained in a general consciousness of conviviality and happiness and, enhanced by the setting, it was as if they had all participated in a magic blending of past and present.

"I hear you went to Corning, Ruth. What did you think of the museum? Knocked your socks off, huh?"

"I'll say! It makes you want to buy up every piece of glassware you see. It's almost a religious experience. I have new reverence for glass."

"And up the price on the things you've got for sale, too. That's what I felt after I'd been there."

"Speaking of price tags," said Sylvie. "I couldn't believe what was on some of the tags in the antiques shops we were in this summer."

"What, the prices?"

"No, what they wrote on the tags, the descriptions. 'Old bowl.' And that's all! Or 'Vintage china bowl.' I mean, why bother? And what the heck is 'vintage' supposed to mean, anyway?"

"The ones that always get me," Marv contributed, "say 'Lovely old bowl.'"

"How about 'Beautiful, old, vintage bowl?'"

"Obviously they don't have a clue to what they're selling."

"My favorite was one that just said, 'Dish.'"

"Where did you get that gramophone, Richard? I love it! It's the sort of thing they'd take in the old Model T out to the picnic grove by the lakeside."

"Where they'd sit on a rug spread on the grass."

208

Richard said, "It will be for sale. The price will be steep, but it will be for sale."

"Maybe Owen should have had it to lure the froggies."

"I bet the froggies are still laughing, huh, Owen?"

"Cut it out, you guys."

"Hey, Owen, what's green and hops?"

"Ruth knows the answer to that one," said Jake, "don't you, Ruth? A rabbit on St. Patrick's Day."

Ruth looked at Jake, smiling enigmatically at her, then at Marv, who gave Jake a puzzled look, but Jake had turned away by then. This time she knew it hadn't been a mistake, what she had heard. But the conversations around her continued and kept her from thinking about it.

"I just want everyone to know the food you all brought is absolutely delicious," Laurel sighed.

"You wouldn't have said that four months ago," Cora commented.

"Four months ago there wasn't fresh picked sweet corn," said Grace.

"When is that baby due, Laurel?"

"November 8th," Jake murmured. Only a few people overheard this remark, but Clair was one of them.

"The first half of November," said Laurel, and beamed at Joe.

The ice cream was served up and eaten. Two big pots of coffee were brought out from the house. The evening drew in, the first chill was in the air. Crickets began chirping and evening smells arose from the cooling of the day and the release of dampness from the ground. As the sun went down, the aroma of foliage and earth provided a subtle backdrop to the gathering dusk. Benches were moved in around the fire pit where a wood fire crackled. It was like being at camp the last day, the last campfire.

The young people went off for an evening stroll, Noel in the middle with Clair on one arm and Rosie on the other. Elaine caught the expression in Jake's eyes as he watched them walking off. A touch of envy, perhaps, she thought. Wistfulness. Jake? It didn't seem likely. She said, "Emmy, your boy is just charming. You must miss him terribly."

"We do," Emmy replied. "But it's our own fault. We have no one to blame but ourselves. We used to take him out of school whenever we went anywhere and then there were Charles's sabbaticals, when we had Noel in British schools, and he just got used to other countries and every time we went to a new one, he'd want to learn the language."

"What is it that he's studying? Economics?"

"History," said Charles.

"What?" Marv exclaimed. "And you haven't been able to talk him out of it, Charles? Do you want him ending up like me?"

"How's that, Marv?"

"Living in the past," Helen answered for him.

"The past sure seems to be alive and well out here," remarked Hal. "It's got me convinced."

Marv cleared his throat dramatically.

Helen warned, "Watch out, everybody. Marv is about to say something profound about history."

The desired effect achieved, conversations ceased.

"The past," intoned Marv in his professorial voice, "is always there, lurking around. If it were a snake it would bite you."

Later, Jake said to Keith, "Hang in with me, buddy. I'm still trying to get a deal on that property."

Chapter 18

For a long time after the Labor Day picnic, a warm communal feeling lingered for the dealers at Cider Run. Andy was the hero of the hour, an honor he only reluctantly accepted, and anecdotes about the picnic were told and retold with inventive elaborations, until the event took on overtones of mythic feasts under the greenwood trees. No one could remember tasting such heavenly ice cream, never was there such a variety of delicious dishes. The children had all behaved, the adults were all witty. Stimulating and entertaining conversation had been the norm. The music from the windup gramophone was the ideal accompaniment and everyone was handsome in the evening twilight. They had come together and fallen under a spell woven by the setting, a place that enveloped them in a rural beauty still enshrouded in the past. It was something to hang onto, to take into the autumn and winter months.

Clair felt excited and privileged to be a member of this select club. As she was newly arrived, it was the defining moment of her involvement: it said it all. From now on, Cider Run was the focus of her energies.

Only one other thing besides her part-time work took up a portion of her thoughts. Clair had known Noel in high school, that is, knew who he was—being a year older, he was in the class ahead of her. She knew he had been the editor of the high school literary magazine and was gone his junior year in England. Then he graduated and went away to college, spending his summers in Europe.

This was the first time she had a chance to get to know him. It was brief, he was leaving to go back to Cambridge in another week. They biked together, enjoyed each other's company, hung out with some mutual friends, did a lot of talking about Clair's experiences in New York and Noel's experiences in Europe. Their conversations ranged from books and music to history and design. He asked her to think about coming to England next summer. Being around him brought out new ideas, another dimension to life. Then he was gone.

At the shop, Clair got to know everyone better. From them she learned about buying and, since she couldn't drop in on the Manhattan thrift shops when her stock ran low, this was an important consideration. Elaine took her out to the parking lot and introduced her to some of her regular sellers. Sally Ann took her to flea markets. Emmy, although Clair still could not bring herself to call her anything but Mrs. Greene, sent several of her little old ladies Clair's way, and Ruth did too. Clair climbed up into attics and brought down trunks, and bought. When Jake's table and chairs were sold out of her area, she realized she needed to replace them. She decided to go to Jake.

Jake, meanwhile, had been buying as well. Late in September he was gone for a week, then returned with a remarkable assortment of European sacred art, crucifixes and statues, small paintings, architectural fragments, most with brilliant colors and gilt embellishments. They made a pleasing complement to his Mission-style furniture. The strong, straight vertical lines and horizontal planes of the oak and walnut were enhanced by the colorful and ornate art objects.

Marv stopped to look at the collection as Jake was arranging it in his area. It was a new direction in antiques and could bring a different class of buyers, Marv figured. "But, Jake," he observed, "I thought you had rejected all that religious business."

"Hey, I sell it, I don't do it," was Jake's reply. "I got some things in Holland last year and they sold pretty well at Christmas, so it seemed like a good idea."

Marv read one of the price tags, whistled, and said, "Pricey."

"Real art is pricey," Jake replied. "And antique art is even pricier."

Clair, who was interested in whatever was going on, noticed the activity in Jake's area and came over.

"What do you think, Clair?" Marv asked her. "You worked at the most prestigious art museum in the country. Are these genuine? Are they old?"

Flattered that her opinion was being sought, Clair picked up a small plaster statue of the Virgin and studied it carefully. "I would say so, yes. Her features are perfect, you can tell she wasn't mass produced, and the colors of the paint look naturally oxidized. She seems to be made out of an old-fashioned type of plaster, the kind that had horsehair mixed into it. And look, right here, you can see where she was attached to something."

"Good girl, Clair," Jake rewarded her. "Oh, ye of little faith, Marv. I paid exceedingly for these goods and I expect to do exceedingly well."

"Looks like they left the back door of the Metropolitan open. These are the sort of thing museums acquire," Clair said thoughtfully.

Marv said, "We're already selling to one museum, that is, when Andy can be kept from giving his things away. Which

213

reminds me, Clair. Have you been to the railroad museum? It's new, only started last year. The curator called to say he'd like to come over and have a look around Cider Run. He's in the market for early 20th century clothing for his exhibits."

"I would be honored," said Clair, "to sell to a museum. But what I need now is to buy a few things, a whole bunch of things, actually."

Jake listened to Clair's concerns about filling out her inventory. A dressing table and seat, a cheval mirror, a small boudoir chair or two would be good additions in the furniture line, over and above restocking her other merchandise. They came up with a list of things that would set off her collection of clothing and accessories. Jake brought her the public sale register for upcoming auctions and suggested that she check the ones that looked promising. She did as instructed and found that several auctions on the same day in different locations held interesting items. She went back to Jake with the dilemma and summed it up by admitting that she'd never bid at an auction before.

"What you do is find out who is going and to which ones. Elaine or Richard, they go to auctions all the time. Ruth, maybe. See who's going where and go along."

"Thanks, Jake. I'll do that." Once again, he had been so kind.

As it happened, it was Keith and Owen who took her to her first auction. Ruth was working at the shop that day, Richard was off to find more Art Deco and Elaine had "bought much too much" last time, so was taking a break from weekend auction-going.

It was a strange combination of goods advertised. Owen was after the "Xmas dec" and the "Lionels w/box," as they read in the advertisement; Keith for the "Ducks, some signd" and knew if there were decoys, there would be more along that line. Also advertised were "Nice oak bedrm. furn." and "Ladys van. Objs and Others." Clair was ready to go.

The auction was held in one of the older towns, a farming community whose last house was probably built in 1920, if that recently. The town was one-street wide and homes lined the three or four blocks of the street, with only a single storefront among them. The houses all had deep, generous backyards leading to barns, now used as garages, which had access off alleys paralleling the main street. Beyond the alleys were fields and beyond the fields rose the hills. The auction was taking place in the backyard of a white clapboard house with a wrap-around porch, a pretty house with big old maples and a garden patch to one side.

It was a warm day for mid-October, the autumn sun coming through the yellow leaves in shafts of mellow light, the hills behind burnished in red, orange, gold, and russet hues. And again, the rows of chairs had their backs turned to the glory of the season.

But none of it was lost on Clair, and for her it was all an extension of the new world she had joined. This was the next degree of involvement and she was eager to experience all the sights, sounds and sensations. With her appreciation of clothing design, she had even worn the compatible colors—a jacket in a bronze tone and a soft yellow shirt with her jeans. As they showed their driver's licenses to get their bidding numbers, Clair felt she had finally come of age.

They were there early enough to have a good look at the items offered. There were smalls inside the house laid out on tables and furniture outside in the yard, and Clair had a moment of despair: she wanted this and this and this and...!

Suppose others wanted these things as much as she did and bid her up to where she had to drop out? She let her eyes rest on the hills and she breathed in the beauty of the day. Even if I can buy nothing, she told herself, it is worth it just to be here.

"See what you want, Clair?" asked Keith, as they met back at their folding chairs.

"More than I could ever get," she sighed.

"It's always that way," said Owen. "But there are several sales this weekend, so the competition shouldn't be too stiff."

Clair sat between them and noticed how they bid. You put your number card up when you wanted to get in, then you simply nodded to continue in the bidding. Right. She was getting the hang of it. The first time, when a box of hats came up, it was all she could do to let the auctioneer come down to a reasonable starting place. And when she could wait no longer and raised her card at "five dollars, five dollars, the whole box here of lovely hats, come on, ladies, who wants to start me out at five dollars?" she had no competition and took the whole hat collection for $5.00.

As the auctioneer's helper came back to her chair and deposited the box in front of her, she exclaimed happily, "I love this!"

Owen and Keith looked at each other. "Uh, oh," said Owen, "we've corrupted her."

"Careful, Clair," Keith warned, "it's habit forming."

Owen and Keith were enjoyable and helpful companions. They kept her from making bidding mistakes, applauded her successful bids and did it without being patronizing. She found most people there were not as interested as she was in used clothing, although the embroidered shawl she wanted went up too high and she had to drop out with a shake of her head. But a fur cape, redolent of mothballs, was knocked down to her on the second bid at only $7.50. She sat rigid with apprehension when what she wanted came up and had to laugh at herself when she realized that Keith and Owen were far more casual about bidding.

The "Ladys van. objs." turned out to be assorted toiletry articles, dresser sets of brushes, combs, manicure tools, hand mirrors, hair receivers, pin cushions, round and oblong boxes and dresser trays. Most were in French Ivory or celluloid, some in a pearlized green with black decorative motifs. There were also gold embellished milk glass items—perfume bottles and crème jars in Art Nouveau designs. Someone had been a keen collector. Clair bid with confidence and was able to get them all, and she was ecstatic. When the auctioneer moved on to newer things that none of them were interested in, they headed for the lunch stand.

"This is really why we came," Owen confided to Clair as they strolled over the leaf strewn grass. "It wasn't the ducks or the furniture or the rest. Forget about them. This is the real reason." He pointed to the food wagon, a trailer pulled in next to the garage. It bore the inscription *Martens Valley Lions Club*. Two apron-clad gentlemen had a big stainless steel pot steaming away on a stove inside the trailer. The aroma was mouth-watering. "Martens Valley ham and bean soup," said Owen. "Best in the world."

"The universe," Keith amended.

Autumn and bean soup, autumn and auctions. Clair sat on a bench with Owen and Keith underneath the yellow-leafed trees, listening to the patter of the auctioneer, watching the people coming and going, and relishing the rich taste of the thick, hearty homemade soup, relishing the day. This was wonderful. Why had she stayed away from Martensdale

217

so long? For an instant Clair wished that Noel were there, then wondered what Jake was doing. Did he go to auctions or did he have other sources for his things?

It was a very successful day and in the late afternoon they drove back to town, doing the kind of postmortem on the auction that comes so naturally.

"Could you believe that guy in the camouflage jacket? Every time anyone bid against him, he'd turn around and give them a dirty look. What an ass," said Keith.

Good, thought Clair, they accept me as one of them.

"How about that woman who kept jumping in on the first bid? Someone should have clued her in," complained Owen. "It just killed anyone's desire to get into the bidding."

"I wish I hadn't dropped out on the last decoy. I would have had an even dozen."

"You're a pig, Keith," said Owen.

"At least the auctioneer didn't spend all his time telling jokes. I appreciated that. Why some of them think they're professional comedians, I don't know."

"Hey, Clair, did you think you'd come away with all that stuff?"

"I couldn't have done it without you guys," Clair said gratefully.

Then the quintessential auction observation: Owen said, "Too bad Clair only got one bid in for the dressing table."

"Yeah," Keith agreed, "but it was the last bid."

Ruth had come in to work Saturday. As was her custom before she went into the shop, she walked across the parking lot for a look at the hills. They were a panorama of softly glowing autumn colors now and even though it wasn't *quite* as bright and colorful as New England, it was quite enough beauty to break your heart. Break your heart. The phrase echoed in Ruth's mind. Marv's truck was already there and she thought, yes, he could break my heart. Then she quickly shook off such a thought to better face reality.

It was a busy day. Marv and Helen were both working and also Jake and Hal. The volume of things sold on a fall Saturday and the types of things, such as the bigger pieces of furniture, warranted the "moving guys," as Richard called them, dealers who could load customers' vehicles and deliver things as well.

They had one thing and another go wrong, then miraculously get solved. The printer refused to print, but a customer knew what to do and got it going again. Everyone seemed to want to pay in cash with twenty-dollar bills and they ran low on tens, fives and ones. The credit card machine got backlogged and held things up for what seemed like ages, and then someone carelessly tugged at it and it got unplugged, with a $325 transaction going off into thin air. The shop phone disappeared and it took forever to track it down. (*Who* had left it in the Men's Room?) Customers were very patient but, as Marv described it later, "We almost had meltdown."

By late in the day when things had calmed, Ruth was taking a breather in the kitchen, finally getting her sandwich, having a bottle of water, idly looking through a Collectors Books catalog. She had kicked off her clogs and was sitting sideways to the table with another chair pulled up to rest her feet on. Marv, who had seen her going to the kitchen door, followed as soon as he got a chance. They had been together for hours but frantically busy, helping customers, helping each other out. There had been much communication between them, spoken and unspoken, which only made him feel more strongly the need to have a quiet moment alone with her, just one moment.

She looked up as he came in. "Do they need me?" she asked with a weary smile.

He sat down opposite her, saying, "No, stay where you are. You look settled and heaven knows you've earned a rest."

"Well, I *am* hiding out," she confessed.

"I don't blame you. It's a jungle out there. We're the hottest game in town. What have we done to deserve this?"

Ruth replied with a laugh, "Just keep that thought, Marv. We'll need it next February."

"Ruth, you know, when you laugh like that your eyes laugh too. They shine." He couldn't help himself. He had to tell her.

Ruth thought, do I make the standard reply and shrug it off? No, Marv is sincere. "Thank you, Marv," she said with a smile, but then automatically added, "I guess." She was still unable to receive compliments from him graciously, and when she heard what she had said, she was annoyed with herself.

"You guess? It's true. You'll just have to live with it." He got up to go. He was afraid he was making her uncomfortable and anyway there were still customers in the shop. But he had to tell her one more thing. "By the way, I was touched by your giving me the Beatrix Potter book." Then he added, "That's not all I liked. I liked the inscription. There. You'll have to live with that too." And he went out the door.

He was making it hard for her, she thought, making it hard not to let herself think about him too much. But she was not in control of Marv. He would feel what he wanted to, say what he wanted to. And she wanted to hear those words and feel the stir of happiness they aroused in her. It didn't mean she had to do anything, she told herself. If her thoughts flew to him, no one could possibly know.

Richard had put on a Cole Porter CD. It went with his Art Deco display and also his mood. Sally Ann was working with him on this slower weekday and in a lull between customers, he was teaching her dance steps, the fox trot to start with, and then they progressed to a Latin beat. She was, as always, dressed appropriately for such an occasion, should it occur, in a print dress that fit tightly at the hips and flared at the hem, with Cuban-heeled pumps. They moved in unison with verve and dash and left a series of dark scuff marks in the grey carpeting. Marv would have been beside himself.

Richard's mood was ebullient: he had met someone on a trip to Baltimore. His name was Trevor. He also collected antiques; his apartment was a study in fifties kitsch. "Not really my decade," Richard was telling Sally Ann, in between turns and dips, "but he's got the right idea."

"Oh, Richard!" said Sally Ann. "I can't wait to meet him. What does he look like? Is he as handsome as you?"

Clair, with some of her new auction acquisitions in tow, came in on the dancing couple as they completed a swoop near the front of the shop. What fun people have here, she thought. "You look right out of a Ginger Rogers movie!" she told an out-of-breath Sally Ann.

"Richard makes me feel like Ginger Rogers," Sally Ann gushed.

"Don't I look like Fred Astaire? You could pay me the compliment too, you know," said a not-at-all winded Richard.

"You are far better looking than Fred Astaire," Clair replied.

Richard said, "Did you know, they used to have dances here? There's a wooden dance floor somewhere under this ugly carpeting. We thought we'd try to locate it. All we'd have to do is rip up the carpet."

The song ended and Richard helped bring in Clair's oak dressing table. Both he and Sally Ann admired it, with its beveled, oak framed triple mirror and curved Empire-style legs. Since it had no damage, all Clair had to do was put a light coat of wax on it. She had also brought in several old leather suitcases, one with alligator trim, to go with her clothing collection. She was abundant in her praise of Keith and Owen, who had introduced her so successfully to the auction game. "It's almost an art form," she said. "It's all in the rhythm and timing of the auctioneer, and the responses of the bidders. It's like music. And look at what I got!"

"Like the tango and the rumba and the cha-cha-cha," Richard contributed.

"You could say that," Clair agreed. "Like a dance contest and you can win prizes."

Sally Ann said, "Richard has been teaching me new steps. We could be dance partners. Oh! Richard has met someone new," Sally Ann enthused. "His name is Trevor. He collects antiques."

Clair smiled at Richard. "I'm envious!" she said warmly. It was close to the truth, she thought. The wasted time with her ex-boyfriend back in New York. And then that nice beginning with Noel, and off he goes. Maybe not envy, really, but certainly a longing for a relationship.

"Honey, I would be envious too," Sally Ann confided, "but only if Richard wouldn't let me dance with him."

Clair got busy in her area, the dance music playing in the background. It's like a party, she thought. This whole place is one big party. She was just getting up off of the floor, where she had knelt to arrange the flounce of a dress, and saw Jake looking appraisingly at the new display. Clair desperately wanted Jake to like it.

"You went to an auction, then, Clair?" Jake asked, indicating the new dressing table. He checked the tag. "You're asking way too low for this."

"But I got it for half of that. Keith said you try to double the price, so that's what I did."

"Do you have another one in reserve? Because at that price, it's going to waltz right out of here before the week is over. No, Clair, double it again," he instructed.

"You think?" Clair asked dubiously.

"Yes," Jake replied, "absolutely," and went on through the shop to the kitchen door.

Clair had the first momentary doubt as to whether she was really the stuff that dealers were made of, but then looked at the table and at the tag and had to agree that Jake was right. $150 was too low a price for such a fine piece of early 1900s oak furniture. She wrote out a new tag doubling the price again and immediately felt stronger about her judgment of antiques.

She glanced at the door Jake had gone through and wondered if she should go tell him that she'd taken his advice. She was on the verge of doing so when a customer came by, admired her area and began to ask her about several things. Clair smoothly became the professional antiques dealer, explaining about dress fabrics and styles, what was worn in the era and the accessories that went with them. It's good to have this opportunity, she thought; this is a good place to be.

Chapter 19

November 8th came and went and on November 10th Helen took a phone call at the front counter from Joe who, with much excitement, announced the arrival of Benjamin Joseph Fisher, 7 pounds, 5 ounces, mother and baby doing splendidly.

"Laurel's had her baby!" Helen shouted to Elaine and Clair. "Joe," she said to the happy father, "please tell Laurel we're thrilled and we can't wait to see him!"

"Give us a few days. We'll bring him in."

Helen hung up the phone and repeated everything to Elaine and Clair. "The first Cider Run baby," she rhapsodized, then wiped her eyes, remembering her first born, the son who had died in infancy.

As the loss of the Yeagers' first baby was well known at Cider Run, Elaine tactfully shifted the subject. She said, "Did you see Laurel when she came in a few weeks ago? Nine months pregnant and she still looked chic and elegant. I was never able to manage that."

"I looked like a cow," Helen confessed.

Clair's gaze went from one to the other. The people at Cider Run were her mentors and role models. What were they saying?

Helen caught Clair's look. "Pay no attention to us, Clair. We'd give anything to be pregnant again."

"Would not!" Elaine retorted.

Ruth came in to do some work in her area and was told the news. She was genuinely happy for Laurel and Joe, reminding herself to let them know she'd be glad to take some of Laurel's days for her. Good for you, Laurel, Ruth thought, and lucky you. A child was a luxury Ruth had not been able to afford, a decision she'd had to make. And for Helen it had been tragic, at least the first time. That was something Ruth found she didn't like thinking about, and she proceeded to immerse herself in redoing her area.

When Clair saw Ruth standing on a chair trying to hang some botanical prints, she came to help and handed up the pictures. "Clair, thank you!" Ruth smiled down at her. I'm happy she's one of us, this nice young woman with her hazel eyes and short, swinging hair, Ruth thought to herself.

Clair was thinking about Ruth in much the same fashion—what a pretty face, that stunning red hair. Does she look so young because she isn't married? Is it from being an independent person? Clair was at the age where she was seeking clues about life, but not yet ready to draw conclusions. Ruth was at an age where she knew many of her conclusions were no longer valid. In a way, they were on the same ground.

Ruth, with Clair helping, got the pictures mounted, and they moved a walnut tea cart into the center of Ruth's area, then loaded it with a silverplate coffee service and a set of linen cocktail napkins. Ruth, by way of explanation, said, "Thanksgiving is coming and we want to give customers all the ideas we can."

"Mrs. Yeager, I mean Helen, says Christmas is frenetic. I can't wait!" Clair exclaimed.

"But after that it gets duller than dishwater for the next couple of months. Gives us all a chance to catch our breaths, go off somewhere if we're fortunate."

"I'm not sure I'd want to leave this place, even for a few weeks. It's too exciting, things keep happening and everyone is so..." Clair searched for the right word, and an image of Jake flashed into her mind, "...helpful." The word sounded lame to her; it didn't express her feelings adequately.

But Ruth apparently understood, because she gave Clair a private sort of smile. "I know how you feel," she said.

A few weeks later Elaine was at the front counter, while Emmy was bringing up purchases for a customer who was still browsing. Sylvie was helping another customer and Jake was somewhere in back. It was getting busy even on weekdays as Christmas approached. The door opened and, with cold air following, one of Jake's dealers came into the shop.

"Sergi!" Elaine greeted him. "Nice to see you. I think Jake's around here somewhere."

Sergi bent over Elaine's hand and kissed it. Emmy looked on with interest. "Sergi always does that. He's from Romania and it's the custom. Sergi, this is Emmy Greene."

Emmy said smoothly, "*Buna ziua. Sunteti din Bucuresti?*"

Sergi gave Emmy a surprised look and immediately replied, "*Da,*" then added, "but I tell myself I will only speak English while I am in America. How enchanting to meet you." He took Emmy's hand and kissed it, and turned to go in search of Jake. Emmy had a slightly puzzled look on her face.

"Emmy, you put us all to shame," Elaine said. "You speak Romanian?"

"Not really," Emmy admitted. "I learned just enough to get by when we were there. 'Good day' and 'Are you from Bucharest?' Things like that. It's a Latin-based language, so if you know Italian or French or Spanish, you can pick it up pretty easily. Noel is really fluent, but Charles and I..."

Elaine was spared the rest, as Emmy's customer arrived to pay for her purchases.

The Christmas shopping season had begun. Hal put lights on the little hemlock they had planted in front and a wreath went up by the door. The Cider Run Christmas card, this time a sketch by Cora of the cider press filled with holly, had been sent out and, like the year before, dealers were kept busy coming in with seasonal items to fill their areas.

Keith, with Clair's inspiration, tied red ribbons around the necks of his decoys. Owen set up a Christmas village and one of the electric trains was allowed to run on the track on a demand-only basis. It was an instant hit, promptly sold and had to be replaced by another.

Cora had Christmas books, from Charles Dickens to Washington Irving to Tasha Tudor, each as desirable for the illustrations as the stories. Grace brought in pewter bowls, candlesticks and tankards, and decorated them with holly sprigs made in the Thirties from cut green velvet and red glass beads.

Emmy put out English silver toast racks filled with old Christmas postcards. "It's a much better use for them than cold toast, like they do in England," she told Ruth.

Ruth laughed in agreement, remembering the English penchant for cold, hard toast sitting primly in the toast rack. She had concentrated on white ironstone pieces for this Christmas season, putting them on a red cloth and filling the creamers, pitchers and toothbrush holders with faux greens, which set them off nicely.

Richard was in dismay. His Art Deco had almost sold out and he had not been able to replenish it, so he didn't know what to stock for Christmas. He decided to go on one more lightning-quick shopping trip and came back with, among other smaller items, a leather club chair and ottoman. "Which I paid much more for than was prudent," he confessed, but it refilled his area, and had a SOLD tag on it before the season was over.

Sally Ann had a bunch of 1940s and 1950s Christmas hankies in a basket. Their brightly patterned holly, poinsettia, and candy cane prints were very jolly and since they were not priced above a few dollars apiece, she had trouble keeping the basket full.

Grace and Cora helped Andy decorate the country antiques in his area with gingham bows in red and green. A metal milk bottle carrier from the Twenties was intertwined with ribbons, and into an egg carrier they put old glass Christmas ornaments. Andy was amused. Town people did the darndest things.

Jake's beautiful and unusual religious items were selling fast, even with the high prices. He had arranged a set of miniature paintings of the Madonna on the fireplace mantel and it gave his whole area the atmosphere of "serious antiques." Customers said that the presence of sacred art lent a museum aspect, and the fact that they could actually own one or more of the pieces made them irresistible.

Clair had done a holiday display with evening bags in silk and satin, beaded and plain, most of them black, but some in silver and gold. She had long ropes of crystal and faux pearl beads, which she draped over the mirror of the dressing table. The fur cape and a pair of black evening gloves lay across a suitcase.

The Yeagers' and the Thompsons' furniture was decked with brass candlesticks holding red candles. There was a folk art wooden sleigh and several wooden bowls filled with pine cones. Elaine didn't worry about decorating; she just crammed more things in. Laurel took this year's holiday off and invited other dealers to use her space for their overflow.

The plates of cookies reappeared along with coffee for customers. One day had been designated as an open house, and Sylvie concocted a cranberry punch which looked heavenly in a sparkling pattern glass punch bowl from Ruth. The assorted pattern glass cups, which were close although not a match, came from Emmy. Both bowl and cups were sold, but not removed, before the day was over. The ladle, alas, was new and thus not for sale; antique ladles cannot always be found when needed.

The impact of seeing antique linens, glassware, china and silver laid out on a gleaming mahogany sideboard, in the manner and purpose for which they were originally designed, was definitely felt by visitors to the shop. Damask napkins, silver napkin rings, crystal wine glasses from a hundred years ago: customers could visualize them at their own homes for tonight's dinner party. The white ironstone sauce boat that graced a table in 1910 could be used to serve gravy for a holiday turkey this year. Even just one piece here and there from yesterday could easily blend in and, at the same time, hold its own. These were antiques to be taken home and used.

It was all part of the spirit of the season, and the dealers at Cider Run did their best to give expression to that spirit. At the holidays, the antiques which dealers sold to their customers, whether to be put to use, to give as gifts, or simply to be kept for posterity, were an embodiment of this essential character. Customers bought antiques not only for their beauty or uniqueness or utility or, often, all three, but because the holidays are a time of great looking backwards and of nostalgia for the past, and antiques make both a tangible and spiritual link to the past.

The season was merry at the shop, and when it was over, dealers carefully put things away for another year and quiet returned to Cider Run. Marv decided it was time to go over shop business, matters that had been neglected during the rush of fall and the holidays. On a snowy day, he, Hal, Jake and Helen got together around the kitchen table, while the few customers who ventured in were helped by Cora and Grace.

Finances were the major topic of discussion. Helen, with her job of doing the accounts, had told Marv that expenses were getting out of control.

"Advertising," explained Marv, "for one thing. We spent more than we thought we would last year. It has paid off in individual sales, but it isn't bringing money into the business."

"Don't forget the expenses we had in regard to the physical plant," Hal started to say, then apologized, as Marv was looking askance at him, "sorry, I mean, the maintenance issues for the building."

"When Hal talks in engineerese, it's more than I can handle," Marv said.

Hal went on, "The masonry work, the parking lot work, is this elementary enough for you, Marv? The landscaping, although the labor was cheap enough, the sidewalk extensions and repairs, re-caulking some of the windows, and I'm sure we'll find more when this winter is over. I had a look at the roof in the fall and I'm afraid there is going to be work needed there."

Helen took up the theme. "The carpeting may need to be replaced. It hasn't worn very well."

"You're right," Marv agreed. "I was noticing, even before the Christmas traffic, there were deep scuff marks all over the place. But what a mess and dislocation it would be to replace it."

"Well, I'll look at our warranty," said Helen, and then went on, "Also, the coffee pot has been used pretty hard and we need a new one. As far as our cleaning service goes..." The cleaning service came in twice a week. One of the partners got to the shop early to let them in for an hour before opening time.

"We can cut that back to once a week for the time being, anyway," said Marv.

"Still," insisted Helen, "the in-go is less than the out-go."

Jake gave Helen an indulgent look. "I love it when you talk in bookeeperese," he purred.

"So, what's the verdict, partners?" Marv persisted. "We need some more revenue to carry on, as far as I can tell. What are our options?"

"There's always the Flow Blue," Hal said with a grin.

"Soak your head, Hal. There's a fortune in antique tools sitting around your house," Marv countered.

"There's the possibility of taking more of a percentage of sales," Hal said. The business took three percent for the express purpose of paying for credit card company fees. It mostly balanced out and the dealers understood the need for it.

"Or we could raise rents," Helen suggested. "It won't be popular, but if we do it gently and only by a small amount, we might not lose anyone."

"Hitting up the dealers should be our last resort," said Marv. "I'd like to avoid raising rents or taking more of a cut of their profit. When we started this partnership, we agreed that if we got into a bind after the first year, we'd all put in more cash. Well, folks, we may be at that point."

"Look, Marv," Jake said. "Let's wait and see. Most of these expenses are over and done with and unless the roof does fall in, we may be all right this year. I'm not feeling all that flush right now, thanks to Annette, and would rather put off having to go to my banker."

"Jake is right. There may be other things we could do as a business to raise money. What about your teaching that antiques class of yours again, on site, whoops, I mean at the shop, Marv?" Hal asked.

"If the advertising for it doesn't equal the tuition, sure," Marv agreed.

They decided to put the question to the dealers. A notice was prepared to be placed by the mailboxes. It read:

HELP!
Cider Run expenses have gone through the roof! And the roof isn't all that great either! Help us come up with ideas to raise some cash. All suggestions will be taken to heart and only thrown out after careful consideration.

There was space below for suggestions and Helen had written in the first one.

Marv's antiques class taught at the shop for a fee.

As the partners emerged from the kitchen after their meeting, Cora reminded Jake, "Don't forget. You're going to sit for me."

Cora had asked, and Jake had reluctantly agreed, to let her do a sketch of him sitting in the Morris chair, a book open in his hand, but with a faraway gaze. It was to be in the style of Charles Dana Gibson and she would use it on a *Winter Reading* poster for a display of books in her area. The Gibson men, like the Gibson girls, represented the height of Edwardian fashion and were handsome, rugged, manly—whatever that means, thought Cora—with brooding look and serious demeanor. Jake was the ideal model, with just the hint of a cleft in his square chin and a cool, lush look in his eyes.

Marv and Hal came by as the sketching progressed. "What do you say, Hal? He looks almost life-like."

"Shut up, Marv," muttered Jake.

"What's he reading? I think he's holding the book upside down."

"He needs a pipe. Didn't they always have a pipe?" Hal asked.

"No," Cora disagreed. "It would ruin his expression."

"Just exactly what is his expression supposed to be? He looks excruciatingly bored to me," Marv observed.

"He's gazing off," Cora explained, "thinking about some fascinating woman. He can't concentrate on what he's reading."

"And you think you're going to sell books with that?" Marv asked with an incredulous look.

"Cora, do you mind if I get up and deck Marv? It'll only take a second."

"I'm almost through. I'll fill in the high collar and the cravat thing later."

When Clair saw the completed sketch of Jake on the poster in Cora's area, she stared at it for a long time. Something about the way he looked, the old Morris chair, the hint of the fireplace in the background, excited her imagination. Jake was the embodiment of Cider Run for her. He brought it together, past to present. And wasn't Jake a nickname for Jacob, the first resident of Cider Run?

Laurel, holding the sleeping Ben, looked at the sketch too. She gave a slight shudder, and the baby stirred.

Chapter 20

Over the next week, the space below the suggestion sheet was well used. Much pent-up creativity must have been present, because the sheet soon got filled.

Have a bake sale.

What about all the apples? Could they be sold?

Hold a flea market in the parking lot. Charge for space. Someone else had added a note: *Then where would everyone park?*

Have a flea market in the orchard.

We could raise rents by 10%. I wouldn't mind.

How much money do we need anyway?

Find another investor, but who?

Find an angel, like for theatre.

Hold concerts in the orchard and/or summer theatre. Note: *Too many insects!*

Have a wine tasting using antique stemware. Note: *Do we need a liquor license?*

Everyone could donate items and we could have an auction for the general public. Note: *Would we need an auctioneer's license for this?* 2nd Note: *We could hire one of the local auctioneers.* 3rd Note: *Their fees would be too high and they're all jokers anyway.*

Charge for parking.

Have valet parking.

And the last entry:

Pony up, you tightwads! We know you're just being cheap.

Of all the suggestions on how to infuse more money into the business, only a few were not tossed immediately. Marv felt, if nothing else, it had been good for the dealers to express themselves, wildly and otherwise. He thought it was interesting that there had been a suggestion about a 10% raise in rents and was pretty sure he knew who had written it, namely Sally Ann. She was financially secure and was always bringing in doughnuts and other goodies to share with everyone and, quietly, without calling attention to herself, keeping the refrigerator stocked with soft drinks and bottled water. Finding another investor, or an angel, was also a possibility. One or more of the dealers, perhaps? It was an idea to have in the back of his mind. There *were* a lot of apples and maybe that was something to think about for the future. As far as the last comment went, Marv scratched his head for a while wondering who the writer was. He put a note after it: *Identify yourself, you coward!* but then figured it was Owen, most likely, getting even for the ragging he'd taken over the frog episode.

They would just have to wait and see, as Jake suggested, and come up with something if expenses started to pile up again. Marv privately thought that more capital needed to be invested by the partners.

In the meantime, winter wore on. There were the indoor auctions to go to and the day-to-day business of running the shop. Almost automatically, Marv found himself checking the calendar to see when Ruth would be working and made it a point to be there. He told himself that he enjoyed her company, so why not? He didn't go beyond that thought, mostly because he wasn't sure how to deal with what he might find, what he knew would be waiting for him in the deep part of his mind. Loneliness, longing. Best not to probe, best to stay on the surface and try to keep his thoughts uncomplicated.

Once again the shop took on the role of gathering place, social club and general hang-out for dealers, both Cider Run's and those from out-of-town, for customers and the occasional friend or spouse. It was cold out, it was warm and sociable within, there was music and conversation. But suddenly one day, there was no coffee.

The coffeemaker had blown itself up as Clair had been going about making another pot. It gave a loud *POP!* then started sparking and smoking. Clair gave a little shriek which was heard by Marv, who was in the office. He came in to find her standing against the wall, trying to put as much distance as possible between herself and the offending appliance.

"I'm sorry, Dr. Yeager, I must have done something wrong!" cried a distraught Clair.

"Clair, don't worry. I've been hearing it mutter and complain about its unhappy lot for weeks and I've grown weary of its threats. I say good riddance and let us get ourselves another. You didn't get splattered with boiling water, I hope not?"

"No, I'm fine. I was just afraid it wasn't through popping yet."

"Well, exploding appliances can be a nuisance." He unplugged the machine. "What do you say we make our explanations to the waiting coffee drinkers and send someone out for a new, improved design?"

It was a bitterly cold day and customers were well outnumbered by dealers. Snows had been heavy over the last week, and although the sun was shining now, it shone on huge mounds of snow that the plow had piled up in the parking lot. But the roads were clear and several dealers had come in with things to put in their areas and to check their sales, and they had stayed for the chance to talk, get caught up, and have a cup of coffee.

Marv announced the recent tragedy. "So, who wants to volunteer to make a mercy run and pick us up a new coffeemaker?"

"What kind do we get, Marv?" asked Richard. "Given the notice about finances that's been posted in the kitchen, the cheapest we can find?"

"You don't want to get cheap. They'll blow up on you," was Elaine's opinion, "like this one did."

"What we need is an espresso maker," Emmy proposed. "When we were in Italy last year..."

"Or a brass samovar. The kind with the Russian imperial eagle on the top. People would come in just to look at it," interrupted Elaine.

"They only make hot water," Emmy stated, "for tea. With an espresso machine you can make cappuccino and latte and..."

"Would we have to use those little cups?" Marv asked. "Ruth, what do you say? Espresso machine? Samovar?"

"Franchise," Ruth replied neatly. "That would kill two birds with one stone. We could have coffee and make money at the same time."

"What a brilliant idea!" Marv exclaimed. "Why didn't I think of it?"

"If we're broke," Richard suggested, "maybe we all ought to chip in to get a new coffeemaker."

The door opened and Jake came in, wearing a pair of dark glasses against the glare of bright sun on snow. Seeing a ready-made audience hanging around the front counter, he stopped and said, "You know how you can tell when it's really cold out?" paused for effect, then went on, "The lawyers have their hands in their own pockets."

There were a few groans.

"And we know which lawyer Jake is talking about," Elaine commented.

"Jake," Marv persevered, "we need a new coffeemaker and we need it now. A decent one will cost at least a hundred dollars. What do you think? Do we break the piggy bank and incur Helen's ire? There's been a suggestion that we pass the hat."

Jake took off his dark glasses. "What happened to the old one?"

"Blew up," said a somber Clair.

"Blew up in front of her. Gave her a nasty turn," Marv elaborated.

Jake looked at Clair. "Come on, then, let's go out and buy a new one. We can put an empty jar in the kitchen for donations."

Clair got her coat and bag and went out with Jake to his still warm truck. It was the first time she had been alone with him and she felt a definite thrill about it. Here was this older man, something of an idol to her, taking her out. Well, not really taking her out, but she was going somewhere with him. She glanced at his profile, pulled out her own pair of dark glasses and put them on.

What Marv and Ruth had felt when they had been in Marv's truck, Clair felt now. It was the sense of closeness, of being shut in together. Anything could happen between them. She was alone with Jake and, as far as she was concerned, they were in their own world. It was intimate, it was marvelously exciting.

Jake said, "Sorry we have to rush this, Clair, but I need to get back to the shop. However, my truck was warmed up and I didn't want you to have to get in Marv's cold, cruel vehicle."

Clair came back down to reality. "I need to get back too," she said. "I'm supposed to be working today. But I appreciate your consideration. It's awfully cold."

"And it sometimes gets colder. I had to make a fire in the fireplace for Laurel one time at the shop, about a year ago, because she got so cold. Hey, here's the store. Let's see what they have."

Meanwhile, at Cider Run, Elaine and Ruth were discussing ways to get the brown stains of age out of white ironstone. "You can't use bleach," Elaine pointed out.

"I know," Ruth agreed. "When I first started collecting ironstone, I tried soaking plates in bleach and it caused a residue that I could never get rid of."

"What you need to do," Emmy said, joining in the conversation, "is have a friend in the chemistry department get you that super high-test strength hydrogen peroxide. You soak it and then bake it in the oven. The impurities get exuded out."

"I have a book on white ironstone that describes the process," said Ruth, "but where do we get the hydrogen peroxide?"

The three were silent for a moment.

"Doesn't Owen teach high school science?" Elaine asked.

Customers came in and were helped. One burly looking man was trying to find a cast iron fry pan. "You know, the kind they used for bacon and eggs for breakfast, then just wiped it out and used it again to cook the dinner."

Ruth said, "I think we have several. Do you want Griswold?" She had learned about the Erie, Pennsylvania mark.

"That's it."

"What size? Seven? Nine? Or one of the smaller ones?"

"Does that refer to inches?"

"Not for Griswold. A number seven measures nine inches in diameter."

Elaine was giving Richard's shoes an appraising look and said, "Richard, are those clogs you're wearing?"

"You like 'em, Elaine? My friend Trevor works in a hospital. He has to stand for hours on those concrete floors. Everyone swears by them, and I can see why."

"Emmy always wears clogs," Elaine went on. She raised her voice slightly, "I thought it was just another Euro-affectation, like the black clothes." Emmy had not been out of earshot. Today she was wearing a black turtleneck sweater, a longish black corduroy skirt with heavy black knee socks and her trademark clogs. "Oh, no, Elaine, clogs are the only thing you can wear when you have to be on your feet all day, particularly on hard surfaces like the stone floors in here. Ruth wears clogs, Clair wears them. Staffers wear them in the museums."

"If I could trot off to Europe all the time, I might pick up a pair or two," Elaine considered.

"You don't need to go to Denmark. I go online to get mine from a place in New York. I'll give you the website."

Jake and Clair returned, bearing the box with the new coffeemaker. Marv came to the front to take possession.

"Not so fast, Marv," commanded Jake, holding the box out of Marv's reach. "We've braved the rigors of winter and we're going to have the luxury of making the inaugural pot."

"Its maiden voyage, eh?" Marv responded. "Then you'll need a maiden." He looked at Ruth and was rewarded by the laughter in her eyes.

"I don't see any maidens around here," Jake observed. "I guess you'll have to stand in, Clair, seeing as how you're closer in age, if not in fact, to the maidenly state."

"No fair, Jake!" Elaine exclaimed indignantly at the sexism.

Clair said, somewhat archly she thought later, "How do you know I'm not?"

"It's that look of lost innocence," Jake sighed. "Here today, gone tomorrow. I've always found it irresistibly appealing."

"Clair, I wouldn't go back into the kitchen with him if I were you," warned Elaine.

"Now, Elaine," Jake protested, "Clair will be perfectly safe. Come and check up on us if you like. Don't think you'll be entitled to any coffee, though."

When the coffee had been made and the pot brought out, Ruth poured herself a cup and offered one to Marv, still at the front counter. For the moment, everyone had scattered. Marv smiled as Ruth approached, wondering, what can I say? He ventured, "Thanks, Ruth. Ah, this is better coffee than that swill the last machine made."

Ruth, in turn, wondered, what can I say? I'd like a real conversation with him. But in keeping with the tenor of the mood, she replied lightly, "Maybe it's the 'almost maidenly' touch."

Marv felt a little guilty. He was the one who made the crack about a maiden. What he wanted was to find out about

Ruth's marriage. What had her marriage been like? Why did they divorce? How long had they been married? How in the world could he ever ask questions like that? He couldn't. Instead he said, "Our Clair seems to be quite taken by Jake. I think he's turned her head."

Ruth replied, "It's the atmosphere around here," and instantly regretted what she'd said. She didn't want to get into a habit of flirting with Marv, even though that kind of good-humored banter with him seemed so natural.

But she knew she'd hit home, because Marv shot her a look and said, "And how!"

It was Hal who, mercifully for the awkward silence that followed the last remark, walked in the door next. He, too, had on a pair of dark glasses, which he was taking off as he came in.

"Our latest celebrity has arrived," Marv observed, "straight from the Coast, still trailing glints of Hollywood glamour."

"I could do with some Los Angeles right now. My fingers are numb," Hal replied. "It's nice and warm in here, though. Is that a new coffee pot?"

"Yes, it is. The old outfit was a casualty this morning. We tried to bury it but the ground was frozen."

"Would you like a cup, Hal?" Ruth asked.

"I'll go back and get my mug. It's in the kitchen."

"Knock first," said Marv, for Ruth's benefit.

What Clair and Jake had been talking about in the kitchen was, as expected, not at all what Marv had hinted at. Jake was telling Clair about some of the artwork he had acquired. He had begun collecting it during and after the trip to Amsterdam, where he'd spent time in the antiques district.

"There was a warehouse full of antique art: paintings, sculpture, statues, frescoes, artifacts—from the sacred to the profane. Have you been there, Clair? It blew me away."

"Not to Amsterdam. But to the *Musee Conde* outside of Paris at Chantilly. They took us into the archives where they do research, one of the storage areas in the basement of the chateau. It was a gigantic vault of a room and from floor to ceiling there was artwork. We were shown drawings and sketches, artists' notes, some going back to the 15th century."

"That's what this place in Amsterdam was like. Floor to ceiling, but the difference was that everything was for sale. Just looking is one thing; having the possibility to buy puts a whole new, exciting light on it. Given the chance to own a part of the 16th or 17th century, well, it's hard to beat that."

"It's funny," Clair went on with her train of thought, "but what I chiefly remember about Chantilly was Mme. *la* curator. *Tres formidable!* She was so very, very, French, so cool, so impeccable in a chic linen dress, looking down her nose at us American students in our shorts and T-shirts. I was very impressionable then." And I guess I still am, thought Clair.

Then she realized, too late, that this wasn't what Jake wanted to hear, because he got up from the kitchen table where they had been sitting and said, "Back to the floor with you, young lady. Time to earn your keep, or else be chucked out into the snow."

Hal had come to meet with Marv and Jake, and the three went into the office. When they emerged, Ruth and Clair were closing up, settling the day's business and turning off lights. It was not yet quite dark and as Marv left the shop, a lovely winter sunset was lighting up the western sky. He came back inside. "Come and see the sunset, Ruth," he invited. "It's just magnificent."

Beyond the orchard, the sky presented a backdrop of glowing red, orange and gold against the black silhouetted branches of the trees. It was a moment that could not be held. The light and colors faded as Marv and Ruth stood looking, Ruth without a coat, her arms wrapped around herself to keep warm. Marv realized she was shivering and because he couldn't do what he wanted to do, put his arms around her, he said, "Ruth, sorry, you must be freezing! I've lured you out here for an esthetic experience and now you'll turn into a block of ice, and it's all my fault."

"The sky is beautiful, Marv. It's worth it, not to miss a sunset like this. How lucky we are to be in this place, up here with the hills and the sweep of sky."

"I wonder if Jacob Smith appreciated it too. Hey, Jacob, are you listening? You done good! Now, Ruth, please, let's go back inside, before you turn blue."

Clair, still musing about her conversation with Jake, was disappointed in herself because she had rambled on about her experiences and obviously turned him off. Well, there's got to be give and take, she thought. But I probably did sound pretty childish to someone as worldly as Jake.

She left the shop right after Marv, and they were followed by Hal. Ruth found some mugs that needed washing and went back to the kitchen to rinse them before leaving. She forgot that Jake was still there. He came out of the office as she set to work.

"Ruth, such a considerate person," Jake commented. "One wonders, how considerate you are to Marv?"

Ruth bristled. She shut off the water, turned from the sink and gave him a stony look. "Jake, what are you trying to say?"

"Only that you could be skating on thin ice, cutting it close, sailing too near the wind, playing with fire. How many trite expressions would you like to hear?"

"I take it you think there is something going on between Marv and me. Well, there isn't." She immediately became the school principal again, facing down an errant fifth-grader, but the effect was not the least discouraging to Jake.

"Ruth, Ruth!" he protested. "Notes in the mailbox, signed with affection, rendezvous being anticipated in the garden, sunset-gazing in the twilight?" Ruth opened her mouth to speak but Jake went on, "Not that I blame Marv. Helen has him on such a tight leash that his need to break free must be extreme. I don't know how anyone could live that way. And you are the perfect safety valve: single, attractive and here."

"He and Helen are devoted to each other. How can you say that?" In truth, she wanted to learn more.

"There's no affection between them. It isn't a secret, as anyone who has known them can tell you. She always tries to put a damper on him, keep the reins drawn in. He has a free spirit; surely you've seen that by now."

Surely, yes, she had. She couldn't counter Jake's arguments, but she was furious with him. How dare he accuse her and Marv? What were his motives in doing this, anyway? "I think it was unconscionable of you to read our correspondence," she managed.

Jake shrugged. "The mailboxes are hardly private. Things practically fall out of those little cubbyholes."

"Are you warning me off? Is that your motive? Altruism? Concern for me or Marv, or is it Helen?" Out of frustration, she ended with, "Your own character..."

Jake interrupted her. "My character is hardly spotless, but I think you two might try to be a little more discreet in the future. It could have repercussions on the business. That's all."

"Self-interest? Fine. But don't assume there is anything."

Jake, with complete equanimity, had the last word. "Yet," he said, as he pushed the kitchen door open and walked out.

Ruth stood shaking with anger, but some of the anger she felt was directed at herself, not Jake. He had, damn it, been on target. She could not even justify feelings of righteous indignation. She was guilty, in her own mind, of everything he had intimated. His disclosures about Helen had only made her aware of more empathy toward Marv. Had Jake intended that? He had been successful, if that were the case. She had a feeling that he would love to fan the flames and then stand back and watch her and Marv...do what? Make fools of themselves?

Ruth shook her head to clear it, got her things together and went out the kitchen door. She gave it a swat and as it closed behind her, the sign in Helen's neat printing, NO ADMITTANCE CIDER RUN PERSONNEL ONLY, swung back and forth with a clatter.

Jake was still in his area and as Ruth left he called after her, "Don't do anything I wouldn't do, Ruth!"

Chapter 21

It rankled. Ruth drove home in a state of agitation, pulled into her driveway, hit the garage door opener with a fierceness it did not deserve, and almost drove through the back wall of the garage.

She wandered distractedly around the house until she realized she needed to settle down. But thoughts continued to race in her head. Jake had pointed out the truth to her. That's what rankled. That and the way he had done it, but maybe someone needed to point it out. She and Marv did have feelings for each other, irrespective of their actions, which were innocent enough. But those feelings seemed to be known to Jake. She had been confronted with them and in someone else's words. Not an easy thing to swallow. What worried her was that Jake might also confront Marv. If he did, how would Marv take it? Then Ruth thought in a panic: Jake wouldn't say something to Helen, would he?

She wasn't due to work again for two weeks. She didn't have to go in, sales were slow. Ruth decided to stay away from the shop for a while. She had things to do: she'd promised to go somewhere with her sister-in-law, she had several appointments with sellers lined up, she wanted to go to at least one auction out of town, and there was a room in her house to paint. Keep busy, she told herself. Don't let Jake get to you.

Richard had once been thinking along similar lines, about not letting Jake get to him. With Trevor now in the picture it was easier for Richard to see things in perspective. He handled Jake's insurance business and participated with him in Cider Run activities, but kept an emotional distance from Jake. Right now, his concern was redoing his area at the shop. Only a handful of the Art Deco things remained—one table, a movie poster or two, some art glass—and he wanted to start anew with another theme. Sally Ann, who had stopped by with a cache of hankies in spring designs, had a solution. She proposed that Richard move what was left into her area, as it would fit in well with her other Thirties things. They moved the Art Deco in and rearranged Sally Ann's display and then went back to Richard's space.

Sally Ann looked sadly at the emptiness. "It's as if you had died, Richard, and there's nothing left of you."

Richard, however, was upbeat. "I look at it as an opportunity. I can go in any direction. I can soar." He flapped his arms like wings.

"But you don't have anything to sell!"

"Sally Ann, the first rule of antiques dealers and my personal motto—in fact, I would have it as my epitaph—is: Selling is all well and good, but buying is a lot more fun," and he went off in search of the *Auction News*.

Marv came into the shop at the point when Richard, behind the front counter, nose in the newspaper, exclaimed, "Ah, ha! I've found it!"

Somewhat distractedly, Marv asked, "Found what, Richard? The key to perpetual happiness? Do share." He was wondering what had happened to Ruth. He hadn't seen her for almost two weeks. Was she sick? Had she gotten a chill the night they stood looking at the sunset? She was due to work in the shop the next day. Perhaps he'd phone her, see how she was.

Richard had already replied and Marv had not heard, so deep was he in his thoughts. Seeing the abstracted look on his face, Richard said, "I repeat, Marv. Bird-in-Hand!"

"Right," Marv answered. "What about it? Worth two in the bush?"

"Bird-in-Hand. Blue Ball. Intercourse."

"Excuse me?" The last-mentioned got Marv's attention.

"Lancaster County. If you look for me this weekend, that's where I'll be. I'm pulling out all stops. If you liked my Art Deco, you'll love my next venture."

"Richard," said Marv, "when you throw yourself into something, we all love it. I wish you the best. Go for it."

Elaine had overheard some of this conversation. "You'll pay through the nose for anything down there, Richard."

"Wait and see, Elaine. What I come back with will be so smashing, so over-the-top, that even you, smoke-befuddled as you are..."

"Is there a shop policy, Marv, about insults? Or do we have to put up with Richard as he is?"

"Marv, tell Elaine there are laws protecting me, whereas you, Elaine, a pawn in the clutches of Big Tobacco, are a persona non grata everywhere you go."

"Stop!" cried Marv. "Go duke it out in the parking lot!"

"And disturb your carefully tended gravel? Wouldn't dream of it, Marv. Would you, Elaine?"

"I hate to see a grown man cry."

It was two weeks since Ruth's self-imposed exile. She had accomplished a lot, including pricing and tagging of items to sell. She had also called Owen and he thought he might be able to help her, mum's the word, on the hydrogen peroxide.

"It's a hazardous waste," he'd told her, "but life is full of hazards." She liked Owen's attitude. He did say another thing that interested her. "Have you seen Keith lately?" he had begun.

Ruth told him that she hadn't been in the shop for two weeks. Why?

"He's trying to buy some property with Jake and hasn't gotten anywhere. I think he's getting antsy; in fact, he's probably at the end of his rope with Jake by now. I just wondered if you'd heard anything."

Ruth said, no, but she wasn't surprised, because in her opinion Jake could be obtuse. She didn't elaborate, and Owen didn't ask, but he seemed to understand. He said, "Doesn't have all his cards on the table. That's what Keith thinks."

Late in the afternoon, Marv decided to call Ruth at home. He had a good reason. He wanted to make sure she was coming in to work the next day. If not, someone else would have to cover for her. He was concerned about her health. He wanted to talk to her; he needed to talk to her.

"Ruth, you haven't been in for ages. Have you forgotten us? We're located on Cider Run Road, out Martensdale Pike, left at the light."

"Marv, I'm sorry. I've been catching up on things. Has a piece of furniture been sold from my area? I assumed I'd be called if I needed to come in." Had Jake talked to him? She didn't like being evasive with Marv, but for the time being, until she got an idea of whether Jake had said something, she held back.

"I was worried. I thought you'd gotten pneumonia, gazing at the sky to humor me." Is she really all right? Her voice sounds strained. Is she angry with me for something?

"I'm fine. I'll be in tomorrow." I'm going to have to warn him about Jake. Suppose Jake is there? "Will you be at the shop? There's something I want to talk to you about," she added.

His heart fell. "Do I need to be sitting down?" She's leaving. She's moving back to Maine.

"Wouldn't hurt. It has to do with Jake." Not entirely accurate, thought Ruth, but there it is.

Marv brightened immediately. "Tell me. I can take it. He's won the lottery. He's been elected Pope. Am I getting warm?"

Ruth laughed. "We'll talk tomorrow."

Marv hung up, feeling immeasurably better. He whistled to the music being played. Richard, who was making a sign to put in his area which said WATCH THIS SPACE FOR COMING ATTRACTIONS, raised his eyebrows.

Ruth hung up, feeling much happier. Why does he care about me, she asked herself. Am I just a safety valve, as Jake would have it? She hoped she and Marv would have a chance to talk, but she felt reticent about telling him all Jake had said.

Helen's car was parked in the lot when Ruth arrived the next day. Had she been scheduled with Helen? She didn't think so. It had been Sally Ann, she thought. But in a two week space, people's schedules can get changed due to unforeseen events. Then she remembered that this was the day of the week the cleaning service came, so perhaps Helen had come in early for that. Ruth forcefully thrust out of her mind the thought that Helen had heard something from Jake.

March had arrived during the intervening two weeks and everything looked a little brighter. There was still snow on the hills, but the sun stood at a higher angle and there were birds calling among the bare branches of the orchard trees. Flea market in the orchard indeed, Ruth thought as she walked across the parking lot.

Helen greeted her warmly and Ruth felt relieved, but not less guilty, as she returned Helen's greeting. Jake had said there was no affection between Marv and Helen, and Ruth thought about it again on seeing Helen. Was it true? How could anyone not feel affection for Marv?

Helen said, "Sally Ann was supposed to be in today, but she's gone off to Lancaster County with Richard. He's got some project up his sleeve and took Sally Ann along for, I don't know, appearances maybe. They promised great things. You should see his area. It's completely empty! Want some coffee, Ruth?"

There were plenty of customers this morning, and Ruth was grateful for a little respite from worrying about what Jake might or might not do. And wondering what she should say to Marv when the time came, if it came. After a while, however, it became clear that she and Helen by themselves were not enough to handle all the business. Helen said, "Marv is supposed to be coming in. Where is he? I can't reach him on his phone or at home."

Was this part of the tight leash she kept him on, Ruth thought uncharitably. She said brightly, "We're just too popular here."

As if in answer to a prayer, Grace and Frank came to the door, each bearing one end of a pine commode. "Frank, be careful! You're going to knock your end into the door," Grace was saying. She had propped the door open with her foot, and it was starting to close on them. Ruth hurried to the door and held it open.

"Frank bid way too high for this. Again," Grace confessed to Ruth as she passed by with her end.

"Grace told me she wanted it," protested Frank, as he went by with his end.

"Grace!" cried Helen eagerly, coming up to them as they placed the commode in Grace's area. "Can you stay for a while? Marv is supposed to be here, but until he comes, we're shorthanded."

Frank answered, "That suits me fine. I'll wander around and look officious."

"That's official, Frank!" Grace called after him, as he walked off. "Ruth, don't ever get married. It's the end of a perfectly good relationship."

"It's a different kind of relationship, anyway," Helen commented drily. "More like a constant struggle against overwhelming odds."

I didn't like hearing that, Ruth thought. But she smiled and went to see if any of the customers needed help, or rescuing from Frank.

Marv got to the shop a little before 2:00. Ruth could see him standing in the parking lot, motioning to a truck slowly backing up as close as it could get to the door. He held up his hand to stop the backward movement, then went to consult with the driver. Ruth was intrigued. What was Marv up to now? If Helen saw, she would come bustling out, frowning. Oh, heavens, thought Ruth, amused. Here I am, wanting to protect Marv from his own wife!

Two men got out of the truck and slowly slid the back door up. A ramp was put down, a furniture dolly unloaded, and Marv went to prop the shop door open. He saw Ruth standing there, watching the activity and smiling at what was going on.

"You won't believe this, Ruth, but I just bought an entire room."

"A whole room? A roomful of furniture?" She knew that Helen would say: "And where do think you'll put it? Our area is already full," but Ruth said, "What's it like?"

"Here comes the first piece now. OK, back and to the left. Ruth, could you show him where to go?"

A partially wrapped oak china cabinet came out first and was wheeled into the shop. Ruth saw that Helen was busy with some customers, so wouldn't notice where the piece was headed. "You'll have to shift a few things, I'm afraid, to make room," Ruth said to the mover. Perhaps, she thought contritely, the comment she had been so sure Helen would have made was probably not that far off the mark.

When the china cabinet was unwrapped, Ruth saw that it was quite handsome and looked forward to the rest. One after another the pieces came in: a sideboard, a dining table with four leaves for extension, six matching chairs and, rolled up, a large Persian rug in deep reds and blues.

But that wasn't all. When Marv said he'd bought a room, he had bought everything in it. A crystal chandelier and two tall matching table lamps for the sideboard came in next. Four boxes of china were wheeled in, and another four boxes that might contain almost anything. Ruth helped move things to try to make some room for them, until Marv came and reminded her about her shoulder.

"You go and reinjure your shoulder on my watch and I'll never forgive myself," he said sternly.

"Where did all these things come from? How...?" Ruth started to ask.

"Marv!" Helen was freed up at last. "What have you done?"

Ruth beat a hasty retreat.

There was no denying it. The Yeagers' area looked like a furniture warehouse, with pieces sitting at strange angles any old way. But what an abundance of gleaming oak, what a find for anyone wanting to furnish with antiques! Not one odd piece, but the whole matched suite. It was probably ordered complete, Ruth judged, in about 1900, from Sears, Roebuck. Price at the time for all pieces, under $300. She had reproductions of old Sears catalogs that showed these, or strikingly similar, suites. She told herself to remember to go hunt up the catalogs and bring them in. In the meantime, Helen was having her say and Ruth stayed out of the way.

When the smoke cleared and the movers had gone and customers had been helped, Ruth found Marv at the front counter. Helen had given up and gone to make coffee.

Marv started right in. "I would have gotten another room, one of the bedrooms, but someone got there first. It was the most exceptional sale, Ruth. The estate wanted the house cleared and told the auctioneer to go ahead and sell it by the room. The house had been sold and the new owner could not wait. I got there late and had to take what was left. It was one hell of a bargain. I don't even know what's in the boxes."

"The suite is quite magnificent. I think it must have been from Sears, don't you? I'll look it up. I have some old catalogs."

"Yes, do, please, I'd like to see them. I had a peek at the bedroom furniture and it was much the same. Damn, I wish I'd been able to get that too."

"Helen would have loved that." Oh, dear, not a nice remark that, Ruth thought a little guiltily.

"She's pretty upset, all right, but at least I didn't take it home. I had them bring it right here."

"Where was this place? In town?"

"No, way up north, almost out of the county. Not quite the end of the world, but you can see it from there."

"How do you find out about these things, Marv?"

Marv tapped the side of his nose and gave Ruth a secretive look. "It's the old student network," he said. "A former student knows I'm interested in antiques and lets me know what's happening. The hills are full of 'em. My ex-students, that is."

Free spirit. Jake was right, she had to admit it.

"But, Ruth," Marv went on, "you wanted to talk to me about something. Jake, was it?" Marv looked around. There were still customers in the shop. "Later, perhaps?"

Ruth had wrestled a long time with what she should say to Marv about the encounter with Jake. Her thinking had gone back and forth, if she should tell him at all, how much she should tell him. If he were outraged, as she had been, would it be because Jake had so overstepped himself, but come close to the truth, or would it be because there was nothing to be concerned about, a tempest in a teapot, and Jake had the audacity to blow it out of proportion? Since she had obviously taken Jake's words seriously, she hoped Marv would as well. But perhaps he wouldn't be as upset as she had been. Perhaps...perhaps she should stop this and play it by ear.

Late in the day, Helen asked if Ruth would mind if she left early. "I need to get groceries. When Sally Ann called last night, I was happy to come in, but I forgot that we're having a dinner party this weekend. So if you don't mind, Ruth. Marv can close things out with you, and I'll be off."

They were finally alone. The door had been locked, the business settled. Ruth was turning off lights, still not sure of what to say to him. Her actions had slowed down. She was in no hurry to hasten their discussion for fear it might backfire on her. As she was reaching to turn off a lamp in Sally Ann's area, Ruth noticed that Sally Ann's basket of hankies was in disarray. A customer must have been going through it and left things spilled about. Ruth started to refold the handkerchiefs when one caught her eye, a hankie from the 1950s. It was entitled "How to Speak French" and was printed with colorful illustrations and words in French and English, phrases that a young lady might need to have at her command when she made the trip to Paris. Ruth sat herself down in Sally Ann's little white rocking chair. This was too good. The crossing, *la traverse.* By ship, of course. A dress, *une robe.* Dressmaker, *couturier.* Fitting, *essayage.* Did people still do that? Go to Paris to have dresses made? Then there was a most poignant one: "This gentleman sent you flowers," *Ce monsieur vous a envoye des fluers.* Had anyone sent her flowers when she was in Paris? Afraid not. What a long time ago that had been. Ruth realized with a little flutter of excitement that Marv was looking over her shoulder.

She turned her head to look at him. "I'm wallowing in the past, Marv," she said, holding up the hankie for him to see. "Or maybe I'm just feeling nostalgic for a time that's been lost. I missed this era, when I first went to France."

Marv read over her shoulder: "'I want to change some money,' *Je veux changer mon argent.*"

Ruth said, "I remember having to do that, change pounds to francs, when we came over on the ferry from Dover to Calais."

"Someday, will you tell me about your trip?" And yourself? All about yourself, he wanted to add. He put out his hand,

Ruth put her hand in his, and he helped her up off the low rocking chair. He released her hand slowly.

Ruth was very aware of the touch of his hand. Such a small thing, so significant. "If you like, though there's not much to tell," she said, reverting unconsciously to her ingrained reticence.

He wanted to hold her hand again, but said, "Now what was it about Jake? Did you say I needed to be sitting down? Come on, let's go into his area. Jake won't mind, seeing as how we'll be talking about him."

They went over to where the settee and Morris chair formed their cozy corner by the fireplace. The hearth had been cleaned after the winter and instead of a fire screen, an Arts and Crafts style hammered copper pot stood in the opening, filled with neatly cut firewood. There was a price tag on the handle.

Ruth took the settee, Marv the Morris chair. He said, "Let's have it."

"This isn't going to be easy, Marv," Ruth began, plunging in far more boldly than she thought she would. "Jake cornered me in the kitchen when I worked last and essentially accused you and me of being indiscreet."

Marv was silent for a second or two. "Is that why you've stayed away, Ruth?" he asked.

"Stayed away?" she repeated.

"Stayed away from the shop. From me."

"No. I mean, yes. Because I wasn't sure what to do about it, what there was to do," she faltered.

"Why do anything? But it upset you, didn't it?"

"Tremendously, because..." Ruth hesitated slightly.

Marv finished, "Because he's hit near the mark."

Ruth looked at Marv, a grateful look.

He went on, "Jake isn't stupid. He might act that way sometimes with all the blarney, but he's very astute, very observant. He's apparently taken a few clues and come up with a theory. He tested it out on you and it proved correct."

"That we've been indiscreet? He actually implied a lot more than that."

"He's waiting to see what we'll do. Damn him."

"I didn't want to tell you, Marv, but I thought you ought to know."

"I'm glad you did. I'll kill him."

"Better not. He may be playing with us, and I guess I rose to the bait. I didn't laugh it off. I couldn't," she confessed.

"Ruth, what I love about you," Marv started to say, and then stopped.

Ruth continued, "The thing I was really concerned about was that he'd say something to Helen. It's the way he hints and insinuates."

"Are you sure I can't just kill him?"

"Not a good idea. What I can't figure out is his motive. Why should he care? He said something about it having repercussions on the business."

"I suppose it could be an aspect of concern for him. Did he mention how he stumbled upon this?"

"He read the inscription in the book I gave you, and he read your thank you note to me." She didn't mention the safety valve part or the revelations about Marv's marriage that Jake had obviously wanted her to know.

"What gaul!" Marv exclaimed. "I showed the book to Helen, by the way, and she thought it was sweet of you."

"She would. I don't mean that in a sarcastic way, either. Helen has that outlook on life."

Marv said very quietly, "Not invariably."

260

Ruth heard what he'd said and got up. She was much too fond of this man. "Marv, thanks." She smiled at him. "Talking with you was what I needed. I don't know what I'll say to Jake when I see him next, but I'll deal with that when it comes up."

Marv rose. Couldn't he just take her in his arms? No. He said, "Please, Ruth, come to me if anything like this happens again, will you promise?"

"I will," she promised.

After Ruth left, Marv went back into Sally Ann's area. He found the French hankie and took off the price tag. He slipped the tag and the $5.00 it cost into an envelope, wrote "Sally Ann" on it, and put it in her mailbox. He'd give the hankie to Ruth when he got a chance. And to hell with Jake.

Chapter 22

Some people always seem to land on their feet. Lucky stars shine down on them, four-leaf-clovers spring up where they walk. A car pulls out of a parking place in front of their destination, with time on the meter. They may be unaware of this providential blessing, but it contributes to a general *joie de vivre*, which is either intoxicating to be around or annoying, depending on one's point of view.

Such an individual was Marv. Once again, fate intervened on his behalf. After a weekend spent with Hal trying to make space for the dining room suite and still having it block his area, and partially block circulation in the shop, Marv pondered his next move. Richard's empty area beckoned, but he knew Richard would not let his space lie fallow for long. There wasn't room in any of the other dealers' areas and even if there were, he didn't want to separate the individual pieces of the suite. By midweek he was beginning to think that Helen may have been right in her disgust about his purchasing excesses. And then a middle-aged couple came in who had recently bought a large Victorian house in the county seat, which they were turning into a Bed and Breakfast and furnishing with period pieces. They saw the oak furniture and bought the whole suite, as well as furniture from other dealers in the shop. They even arranged to have everything transported by a moving service.

"What really gets me," Helen confided to Ruth a few days later, "is that something always bails him out. Marv does these outrageous things and then it's all made right." Helen was obviously no longer intoxicated, if she had ever been.

Ruth, on the other hand, was enchanted by Marv's impetuosity. Ever since last spring at the farmhouse, when she had seen first-hand what he was capable of pulling off, she looked forward to what he would get up to next. Living with someone like that for many years, though, would it grow thin? She could not take that step in her mind and merely murmured something vaguely sympathetic to Helen.

"Some days I'm ready to give up," Helen went on. "He should have better sense than to keep doing things like that," she waved a hand in the general direction of their area, "but Cider Run has just given him an excuse to run amok. Lately he hasn't even been acting his age."

Ruth hardly thought Marv was running amok. Not acting his age? Poor Marv, she thought, to be regarded in such a light. What occurred to Ruth was that Jake had been right in his assessment about Helen's attitude. Score another point for him.

"We've always loved antiques, but now it's almost as if he's going for volume and the bigger the better. A whole roomful of furniture! What next?"

Ruth had come in to leave a few things in her area, but she had also cut some branches from her forsythia and brought them in. She had put them in a pot of water and set it on the front counter, where the tight yellow buds would soon be full blossoms. They brought a springtime touch, but Helen was so preoccupied with her complaining about Marv that she took little notice. Ruth decided to go see what Richard was doing, as he and Sally Ann had returned from their shopping trip and much activity was going on in his area.

"Ruth! Come and see the latest!" Richard greeted her.

From the highly stylized, sophisticated elegance of the Art Deco period, Richard had returned to the rural farm-and-buggy genre of the Pennsylvania Dutch. He and Sally Ann, not content with only attending an auction in the Lancaster County area, had driven the back roads and country lanes, had bought out of farmhouses and barns, junk shops and garage sales.

"There was even a town-wide yard sale going on in one place," Sally Ann said excitedly. "I didn't know where to start. There were things laid out everywhere I looked!"

Richard added, "I was afraid all the antiques had been cleaned out long ago down there, but not so. Tourists want the new stuff, the crafts. We bought old quilts off clothes lines. Sally Ann has that technique perfected."

"And Richard bought horse shoes out of a barn," gushed Sally Ann.

"And a wooden hex sign," he held it up, "which was underneath this box of Boot Jack Plug Tobacco," he held this up too, "which was covered by this horse blanket," he pointed to the horse blanket, "and this horse collar," which he indicated with his foot. "There's a coal-burning buggy heater somewhere around here too."

Richard had come back with a wonderful collection. There were sturdy pieces of farmhouse furniture—a rubbed pine kitchen table, an assortment of plank-bottom and caned-seat chairs, a blanket chest, painted white and decorated with flowers and birds, a rocking chair that was bought right off the front porch, "still rocking," Richard said. "We bought

Amish, Mennonite and English, and everything in between."
He had bought quilts too, which were set off nicely by being
in their element.

"Richard, it is stunning. I am very impressed," Ruth
complimented him. She approved of Richard's tags too. Like
her own, he gave the customer whatever information he had
on the individual piece. Ruth saw that a number of them
said "from a farm in Lancaster County, Pennsylvania."

Richard had also gotten a few pieces of Stiegel glass, the
glassware that was first made in the 18th century in Manheim,
Pennsylvania. There were two tumblers and a bowl with red,
white, blue and yellow flowers and hearts, hand-painted
designs characteristic of Baron von Stiegel's glassworks. Ruth
started to reach for them.

"Are you bonded and insured?" warned Richard. "Those
were not a bargain. Still, they were absolutely necessary to my
well-being. Once I saw them, I knew they needed to be here.
They will be in a locked case before the day is done."

"I should say, Richard. I saw Stiegel glass like this in the
Corning museum last summer. Where did you get them?
Antiques shop?"

"Antiques shop? Far too commonplace. We were over
the hills and far away, searching out the byways and little
known lanes, the back country, the winding ways, the roads
less traveled. Antiques mall, actually."

Sally Ann was placing at least a dozen umbrellas of
differing sizes, styles and eras in an umbrella stand and Ruth
stopped to look at them. "It was at the yard sale," Sally Ann
explained. "They were only a dollar apiece, can you believe
it, Ruth?"

There was great variety. The fabrics were silk and treated
cotton and 1940s nylon, some child-sized. There were solid

colors, plaids, stripes and prints, with handles of celluloid, Bakelite, wood and plastic in various shapes. Sally Ann had made a sign that said *April Showers Bring May Flowers*, and had decorated it with flower stickers.

Ruth admired the display, then remembered, "Sally Ann, there's a hankie in your basket I'd like to get."

"Help yourself," Sally Ann invited and handed Ruth the basket.

Ruth searched among the array of springtime florals, but failed to find the "How to Speak French" hankie. I guess it's been sold, she thought sadly.

Richard took a long time putting the finishing touches on his display, but when he was done, it had the look of a Pennsylvania folk art museum, except arranged in a more casual and inviting manner. He was pleased with the effect and also with his strategy. Taking Sally Ann with him was a big part of what had made the foray so successful. Not only was she a fun companion, but she was also a natural when it came to sweet talk and had convinced several farmers to sell their antiques. Further, they had the appearance of a couple which, in the conservative area they went to, was necessary. Richard didn't mind this bit of subterfuge and Sally Ann had enjoyed participating in the masquerade, wearing a longish denim skirt with flats and a sweater and jacket instead of her usual modish dresses and high heels. "Honey, I felt absolutely in disguise," Sally Ann had said. "If I'd seen anyone I knew, they never would have recognized me, or if they did, they'd wonder if I was well."

The other reason for Richard's good mood was that Trevor was coming into town for the weekend to visit him, be taken to the shop and get a taste of Richard's life. Richard was looking forward to this and hoping it would go well. He was planning dinners in his mind and was about to leave for the day, when Jake came in. Richard heard Helen make a fuss over him at the front counter, the way she always did, then Jake came back and stopped to have a look at Richard's new display.

"Not bad," Jake admitted. "A little touristy, perhaps, but not bad. By the way, about that insurance policy: I want to add a few things."

"Fine. When do you want to get together on it?"

"How about this weekend? I'll be here."

"I've got a friend coming this weekend. I may be bringing him in. How long do you think we'll need to talk?"

Jake gave Richard a scornful look and with a little sneer said, "By friend, I assume you mean one of those 'boys' your type is so fond of?"

Richard drew in his breath sharply, then turned on his heel and walked out. He'd take care of Jake's insurance, but not take his insults.

Ruth had left the shop in an unsettled state of mind too. She had missed running into Jake, at least, but the conversation, the one-sided conversation with Helen, bothered her. Ruth got into her van and started it. It turned over, but the engine still sounded bad. It was running rough; she'd have to take it in to her mechanic. She told herself she wouldn't think about Marv, but Helen's words came back to her. "Some days I'm ready to give up." Helen, she thought, do you realize you are holding the door open for me? This gave her an uncomfortable guilty feeling, and she instantly rebuked herself for being so presumptuous.

When the first of April came, Sally Ann celebrated it by wearing one of her tropical dresses. It was made of rayon and had a hand-painted look with a large print of green palm trees and pink flamingoes on a white background. White snakeskin pumps with open toes completed the look. It was an eye-popper.

The day was active with customers and sales. People came in to look for Easter dinner table settings and interesting additions for a special Easter basket, and also to get the basket itself. Dealers had all sorts of Easter things in their areas and several had put green cellophane grass in handled baskets and in mixing bowls. Owen had brought in a collection of small cast iron toys—a miniature tractor and a Model A truck, among them. Porcelain and earthenware rabbits and ducks had appeared in several of the dealers' areas. Emmy had two glass candy containers in the shape of rabbits. Grace had rabbits in papier-mâché. Cora had a wooden duck on wheels. Bunnies, fuzzy chicks and a dish of jelly beans sat on the front counter.

Toward the end of the day, Elaine was behind the counter, eating jelly beans in lieu of smoking. Marv was on the computer, checking sales. Sally Ann, after a day of receiving compliments on her outfit and being on her feet, lolled at the counter. Richard came in, and on catching sight of Sally Ann, stopped short. "Words can neither express nor do justice to your incomparable ability to knock 'em dead!" he declared.

"Well, honey, I feel dead. It's been a long day," sighed Sally Ann. "But you're a sweetheart to say that."

"Where, where did you find that dress?" Richard persisted.

"Richard," said Elaine, "you'll never fit in it, so don't get any ideas."

"I was thinking that it makes one wish to go back to the Forties," Richard said, "if you want to know what I was thinking."

"Or at least to go to Florida," Marv added, his attention riveted on the computer screen.

"You might. Not everyone would," Richard said.

"Who wouldn't?" Sally Ann wanted to know.

"Ruth, for one. She had the worst time of her life in Florida. A life of abuse and despair, and..."

Marv looked up, suddenly alert and quite serious. "What happened to Ruth in Florida?"

"There you go again, Marv," Richard pouted, "trying to pry information out of me."

Elaine said, "Richard, if you know something, for heaven's sake tell Marv. Last year you dropped the bomb about Ruth being divorced, now you hint at unpleasant goings on. Sally Ann and I will retire to the back of the shop and do our nails."

"Wait!" Sally Ann protested, "I want to hear."

Marv asked again, "What happened in Florida?"

Richard sighed. "Look, Marv, I only know what she told me. Her husband..."

"Was a brute?" Marv interrupted.

"No, not really, but let her take a lot of crap from his relatives. They all had it in for her because she was from the wrong side of the Mason-Dixon Line and stole away their fair-haired boy. Something like that. You'll have to ask Ruth."

Elaine said, "That would be cruel, don't you think, Richard? To reduce her to tears, forcing her to remember what she probably wants to keep buried in the dim, dark past?"

"She was very forthcoming about it when she told me and I saw not one tear. *Au contraire*, she was smiling as she told the tale. However, if you wore that dress around her, Sally Ann, Ruth might, she just might, get homicidal," Richard finished.

Marv couldn't get the picture of Ruth being made unhappy out of his mind. It hurt to think about it. At the end of the day, when everyone had left, he went into Ruth's area. He felt closer to her, even though there wasn't much of her there, only things that had once belonged to other people. He looked at the white ironstone. There was something pure and tough about ironstone. Yes, that was like Ruth. He looked at the pattern glass tumblers and pitchers, sparkling and translucent. He thought about her eyes, her laughing eyes. They were the color of the sea, and sometimes looked blue and sometimes green. How could anyone be unkind to her? He hated Ruth's unknown ex-husband. He had a moment of uneasiness: was he being unkind to her himself, by showing how he felt about her? How did he feel about her? Was it only affection and, he dared hope, affection returned, or was it more than that? He thought perhaps it would help to get another opinion and decided to explore the situation with Jacob Smith.

"Jacob," he ventured, "are you still around?"

"Aye, yup, Marv. I'm here. You want to parley?"

"I would appreciate it. I can't really talk to anyone else about this."

"Well, Marv, I'm available most times."

"Jacob, perhaps you've noticed, or maybe you haven't, but there's this lovely woman, Ruth, and I can't stop thinking about her."

"Yup. She be a mighty pretty little thing all right. Puts me in mind of when I was courting."

"But you, at least, weren't bound and fettered like I am."

"We had our problems too. Everyone was agin us. But we didn't take no account on it and went ahead anyway. Ah, but she were nice. I recall me the first time..."

Marv decided this was not an area he wanted to explore and quickly backtracked. "I'm afraid I'm not so lucky," he said.

"We got into a peck of trouble. I s'pose you heard."

"Yes, it has been told of."

"Writ down, was it? Did they say who done it, started the fire?"

"Not precisely. I guess, Jacob, what I'd like to know is, was it worth it? Would you two have done what you did all over again?"

There was a pause while Marv searched his mind for Jacob's answer. "Oh, aye, Marv. There weren't no stoppin' us."

Marv nodded. That would be how it happened. He felt comfortable with Jacob's answer. "Thank you, Jacob," he said. "Good night."

"Good night, Marv. Be seein' you."

As Marv turned out the lights, he realized that he'd have to think it out, think where he meant to go with this, and how not to hurt anybody.

Sally Ann's new umbrellas had attracted Clair. Some of them were old enough to be compatible with the era of her things, and when Clair asked if she could put them in her display, Sally Ann said, "Go right ahead, honey. You don't even have to ask." One was obviously for someone in mourning, black with a fringe around the edge. Another was much more of a parasol, in a pale color and a silk too flimsy to repel rain. A dollar a piece, Sally Ann said they had cost. Clair thought she'd take more notice of yard sales.

Laurel had come in with the baby earlier in the day and everyone had been admiring him. She was starting to get

271

things into her area again and the baby was good enough to let her work half-days without getting too fussy.

"Here, let me hold him," Sally Ann offered, "and we'll follow you around, so Ben can see what his mother is doing. He's so big, now, Laurel!"

"The miracle baby," Laurel laughed. "That's what Joe said. It was miraculous when I finally got pregnant after so long, and with his having to be at the hospital so much. But, you know, I'm not sure I was old enough to be a good parent before now."

Sally Ann said, "Honey, I was only nineteen when I had Rosie. I knew I wasn't old enough, but Rosie didn't know it, so it didn't matter. She thinks I was the ideal mother. Babies always do."

Laurel was just leaving when Jake came in the shop. He was amiability itself, greeted her cheerily and gave the baby an indulgent smile and a pat on the cheek.

Laurel was pleased. Jake had been very courteous to her since the difficulty she'd had with him, the afternoon in the kitchen when she was pregnant. It seemed he had forgotten the things he'd said to her. She was still embarrassed over her own behavior and very embarrassed about the feelings she'd had for him. But it had been something she had simply not been able to control, those feelings, and she only hoped he hadn't guessed the extent of them. She automatically gave Ben a kiss on the cheek and, at that, Ben turned and put his arms out to Jake.

"You don't want me to take him, Laurel," said Jake, while the squirming Ben gave every indication of wanting another adult's attention. "I may not be able to give him back."

"That's the way I felt when I held him," Sally Ann interjected, unconsciously rescuing Laurel from having to respond to Jake.

"Ben and I must say goodbye, but he'll be happy to wear out his welcome again soon," Laurel said and the two left.

There was a quiet pause in the wake of Laurel's leaving. Then Clair said, "What a beautiful baby! Those blue eyes and that blond hair."

"Yes," added Jake, "and isn't it odd, because both Laurel and Joe have such dark hair." Then he went on, "Clair, if you have a few minutes, I'd like to talk to you about some artwork," and without waiting for her answer, he went back to his area.

Since the first time Marv had asked her opinion of Jake's artifacts, Clair had been studying the things in Jake's area. The Arts and Crafts furniture and other items she recognized as being exceptional. She had some background in that period of craftsmanship, and had seen exhibits at museums in New York. She had reference books on Stickley, Roycroft and other American makers of furniture and associated art objects in metals and pottery. She was excited that Jake wanted her knowledge and eagerly followed him.

But it was the European art he wanted to talk about. "Clair," Jake began, "how much do you know about Renaissance and Baroque artists' work? Could you tell a real one from a fake?"

Clair wondered if she could. "I don't know. I might be able to, if it's a recent copy. But I don't see any artwork of that period in your area," she said, looking around.

"It's not here. Some of it is at my house, some hasn't been delivered yet. I was thinking that I could bring it in and you could have a look. It's sort of tricky and I don't want something that isn't genuine. Do you think you could, Clair?" he asked, and to Clair it almost sounded plaintive.

Clair felt honored. "Of course," she said, "I'd be more than happy to. I could lead you astray, though. I might not be able to tell if it isn't authentic."

Jake smiled and a new and different look came into his eyes. He said in a lowered voice, "You could lead me astray anytime, Clair. I would be delighted to have you lead me astray." He gave her a long look, and then went on back and through the door to the kitchen.

Clair stayed where he left her, transfixed, rooted to the spot. Jake had almost said, almost said, what? That she was interesting to him, not just a kid. Did he mean it? Was it possible? This place, this Cider Run, grew more exciting every day.

Chapter 23

On the next Saturday that Keith and Owen had signed up to work together at the shop, Owen got there after Keith and Hal had already arrived. "Sorry I'm late," Owen apologized as he came in, struggling to get himself and several large objects through the doorway.

Keith looked up from his job of counting out the change preparatory to the day's business, started to snicker, and it soon grew into a roar of laughter. Owen was pushing two white wicker doll baby carriages, one of which had a pink-bonneted baby doll in it. Although Keith had willingly participated in Kristine's play when she was young, something about seeing the athletic, dark-browed Owen concentrating on wheeling baby buggies was too much to let go. "Lady," he managed between guffaws, "you've got to be one of the ugliest moms I've ever laid eyes on!"

"Just shut up, Keith, will you?" countered Owen. "They're Lynn's idea. She says I mostly have things that boys like and I ought to have some things for girls."

Keith couldn't help himself. "Will you be requiring a private place to nurse your child, Ma'am?"

Hal came to the front of the shop to see what was going on and started laughing so hard he had to hold his sides. "Knock it off," scowled Owen. "These are antiques. They're for sale."

Hal looked at Keith. "He wants us to believe that? Look how smartly he's pushing those carriages. Anyone can tell it comes from a childhood of playing with dollies."

"And we thought last summer he was interested in froggies. Well, now we know."

"Go to hell," said Owen, heading off to his area.

Keith called after him, "Can we play with your trains while you're playing with your dolls?"

In the well-worn tradition of running gags, when there were no customers within earshot, Owen was subjected to more jokes at his expense. Marv came in and then it was three against one.

"Owen," Marv ventured with a concerned look, "Keith and Hal think you've been working too hard and need a little break. I told them I was sure this cross-sex disorder was probably only a temporary phase and..."

Owen made an obscene gesture in Marv's direction.

"It almost makes you sorry for him, doesn't it?" Hal commented. "He looks so normal otherwise. You never would have thought."

"So help me, I am going to get even with you guys," muttered Owen between clenched teeth.

Since it was Saturday, the shop was busy, fortunately for Owen, and the remarks finally petered out. When there was a lull in business, Hal and Marv left to deliver several pieces of furniture. Keith had finally stopped joshing Owen and took the opportunity to talk to him about the real estate deal. "I've been meaning to tell you: I have another realtor working on the property now. I've given up on Jake."

Owen nodded. "Well, I guess you gave him plenty of time. It is still for sale, I take it?"

"It seems to be. I took June and the children out there the other day and they loved the place."

"I'd like to go see it again. I'm still interested in what you had in mind, if you want a partner."

"I do, and I've got an idea. When it gets warm this spring, let's all go out and have a picnic there: you, Lynn, the kids, us. What do you say?"

"Yes. I'd like that, and so would Lynn, I know. I told her about it after we were there the first time. She said it sounded almost enchanted."

"It has that quality about it. Damn Jake. It could have been in the bag by now."

Keith then went on to talk about his plans. He was graduating and getting his business degree next month. He'd already gotten a job offer as assistant director of housing and food services at the university. "I'm thinking I'll go ahead and take the job, because it means we can stay here. June doesn't want to leave and I don't want to pull the kids away either. Also, we can start to develop our ideas for the property, partner."

Marv and Hal, the moving men, got back, telling tall tales about what took them so long. The house was almost in the next county, they had a flat tire, there was a roadblock, a bridge was out, the map was wrong, they ran into a plague of locusts.

Marv still had, sticking out of the pocket of his shirt, a card with a bidding number prominently written on it. "OK, Marv," said Keith, pointing to the bidding card, "what did you get?"

"We only dropped in at the auction for a minute," Marv said in an innocent voice.

"We had no idea there was an auction going on," added Hal

"The road went right by it. Imagine our surprise."

"Marv bought a four-poster. It's in the truck. Can you guys help us bring it in, if you're through playing with the doll babies?"

Richard came in while the bed was being moved into Marv's area and watched while it was reassembled. It was a massive piece in mahogany, with tapering posts and an arched headboard carved in a high relief of foliage and scrolls. Larger than the average bed of the mid-1800s, it could accommodate a modern-sized mattress. They laid out the boards on which to put the mattress, but when he considered it, Marv realized that it didn't show very well without a cover of some sort.

"Can anyone think of some way to make this look more appealing? Helen is going to be unhappy enough with all the room it takes up in here."

Richard offered, "Take one of my quilts and lay it on top. That should do the trick."

"Richard! Perfect, as always. Thanks, old friend. If there's anything I can do for you, you've only to ask."

When they had a moment later, Richard said to Marv, "Actually, there is something I want to talk to you about. Can we go into the office? I may be committing a breach of confidence, but I think you ought to know what Jake is up to regarding his insurance policies."

April, living up to its reputation, brought sweet showers and the first tentative green appeared on the hills. By the third week in April, spring was well underway and when Ruth came in to work at the shop, she brought with her a bunch of pussy willows to deck the cider press and a bouquet of daffodils from her garden for the front counter. Music was already playing. Emmy, when she was working at the shop, always put opera on the CD player. Today she had Mozart, *Cosi Fan Tuti*. "Not my favorite Mozart opera," she told Ruth, "but I can't be helping customers when the arias from *The Magic Flute* or *The Marriage of Figaro* are going on. I would not be able to concentrate on anything else."

Ruth and Emmy were on today. Helen was there for the morning and Marv had promised to come and relieve her for the afternoon. Apropos of the music, Helen said, "I remember once I was doing the year-end checks and there were requests for donations to the Cancer Research Fund and the Opera Guild. I asked Marv which we should give money to, as we couldn't do both that year. He said the opera, because without opera life isn't worth living." She shook her head in a deprecating manner as she said it.

"I definitely agree with Marv," Emmy stated. "Charles and I always get our Met tickets ..."

"Really, Emmy?" Helen countered. "I argued with Marv over that for the longest time. I thought he was just being funny, but he was serious."

Emmy said, "One time we had tickets for *Der Rosenkavalier* at the Met and there was a big snow storm and we couldn't make it to New York. It was terribly sad." And, recalling her distress, she did not go on.

Ruth took advantage of the pause. "I'll never forget the time I was driving on the Interstate and they were doing *Tosca* on the Met broadcast. As the tenor's last aria reached its peak, I looked at the speedometer and I was going 85."

Emmy nodded. "Puccini will do that to you," she said matter-of-factly.

Predictably, Helen was miffed at the big four-poster sitting in the middle of their area. She said to Ruth, "He's done it again. If there were a bigger, higher or more massive bed, I don't know what it would be."

"It's a stunning one, though," Ruth pointed out. "The carving is in excellent shape. Most of the time those leaves and curlicues have missing edges."

"Let's hope someone else feels the same as you and has plenty of money. I forgot to ask Marv what he paid for it, not that he'd give me an honest answer. I'll have to wait for the bank statement."

Ruth couldn't help herself and immediately came to Marv's defense. "But, Helen, he's one of the most honest people I've ever known!" She said it with a smile, what she hoped was a mollifying smile.

Helen said tartly, "When it comes to antiques, he can be very devious."

And Ruth, remembering the dry sink, couldn't dispute it.

Marv came in after lunch and one of the first things he said to Ruth was, "Have you seen the bed? Isn't it something? Hal and I figured it was custom made. There were probably other pieces too. That must have been quite a bedroom suite."

"It does look custom made, definitely hand-carved applications. What kind of place was it that you bought it from?"

"Not its first home, that's certain. We had a feeling it was originally from one of those big steel factory owners' summer homes in the mountains. A lot of looting went on when they were closed up for the winter. I've seen the most incongruous pieces of furniture coming out of workers' little row houses in towns up there, pieces that you know didn't belong."

Marv had a faraway look in his eyes as he said this. Ruth knew what he was talking about. She had felt it too, that the little towns she drove through had wonderful things hidden away. She said, "And even common ordinary things from a century ago are still in the backs of cupboards and on kitchen shelves and stored in attics and basements and haven't seen the light of day in decades." And she sighed.

Marv, in turn, recognized the sigh. "There was a customer who came in here last year; I don't think you were in that day, Ruth. A black fellow, older, who was telling me about the things he'd collected. He said when he was young he had worked for a firm in Philly that was re-habing some of the old houses in the Germantown section. When they tore out walls and floors and closets they'd find things going back to the 18th century. He said he had tools, clothing, children's shoes, kitchen ware, bottles. He said he kept everything, but the other guys just threw the stuff in the dumpster. It nearly killed him. What really intrigued him were a set of diaries he found. They were from the period before the Civil War, talked about slavery and how odious it was. He said reading about the everyday descriptions of life—how long it took to get somewhere, who died, who was born, the weather—made him feel close to the people who had lived there. He couldn't believe one thing he read in there: from their home in Germantown, the early residents could see all the way to the Port of Philadelphia and the masts of the ships."

"I wish I'd been in that day. You want to shake him by the hand and thank him for saving those things."

"I believe that's just what I did, Ruth. I also wanted to hire him to go out and find more. But about the diaries: next time I'm in Philadelphia he is going to let me have a look at them."

"Lucky you!" Ruth's eyes shone with happiness for him. She could see the excitement this offer had given him. He was not ready to give up being the historian and she was glad.

What with daylight savings time, it was still bright when the shop closed. Helen had stayed the afternoon, as Emmy had to give a make-up piano lesson she hadn't been able to reschedule in time. "Don't come back, Emmy. I'll stay on," Helen told her.

Ruth got ready to leave after doing what she could to help close out the day's business. Helen had told Marv she would lock up, and he had gone back into the office. Ruth bid Helen goodbye and went out into the late afternoon spring sunshine.

There is a quality to the light at the end of the day in early spring, a quality that has something to do with April's proximity to the equinox. But it is not at all like its counterpart in early October, when the afternoon light is long and low, penetrated with the first chill of autumn. This spring light is clear, sweet. It's a shining softness that holds warmth and a promise of more to come. A promise of things to come, Ruth thought. She went over to look at the hills where the new green was starting. She wished she could share this beautiful early evening light with Marv, as he had shared the winter sunset with her. Ruth felt the warmth of the sun on her face, and thought how she wanted to hold onto it, the promising, caressing light. She closed her eyes and thought how she wanted to take it inside her, wanted to...take him inside her.

"Oh, no!!" Startled, shaken, Ruth's eyes flew open. "Oh, no," she said aloud, closing her eyes again. It wouldn't do, it just wouldn't do, thinking about him like that. It was the first time her thoughts of him had presented themselves in such a thoroughly sexual manner and, as excruciatingly pleasurable as the thought had been, she could not, simply

282

could not do this to herself! He was married to Helen; she'd just spoken with Helen. Ruth walked back rapidly, unnerved, and climbed into her van.

This time the engine did not even turn over. She tried again and again and, fearing she'd only run down the battery, went back into the shop. Helen had heard the sounds of Ruth's unsuccessful attempts to start the van. "Didn't start?" she asked.

"It's died," Ruth nodded. "I'm going to have to get it towed to the garage and then figure out what to do."

"Look, Ruth, Marv can stay here until the tow truck comes and then take you home. I hope it can be fixed, but you know there comes a time."

"Thanks, Helen. Shall I go tell Marv?"

"No, I will. You call the garage and I'll tell him what we've decided."

Ruth thought this might be the usual way Marv's life was ordered, then wondered if, once again, she was giving herself reasons to justify her feelings for Marv. She thought she'd better deal with the car first.

After Helen had gone, Ruth and Marv stood outside in the soft light of the spring afternoon, as she had earlier wished for. But it was less than a few minutes, and then the grinding noise of the tow truck could be heard making the turn up Cider Run Road and into the parking lot.

The tow truck driver tried to start the van, but had no luck either. He hitched it up and took it away. Ruth stood gazing after it, having the strange feeling of not being sure whether something had ended for her or had just begun. Marv held the door of his truck open and she got in.

He didn't start the truck immediately; he looked over at her. Henry Ford's double blessing again, the intimacy of a car's interior, the possibilities, the ability to be remote if they wanted, if only they could. But he said lightly, "Where to, Madam? The Palace? The Astoria? The Martensdale Diner?"

She didn't answer right away, trying to get a perspective on how much different this was than the last time she'd been in his truck, the day they went to the nursery to get plants and then on to the farmhouse, a year ago.

She must have been looking at him in an odd manner, because he said, "You're supposed to say 'Home, James,' I believe, or something like that. It's déjà vu, isn't it? You remember being here once, but can't quite place it."

She said, "Yes, I was thinking of that, thinking how different it is now. I mean, how much better we know each other. I'm not putting this very clearly, am I?" She looked away from him. It's not just that we know each other better, she thought. It's far more than that.

"It's been a year. We know each other a year's worth more. But not nearly as well as I'd like." He started the truck. "And I have no right to say that." He shifted into reverse and backed up. "And yet I do." He shifted into low. "By the way, where are we going?"

"To my house, please, and try to sort out transportation options."

"What are you going to do about your van?" Marv asked as they sat in Ruth's living room. She had poured them two glasses of pale ale, as it seemed just right for their companionable mood.

"Do you have any suggestions? I think it's had it, and anyhow it was a terrible gas guzzler and really too big for my needs. I'd like a smaller van or something else. I don't generally haul big pieces of furniture around."

"You mean like someone else you could mention but are too tactful to do so?"

"Oh, *that* person? The one with the dining room suite, four-poster bed, oversize wardrobe?"

"You got me," Marv admitted cheerfully, making the gesture of slitting his throat.

"The problem is," Ruth went on, "I need something soon. I've planned to pick up Ruthie from her college when the semester ends in May, and we're going to take a week to visit relatives and old friends and do a little antiques buying up in New England."

Marv had a twinge of apprehension. Suppose it looked good to her, being back there again? He needed to be with her as much as he could before she left. He said, "May I be involved? In finding a new vehicle, that is, not in coming between you and Ruthie. We could look at a few vans and maybe SUVs."

"Thanks, Marv, but I'm sure my brother..."

"I'd really like to, Ruth, and then I could point to it proudly as you drive down the street, knowing I was implicated in the circumstances surrounding its ownership."

If we can keep this up, Ruth thought, we won't talk about what is really on our minds. She said, "I'd be happy for your help."

Marv thought, can I trust myself sitting here with her like this? Not if we start to get serious. But he did ask, "Ruth, have you had any more talks with Jake?"

"No. I've seen him around and he's been his usual self, pleasant enough. But sort of distant. Distracted. I didn't think it had anything to do with us, though."

"He's been acting that way for a while. Hal thinks it has something to do with Annette, but I don't know. Richard has concerns about him too."

Ruth commented, "As long as he leaves us alone," then realized what she'd said.

Marv heard the words and immediately interpreted them to coincide with the thoughts uppermost in his mind. He said in a softer voice, "I'd like that more than anything in the world, Ruth, to be left alone with you." Then he got up hastily, saying, "I must go, and go now. Thank you for the brew. I'll call you tomorrow morning and we'll go pay our respects to the deceased at the garage and then find you some new wheels."

Ruth washed the glasses after Marv had gone. She felt quietly happy as if everything were flooded with a soft glow.

Marv drove home, running a red light and nearly missing his turn. And we think Jake is distracted, he said to himself.

They were together for much of the following day, and even though they stayed strictly to their task of finding a new car, it had the feel, for both of them, of a holiday. After they learned at the garage that the van would cost more to repair than Ruth was willing to invest, she and Marv went to several car dealerships and test drove various vehicles. They settled on a new SUV hybrid that filled Ruth's needs, handled well, was environmentally friendly and low on fuel consumption. In a festive mood after such a successful venture, they celebrated by having a late lunch at a taco place, sitting outside in the warm April sunshine at a humble plastic table.

"This is almost as good as an auction, having lunch outside," Marv observed. "I've often wished I could get tacos at an auction, haven't you? Auction food can be good, but the choices offered by the ladies of the church are so predictable."

"Unlike you, Marv," said Ruth boldly. "No, wait," she hastened on as he started to protest, "I mean I like your unpredictability. It's a quality that few people value because it makes them nervous. What will you do next? You keep them guessing."

He looked across the table at her and said, "And how long will you keep me guessing?" That was a rather forward remark, he thought after he said it, but it somehow seemed appropriate for the sunshine and the tacos and their lighthearted mood.

And to Ruth it was just right. She could not, of course, answer it. Instead she did exactly as he had desired, laughed in her appreciation of him.

Alone that evening, Ruth basked in the happiness from the day spent with Marv, from the unfamiliar, heady certainty of being wooed. In its wake sober thoughts of ethical behavior and moral obligations faded. But her conscience would not let her off so easily. How can I be so callous? We could cause irreparable damage to both of us, to all three of us. In two weeks she would be going to pick up Ruthie in a brand new car, a car indelibly associated with him, as had been his intention, she knew, and she smiled at that. But when she returned, then what? And would her heart be broken?

Only two more weeks, thought Marv, and she'll go off. Maybe there will be someone, one of those old friends she is planning to visit, someone from her past. She wouldn't move back there, would she? If I were to show her how much I care about her, would it keep her from moving away, or would it frighten her? He had to take the chance, if he were lucky enough to have a chance.

Chapter 24

On the first day of the month, the checks for the last month's sales were ready and many of the dealers came in early to get them. When Ruth, driving her new car, arrived at the shop on the first of May, it looked, with all the vehicles there, as if a major event were taking place. She parked down the line next to Emmy's station wagon and, as always, walked to the edge of the parking lot to gaze for a minute at the hills.

The redbud was in bloom. Ruth had learned to look for it, because it was only for a short time in early May that this small tree could be seen dotting the countryside with its deep pink blossoms, before it lost them to become green-leafed and blend into the rest of the foliage. Redbud was new to Ruth; it didn't range as far north as New England and, like other Pennsylvania flora, it surprised and delighted her. Resting her eyes on the closer slopes, she could pick out its wild pink interspersed among the brazen yellow of forsythia bushes, the light greens of newly-leafed trees and the grays and browns of still-bare branches. By the time she got back from her trip, she knew, the redbud's blossoms would be gone, but dogwood and then mountain laurel would be starting up in all their loveliness. It was a beautiful place, this part of the world. She wondered how New England would look to her after her long absence. One thing, she thought, as she turned to go into the shop, spring would not be nearly so far advanced.

As was the custom, everyone was in the kitchen where the coffee and the checks were, and also a sign-up sheet for work days for the next few months. Vacation schedules were being discussed and it was noisy and cheerful.

"Can anyone work an extra day for me in June?" Cora requested. "I can make it up to you in July or whenever."

"Where are you going? Some exotic place?" Sylvie asked.

"Hardly. We're babysitting the grandchildren while their parents have a vacation."

"I'm going to be doing that this month," Helen volunteered. "I'm really looking forward to it."

"Hey! I hear Ruth got a new car." Richard announced. "Can we see it?"

Ruth was happy to respond, "It's out in the parking lot, down near the end."

"Do we get rides in it?" It was Keith who asked. "Seriously, I'm going to be in the market for a new car."

"I'll take you for a spin any time," Ruth offered.

Marv, ready for such a remark, spoke up, "I have a proprietary interest in that car. I will go along and sit in the back seat to make sure everything is on the up and up."

Jake raised his eyebrows, but said nothing.

Sally Ann came in saying, "Whose car is that parked next to Emmy's? It looks brand new."

"It's Ruth's, but to hear Marv tell it, he has a prior claim," Richard stated.

"Well, I just love it, Ruth," Sally Ann enthused. "If I hadn't promised Fred I'd only drive a Mercedes, I'd get one like it."

Sylvie asked, "Sally Ann, I've always wondered, how do you get furniture in that car of yours?"

"Honey, I don't. There's always someone who is so sweet and delivers it for me."

Some of the dealers had drifted out and since it was past opening time, customers were starting to arrive. Ruth went to have a look at her area. She'd need to bring in a few more things to tide it over while she was gone. In less than a week she'd be leaving. Her new car was so splendid. It suited her in every way. She thought she'd like to do something for Marv, to thank him for helping her with the car. Dinner for him, and Helen, of course. She would make a nice little dinner party for them right before she left. Now wasn't the time to ask, people were still milling around, chatting, talking about their schedules for the summer. As Ruth stood musing, Jake separated himself out and came up to her. She looked at him warily and he interpreted her expression immediately.

"Don't look so affronted, Ruth," he said. "I was just going to congratulate you on your new car."

Giving him the benefit of the doubt, she responded, "Thanks, Jake. I like it very much."

"As you do the person who was instrumental in your getting it," Jake added.

"Yes," she said calmly, "it's true, you know I do. And so do all of us, like him very much." There, Ruth thought. That ought to put an end to it.

But Jake was not through. "Ruth, I don't dispute it in the least! We all love Marv in our own ways. It's just that some of us love him differently than others do, wouldn't you agree? Take Helen, for instance. She worries about him all the time, what he's up to, what he'll do next. What will he do next,

Ruth? Do you know?" And true to form, he walked away on this last remark.

Ruth simmered, but let it pass. She was less bothered by Jake's comments than the first time, but she wondered again why Jake was doing this, getting on her like this. Was he simply amusing himself at her expense? Perhaps setting the stage for something, laying the groundwork to be able to say at some future time, "I warned you, but you didn't listen to me." Or maybe, she thought, it's my own conscience that's needling me. But I'm just going along with things, seeing what will happen; I'm not really doing anything. Or am I fooling myself? Yes, she thought guiltily, Jake had her figured out all right. She may as well be transparent.

She did, nevertheless, decide to invite Marv and Helen for dinner. She had gone to the shop the next day to leave a flowered teapot with six assorted cups and saucers and was heading back to her car when Marv drove up.

"Don't go away mad, Ruth," Marv called by way of greeting as he got out of his truck.

"Just go away," she answered, coming alongside of him.

"And when are you going?" he asked, outwardly smiling, but once again inwardly chilled by the idea of her being gone.

"Not before I have you to dinner, I hope."

"What a nice thought!" he exclaimed, his inward state beginning to equalize itself.

She explained when it would be. "It won't be grand, since I'm leaving the next day. But I'd love to have you over, to thank you for helping me get the car. I'm afraid that's the only day I can do it before I go and I'd hate to put it off for too long. So please check with Helen and let me know."

"Ruth, I'd be delighted and honored. However, it will only be me, because Helen will have left by then for Bucks

County to be at our daughter's and I'm not going over until later in the week. So if you don't mind being alone with me, I promise I will be on my best behavior. Or would you rather go out? We could go first class and take your new car." They would be alone together! How could he live until then?

Ruth felt a flush of emotion, but managed to say smoothly, "No, I do want to fix dinner and besides, I need to use up some things that might spoil while I'm gone. Wait, that doesn't sound very appetizing, does it?"

"I don't know when practicality has ever sounded more appetizing," he replied with feeling.

Her last day in town, Ruth had packed for the trip, made her arrangements about the mail and the paper and spoken with her family. She had tried to concentrate on her chores and had succeeded, mostly. But after she had showered and dressed and was putting dinner together, she came to a standstill. She poured herself a glass of wine and had a little talk with herself.

She knew there was a possible outcome of the evening and needed to examine her feelings about it, whether she was ready for it: the hitherto-unconsidered prospect of their making love, a thought which, before now, had not seemed imaginable. Not quite accurate, Ruth, she admitted. It was there in her imagination, but she had not let herself luxuriate in it because what good would that do? Sexually, there was no question of being ready. Her attraction to Marv was undeniable, the excitement he aroused in her warm and thrilling. But what about the consequences? He *was* married. Making herself miserable was one thing, but having him miserable too, not to mention Helen? Could that be kept from happening? And suppose Jake was right about Marv only needing a safety valve? But her instincts, based on the last two years of being around Marv, suggested that he didn't view her that way. Well, this was all speculation anyway; she would see how the evening unfolded. And having wisely decided not to decide anything, she went out on the patio for a breath of fresh air.

Marv was having a talk with himself as well. He would not, truly not, try to seduce her. It wouldn't be fair. "Oh? And what makes you think you could?" the contrary part of his brain said annoyingly. He ignored this little jab and went on with his thoughts. It wouldn't be fair because she is just getting to know me and I want her to like me. Let's be honest. I also want her to want me, but at her own pace. Otherwise, it's no good, it's demeaning to her. No, pressuring her is not what I want to do. But how I want her! Nonetheless, he solemnly vowed to behave like a gentleman and not do anything rash.

The evening was mild and the sky still held a clear, soft glow. The scent of blossoms filled the air, as only it does in May. Ruth, out on her patio, took a breath of the blossom-scented air and went back to the kitchen. Marv breathed deeply, got into his truck and drove over to Ruth's.

"Beer and bratwurst would have been fun," Ruth said to Marv over dinner. She had fixed chicken tonight, sautéed in olive oil and wine over brown rice. "But that's really for high summer, picnics on the patio, potato salad and coleslaw."

"And so very Pennsylvania; you've adapted well. But, Ruth, this is excellent, this is superb. I thought you were an elementary school principal. Do elementary principals cook with wine?"

"You'd be surprised what goes on in the school cafeteria after the kidlets have gone home."

"What? Experimental cookery? Things you'd never let on to the school board."

"Well, you know, in New England there's a need for great, creative endeavors to counteract the effects of the long, bleak winter. Food, mainly."

"Is that why you have pie for breakfast up there? I could never fathom that."

"There's nothing wrong with pie for breakfast," laughed Ruth.

Marv realized he was supremely relaxed being with her. Everything was complementary: the dinner, his delightful companion, the 18th and early 19th century furniture. They were dining at a polished pine farm table using white ironstone plates, each slightly different, all at least a hundred years old. They had a salad with the entree, they had Stilton with sliced pears after that and Ruth made coffee, which they took out to the patio. The silver crescent of a new moon was setting in the western sky against a backdrop of azure blue.

Marv looked at Ruth and thought how enchanting she was. Instead of slacks, which was what she wore at the shop, she was wearing a skirt which was cut in a light, soft sweep and a sweater in the blue-green that matched her eyes. What can I say that she won't reject, he wondered? He plunged in. "Ruth, even though you deliberately bribed me by feeding me that elegant dinner first, I will say it anyway: you look lovely tonight."

"Thank you, Marv," Ruth smiled at him. "You know, you said that once before to me. A long time ago."

"I remember. It was at that wine and cheese party we had in the shop, when we were just starting out."

"I didn't know what to say then. I thought you were, well, that you said it to everyone."

"But I don't. I'm not like Jake."

Ruth sighed. "Jake had a few words to say about us again the other day," she told Marv. "Is he mad at you for something? I don't understand why he's doing it."

"What did he say, Ruth?" Marv looked concerned.

"It was rather vague, but I had the distinct feeling it was a threat. He said Helen worries about what you're up to and insinuated that I know—what you're up to, that is."

"It's common knowledge that Helen worries about me. She tells everyone. I think it's time I had a talk with Jake, get him off your back."

Ruth put her hand on Marv's arm. "No, Marv," she implored. "It will look like you've got some reason to defend my honor. It doesn't need defending, I shouldn't think."

"Ruth, I don't want you to have to take this from Jake." He put his hand over hers. "You've had distressing enough things happen before in your life."

Ruth, startled, took her hand away and could only say, "I what?"

Marv immediately knew he had struck upon a delicate matter and had done it in the clumsiest way possible. "Can I retract that?" he asked.

"Not entirely," said Ruth, a slight chill in her voice. "But let's go in. I'll make some more coffee and you can explain that last remark."

Ruth knew she had started to revert to her former guarded behavior, and wanted to keep that from happening. Instead of coffee, she poured Irish cream into two cordial glasses and they took them into the living room. Marv sat at one end of the sofa, Ruth at the other end. She had taken off her sandals and had her feet tucked up under her. But there was a tension between them, a tension Ruth did not want but couldn't seem to help.

Marv started off at once by apologizing, "Ruth, I'm sorry I blurted that out. Please forgive me." He said it earnestly, hoping to clear the air.

"These distressing things you alluded to: what exactly did you hear?" Ruth asked.

"Richard made some comments about your having been in Florida, when you were married, and I guess he dramatized it. I got the impression it was pretty awful."

"And so it was, but it isn't something I want used as general entertainment." Ruth was unsure where this was leading.

"No, that wasn't it at all. Richard dropped some hints when Sally Ann wore her palm tree and flamingo number. I was the one who asked him for details. It's not Richard you should blame." He looked appealingly at Ruth. "I just wanted to know more about you."

"Then you should ask me, Marv. I have no secrets I'm trying to hide."

"That's what Richard said, I should ask you, but how could I? And what would you think of me if I asked you to delve into your past?"

"What *are* your reasons?" Ruth, unable to counter her defensiveness, heard herself saying. She felt her cheeks starting to get hot. "Idle curiosity?"

Marv put his glass down on the end table. He turned to face Ruth and decided to be truthful, insofar as he could get at his own feelings. "I'm not sure I can answer that question without taking a chance on your friendship," he began. "It's not idle curiosity, certainly. It's genuine interest in you."

Ruth frowned slightly. "But interest in me now or interest in my past, which doesn't enter into our relationship, as far as I can see."

"In both, really. How can I get to know you if I'm in the dark about you?"

"This is unfair, Marv," she said, turning her head away.

"Why is it unfair? To tell me about your life?" He was pressing her and he knew he shouldn't. He wasn't prepared for her reaction.

She straightened her back, raised her chin. "Very well. Fine," she said with a rising anger she couldn't control. "Details, is that what you'd like? Where shall I start? With Brad in England? Or maybe you'd rather hear about the affair I had with the superintendent of a school district in Massachusetts? That went on for years. Would you like to hear about that?" Ruth asked, feeling cornered.

"Ruth, I'm sorry," he said bleakly. "I have no right to ask about your personal life." He had overstepped the bounds and was paying the price.

"Oh, you shall know, if you must." Was she trying to make him angry too, or maybe even jealous? But she had gotten agitated and couldn't stop herself. She went on mercilessly, "I met him when I went back to the university to get my master's degree and principal's certificate. He was getting a doctorate in education and his superintendent's credential. We lived in different parts of the state and got together in Boston when we could. Am I filling you in on enough details to satisfy you? Or would you like to know what we did when we were together in Boston?"

"Stop. No," Marv protested, looking at her in abject misery.

Ruth knew she was being unkind, but needed to finish. "He was between wives at the time and neither of them was me. I don't know if I was sorry or relieved when we finally called it quits." Ruth ran out of steam and was annoyed with herself. Losing her temper with Marv was so unexpected, not at all what she had visualized for this evening. What had happened to her? She was usually so self-possessed. "Marv," she begged after she was in control of herself again, "why are you doing this to me?"

"I'm doing it to myself too. Believe me, upsetting you is the last thing I wanted to do and now I've done it." He decided to take the gamble. Looking into her eyes, he held her attention and, with all the sincerity he could muster, said, "I want to learn everything I can about you, who you are, what you've done, what's happened to you. Don't you see, Ruth? If I can't have you, at least I can know about you."

Ruth was speechless. *How in the world can I be angry with him?* She got up, both to regain her composure and to put off responding to his last statement. What could she say to that? He had let her inside. He had shown her his need for her. With a hand less steady than before, she poured liqueur into their glasses and sat down on the sofa again.

Marv continued, "That's as honest as I can be. I can't say enough how sorry I am. You can kick me out now, or let me finish my drink and I'll go quietly."

"I'm the one who should apologize," Ruth admitted. "I had no call to get so worked up and unleash my sordid bit of history on you like that." If he were going to be honest, she would be honest in return. "I could have controlled myself and kept it light," she said, "but I had gotten to the point where I was too far gone to stop." She looked at him squarely. "And that's the truth, Marv. You have gotten to me, straight to the core, and I am in far too deep."

And it is right here, Marv thought to himself, when she has let me know how she feels about me, that I should follow through, press my advantage, take her directly in my arms. But instead he stood up, leaned down and smiled at her. "Just hearing you say that makes up for everything. I can leave knowing you don't despise me. That's all that matters."

She looked up at him. "I could never despise you. But it's a wonder you aren't completely disgusted with me for the way I went on." She smiled for the first time since this conversation started. "I guess I forgot. History is your field, after all," she said in a much lighter tone.

His confidence restored, Marv said, "I think you've led a shameful life and I will personally undertake your rehabilitation. By the way," he reached into his pocket, "I thought you might like this." He unfolded the "How to Speak French" hankie and handed it to her. "I promise I haven't used it."

Ruth was flabbergasted. "How did you...?" she began, then started laughing and Marv sat back down next to her.

"That comment was all anyone could wish for," he said happily.

She looked gratefully at him. "You know, I searched for this in Sally Ann's area, but it was gone. Thank you, Marv. It made me nostalgic when I first saw it, but now it reminds me of you," she confessed without any difficulty.

"Although we haven't been to France together. But I'd like to. Ruth, I'm so sorry I made you angry. Will you forgive me?"

"You make it impossible not to. I just hope I didn't disillusion you too much. It couldn't have been very nice listening to what I said."

"I asked for it. I'm sadder but wiser, and I like you more than ever."

"And you know you can get to me," Ruth said with a laugh. She got up and Marv realized it was time for him to go. He rose and took her hand. They walked to the door.

"I'll miss you next week," he confessed. "I've been dreading it, afraid you'll decide to move back up north. Promise me you won't, Ruth."

"The thought had not entered my mind. Quite the contrary. I'll miss you, in spite of the harassment," Marv looked guilty and she went on, "and the complications, and Jake..." she trailed off. She had said more than she meant to, more of what was on her mind about their relationship. But Marv was still holding her hand. She particularly didn't want to think about Jake.

Marv took her other hand in his. "Thank you for dinner. It was delicious and perfect. Like you. Like your home. Will I be given another chance? Can we pick up again where we left off, without having to go back to the beginning?" He looked entreatingly at her, but there was the glint of laughter in his eyes.

"Or at least skipping the middle part," she proposed. "Goodnight, Marv."

"Goodnight, Ruth. Take care. Come back." He let go of her hands, opened the door and left.

Ruth closed the door and turned back to the living room. She picked up the hankie. Under the heading *Rendezvous* it read, "You are charming," *Vous etes charmant.* Ruthie's words from a year ago came back to Ruth: "He's very charming, Aunt Ruth. I can see why you like him so much." Yes, thought Ruth, and I said, "Charming and taken," if I remember correctly. She looked at the hankie again and read, "I do not know you, sir!" *Je ne vous connais pas, monsieur!* She heard Marv's truck door close. Did she know him? He had said, "If I can't have you..." How disarming that statement was! If he only realized the effect it had on her. She thought, he's completely broken through my reserve and now he knows it. And I'm ridiculously happy. I only wish I could tell him. No, that's not all I wish.

Marv got into his truck and started it. But he couldn't bring himself to drive off. She made him happier than he could remember, being around her, watching her reactions. It had been a challenge at first, her quietness, her reserve, but it went beyond that. It wasn't merely that she was beautiful to look at, which she was. He liked the whole person he saw. Her good humor about things, even her anger had been beautiful, and then her acceptance of him in spite of what he had done to alienate her. He knew he had touched something in her tonight. She'd confessed her feelings for him.

Or had he forced it out of her? Had his candor, had that insufferably self-serving statement about why he wanted to know her, really been accepted by her? And after he'd essentially coerced her into talking about her past. He had been so heavy-handed. What a cad he was! He had to explain and he wouldn't see her for, how long? A week? He had to know what she was thinking. He turned the truck off and got out.

Ruth heard the engine stop. She went to her front door and opened it. Marv came inside and shut the door behind him.

"Ruth," he began, "there's more I need to say." She stood very still and he took her hand in both of his. "Listen, you probably don't trust me anymore and I can't blame you. You must wonder why I said what I did."

Ruth knew, but said anyway, "About not having me?"

"I used it like a sledge hammer, didn't I? I hit you over the head with it. I have so much to apologize for, I don't know where to start."

"Marv, you have met me honestly and without pretense. You haven't bludgeoned me. You've made me feel," she paused, "wanted, needed, and that's a wonderful feeling."

"And it's true. I do want you and I do need you. I don't know how it happened, but it did." Then, more quietly, he added, "I do know how it happened. I wanted it to happen. I willingly encouraged it."

Ruth looked into his face, saw both the hope and hopelessness he felt, both yearning and constraint. "What are we to do about it, Marv?" she said softly. "I have far less to lose than you. No," she shook her head, as he started to interrupt her, and she put her hand up to his lips to silence his inevitable protest. He took her hand, turned it over and kissed it. At the touch of his lips, Ruth felt the last shred of any resistance disappear. "What are we to do about it?" she said, her voice low and steady.

To hell with everything else, Marv thought to himself. He put his arms around her and drew her close. He said in a burst of relief, "I've wanted to hold you for so long. I've wanted you for so long. I didn't realize how strong it was until now. Ruth, may I stay?"

Before she could answer, he released her and took both her hands in his, eyes searching her face. "But if I stay, you must know," he said, the words plain but eloquent in their significance, "I am going to make love to you." He reached for her again. "May I stay, Ruth?"

"Yes," she whispered.

Whatever his hopes had been, Ruth's response to his first kiss, the way she melted into him, was all he could have wished for. It was like a gift given him after he had long ago stopped believing he could find happiness, and it was Ruth, here, in his arms that made the difference. They climbed the stairs and in the semi-darkness of her bedroom, it seemed to Marv that time and history hung suspended, his own past disappeared and everything came down to this one moment, a charmed space in which were distilled all desire, all happiness. He made love to her with passion and great joy, the pent-up emotions released, shaping themselves to her, and she let herself get carried away in a wave of warmth and exuberance.

They lay afterwards lazily, easy with each other, against the pillows, Ruth with her head resting close to his, Marv with his arm around her telling her how much she meant to him. "Thank you, Ruth. Thanks for being you, wanting me." Then, turning to look at her, suddenly concerned, he said, "You weren't just humoring me, were you? You did want me, didn't you?"

She smiled. "I think I've wanted you for two years, although I couldn't admit it to myself. I do know I was becoming more and more fond of you and as long as I could call it fondness, I thought it would be all right."

"Ah, Ruth, it's a good thing I didn't know that or I might have done something alarming. I thought I was locked in a one-sided infatuation. Do you remember that first time you walked into the shop, when we were still doing the remodeling? You introduced yourself and we shook hands and I thought, with her around, this Cider Run venture is going to be far better than I ever dreamed. I know I've wanted you for two years."

"We've been the picture of restraint."

"I almost lost my restraint once, though. It was after you'd had surgery on your shoulder. We were on the patio, that afternoon when I'd chased the rabbit around."

"I was laughing very hard, I'm afraid," she admitted, remembering with pleasure how he had endeared himself to her that day.

"Yes, and so was I. But then I looked at you trussed up in that sling, sitting there so helpless with your arm out of commission. It was all I could do to keep myself from ravishing you on the spot."

"But Ruthie was here."

"The only thing that stopped me." He gazed into her eyes and said seriously, "As long as you want me, nothing is going to stop me now."

Chapter 25

He called her in the morning before she left town and thanked her for the dinner and over and over again for the night. "Do I sound grateful? I am so grateful for you, Ruth," he said. He wanted her to know this, he wanted her to know everything: how perfect she was, how happy she made him, uninhibitedly returning the intimacy he had wanted so badly from her.

That she made him happy, Ruth admitted to herself, meant more to her than anything she could imagine. But what happiness he had given her too, and not only the bliss of last night. She was feeling a new and unforeseen joy, as if, because of him, she had shrugged off years of being on the sidelines and was now into the stream of life, the rich, keen, rewarding world of possibilities, of anticipation and excitement. "Marv," she said with a little sigh, "I'm so glad last night happened, that we let it happen."

"You will come back to me?" he implored.

She laughed. "I'll be back."

"Good. I'm counting on it. I'm more than counting on it. I'm living for it."

Driving northeast to her niece's college, Ruth had time to let her mind return to last night. She went over it again, what she'd said when she'd been so angry, horrified at herself for losing her temper. And he hadn't gotten upset with her in return. He had said goodnight, so gentlemanly, and then he came back, unable to say goodnight after all, and she thought of the way he had announced his intentions. Those few words and the way he said them: it was the most seductive thing anyone had ever said to her. "I am going to make love to you." He was, unquestionably, a lover, Ruth thought with a thrill, and better than... She wondered, do women always compare? I guess we do, she decided, because men have such different approaches, want different things from us. But us, we wait to see what they're up to and respond. And responding to Marv was so, so easy. She felt again the warmth flood through her, let herself relive their lovemaking. What had started out almost tentative had grown until there was a rush, an unrestrained quality to it, as if they could never get enough of each other. That it had been building up for two years was one of the reasons, she knew. But even more than that it was Marv himself, his need no longer held back and that enthusiasm of his able to be freely expressed. What had been her expectations? She'd had none, and because she had steeled herself from thinking about it beforehand, it came as a surprise that he was so very loving. A serious word that, loving, but appropriate, she reflected, and now all she wanted was more of him. She marveled that she was able to have these thoughts and still stay on the road.

When she reached Ruthie's college, the new car heartily approved of by Ruthie, and the two of them were starting the drive north, Ruthie turned and gave her aunt a long, appraising look. It was all there, she thought with growing certainty, no doubt about it. The softness around her aunt's pretty eyes, the smile faintly hovering on her lips, the lapses in conversation, the slightly distracted air. And it must have been quite recently. "You've slept with him, haven't you, Aunt Ruth." Ruthie made it a statement, not a question.

"Ruthie!" exclaimed Ruth. Then, "Does it show so much?"

"All over the place. I think it's cool."

Marv had a meeting with Hal and Jake at the shop at 9:00. That was one of the reasons he had stayed while Helen left for grandchildren duty. The other reason was Helen did just fine without him, so much so that she always made him feel he was in the way. When they went to Bucks County he usually spent his time scouting out the antiques scene and that was their compromise. Now he was so thankful he had stayed behind he could hardly contain himself.

As he brought the truck to a stop at Cider Run, even the gravel in the parking lot seemed benign. He jumped out and looked appreciatively at the blue sky, the hills beyond. Never had there been a more beautiful spring morning, never a more beautiful spring. What an unimaginably sweet interlude last night had been, how enormously satisfying it was to be with Ruth, making love. She could have anything she wanted from him. What the future might hold for them he didn't know, he admitted, but he still wanted her and would go on wanting her. He also knew he'd better pull himself together before he met with his partners.

Hal and Jake were already at the shop, in the kitchen where Hal had made a pot of coffee. Marv came in and tried to look normal. "What a beautiful morning!" was his greeting. He poured himself coffee and sat down at the table.

Hal said darkly, "You wouldn't say that if you knew what I know about the roof on this place."

"But you would say that if you were Marv," Jake declared. "Wouldn't you, Marv?" he added in an insinuating manner.

Marv almost choked on his coffee. "What's that supposed to mean, Jake?" he demanded.

"It means that your truck was still parked in Ruth's driveway after one o'clock this morning, that's what it means. Marv, have you lost your senses?"

Hal started grinning. Marv gave him a threatening look. Hal tried to wipe the grin off his face, but it kept returning. "Hal, if you can't behave, you'll have to leave the room," warned Marv.

"Marv, you old dog," said Hal in a respectful tone.

Marv turned to Jake. "I don't know what you were doing in Ruth's neighborhood at 1:00 AM, Jake. But it concerns Ruth and me, no one else. Is that understood?" he said, dead serious.

Jake raised his hands in protest. "What you do in your private life is your business, as what I do is mine. I'm just saying that everyone knows your truck and you can't keep secrets in a town this size."

"Marv, you dog," said Hal again.

"You too, Thompson. It goes no farther. Are we clear?"

Jake persisted, "You're playing with fire, Marv, and if it got about, it could easily affect the business, put the shop in a bad light."

"And you, Jake?" Marv shot back. "Fire? What about Laurel and you that night of the snow storm, almost nine months to the day before she had a baby? Everyone has heard how you made a fire to keep her warm. Your lack of reticence about that was rather obvious. Are you denying it?"

Hal said, "At least Marv doesn't have to worry about Ruth getting pregnant. Marv, I still can't..."

"Well, forget it, Hal! And, please, for God's sake, don't say anything to Sylvie."

"No, no, of course not," Hal shook his head. "You and Ruth. I'll be damned!"

"Can we get on to the purpose of this meeting and stop dwelling on last night?" Marv said angrily. Although that's what I'd rather do, he thought to himself. But how upset Ruth would be if she knew Jake had been there, driving by her house, watching. It gave Marv a distinctly distasteful and unsettling feeling.

"As I was saying, Marv, before your love life became the hot topic here," Hal started.

"Damn it! One more word out of you about that and I'll damn well break your neck!" said Marv with vehemence.

"No need to be so touchy, Marv," protested Jake. "These things do have a way of grabbing center stage."

"That goes for you too, Jake, and double, for giving Ruth a hard time."

"A hard time? Is that what she said? I was only trying to head off trouble, and now look what you've gone and done."

"Simmer down, you two," Hal said at last, "We need to figure out how we're going to pay for a new roof, plus meet our other expenses."

Marv, with one final glare at his partners, got back to the business at hand. He said in a more controlled voice, "I think it's time we all put in another $5000, as we agreed to do when we started out. That should give us some cushion, until we either raise rents, rent out some more space or take in another partner, silent or not."

Jake was not done yet, however. "I think you can pay my share, Marv, for putting the business in jeopardy with your reckless behavior." He got up. "If you need me, I'll be at my office selling real estate, hoping I won't have to deal with fallout from your latest indiscretion," and with that, Jake left.

Marv and Hal looked after the departing Jake, watching the kitchen door swing to and fro until it stopped.

"If I didn't know better," Marv observed, "I'd think that sounded like blackmail."

"He must be in some financial straits if he's resorting to threats like that. I wonder what Annette is holding over his head? Or what difficulties he's gotten himself into? Well, he's not likely to tell us. I guess we'll just have to muddle ahead, you and I, as best we can. When is Helen getting back? Oops, sorry, I didn't mean to bring that up," Hal apologized.

"It doesn't matter. Ruth is gone for a week with her niece."

"Did Jake really get on Ruth? How did she take it?"

"He was blunt, warned her about being indiscreet. With me. Now I'm sure he feels fully justified."

"Maybe it's time someone talked to him and tried to find out what's going on with him."

"If you can get a straight answer, which I doubt. Richard let on that Jake told him Annette has a new boyfriend and wants to get married. There has to be an annulment and Jake is worried she'll try to get at his assets. So I gather he's hanging back on that and she's not at all happy. But I can't sit in judgment on them after what I've done."

Hal said, "Look, Marv, we've known each other for years. I also know this isn't the first time you've gotten entangled with someone, and you managed to get yourself disentangled gracefully. How, I don't know."

"Graceful only because she left to take a teaching position at another university. Otherwise, it would have been decidedly graceless. This is different. Not only is Ruth here, but I care about her a lot more than I ever imagined. I really do, Hal. And as you know, Helen and I aren't, well, there's no closeness at all," Marv admitted. "But I didn't mean for this to happen. I thought I could at least control my actions, if not my feelings. I tried, anyway."

"But not very much?"

"No, really, I told myself I'd act like a gentleman and not pressure her in any way. We said goodnight rather chastely and I got into the truck and started it up and then needed to tell her one more thing, so I turned it off and went back. Just to talk, just to clarify something I'd said earlier. But then she was in my arms and..." He looked at Hal and hoped he hadn't gone too far.

Hal responded, to Marv's relief, "Whatever you decide to do or not to do, I'm totally behind you, as far as you and Ruth go, and I mean that, so you can count on me." That Hal knew how difficult Marv's marriage had been was implicit. But Hal also felt that Ruth was one in a million. And so is Marv, he thought to himself.

"Thanks, Hal. It's not as if I feel vindicated in what I did. I feel guilty as hell. I pursued Ruth and wouldn't give up. But I don't want to hurt anybody. It was something that, after all, I simply couldn't help, we couldn't help. And, God, I wouldn't have missed it for the world! Quit that damn grinning, Hal!"

Marv put this conversation out of his mind for the rest of the day, as the shop kept him occupied. He had decided to drop the price on the four-poster bed and as a result the customer network went into action. Someone came in and noted the lowered price and made a phone call. Next, her ex-boyfriend arrived to check the bed out, then he also made a phone call to a friend who had expressed interest in it. Marv had an idea what was going on, but stayed out of the way. When the day was done, the third customer in this network had bought the bed. Word gets out, Marv mused, when there are good deals in the antiques world.

Keith came in late in the day, looking for Jake. He seemed very upset about something and Marv asked if he could help.

Since no one else was close enough to overhear, Keith did not mince words. "That son of a bitch," Keith swore softly.

Marv's attention was alerted at once. "I think you may not be alone in that assessment," he agreed, "but what's he done?" He wanted to add "now," but refrained. "Let's find a quiet corner and you tell me about it," Marv suggested.

They settled themselves in Jake's area, the most private spot at the moment.

Keith said, "It makes me feel uncomfortable being among his things." He looked around at Jake's expensive Arts and Crafts pieces. "I understand you and Hal didn't know him all that well when you bought this place."

"If anyone knew him all that well. Very likely Annette didn't either," Marv added. "What we didn't know, we are all learning now. And it has something to do with money, we think."

"That's what it looks like," Keith agreed. "There's a piece of property Owen and I were planning to buy. Jake knew I wanted it. In fact, I had worked with him at first to try to put a deal together. He kept stalling and after a year I gave up on him and found another realtor. It's a real piece of history, an old CCC-built hunting camp hidden away up in the Nine Mountains area."

"I think I know the place you're talking about," Marv said with interest. "Is it the one with the stream dammed up to form a pond? It has stone cabins? Yes? It's famous! Gentlemen hunters used to come there from Philadelphia and they'd bring their own chef."

"I can believe it. We thought it would make a great summer camp, primarily for kids who have lost a parent, Owen and I, then we got Andy interested in it too. We all went out with our families and had a picnic there last weekend. Everyone was so enthusiastic and then this happened."

"What?" asked Marv.

"My realtor just informed me that Jake has bought up an option to get it himself. He said he'd sell it to me, but at an inflated price. That son of a bitch."

"What a nasty thing to do! I don't know if it's even legal, certainly it's unethical, if you had already started negotiations with him for it. What does your realtor say?"

"He was thoroughly disgusted. He's going to see if there are any loopholes. Then it's the real estate association's Board of Ethics. Damn! I'm sorry to dump this on you, Marv. But how can you be a partner with a guy like that?"

"I'm beginning to wonder myself. You haven't been able to talk to Jake, I take it. He's not at his office?"

"No, hasn't been in. Well, I'm going to track him down sooner or later. I haven't told the others yet. That's going to be grim." He paused. "I feel tainted sitting here."

Marv had to agree with that feeling. He asked, "You'll be graduating soon?"

"This coming weekend, and I start my new job too."

"I heard you'll be working at the university. Congratulations."

Keith thanked Marv, then went on, "So, this intervening time is when I'd like to pull things together on the property, as would everyone else."

"Look, Keith," said Marv, "let me or Hal know what happens. We're interested in what's going on and if there's any way we can help, we'd like to. I'm very much in favor of your getting that place. I've never seen it, only heard about it."

Keith said, "Thanks, Marv. Sorry again for getting carried away." He got up. "If we beat this s.o.b. at his own game, we'll have the next Cider Run Labor Day bash at the camp. Minus one."

After Keith left, Marv pondered Jake's strange dealings. What would cause him to act so unethically? Jake had gone to law school; surely he knew the consequences of such behavior. But that got Marv back to thinking about the consequences of his own behavior and right now he was, as he said to himself, too fresh from Ruth's bed to be rational. The thought of Ruth and last night came back to him. He sighed and it was overheard by Sally Ann, who was working the day with him.

"Honey," she said sympathetically, "I heard that sigh. You're worrying about money again, aren't you?"

"How did you guess?" Marv responded convincingly. "Hal just told us we need a new roof."

"Well," Sally Ann went on, "I've been doing a lot of thinking about Cider Run and our money problems. I may not know how to manage a business, but I do know I love Cider Run and I'd do anything for it."

"Just being here with your bright smile and knockout clothes and your wonderful collection of..." Marv searched for the words, "...color, verve and fun, you add so much zing to this place."

"You are sweet to say that, Marv," Sally Ann cooed, "but as I said, I've been thinking. What I want to do is be a silent partner. I think that's what it's called."

Marv started to interrupt, but Sally Ann silenced him with a determined shake of her platinum blond curls and a terribly earnest look. "No, I truly want to. You know, Fred left us so much money and we can spend it on anything we want, and Rosie and I would like to invest in the business. We just want it to be nice here and stay nice and we trust you to do the right things."

She finished and looked so pleased with herself, that Marv could only give her a big hug and a kiss on her pink-blushed cheek.

"Sally Ann, you are a jewel, an angel, a true princess. Hal and I accept your offer. I can't speak for Jake, as he's nowhere to be found, but we'll be more than happy to have you for a partner. And you don't have to be silent. You can speak up anytime you want to."

"Honey, I already do, speak up. But I'd just as soon no one else knew, at least for now. I wouldn't know how to *act* like a business partner, so I'd rather no one thought I *was* one."

Bless Sally Ann, thought Marv later, as he closed up the shop. He'd call Hal that evening and tell him the news. Jake. He'd have to be told too. Marv decided to let Hal handle that, preferably after he'd already left for Bucks County. He couldn't face another conversation with Jake right now. And for the time being they would keep Sally Ann's offer among themselves, as long as she was serious about being a silent partner. What a fine person Sally Ann was. He was even beginning to appreciate her taste, since he'd been so well-rewarded for giving Ruth the hankie. Ruth, he thought, where are you now? Are you thinking of me?

Marv continued to go around the shop, turning lights out. He stood for a while looking at Jake's things. Jake had brought in a few more pieces of early 1900s Craftsman furniture, a handsome Limbert oak server with a plate rail, and a double-door bookcase, which on closer inspection turned out to be Stickley Bros., and an Arts and Crafts daybed, oak, quarter-sawn, newly cushioned and upholstered in a loose-woven linen. Marv guessed they were from Jake's private collection. He must be selling off some of his own furniture and Marv wondered why. The pieces were all of the highest quality and design. Not surprisingly, the prices listed on the tags took Marv's breath away, but he was sure they would sell readily.

He thought about Keith too, and what would happen with the property. Keith was a veteran and Marv was pretty sure he was not one to take crap easily, which was what this double-dealing of Jake's certainly was. In a way, Marv wished he weren't leaving the next day, wondering as he did about what Jake was going to do, but he had promised Helen he'd be there and he had guilt enough where she was concerned. It wouldn't be all that pleasant in Bucks County, he guessed, but he'd find things to do and when he was able, he'd let his mind go back to Ruth.

Now as he stood in the shop, the lights mostly turned off, he felt uneasy. It was as if the disparity between the exultation from last night and the guilt for the coming week was beginning to take its toll on him. He decided to seek help.

"Jacob," Marv said, "have you got a minute?"

"Aye, Marv, all the time in the world. Ain't got much else going on."

"You're a good man, Jacob," said Marv. "I've been meaning to tell you."

"Now, that's right kindly an' so be you. I've got a hunch, though, you have landed yourself in a quandary like. You and that little gal, now, you two have bedded, am I right?"

Marv wondered where these quaint phrases came from, then remembered all the oral histories and primary source documents on Appalachia he'd studied doing historical research. Jacob may actually have been more Dutch-sounding than Pennsylvania Scots-Irish, but the dialect seemed to suit him.

"Blissfully so, Jacob," Marv sighed.

"I sure am relieved to hear tell of it. You was sufferin' somethin' awful last time we spoke."

"The thing is, as you know, I'm married, and despite the fact that Helen and I, well..." Even Jacob ought not to be burdened with this. "I'm feeling guilty about her."

"Maybe she don't care. Seems as though she acts that way, far as I can tell."

"I often think so, although that doesn't make me feel less guilty."

"There be times you just have to go along, leastways 'til you can settle things out like."

"Settle things out? You mean, make a break?"

"That's the way of it. You think you and that little gal can get on together? You know, can you keep her happy? That's what counts."

Marv was taken completely off guard by this astonishing insight. He had only been thinking about his own happiness, how happy Ruth made *him*! He hadn't even thought about making her happy, although she said he did. Jacob had raised the crucial point. Could he keep Ruth happy? There wasn't anything he could do now, nor had he been able for many years, to make Helen happy. He decided that from this time on he had a goal. To make Ruth happy, to be worthy of her, worthy of the happiness she gave him.

"Jacob, I don't know how to thank you. I've been a self-centered bastard ."

"No need to curse yourself out, Marv, and anyhow, you don't never know when someone might be listenin' in."

Marv looked around the shop, laughed, and said, "Good night, Jacob. I think I'm going to be all right now. And thank you for keeping an eye on us."

"I'm proud to help, Marv. Good night."

With a final pause in Ruth's area, he turned out the rest of the lights and left.

Marv drove to Bucks County the next morning. He had been looking forward to this time when he would be alone to think about Ruth and their night together and daydream a bit, but as he drove east, he found himself thinking instead about Jake. He had to admit that Jake was right about one thing. It was a small town and Marv knew hundreds of people. Nothing could be kept quiet. He remembered what Ruth had done in the past, escaped to Boston to meet her lover, and at the thought of the anonymous superintendent, Marv had a sudden and severe feeling of revulsion. Remind me in the future, he told himself, to avoid Boston like the plague. He had no wish to repeat a life of clandestine meetings, but what could they do? Jake: what a problem he was presenting. Maybe, thought Marv, I should turn the other cheek. Seriously. Maybe I should offer to help him out of whatever difficulties he's in and befriend him. I've been so preoccupied, I haven't thought about anyone else but myself and Ruth. And mostly about myself. But the conversation with Jacob had straightened him out, and he knew now how he intended to go on with Ruth.

Still, Jake was a concern. Helen just loves Jake, thought Marv. Jake could so easily gain her confidence. Well, nearly anyone could gain her confidence, except him. And, he told himself, I've certainly earned that vote of no confidence. His thoughts ran around, from Ruth to Jake to Helen. Jake could cause a terrific amount of mischief or worse. He would have to decide what to do about Jake when he got back.

Chapter 26

Marv had been right. Jake could cause all sorts of mischief. As it turned out, Hal was next to find himself on the receiving end of Jake's unpredictable behavior. Hal and Sylvie had gone to a sale earlier in the spring and bought several pieces of furniture. One, an oak library table, had a large, rather garish tile glued down on the top, probably, Sylvie figured, to cover an ink stain. The auctioneer thought it could be removed if someone wanted to refinish the top and then, he declared, "It will make a right sweet piece." Sylvie worked on it and finally got the tile loose, but the back of it was slightly defaced. However, because it was unusual looking, she brought it into the shop and put a price of $50 on it.

Jake, coming back to the shop in the evening, saw it and put a HOLD tag on it. It wasn't until the next day, when Sylvie was there, that Jake was able to talk to her about it.

"Do you want that tile, Jake?" Sylvie asked. "It may have the potter's mark on the back, but the glue made a mess and I didn't take the time to try to clean it up. You can have it for $35 if you want."

"No, Sylvie, it's quite interesting and I don't think that would be fair. Even $50 is a little low. I'm sure it's worth over $100. Why don't I give you $65 for it?" Jake offered.

"That's awfully nice of you, Jake, seeing as how you'll have to do some work on it." Sylvie was a furniture person; pottery was not her forte. And the tile was really pretty ugly, she thought. It was black and blue with lightning bolts and the word "JAZZ" in twisted letters. She was glad not to have to look at it anymore.

Jake, on the other hand, knew pottery, especially this piece. It appeared two days later in his area, cleaned up and displayed in a plate stand on the mantelpiece, with a tag that read, "Rare, high-glaze Cowan Pottery plaque, designed by Viktor Schreckengost, c. 1931 $850 Firm."

Although Sylvie did not complain, Hal was incensed when he found out what Jake had done and confronted him immediately. "You were treacherous to take advantage of Sylvie like that, Jake. This is not how our dealers treat each other, to blatantly deceive and profit from them in such an unfair way."

"If you'd bothered to do a bit of research, you could have found out about it. I'm just more informed, that's all," said Jake in a condescending tone. "Are you going to tell me next that I shouldn't bid against you at an auction if we both want the same thing?"

Jake must have made some phone calls to potential buyers, including members of the university's art department, because several people came in specifically to see it and the tile was sold for the asking price within the week.

Hal felt burned. He was angry at Jake and, at least until he got over it, wanted to avoid him. As a result, he kept postponing informing Jake about Sally Ann's offer, which he and Marv had already accepted. Serves Jake right, Hal thought, to be cut out of the loop. He did, however, tell Sally

Ann how happy he and Marv were to have her as a partner, and could see that it pleased her very much.

May had started out warm and fair but as it continued, clouds began to build. Richard, coming in to work at the shop on Monday, announced to Elaine that the atmosphere was oppressive.

"It is now that you're here," quipped Elaine.

Richard chose to overlook this remark. "And just where is everybody?" he asked. "We usually have dealers all over the place, hanging out, eager to swap stories and brag, show off, complain, gossip, make nuisances of themselves. Has Cider Run become passé, are we out of fashion?"

"You are, Richard," responded Elaine, predictably. "I've been out of fashion for so long I'm back in. That's what Clair has told me. She says if I were to show up in New York, I'd be followed around and interviewed."

"Why? As having survived with your obnoxious habit for so long?"

Elaine was unruffled. "It's my late-Fifties-early-Sixties style, so she says. It's extremely chic right now."

"Well, you've always looked very Peck & Peck to me, but I'd hardly say that's a compliment. But again, where is everyone?"

Elaine counted on her fingers. "Marv and Helen are in Bucks County. Ruth is in Maine or some such place. Emmy and Charles have gone to Sweden to pick up their new Volvo. Grace and Frank are at the Finger Lakes getting their summer home in shape. Andy has already been in this morning and gone. Sally Ann called to say she'd be in soon and could she bring some doughnuts? Laurel is doubtless at home playing with the baby. Owen is at the high school teaching ungrateful adolescents. I don't know where Keith is, or Jake. Cora worked yesterday and is on again tomorrow, so I imagine she's home with her feet up today. Hal is doing whatever it is that engineers do. Sylvie is most likely in her workshop, up to her elbows in that beastly furniture solvent, or has she gone to pick up their daughter from college? And Clair is in the kitchen making coffee. Have I missed anyone?"

"That was amazing, Elaine, given your age and the ravages over time of cigarette smoke on what's left of your brain cells."

"Coffee?" asked Clair, coming up with a full pot, just as Elaine threw a copy of *Antiques Weekly* at Richard.

Clair was filling in for Emmy, as well as being available for any others who needed someone to work a day for them. She was happy to do it, as her other part-time jobs were not demanding at present. She was also happy at Cider Run in general. Being around other dealers and interacting with customers in the capacity of a professional antiques dealer gave her a great deal of satisfaction. It was also at the shop that she would see Jake.

Clair had only admiration for Jake. He had been so kind to her, had helped her get started, given her guidance on buying and pricing, and his advice was always right on target. To Clair, Jake was the shining star of Cider Run and whenever he was there, she watched and listened and learned.

Most of what she learned was beneficial and useful, mainly knowledge of antiques outside her area of expertise. Jake knew about so many things. She waited hopefully for him to ask her again to look at his artwork, and in the meantime she assembled some museum catalogs and reference books in order to be better prepared.

But she also noticed other things having to do with Jake, such as the barely disguised contempt he manifested towards Richard and the way Keith scowled when Jake was mentioned. Jake seemed to rub Ruth the wrong way too and Hal was lately upset with him. Clair didn't ask herself why. She thought Jake was such a superior individual that others must have difficulty dealing with him. Nor did she question the innuendos about Laurel's baby.

And Clair was out-and-out vulnerable. She had been recently unlucky in love and had been hurt. She left New York not only because of disappointments in her job, but also because the city was permeated with bitter memories of her ex-boyfriend. The brief time with Noel was stimulating and fun, but he was so far away and, though they corresponded online, it wasn't the same. Jake was so *present*, he was here, loomed larger than life for her. If there was an operatic aria playing, he sang along with the tenor and she let herself imagine he was singing to her. When she thought of what he had said to her about leading him "astray," she felt weak in the knees, although she couldn't make herself believe that he meant it seriously.

But Clair, if she wanted more from Jake, didn't know exactly what. Making love with him? She had thought about that often enough when she looked at him. He was downright gorgeous. His smile, his eyes, the strength and grace she saw in him. But his wanting her was way beyond her dreams. He was so experienced, so sophisticated. What would he ever see in her? Maybe when she was able to help him in return for all the help he had given her, she would be more of an equal, could feel more on a par with him. Clair knew she was young for him, but decided not to let that get in the way of a relationship she hoped to establish.

That afternoon, Jake had come in for a few minutes and had a private conversation with Richard. As he was leaving, he caught sight of Clair.

"Clair! Just the person!" he exclaimed.

"You leave Clair alone, Jake," Elaine warned. "You're not to be trusted."

"Why? She's practically an urban guerrilla. Look at that outfit she's wearing."

It was true. Clair had on one of her black T-shirts and her olive drab cargo pants with half a dozen pockets. She immediately wished she'd worn something else.

"Clair," Jake went on, "can you stay after the shop closes? I need to talk to you."

Clair agreed readily and tried not to look too eager.

"Fine," said Jake. "I'll see you later," and he left.

"I hope for your sake you have some urban weapons in those pockets," Elaine remarked.

For the rest of the day Clair hid her excitement as best she could, but Elaine and Richard were aware that something was happening and both of them were concerned about Clair's ability to hold her own with Jake.

"Should we stick around?" Richard suggested quietly to Elaine, "or come back, saying we'd forgotten something?" Richard would have liked to thwart Jake, to get back at him for the slighting and insulting remarks he had made, but he didn't want Clair involved in his tactics.

Elaine shook her head. "Clair's had a year to watch Jake's modus operandi. If she isn't wise to him now, she'll just have to learn from experience. But I will have a little talk with her before I leave. Stay out of the way, Richard."

"Ooh, girl talk. Can't I listen?"

"And what good do you think it'll do you?"

Right before Elaine left for the day, as they were standing at the front door of the shop, she said to Clair, "You know, I might make disparaging remarks now and then about Jake, his motives, trusting him and so forth."

"That's all right, Elaine," Clair responded sweetly.

"Well, I want you to know I mean every word of it."

Clair opened her eyes wide.

"So, be on your toes, kiddo. That's all. See you later," said Elaine, and Clair locked the door behind her.

While this piece of cryptic advice was not completely lost on Clair, she didn't worry over what Elaine had said. She had no reason to feel anything other than confidence in Jake as far as her own experiences with him went. However, what did bother her was that he had seemed more distracted of late. She hoped she could learn the reason and maybe even help to alleviate the problem. It was more than wanting to give him something back and prove that she had worth for him. Being around him this past year had given her some insights, and they had to do with a quality he had of seeming to be almost driven in what he did. It was as if he were operating at a higher level of activity than anyone else in all dimensions—mental, physical, social—but under a kind of compulsion. Maybe she was mistaken; at any rate, she would probably never know. But she readily admitted to herself that she was fascinated by him.

With anticipation of what Jake wanted to see her about dominating her thoughts, Clair worked in her area, making room for a new display she planned to bring in the next day. She looked at the time. It was close to 7:00, then 7:30. She wondered if she were being naïve to wait. How long should she give him? It was getting late, she was getting hungry.

326

Elaine's words about not trusting Jake came into her mind. Elaine may be right, she thought.

About a minute later, Jake breezed in the front door, saying, "Supper!" as he handed Clair a stack of take-out cartons. Then he went back outside with the furniture dolly, returning with a large blanket chest, which he unloaded in his area. After he had relocked the door and stowed the dolly behind the front counter, he came back to Clair, still standing where he left her, holding what he had given her, dazed by the whirlwind of his movements.

He laughed at her seeming immobility. "Now, shall we eat?" he asked and, putting his arm around her, ushered her into the kitchen.

With a practiced hand he laid out dinner for two on the table. There were slices of artichoke quiche, a salad of Romaine lettuce and tomatoes with an olive tapenade, a baguette of French bread, and a small carton of strawberries, about which he said, "I'm afraid they're still California berries, but at least they're organic." He got a bottle of Chardonnay from the refrigerator and began to take out the cork. "You didn't notice that I brought this in earlier," he said with a pleased smile.

Clair was completely in awe, she was floored. She was so impressed with Jake that the rest of the world simply ceased to be.

"Clair, find us some glasses, will you?" Jake asked, setting the cork aside.

She mustered all her self-command to appear composed as she brought down two glasses and, seating herself, she said gratefully, "Jake, this is lovely. You are so kind." Stop there, she told herself. Don't gush.

"It's all part of your compensation. Remember, I asked you to have a look at my artwork? I've brought some things in and we can go over them tonight. But first we need to fortify ourselves." He raised his glass. "To a successful evening. And I mean that in every way possible."

"I'll do my best," Clair promised.

"I'm sure you will. I'm counting on you, Clair. How does that feel? To know you have the power to make or break me? To lift me up to the heights or bring me down to the depths?"

Clair thought, what do I say to that? She did not feel at all equal to his level of conversational wit and playfulness, but she could meet him with sincerity, and hoped she didn't sound too mundane. "This is delicious, Jake. It couldn't be better or more welcome. It's been a long day."

"And I need you to be sharp, on your toes, discerning. Have some more wine. I may change my mind and not want you to be too alert." He gave her one of his beguiling smiles and Clair smiled back.

How could anyone be more engaging, she thought, more desirable? She tried not to gaze at him all the time, but it was difficult. He was wearing khakis and a madras shirt in a soft blue and grey plaid. It was open at the throat and she was aware of his pulse, his breathing. She took her eyes away with effort.

Clair managed to meet his repartee while they ate dinner and gradually was put at ease, realizing that Jake had done so intentionally. She admired him all the more for that. He did know how to please a woman, she reflected. He obviously had intended to please her and she felt almost humbled. I will rise to the occasion, she told herself.

"Tell me about the things you brought in," she said, not wishing to make the same mistake she'd once made, talking about herself. "When will I get a look at them?"

"They can wait. I'd rather look at you," he returned, lifting his glass to her.

She said with a smile, "So the real purpose of this dinner is?"

"To butter you up, put you off your guard, win you over."

"You're very adept at it. I couldn't be treated more royally."

"Whatever it takes," Jake said in honeyed tones.

Clair laughed, delighted, and was sure Jake knew how delighted she was with him.

They had the strawberries, dipping them in brown sugar. Then Jake produced a piece of very rich, very dark chocolate cake, which they shared.

"You've overwhelmed me, you know," Clair admitted.

"That was the general idea," Jake said smoothly.

He made a pot of coffee and poured two cups for them. They took the coffee out to his area and he seated himself on the daybed, indicating to her to sit next to him. Clair looked unsure, afraid she might spill coffee on the linen-covered cushions.

"Don't worry," Jake responded to her hesitation. "It's to be used, by us or someone else, although if anyone wants to buy it, they're going to be in for sticker shock."

Clair looked at the price tag, which gave a paragraph of information about the designer, company, style, dates, and origin of the individual piece and ended with the price, $4500. She emitted a little whistle of exclamation.

He laughed, "That comment was perfection! I feel I've priced it high enough."

"In that case, since I have your confidence, bring on the Renaissance or whatever you have hidden away for me to see," she said boldly, sitting down by him.

"But have I got you properly in the mood? I'm not so sure. I need to have you entirely in my corner on this."

"I thought you wanted an unbiased opinion," Clair pointed out.

"And I do," Jake insisted, "but I want your understanding too. That's a very important part of it. Do you want to look first or hear the story first?"

"There's a story? Just let me see one or two things, so I can get an inkling of what we're talking about. Would that be all right?" she asked imploringly.

"When you look at me like that, Clair, I would do anything for you," Jake answered, further bringing her into his spell.

He got up and opened the lid of the blanket chest he had just brought in. It was oak, Mission style, nearly sixty inches long and quite deep. He reached in and took out a painting, wrapped in the blue padding they all used and, unwrapping it, turned it so that Clair could see it. She stared and her breath caught in her throat.

"Tell me about it," Jake instructed, his voice and his look now very serious.

Clair was stunned. She took the painting with its glowing, jewel-bright colors and held it in both hands, studying it. "Flemish, Ambrosius Benson," she said in a hushed voice. "Oil on wood panel, about 1530. *Mater Dolorosa*." She looked up at him. "But, Jake, this is a painting that was ..." she started to say, distress in her eyes, entreating him not to make her commit herself further.

He gently took it out of her hands and put it back in the chest. "You see the dilemma then," he said. Clair was quiet and Jake went on. "That's what I thought you'd find. It couldn't be a fake, could it?"

Clair shook her head. "No, I don't think so. I think it's... it's the real one," she said in a whisper.

He brought out a Russian Orthodox icon, which Clair turned over in her hands, then held up to the light. She said, "I've seen this somewhere. I think it's in a guidebook I have at home."

"Can you bring the book in?" he asked eagerly. "I'd like to find out more about it."

"But I don't think you are going to want to know the answer," Clair responded.

"And this?" asked Jake, who was holding a triptych, its three-paneled miniature paintings outlined in gold.

"Yes, that too," Clair acknowledged.

"All right, one more thing for now, and we'll wait until you bring me your reference books."

He took out a small canvas, about 24 by 36 inches, clearly a portion of a larger oil painting, but still big enough to be seen for what it was. It held one figure, the young and beautiful angel of God, his dark curls framing the boyishly innocent and expressive face, rendered so sensitively by a master whose own homosexual yearnings had taught him about male beauty. His head turned slightly, the angel is looking poignantly at someone on his left, someone who had been painted on the other half of the canvas. But that half of the painting was no longer there.

Unmistakable.

"Caravaggio," Clair murmured, and closed her eyes.

Chapter 27

Jake carefully put the canvas back in the chest, as Clair sat mute, in pain. "You see, Clair, why I want you on my side?" he entreated. "I need to know I can trust you. Now, do you want to hear the story?"

She nodded, unable to speak.

He sat down again next to her. "Do you remember that warehouse in Amsterdam I told you about? There was an annex in another location, and in the annex there was a special locked room, and in the room were these," Jake pointed to the contents of the chest, "and things like these. They were for sale. I bought. I didn't know where they came from and I didn't ask. After I got back, I was contacted by a dealer who said he had more, so I went to meet him in Philadelphia and bought more things. Some were better than others, much better. Those I kept, the rest I sold. You probably remember the small statues and other religious artifacts from Europe that I brought in. You even helped authenticate them. They might have been obtained legally or they might not have."

Clair had found her voice and said, alarmed, "Jake, but how could you, knowing?"

"But I didn't know, that's just it. I believed what I was told, that churches sold things to make money, and I was simply redistributing them; otherwise, they'd go to collectors in Europe or Asia. The prices they could command here were good. And I was buying to resell...at first." He opened his hands in an appealing gesture. "Even if I suspected that they had not been gotten legitimately, I wasn't in a position to know for sure. After all, the monasteries and churches of Europe have been looted thousands of times over the centuries." He paused a moment, as if considering whether he should go on. "But after I realized what I had, I wanted more. Then something happened. My first contact disappeared and the person who took his place had mixed in some fakes. Even I could tell that. So I needed you to corroborate what I thought, that these were real. And you have. Thank you."

"Real and stolen," said Clair, in a very hushed voice. "From museums all over Europe. The Hermitage for one. There's a listing of what was stolen from there."

"Which you'll show me?" Jake asked.

"Yes," she affirmed, "and then we'll have to decide what you should do."

"Then I'll decide, Clair."

She looked up at him sharply.

Jake said, "Do you know what it's like to own a Caravaggio? There are more like what I've shown you. There's a little Canaletto; I can hardly take my eyes off it."

Clair drew her breath in and looked at Jake in disbelief. "From the museum in Venice?" Part of her job at the Metropolitan had been to keep up with missing and stolen artwork and by habit she had continued to check the websites after she left.

Jake continued, "Do you think I knew, or cared, where it came from when I bought it? It was later that I researched what I had, as best I could. All of its history, all of its beauty are mine now. To possess something that graced the private chapel of a palace for close to three hundred years: the feeling is incomparable."

He put his hand over hers and she felt herself grow rigid.

"You haven't heard the whole story yet," he told her.

"I don't know if I want to," Clair said in a distressed voice. "The Caravaggio: it's one of the studies for *The Sacrifice of Isaac*. They cut up the canvas, cut off Abraham and Isaac!" She looked at him and this time tears sprang, stinging, in her eyes.

Jake put his arm around her and, to her horror, she began to cry in earnest. This is not what I want to do, she thought to herself, but could not stop, feeling the sadness, the pathos of the lost half of the painting and the outrage at such wanton destruction of a masterpiece. She stood up, reached into one of her many pockets, got a tissue and blew her nose. "I'm sorry," she apologized. "I fell apart." Slowly, she sat back down. "Jake," she said. "I can't let you do this. I can't let you be, be...You're receiving stolen goods. Do you know what can happen if you're caught?"

"Do I know they're stolen? Have I proof? And what makes you think I'd get caught? Are you planning to turn me in?" Jake asked with a slightly amused look.

She didn't say "no," as Jake had apparently expected. She sat staring straight ahead, tremendously upset, already feeling implicated in some corrupt European art fraud. She wanted Jake to refute it all, to make it aboveboard. Maybe she should hear what else he had to say. But she was afraid to hear more because the more she knew, the more she felt complicit in the thefts.

Her silence must have worried Jake, because he said, "Why don't you wait in your judgment of me until we have a look at your reference materials and you see what else I have? Maybe you're mistaken and they are only copies. What do you say?" He gave her that appealing look he had and Clair felt herself relenting. "There's some wine left in the kitchen. Bring out the bottle and our glasses and we'll talk about something else."

What hold had he on her? She was confused and, even though she was thinking clearly about the artwork, he still could elicit the responses of wanting to help him, wanting to please him, simply wanting him. There wasn't a question in her mind of not doing things for him. As he had been talking with her, Clair had begun to shift away from thinking about herself and her relationship with him, to thinking more solely about him. And from this arose a feeling of compassion for him, of realizing there was something troubling, something haunted, as Owen had earlier observed, in Jake's deep, beautiful blue-grey eyes.

Glad for a break from the tension, Clair got up and went into the kitchen for the wine. She felt the weight of what he had told her, felt the heaviness on her as if it were her burden. He *had* burdened her with it. And she knew that she was more and more drawn to him. But she had stated her opposition, had told him it was wrong, and had not been afraid to do so.

When she returned, Jake had turned out all the lights except for a few lamps in his area. It had gone dark outside and the soft glow of the lamps changed the mood from confrontational to compatible.

Jake filled their glasses. "Clair, you are brave and true, and I drink to you," he said graciously.

She shook her head. "Not really. I think you're the one who is brave. You were willing to take a chance."

"Take a chance?" he repeated.

"Yes. With me. With yourself. Letting yourself get in so deeply, get so emotionally attached to these works of art, letting them affect you like this. Something similar happened to me once. I fell in love with an impressionist painting when I first went to work at the museum. There wasn't a day that I didn't stand in front of it, captivated. Of course, I never had a chance to buy it or I might have, just like you. And not asked any questions."

Jake seemed to digest this for a moment. Then he said, "And how am I taking a chance with you?"

"You don't know what I'll do. I could tell you lies. I could say the paintings are real when they're not. Or I could tell you they're fakes when they're genuine."

"Why would you do that?"

"To make it right, so you'd give them back, get rid of them."

Jake laughed. "You're far too honest to do that. Honest and conscientious, but I think you're pliant too. "

"Or I could call someone I know in New York."

He gave her a serious look. "But you wouldn't, because of the way you feel about me."

And it's true, Clair thought to herself, and he knows it. She found herself asking rhetorically, "And how do I feel about you?"

Jake got up, gave a little shrug, and said, "I'm going to tell you something. It has to do with the Caravaggio and it has to do with me."

Clair said hesitatingly, "I wondered about that, seeing as how you feel about Richard, that is, about his being gay."

Jake sat down in the Morris chair facing her. "I was brought up in the Catholic Church. I think everyone at Cider Run knows that."

"Yes, it seems to be common knowledge," Clair agreed.

"I was a choir boy. Is that common knowledge too?"

"Well, Mrs. Greene, I mean Emmy, did mention something about that."

"And did she say anything else?"

"Only that she thinks you have a lovely voice and I couldn't agree more," Clair confessed.

Jake acknowledged this with a nod and went on, "I grew up in Pittsburgh and my best friend and I were both in the church choir. There was weekly choir practice. I liked it well enough. He hated it, hated to go. I couldn't figure it out. He and I were very close friends, but he wouldn't talk to me about why he had such an aversion to being at the church. One day, when we were twelve, he was supposed to be over at my house in the afternoon and he didn't come. I went to his house to find him, and I did. He had committed suicide. He had hanged himself in the garage." Jake stopped and put his hand over his eyes.

"Dear God," Clair whispered.

"He left a note, to me. In it he said he had been molested and taken advantage of for years by one of the priests, and he couldn't live with it anymore." Jake raised his eyes to Clair. "But I have lived with it all my life now, the knowledge, the image I have of him...hanging there. If I am horrified by homosexuality, that's where it came from."

Clair wanted to protest, to say that consenting adults was different altogether, but she could not. Jake, she could tell, was hurting still. The effort required to talk about it must have brought back the old pain and cost him dearly. She went over to him.

He looked up at her. "So I guess it's somehow ironic that I have a Caravaggio, isn't it?"

She stood close to him, her heart going out to him. "Jake, it's just a painting, just a fragment. It doesn't matter."

"No. It's revenge."

He got up, poured the last of the wine out, took her hand and led her back to the daybed and they sat down again side by side. He reached up and turned off the lamp nearest, finished his wine and put the glass down.

"Come, Clair," he said, turning to her. "Come take these thoughts out of my mind. Take my mind off everything but you."

With the most delicate of touches, Jake put his hand under her chin and gently brought her face to his, her lips to his. She had no idea what he would be like, but was not prepared for such gentleness, such unhurried ease, so soft, so tender a kiss, the merest token of what was to come. He was unlike all the boys she had known, who were always in a rush, so eager. This kiss, his touch, were in a class apart.

Hardly conscious of what she was doing, Clair leaned back ever so slightly so she could savor the moment, savor him, could take in and behold what would, unbelievably, be hers. She put her hands on his shoulders, and slowly ran them down his arms, feeling the hardness of muscle, the warmth of his skin, the soft blond hair on his forearms, then continued all the way to his fingertips. These arms, she thought with wonder, will be around me, these hands will be on me. He did not move, but sat still, letting her do what she wanted. Almost in a trance, she unbuttoned his shirt and laid two fingers at the hollow of his throat, where her eyes had rested again and again during the evening. She looked into his face. Was this true? Was she really here with him? She placed the palms of her hands on his chest and felt his heart beating, not racing, just beating. She wanted to cry. He was so perfect.

Jake took his time, gently and without haste, bringing her lips to his again, still with tenderness, but gradually becoming deeper, warmer, then slipping his hand around her back and guiding her down on the daybed's cushioned surface. So easily, every movement graceful and paced, it was as if he had all the time in the world and was content for this to last as long as possible, as long as he wanted.

Clair had never had anyone like him, so able to make her respond, to want more and more of him. She acknowledged to herself that it was he who was in control, but he was quietly and deliberately leading her into an increasing awareness of him. Clair could only think how exciting he was, how much he had to teach her and, finally, that she must have him.

He held her so carefully, so gently, and when he entered her, let her have full measure, before he at last gave in to his own release.

There was a second bottle of wine that Jake had brought earlier in the day, and he got it now and poured two glasses for them while Clair made a trip to the restroom. She looked at herself in the mirror, her face flushed and her eyes luminous, and knew Jake had won a victory over her former misgivings. But she had been victorious too. He had been hers, at least for a while, and he had been exquisite.

They shared the wine and Jake said simply, "Thank you, Clair."

"Why do men thank women?" Clair asked abruptly, confident with the wine and the moment.

Jake threw back his head and laughed at this rather charming bit of naiveté. "So they'll feel appreciated, young lady! Would you want to make love again with someone who didn't appreciate you?"

"No, what I meant was, I should thank you, shouldn't I? You gave me yourself too." She wanted to add, "And it was glorious," but kept herself in check.

"In fact, tonight I have given you more than you know. I have trusted you with my honor, my freedom." He gazed thoughtfully at her. "I do have your heart and mind, don't I?"

"Jake," she said, still glowing from his touch, "can you doubt it? Oh, gosh!" she exclaimed. "I can't get pregnant, though!"

"You don't have to worry about that with me. I had a vasectomy. I don't need or want a family. My brother has children enough to spare. Brian has all the progeny any family could need."

"But didn't...?" Clair wasn't sure what she wanted to ask.

"A little joke on Annette, who thought that by getting pregnant she could keep me. And another joke on her is that all the family property goes to my brother and his children. She can't touch it."

Clair wasn't sure she should be privy to this information, but was flattered that Jake confided things to her. "What else do you want me to know?" she asked.

"That's all for now, child," he said in a light tone, but he looked at her as if she were anything but a child. "Tomorrow night then, Clair? If you would bring your references, whatever you have. I'll be here, but it will have to be late, say, closer to 11:00. Is that all right?"

"And in return?" Clair asked, matching the light tone and the underlying seriousness.

"You get me," he promised.

Chapter 28

But the next morning, that Tuesday morning, came like a reckoning for Clair. When she first awoke, she lay dreamily immersed in remembering Jake's lovemaking, his gentle, unhurried, almost restrained, yet deeply arousing lovemaking. But other thoughts began to intrude themselves and became more and more insistent, until she had to look at them. They had been there all along and she knew now she had to deal with them.

Her initial concern was about the artwork and what she should do in regard to it. She got out one of her references, *Treasures of the Hermitage*, and almost immediately found icons and triptychs strikingly similar to the ones Jake had shown her. She looked at the listing she'd downloaded some time ago on stolen items and they were among them. She knew when she checked on the Caravaggio and the Benson she would find she'd made no mistake and they were missing from museums in Rome and Madrid, respectively. When she saw him tonight, what should she say?

Then, in spite of the lingering aura of his charm and the desire he had generated in her, she thought of Elaine's warning. How much could she believe of what he told her? That story about his friend committing suicide: it clearly had the intended effect on her. She had fallen directly into his arms after that, when before she had her back up about the artwork. Clair had to smile at herself. She would have fallen into his arms happily after that heavenly supper he had given her. But was that tragic story true, or was it only a ruse, intended to elicit her sympathy for him and justify what he had done?

And, finally, there was the vasectomy. What a horrible thing to do to Annette, who was surely of an age when she would soon not have the option of pregnancy. That he was capable of almost monstrous cruelty toward her bothered Clair in a distressing, disquieting way. Yet, was he telling the truth about it? That could concern her very personally, but how to find out? Medical records were private. There might be a way, though. There was Laurel's husband, Joe. She decided to try him and called the hospital, leaving word for him to call her. Then she tackled the other problem, Jake's childhood friend's suicide.

When Clair first started college, she had signed up for a double room in the dorm and was assigned a roommate at random. Sheree, as it turned out, had done the same thing, which was gutsy on her part, as it was a time when African-Americans seemed much more comfortable with each other. One white girl and one black girl moved in together and hit it off from the beginning. They became best friends and went on to share a room until graduation. When Sheree got married, Clair was one of her bridesmaids.

Sheree North. Clair remembered Sheree telling her how North was the name one of her ancestors had chosen for the family when they left the South after the Civil War, heading for Pennsylvania and a new life. Now, Sheree was absolutely rolling in money, as her husband played professional football for the Steelers. But she still liked working at her job on the *Pittsburgh Gazette*.

Clair reached her at the newspaper office and they had a nice catch-up conversation, then Clair asked if she could do some research for her and told Sheree what she was trying to find out.

"He's thirty-eight or thirty-nine now and this happened when he was twelve, so it would have been about twenty-six years ago."

"You got it, babe," said Sheree, lapsing into the way they used to talk to one another. "But, you know, if it was suicide, and you say he was Catholic, they'd never mention that. So what I'll be able to find is probably only an obit. A twelve-year-old boy. Sometime in the period of 26 to 28 years ago."

"Sheree, you're the greatest. Just whenever you get around to it."

"Hey, pretty girl, I'd do anything for my old college roommate. So, how's your love life?"

Clair laughed, "Nonexistent, until last night. Then it was so unspeakably wonderful I could hardly believe it."

"Now wait a minute, you don't mean with the guy who's nearly forty?"

"That's the one. The only thing I can figure is, by the time they're that old they know what they're doing. They have all the moves down."

Sheree said, "You go, girl! I'll get back to you."

Clair spent some time online looking up references and it wasn't until afternoon, when she was getting ready to go to Cider Run with the things she was taking in for her area, that she got a call back from Joe Fisher.

"Clair," he said, "I've never thanked you properly for working those days for Laurel when Ben was born. We both appreciated it very much, but we were so tired all the time, I'm afraid we forgot our manners."

"Don't give it a second thought," Clair answered. "I was glad to do it and please tell Laurel to call me anytime she needs me. Right now, however, it's you I need."

"How can I help?" he asked, a little warily, Clair thought, as doctors sometimes seem to be. She plunged in, though, trying to word the request in a way as uncharged with emotion as possible.

"It's about Jake Gennari," she started to say, but Joe interrupted her.

"If it's what he's been implying, I've heard about it," Joe replied in an angry voice.

Uh, oh, thought Clair, but she went ahead, "I didn't call about that, but it could be a part of things." She wasn't sure how to handle this terribly sensitive subject.

"Don't get me wrong, Clair. I'm not mad at you. He's the one who's responsible for this rumor. It is absolutely false and exceedingly unfair to Laurel."

And to you too, thought Clair, and I halfway credited it. She went on, "I guess what I want you to do might be unethical. But Jake told me he'd had a vasectomy and I really need to learn if it's true. If there is any way you could find out if, and when, I'd be very grateful."

Joe's tone changed to one of interest and determination. "You aren't the only one who'd be glad to know that little piece of information. Don't worry. I'll find out. ASAP. I have a score to settle with him."

It was overcast, the sky beginning to darken, but it had not yet started to rain. Clair brought her things into the shop—a box of summer garden party hats, which she arranged on a wooden hat rack, and a white wicker-framed oval mirror which she hung nearby. She also had brought a white wicker dressing table with a matching seat, and when everything was placed, her area looked fresh and bright and ready for summer.

She paused for a minute by Jake's area. The large oak chest was closed and what looked to be an altar cloth was laid on top. Two Russian Orthodox icons and a triptych were on the mantel, although not the ones she had seen last night. She looked at the daybed and closed her eyes briefly, remembering last night. Then she went to the front counter.

Cora was working the day, filling in for the absent Grace. She was scanning "Garage Sales" in the *Martensdale Times* classified section and making notes. Hal was there as well, taking the place of Sylvie who had gone to pick up their older daughter from college.

Cora told Clair, "Hal's been worried about the roof all day. It's like Marv used to be about the gravel in the parking lot."

"If it rains as hard as predicted tonight, we'll all be worried about the roof. And the gravel parking lot could be a mess too," Hal said with a gloomy expression.

"Are we going to get the roof fixed soon?" Clair asked.

Hal's face relaxed. "Yes, actually, we have roofers scheduled."

"Then our money troubles aren't as bad as we thought?"

"Haven't you heard? Well, there's a little surprise that will be revealed shortly. But, yes, we can afford to get the roof fixed and even pave the parking lot." Hal looked happier and Clair wondered where the financial transfusion had come from.

"Do you know?" she asked Cora, when Hal had gone off to help a customer.

"Some lovely person has come through. It's one of us, but they're not saying who it is yet."

Clair felt her mood lighten, knowing that the shop was no longer having money problems and as she drove home, she realized how down she had been all day. It certainly wasn't from the aftermath of making love. That sent a thrill all through her and the thought of Jake again tonight, well, it was too much to even consider while negotiating the busy Martensdale Pike. No, she had felt down because she had doubted Jake and doubted him so much that she had acted on her suspicions. She had set things in motion to find out if he had told her the truth. It was as if she had betrayed his trust, after he had trusted her and given of himself so freely last night: first supper, then unburdening his past, then the inexpressible delight of his lovemaking. So far she had not betrayed him about the artwork. What to do about that was still to be faced. Should she risk his displeasure by being firm about it, or should she make more of an effort to understand his position? Either way would not be easy. And what should she wear this evening to look older and more sophisticated?

Marv's outlook began to improve as he drove back to Marten County. Being in the eastern part of the state had turned out better than he'd anticipated. In the first place, Ruth was away herself, so he wouldn't have been able to be with her all week anyway. Then, he had gone to Philadelphia for a day and met with the customer who had the 19th century diaries. The result was that the diaries were now with Marv and they had agreed that he'd edit them, write a preface and prepare them for publication. It was a rewarding project and the sort of thing he had missed since he'd retired. Also, more immediate, there was, covered by a tarp in the back of his truck, the most beautiful early Bucks County corner cupboard, a real steal, and with its original red buttermilk paint. Fortunately it came apart, so could be put in the shop without difficulty. All this and Helen had decided to stay on with their daughter for a few more days. Ruth should be home by now and, then, happiness. He'd be with her tonight.

He'd thought about her constantly and again he worried, had she regrets? What in the world were they going to do, assuming she hadn't already decided to move back to New England? But the thought of seeing her again was so delicious, so heady, that he felt a glow of joy in spite of his fears.

He had also come to a decision regarding Jake. He'd talk to Jake as soon as he could and try to work something out with him, see what he could do to help him with whatever difficulties he was in, financial or otherwise. It wasn't buying Jake's silence about Ruth. It was in order to return to the friendly, easygoing relationship they used to enjoy, bring back the harmony to Cider Run and eliminate the unhealthy friction. Now that Sally Ann had put a substantial amount of money into the enterprise, they could afford to be less demanding on Jake and that should ease things.

He drove west into heavier skies and by the time he reached home, the rain had started. He pulled the truck into his garage and thought he'd better wait a while before taking the corner cupboard to the shop.

Ruth, having gotten back a few hours previously, was still at her brother's house after unloading Ruthie and her things. They'd had a leisurely trip, enjoying each other's company, seeing relatives and old friends, and buying antiques. It was good to get away, to get a little perspective on what Ruth recognized could be the start of something serious. But the perspective she had gained was only to realize how strongly she cared about Marv, how thankful she was that he had come into her life. While she was having supper with her brother and his family, she knew that she wouldn't want to leave Martensdale, nor would they want her to leave. But could she stay here, feeling as she did about Marv, feeling as they did about each other? It could become too painful, being around him and Helen. She put off going home, knowing she would either call him or he would call her, and then what? Would they be able to see each other? She longed to see him, a longing filled with anxiety.

She was due to work at the shop tomorrow and her car was loaded with things to take into her area. She would need help unloading them. That was enough of an excuse to call and if Helen answered, she'd be friendly and natural, even though one week ago she'd made love with her husband and wanted nothing more than to make love with him again. Life, she thought, may have spun out of control, but I am glad.

When she got home she methodically went through the messages on her answering machine, none critical until the last, which was Marv, who had called fifteen minutes before. The message was brief and to the point: "Call me, Ruth. I need you." There was no question in her mind of not calling him.

His words came with a rush. "Have you missed me? You've no idea how much I've missed you. Was the message I left too brash? Oh, no! Ruthie wasn't there with you, was she? Does she know? Ruth, may I come see you?"

Ruth was almost out of breath listening to him. "Helen's not there?" she ventured.

"She's staying with Shirley for another few days. You do want to see me, don't you?"

"Only for this entire week," she answered truthfully. It's both of us who need reassurance, she thought.

348

"In that case, I'll be there momentarily, or sooner," he said happily, then amended, "although I may stop by the shop for a minute first; is that all right? And one other thing, can I park in your garage? I have a rather nice piece of furniture in the back of the truck and I'd rather it didn't get ruined." That was only half of it; he'd tell her the rest later.

When Keith drove into the parking lot at Cider Run about 9:15 that evening, he was surprised to see other cars: Richard's, Hal's, one he didn't know. Jake's truck was not there, however, and he had come specifically to talk to him, Hal having told him earlier that Jake would be there. He unlocked the door and walked in to see Richard, standing still in the middle of the shop, listening intently. He could hear angry voices coming from the direction of the office in the back.

"What's up?" asked Keith.

Richard tilted his head toward the sound of the argument. "Hal and Jake. It's about the partnership. They want to add a partner and Jake's not too happy about having his share reduced. Something like that."

"I didn't see Jake's truck."

"He's parked it around back, must have been unloading something."

"I need to talk to him. I wonder how long they'll be at it?"

"Well, take a number," said Richard acidly. "We all want to talk to him. We're lining up here. Laurel's husband wants to talk to him too."

"I'll bet he does," Keith agreed.

Joe, who had been paged from the hospital and was on his phone by the front counter, came back and joined them.

He shook hands with Keith and asked if he had come in to work in his area.

"No, I have a bone to pick with Jake. I didn't realize we had a waiting list here."

"Keith, you too?" Joe remarked. "How many people has this guy managed to piss off?"

"Everyone he's ever come in contact with is my guess," Richard volunteered.

The voices in the back room had ceased and Hal came out. He stopped when he saw the others. "Damn, I wish Marv were here," he said. "Then at least it would be two against one. Well, I leave you to him."

"Not me," Richard said with a shake of his head. "It can wait. I don't have the stomach for any more shouting. I'll talk to him later." He made his goodbyes and left.

Hal went out next, locking the door. Keith turned to Joe, "Go and talk to him if you want. I can stay and I'll lock up after you leave."

"Thanks, Keith, but I have Laurel's key."

"In that case, I'll let you speak to him in private and I'll be back later," Keith offered.

"And if I wring his neck while you're gone, in spite of the Hippocratic Oath?"

"Then you'll deprive me of the satisfaction," Keith grinned.

Marv pulled into the Cider Run parking lot and noticed a car parked there that he didn't immediately recognize. He drove around back and saw Jake's truck parked near the kitchen entrance. It would be good to talk with Jake, he thought, get things straightened out. But he wasn't sure who was there with him and didn't want to take a chance of embarrassing someone. That would be like Jake, to have some assignation going on in the shop. Fine. Marv had far, far more enjoyable things to do. He'd see Jake later on tonight, if he could tear himself away from Ruth, or more likely tomorrow.

Clair got out of the shower, her mind still going over what to do about Jake's collection of stolen art. She was getting dressed when her mother came upstairs to let her know she'd had a phone call while she was in the bathroom.

"Do I need to call back?" Clair asked, anxious lest it be Jake saying he couldn't make it.

"No. It was Laurel Fisher, who asked me to give you a message. She said to tell you, 'It's true,' and 'Five years ago.' That was all."

"Thanks, Mom," Clair smiled at her. She felt infinitely better, not only because it was a fact, but because she could believe what Jake told her. And bless her mother and father: they rarely asked questions. She couldn't have more understanding parents.

It was a cool evening and it was raining. No night for a swishy skirt and low-cut top. Clair decided to wear jeans, but a soft linen shirt instead of a T-shirt. She put the reference materials in her oversized shoulder bag and, as an afterthought, tucked her camera in the bottom. It was 10:30 and she drove out to Cider Run.

She didn't see Jake's truck in the parking lot, but she was not concerned, by now being used to his ways. As she let herself in and locked the door behind her, she thought she heard voices, then realized that the CD player was on. She put her bag down and saw Jake coming from the back of the shop towards her.

"Clair! You didn't disappoint me," he greeted her.

351

He sounded his typical vigorous self, but Clair thought he looked tired and it aroused anew her sense of compassion toward him. "I'm a woman of my word," she replied. "But where's the truck? Don't tell me it's broken down."

"No, I parked it around back. I had the misguided notion I'd be less likely to be disturbed, but it has not had the intended effect. People have been showing up here all evening, on my case about one thing or another. You, however, are welcome and a sight for sore eyes. Let me look at you." He took her hands and extended her arms out in a way that made Clair feel a rush of anticipation go all through her.

"I thought I had to earn that," she said demurely.

"You do. Now, what have you brought me? Besides yourself, that is?"

They walked back to Jake's area and Clair took the reference materials out of her bag. She asked, "Are there more paintings to look at?"

"In the chest," he said. "I'll tell you what, you have a go at them. I'm going to make coffee and finish up some paperwork I left in the office. Then we can talk about the things and, if you're very, very good," he said in a steadily lowering voice, "you can have your way with me." He looked at her, his head to one side. "I wonder, will you unwrap me again, like you did last night? Or maybe it will be my turn tonight." He gave her one of his dazzling smiles and went back to the kitchen door.

Clair blushed furiously. It was true; she had done just that. Without thinking what she was doing, she had unwrapped him as if he had been an irresistible present meant for her. That it had amused Jake and pleased him made her feel slightly shy, although he clearly wanted her to know he liked it. Would it be different tonight? Snap out of it, she told herself, and attend to the job at hand, and she opened the lid of the chest.

In addition to the artwork she had seen last night, there was another triptych and three other paintings. While he was occupied, she decided to photograph them. Just in case. Just in case what? She didn't know, but she quickly took pictures and put the camera back in her bag. Then she had a look at what he had brought.

The paintings were indeed priceless works of religious art. She studied the ones she hadn't seen before. There was a small Raphael in what looked like its original frame, unsigned but unmistakable, and she was almost afraid to handle it. There was a Virgin and Child done by Tintoretto and one by Bellini, neither of them framed, but she could see where the frame had been for centuries. Could they be real or were they copies? The Canaletto was not among them and she wondered if there might be more he didn't bring.

She was thoroughly shaken by this time. These were pictures she remembered as missing works of art. But suppose they were not the genuine ones? This wasn't the best light. She took the Raphael over to a lamp and was studying it when she thought she heard a muffled thud from the direction of the kitchen. Hoping it was not the coffee pot blowing up again, her mind went back to that day last winter. She recalled her consternation when it happened and how Jake had taken charge of things so masterfully. The way he does everything, she thought, and let her mind drift for a minute or two. Then, looking up, she saw Jake coming back in, carrying two mugs of coffee. She disengaged herself from her reverie. Here he was, even more exciting to her now, but she focused on her task.

She indicated the painting she was holding, "You know this is a Raphael, don't you?"

"I know. I also know it cost me a small fortune. But it's for you to tell me if it's a copy or not."

"As I said last night, I do think they're originals. But I don't have proof."

She put the painting down carefully and he handed her a mug of coffee. "Here, take a break," he said. She sat on the Morris chair and he sat down on the daybed.

Clair needed to express her concerns and came right to the point. "Jake, you can't prove they are genuine until you have much stronger light and use a magnifying glass to examine them inch by inch. You need to scrape samples of the paint to have analyzed, and analyze the canvas and even the frames they're in. I haven't the skills for that. You'd need a lab to do the technical analyses. The only thing I can say is that I'm quite certain all of these are here," she pointed to the lists she'd downloaded, "as being stolen."

"That's not really news to me," he said.

"I'm sorry to disappoint you but, truly, I can't authenticate them for you. And if you were to go to someone else, well..."

"They'd turn me in or try to blackmail me." He gave a short laugh. "I'm in an impossible situation, as far as this goes."

"If they are the originals and if you return them, there are rewards. The reward for the Benson alone is $5000."

"Clair, I paid ten times that for it. I've spent close to a million dollars for these things. And if it is in my power, I'm not through yet."

She could well believe they had cost him that much, but she could only whisper, "Why?"

He shrugged. "Because I could, that's why. Because they are more than a pretty face, more than mere embellishment.

Because they are immortal and will go on, while we must die." Then he made his final point, "And because if I have them, I can look at them whenever *I* feel like it, not some damned priest."

She turned away from him and slowly rewrapped the paintings, leaning them carefully against the chest. He had picked up the book from the Hermitage and was looking at it, idly rubbing the knuckles of his right hand. She sat in the Morris chair and drank coffee and watched him. The rain came down steadily, sighing, shushing. She could hear it through the chimney as it fell on the trees in the orchard. The CD player had Bach's lovely *Arioso* on, the sweet-sad melody complementing the rain's sound, and Clair was sensitive to the mood it evoked.

"Jake," said Clair softly. He looked up at her, still partly distracted by what he had been reading. "Jake, don't do it."

"Don't do what, Clair?"

She took a deep breath and decided to say exactly what she had been thinking, hoping he would understand. "You are so beautiful, so complete. You're incredibly perceptive, you're gifted, bright and discerning, fascinating to be around and heaven, heaven itself to make love with. I mean it. *You* are a work of art. Don't throw yourself away by getting obsessed with these. They belong in museums. They aren't in churches anymore. You didn't steal them. You're an antiques dealer. You bought, thinking they were early copies. Please," she said, with all the force she had, "send them back where they were before they were stolen, take the reward money, let them go."

"I can't," he said. "It's too late."

"It's not too late. I'll help you." She got up and went over to him, took the book away and tossed it on the floor. As she

355

did, she was suddenly aware that the Bach piece had ended and in its place the hushed, stirring adagio from Rodrigo's *Concierto de Aranjuez* had started. At the first arresting notes, Clair lost her resolve, and knew at once that Jake had sensed it.

He drew her down onto his lap. "See, Clair?" he said. "This music was composed for us to enjoy, just as the art was meant for me to enjoy." She found she could not answer him and he went on, "You know you don't want to fight me on this." He kissed her, a kiss as soft and tender as the first time, and Clair felt herself giving up the fight, melting to him.

"Now," he said, "I believe it's my turn. Come, let me unwrap you."

Whoever had programmed this CD must have had a genius not only for understanding the evocative power of the music, but also for choosing the order of its progression, each selection contributing to and compounding the total effect. While the Bach had set things in motion with its lilting, compassionate air, the Rodrigo immediately heightened the senses and created an atmosphere of intense and compelling intimacy. Clair could only give in and be led into its midst, into the center of its superbly calm and forceful beauty. And within this center was Jake.

Slowly, deftly, he unbuttoned her shirt and kissed the hollow of her throat, that spot which had so drawn her to him last night. It was, unquestionably, the symbol of surrender and Clair surrendered, willingly, gratefully to his kiss. Then Jake stood her up in front of him, and unhooked, unzipped and eased everything off her. His touch was light but sure, and when he had finished, he did what she had done to him the night before, putting his hands on her shoulders and running them slowly down to her fingertips, then he placed his hands, cupped, over her racing heartbeat. The music, an accomplice, gave its approval, each chord, each stroke of the guitar, bidding her to submit to his will.

He said, "Isn't this better than arguing?"

She could hardly talk, but just managed, "Better than anything in the world." The music echoed her thoughts, reinforced her words.

He gave a soft laugh. "There's something so enchanting when one of us is fully dressed and one of us is fully undressed." To the accompaniment of the rain and the Rodrigo, with his hands, his eyes and his mouth, Jake gently, caressingly, laid claim to all of her, until she was dizzy, breathless, and then he leaned back on the daybed and brought her down on top of him, his arms holding her fast. The rain grew stronger, its sound mingling with the music winding around them. Finally, at last, more urgently, Jake said to her, "Now, Clair. Take me now."

And with his words, and as the rain lulled, she realized that the music had changed again, this time to the magnificent, tragic *Adagio in G Minor* attributed to Albinoni. Like a summons, Clair felt its immense sadness wash over her and everything came back to her, Jake's past, his obsession, the pain he still carried. While the music swelled to its climax, she took him, deeply and wholly, wanting only for his pain to be gone, as if her strength, as if surrounding him so tightly, could overcome it for him. And for a few moments, although she couldn't be sure, for a few moments she felt she had set him free.

But then the tones diminished and quieted, and she lifted herself from him and got up. He turned onto his side and closed his eyes. Had she ever seen him with his eyes closed like that before? She thought not. He looked peaceful, but so defenseless. She knelt down on the floor by him and with her lips brushing his cheek, she whispered one more time, "Please, Jake, for me. Send them back."

He half opened his eyes and, with a sleepy smile, murmured, "Clair, I don't want to." Then he closed his eyes again, and she gathered up her things and left.

She walked slowly to the restroom and stayed there for a long time, trying to put herself back together, trying to compose herself, the rain loud overhead. I have failed tonight, she thought, but I must, I must try again to convince him. As she repacked her bag, she noticed that a couple of her books had been left in Jake's area, but she didn't want to get them now. She also knew she'd start crying any second and quickly went out the front door, barely managing to get outside before she began sobbing. The final selection on the CD was just finishing, Bach again, the stately, cadenced melancholy of *Come, Sweet Death*.

It was raining heavily and she got into her car. But she just sat there, letting herself cry it out, cry because she liked him so terribly, cry because he was so lost. Ten minutes? Fifteen? She didn't know how long it was. Long enough to quiet down a little, the rain drumming on the roof of the car, the windows steamed up. She thought at last she might be able to drive, then realized she had forgotten to lock the front door of the shop.

She hesitated at the door with her key. Should she try to talk to him again? Not with these awful teary eyes. She locked the door and drove home.

Chapter 29

The rain was over and the morning sun shone on the new greens of the hillside and on the sweet pink of the apple blossoms in the orchard at Cider Run. The building itself basked in the sunlight, as if each individual stone had taken in the light and given back a warm, soft hue. Birdsong filled the air. Everything was new, newly washed, newly bright. Everything was old, gnarled trees, ancient stones. The past was almost palpable—that which had happened long ago and made this place, and that which had happened in the last two years, and also that which had happened as recently as last night.

At 9:30 Ruth pulled into the parking lot and backed her car close to the door for easy unloading. But she would not unload it now; she'd wait for Marv, who promised to be in early. She was surprised that she'd been able to get to the shop on time herself. He hadn't left until, when? Was it 3:00 AM? How little sleep matters, she thought, how much he matters.

Last night they talked for a long time. He told her that Jake and Hal knew about their relationship and how that came about. He apologized to her for it, as if it were his fault. Ruth assured him she understood, and thought how Jake's behavior had been unconscionable.

"And that's why you wanted to park in my garage," she said.

He nodded. "I hope he doesn't feel he has to resort to any more reconnaissance. I'd hate to think what form it might take."

He told her about his resolve to try to help Jake, and seek solutions with him to what was causing such difficulties. She agreed that it was a good idea, but confessed she was not terribly optimistic. He also told her about the financial boost from Sally Ann and about the corner cupboard and his new writing project. And, last, he told her he had fallen in love with her.

"You mustn't," she said gently, troubled at what this could cost him, but at the same time filled with a sense of quiet joy at hearing him say it.

"But I have, and that's that."

They didn't talk about the future. It was enough to be together, to be this comfortable with each other. He kissed her before he left, saying, "See you very soon. Don't unload anything until I get there."

She smiled at the thought of last night and, as she got out of the car and took a breath of the apple blossom-scented air, it seemed to Ruth as if this were the very first spring of her life. It was all that spring should be, intense, joyful, forward-looking. "I've fallen in love with you," he had said, a phrase to be savored again and again. The orchard was full of birds, trilling, calling, filling the air with song. How beautiful everything was. Even the puddles from last night's downpour sparkled lavishly in the sun. Life was rich and the richness around her echoed the feeling of richness within.

Ruth walked to the edge of the parking lot to look across at the hills. They shone back at her in the sunlight, covered now in a light yellow green, the deep pink of the redbud gone. Weeks would follow of steadily increasing growth, more and more trees flowering, and then the wealth of summer. She thought of the pioneers going through these hills toward new homes in the west and she thought of the goods they carried with them to their new homes, goods she now sold for others to enjoy.

A perfect morning, a morning for new beginnings. For a moment she thought of the problems they might cause themselves and others. First among their problems, and most immediate, was Jake. She hoped Marv would be successful when he talked to him. Otherwise, things might be unpleasant. But it was too fine a day for those thoughts. Ruth took one more deep breath of the spring air, and then walked back and unlocked the door of the shop.

As always upon opening the door first thing in the morning, she was greeted by the shut-in smell of the shop, a pleasant combination of aromas—old building, aged wood, furniture wax. It also smelled damp, musty. She sniffed the air: close, it smelled close, she decided. It was a good smell, an antiques shop smell and it added the necessary dimension of the senses in the overall experience of being among old things. It complemented the visual. The sixth sense was brought into play by the implicit awareness of the past. And the sense of hearing? She saw that the CD player was still on, although nothing was playing. Opera, classical music went best with antiques, she thought. But, of course, others had their preferences, which made her remember who she was scheduled to work with today: Sally Ann. That's good, she thought, anyone but Jake. And she'd rather not have to face Hal quite yet either.

Ruth switched on the overhead lights, the computer and printer and the surveillance monitor. She stashed her bag behind the front counter, saw there were no phone messages, looked up to make sure the red security light for the back door was off, and headed into the dealers' areas to turn on individual lamps and display lights. It was tempting to check her sales for last week, but seeing what was new, what had been brought in, was even more interesting.

As she went about turning on lamps, she noticed that someone had forgotten to turn several of them off the evening before. Marv had told her that when he stopped by last night, Jake and someone else were here. The description of the car sounded like Laurel's husband's, unless Laurel was driving his car because hers wasn't available. And would Laurel have been here to be with Jake? There were rumors. These thoughts brought her uncomfortably close to her own situation, so she put them aside.

There were many changes in only a week. Marv's ornately carved four-poster bed was gone, but he'd have to do a lot of moving things around to make room for the corner cupboard. Sylvie and Hal had brought in a Hoosier cabinet and stocked it with green Depression glass. Richard had a pine blanket chest she had not seen before, the top thrown back, with a Mennonite quilted coverlet in shades of green and blue folded over the edge. There was green transferware in Grace's area. Green, for spring, seemed to be the theme.

Ruth had come to Jake's area and saw that he had recently brought in some Arts and Crafts furniture. She noted once again that he had elegant, refined taste. In antiques, at any rate, she thought to herself. Refinement in other matters was apparently not his strong point, certainly not in the way he had acted towards her, and spying on them was the last straw. She saw that one of the pieces, a handsome daybed, was pushed up close to a large oak blanket chest. She pushed the daybed back a bit, in order to give both pieces more room in between, and when she did, she found a paperback booklet lying on the floor. It was a richly illustrated guide to the Florence museum, titled *Masterpieces of the Pitti Palace*, and had Clair's name written in it. She took it along with her to give back to Clair. Ruth had noticed that Clair's area had a bevy of straw hats and white wicker and looked very summerlike and tempting. She thought about Clair's good taste and artistic touch and hoped to tell her soon how nice her display was. And so Ruth came to her own area and stood, deciding how she'd rearrange things.

At 9:45 Sally Ann drove in, parked slightly askew and backed herself out of her car, withdrawing a carton of doughnuts and a partially-full coffee cup as she emerged. She was dressed, as always, with dash and color and this Wednesday morning in May wore a creation in bright spring yellows and pinks, complete with fuchsia pumps and matching bag. Sally Ann believed in honoring the occasion and, if there were no occasion, her outfits provided one.

She walked gingerly over to the edge of the parking lot to stand gazing at the hills in the sunlight and reflected with amazement, not for the first time of late, that she was a partner now. It was a thrilling thought, but daunting. How should she conduct herself as a partner? Should she be wearing grey pinstriped business suits from now on? These were challenging questions, but although her status might have changed from mere dealer, she was not going to change her style. No, never, unless, and only unless, some lovely man came into her life and a new style presented itself to her. But he would have to be something really special and at least as good-looking as Richard. She could not see this happening today, but one could always hope.

About today then: she had recognized Ruth's new car and remembered she was working with her. There was a time when Sally Ann despaired of Ruth's wardrobe, but over the last year she thought Ruth was dressing much more attractively. It almost seemed as if she might have a romantic interest. Could it be? Maybe something exciting had happened on her trip last week too. With these thoughts uppermost in her mind, she walked back to the shop, unlocked the door and called, "Ruth, I'm here!"

Sally Ann was pleased when Ruth immediately complimented her spring outfit. And in turn noticed what Ruth was wearing—slacks, as usual, but with, good heavens, was that a camisole peeking out underneath a pale green blouse? Definitely romantic! Ruth *must* have a new interest and Sally Ann felt a little thrill of empathy. Ruth, for her part, saw a new dimension of confidence in Sally Ann, and although Ruth knew why, she didn't let on. Sally Ann was as chatty and bouncy as ever and Ruth was glad to have her as a distraction.

At 10:00 Sally Ann hurried to open the front door and Laurel came in, Ben on one hip. They had a brief conversation, then Laurel went to her area to add some things and switch others around, putting the baby down on a small rug. Ruth went back to redoing her area after greeting Laurel and the baby. As there were no customers yet, Sally Ann took the moment to wander around the shop, sip coffee and have a doughnut. She paused when she came to Jake's area. There was a large oak blanket chest she hadn't seen before. But it was closed. Sally Ann thought that it really should be open to show the inside. Perhaps it was fitted with a candle till and maybe even a secret compartment. She attempted to lift the lid, but it seemed to be stuck. She got down on her knees and tried pushing it up. "Ruth," she called, "come and help me."

Marv drove up Cider Run Road and turned into the parking lot. The sun was shining, his spirits soared. He noticed how beautiful the orchard looked with the branches covered in blossoms. It was time to get the picnic tables under the trees. Warm weather was coming and the dealers would want to sit outside. He loved each and every dealer, he loved the whole world. Most of all...but he wouldn't let himself think about last night, as he saw Sally Ann's Mercedes parked off at an angle, and Laurel's car, as well as Ruth's car, in the parking lot. He couldn't wait to see Ruth, but told himself he would be circumspect all day. Until tonight. And then he could say all the things he wanted to say to her, do all the things he wanted to do. He got out of the truck, and with a glance at the hills, walked towards the shop.

With a great tug at the lid, Sally Ann got the chest open, swiveling around as she did to tell Ruth triumphantly, "I got it!" She turned back to the chest and let out a piercing, horrified scream and scrambled to her feet.

On his side in the chest lay Jake, his eyes closed, his handsome face ashen, an antique ice pick buried deep in his right ear.

As Marv approached the shop, he saw Sally Ann rush out and vomit into the bushes. Oh, dear, he thought, such a lovely day to have to be sick. He gave her a sympathetic glance and went on to where Laurel, holding the baby, and Ruth had come out and were standing by the door.

"What a perfect morning!" he exclaimed, looking up at the clear sky. Then he saw their drawn faces. The baby was wailing. "What is it?" he asked Ruth.

365

"It's Jake," she said, her voice unsteady. "He's been killed. Somehow." But she knew how. The question was who.

Marv saw she was shaking. He put his arms around both Ruth and Laurel, and the baby instantly quieted. Sally Ann continued to be sick. They stood there for a minute or two, silent. Sally Ann came over to them and was taken into their group. Finally Marv said, "Tell me."

Chapter 30

They had left the lid of the chest open; they did not feel they should close it again. Marv had called the police, fighting a choking sensation of nausea at what he had seen. The group waited by the door, not wanting to go back inside. They said little and there was a stiffness in their silence, all of them with the picture in their minds of Jake lying so still in the chest, of the ice pick, its price tag still attached, dealer code AK. No blood. So clean, so swift and sure a death.

Detective Paul Willard, sad-eyed and courteous, along with his sergeant, Jim Garcia, and a contingent of others, including the forensic unit from the county coroner's office, arrived at Cider Run. In the hours that followed, Ruth, Laurel and Sally Ann stayed out of the way, only answering questions as asked. They corroborated that the cash drawer was untouched, the back door security light off, that everything seemed as usual when they arrived.

Marv gave the police information about Jake and went with them into the back of the shop. Jake's jacket still hung in the kitchen, his wallet in an inner pocket containing close to $100 and what appeared to be all his cards. His briefcase, with his phone inside, was in the office. The office safe was as it should be. There was no damage, nothing obviously missing.

Laurel went to her car to feed the baby and Sally Ann and Ruth sat gloomily on the church pew by the front door, answering the phone occasionally to tell customers they were not open today, before they gave up and let the answering machine take over with its standard message.

Finally, the medical examiner and the photographer had finished, the other procedural necessities had been completed, and the body and the chest taken away. When only the detective and his sergeant and two officers on guard outside were left, they reconvened, drawing up chairs from the shop and huddling around the church pew.

Detective Willard began with an apology. "I'm sorry to have to keep you folks here for so long," he said, "and I'll be as quick as possible, so you can get that baby home for his nap," he smiled at Laurel, "and I would suggest that the shop remain closed for the rest of the day."

"I think there's no question about that," Marv agreed.

"Good," the detective replied. "As I think I mentioned, I have posted an officer in a squad car at the entrance to the parking lot and she will stay for the day. She's been instructed to tell people who drive up that there has been an accident here and that you will be closed."

Marv nodded and the detective went on, "Now, I'd like to find out a few things, if you all will be so kind. There is a truck parked by the back door."

"Oh, gosh, I forgot, that's Jake's truck. He had it parked there last night."

"You were here last night?" the detective asked.

"I stopped by to talk with Jake," said Marv, "and drove around back to see if he was here. He sometimes parks there when he has things to unload. But I didn't go in. Another car was in the parking lot, so I left." Marv did not say whose car it was, although he knew by now it was Joe's.

"And what time, approximately, was that?"

Marv tried not to look at Ruth. "9:30, I think," he answered.

"Did you by any chance recognize the vehicle you say was parked outside in the parking lot?"

There was an awkward silence before Marv replied, "No, I didn't recognize it at the time."

"But on further thought?" the detective prompted.

Laurel spoke up. "It was my husband's," she said. "He came by to speak with Jake."

"And when did you see him again?" the detective asked Laurel.

Laurel said, "He went to the hospital after that; he's a doctor and got a call. He didn't get home until nearly midnight. But I'm sure the hospital..."

"Thank you. Yes, we'll check if necessary. Thank you, Mrs. Fisher. If you want to go now, please feel free. I don't want to keep you and the baby any longer, unless there is something else you think may shed light on what happened."

Laurel shook her head.

"Will you both, er, all three of you," he smiled, "be so kind as to not leave town? Thank you so much for your help."

Laurel got up, settled Ben on her hip, went over to Ruth and Sally Ann, gave them each a hug, and left. Sally Ann excused herself and went to the restroom.

Detective Willard cleared his throat and began anew. "Now, the question of access. Ms. Arden, I believe you were the first to get here this morning. You found the door locked and upon entering noticed that the security light was off, indicating that the back door was also locked. There is no way to lock or unlock the back door from the outside, I think you said. It has an inside hand-turned deadbolt lock only, and the light goes on when the deadbolt is opened. An alarm will also sound if it is not deactivated at the front of the shop first. Is that correct?"

Ruth agreed with a nod.

"I have the deceased's keys here," he produced a plastic bag. "There's a car key matching the make of the truck, and what looks like a house key, two keys with the name of his realty company on them, and this non-duplicable key. Is this the one to the shop?" He held up the Cider Run key and Ruth nodded. "We're going to have another thorough look around to see if there is any forced entry, but for the present, it doesn't look like it. So I must ask now, besides the two extra keys you keep in the safe, how many keys are there to the shop and who has them?"

Marv answered, "There are seventeen dealers, I mean, sixteen now. They each have a key." The detective looked a little taken aback, but rallied and said, "All right. We need to account for each key and we need to account for each dealer last night. Can you help?"

"Yes, of course. However, I only got back yesterday from five days in eastern Pennsylvania. I know some of the dealers were and still are out of town. If you don't mind, Detective, I'd like to call our other business partner. He needs to be informed and he will be helpful, I'm sure."

"By all means," said the detective and Marv went to the phone. Sally Ann came back and seated herself next to Ruth, and Ruth took her hand. Sally Ann had gotten some color back, probably applied from her makeup case, but she was looking much better.

The detective turned to Sally Ann. "Mrs. O'Neill, did you by any chance stop by the shop last night?"

"No, Detective, I didn't. I was in on Monday, the day before yesterday."

"Do you, and I'm sorry to have to ask you this, but do you have anyone who can vouch for your whereabouts last night?"

"What?" said Sally Ann, eyes open wide.

"Were you with anyone last night? Later on, say from midnight to 2:00 AM?"

"Certainly not!" Sally Ann replied indignantly.

"I'm sorry," Detective Willard said, consulted the notes again, then looked up at her. "I want to thank you for staying. You've had a terrible shock and I appreciate your being willing to help us in spite of the way you must feel. You can leave if you wish, but you'll stay in town? Good." He gave her a smile and, as Sally Ann hesitated, repeated, "It's fine, really. You can go if you want."

Sally Ann gave Ruth a hug. "Do you want me to call you later, Ruth?" she asked.

"Yes, do," said Ruth, and she watched Sally Ann as she walked, back straight, head held high, out the door. Ruth noticed that the detective's eyes followed her. Well done, Sally Ann, Ruth thought.

Marv had finished on the phone and came back, sitting down next to Ruth. The urge to put his arm around her was strong, but he controlled himself. He said, "Hal will be right over."

Detective Willard asked a few questions about Hal and then turned to Ruth. "Ms. Arden," he said. "I'm afraid I have to ask about your whereabouts last night too, as you are one of the holders of a shop key."

"I was not here at the shop, Detective. I had just returned from a week out of town and was home from 8:00 on," Ruth volunteered.

"I have to ask, and again I apologize, but were you with anyone in the hours between midnight and 2:00, as this seems to be the approximate time of death."

Ruth did not answer immediately. She looked at Marv and the look was noticed by Detective Willard. He said, "If you like, I can ask you privately. Be assured, no one else will be informed of your answer, unless it is absolutely necessary."

Marv said, "That's all right, Detective. Ruth and I were together. At her house. Until after 3:00 AM."

The detective did not raise his eyebrows or give any other indication of surprise, for which Ruth was grateful. She said, "I would appreciate it very much if this information were kept quiet, Detective. There are people it could hurt."

"I understand," he said, and it seemed to Ruth that he did. "If you want to leave, Ms. Arden, you are free to go. Thank you for helping out. I don't have to ask you if you would be so good as to not leave town, and if you think of anything else pertinent to what happened that you will let us know."

"You have been most considerate, Detective. Please keep me informed too, as I am as anxious as all of us." She turned to Marv, "Call me later?"

Marv got up and walked with her outside, just as Hal pulled in. He didn't care; he put his arms around her and held her close. She murmured, "You didn't come back here after you left me last night, did you? I keep thinking..."

"No, Ruth, it wasn't me." He kissed her cheek, in spite of Hal, and she walked to her car, saluting Hal with a sad little wave as she passed him. All this was observed by the detective standing by the door and he nodded to himself.

Hal and Marv greeted each other wordlessly with a firm handshake and walked into the shop together. Marv introduced Detective Willard and his sergeant to Hal and they sat down. The detective apologized again for having to ask the inevitable. Hal answered, "I met with Jake here at the shop at 8:30 or so and left shortly after 9:00. I went straight home, since our teenage daughter was home alone. My wife is out of town. And I went nowhere last night after I got home."

"Thank you. Was anyone else here at the time you were in the shop?"

Hal said, "Yes. Three others. Richard Keating, one of our dealers, Keith Mackinnon, another dealer, and Joe Fisher, the husband of one of our dealers. Richard left the same time I did. Detective, I know all these people and none of them..."

"I'm sure you do and that's good to know. But we have a problem of access here. The doors were both locked and the key of the deceased was in his pocket, so it would seem that someone had to gain entrance by key. Unless we find another way in, or out, for that matter."

Hal shook his head. "Not that I know of and I've been all over this place. When it was a restaurant, actually a speakeasy, they had the holes plugged. And since we're somewhat isolated, when we remodeled we tried to make things as burglar-proof as possible. Most of the windows don't open, for example, and those that do have bars. Jake could have let someone in, though."

Marv said, "We've already thought of that. The door was locked when Ruth opened up this morning."

The detective said in agreement, "So you see the importance of speaking with everyone who has a key, or has access to one. I assume you'll be wanting to contact the other dealers?"

"We would like to talk to them, if you don't object. It would be better to hear from us first," Marv emphasized. And he was desperately hoping they could somehow keep things quiet, keep it among themselves, at least until they could get a better handle on what happened.

"Yes, I understand," the detective responded, "and also, I'm afraid you'll have some publicity, which could affect your business. I can keep this out of the news for a while, a day or so anyway, to give us more time."

Marv breathed an inward sigh of relief. "Thank you. We'd greatly appreciate that," he told the detective. "Now, can we give you any more information about Jake? I already gave them all we had," he said to Hal, "his brother's name and address, the realty office."

"How about Annette?" Hal asked.

"Darn. I forgot about her," Marv admitted. He looked at Detective Willard. "Jake was married, but separated. His wife lives in Washington D.C., but we don't have her address."

"We'll be having a look around his house. The information should be there if his office or his brother can't supply it. Is there anything you can tell me about her?"

"Only that she wanted to have the marriage annulled and Jake was in no hurry. The person to talk to is Richard Keating, one of the dealers mentioned earlier. He handled Jake's insurance business," Marv said.

"By the way," Hal added, "we are in the process of adding a new partner and it is not yet general knowledge."

"May I ask who the partner is? I should talk to him too."

"You've met her. It's Sally Ann O'Neill. She wishes to be a silent partner for the time being," Marv explained.

374

"I see. Noted. Well, gentlemen, shall we go on to the murder weapon? And by the way, we'd rather you didn't mention what it is when you talk to your dealers. Now, what can you tell me about a dealer whose code is AK?"

"Excuse me, sir," Sergeant Garcia spoke up, "but it's nearly 2:30. These people haven't had anything to eat for hours. I don't mind for myself, sir, but perhaps it would be a courtesy."

Detective Willard looked at his watch. "Oh, I'm so sorry. Yes, certainly. We'll need to be in and out, however, while you're gone, but I'll have two officers here at all times. I hope that's all right? Thank you. Would it be possible to continue this discussion after lunch? Say, 4:00? We'll see you later, then."

Detective Willard watched Marv and Hal leave and when the door had closed behind them, he sighed heavily. His sergeant looked up from the notes he had been working on.

"What is it, sir?" Sergeant Garcia asked.

The detective shook his head. "Sixteen dealers, sixteen keys. What a nightmare! Well, Sergeant, we have work to do. We'll go get ourselves a bite to eat and then tackle the victim's real estate office. And try to get ahold of the wife and the brother. And start back up with the folks here at 4:00. Maybe by then we'll have some information from the lab."

As they got ready to leave, Detective Willard was still shaking his head and muttering, "Sixteen dealers, sixteen keys..."

Chapter 31

Marv and Hal walked slowly out as if they were in a daze. They got into Hal's car and sat silent for a few moments. Finally Marv said, "I don't think I have much of an appetite. God, Hal, you can't imagine how ghastly it was, seeing Jake lying there. I don't know how the women managed to hold up, but they did beautifully."

"You said Sally Ann was OK?" Hal asked. "I'd worry most about her."

"Other than losing her breakfast under the Cider Run sign, she did well. Laurel was white as a sheet. Not surprising. She was worried about Joe. You could tell that."

"And Ruth?" Hal knew that asking about Ruth came close to being a very personal question, but he needed to know how things were.

"She was worried about me. I was with her last night. You probably figured that out when I told you on the phone that Helen was still in Bucks. I didn't leave until 3:00 this morning, so unless they change their estimate of the time of death, I have an alibi. We both have an alibi. But I wouldn't want that to be known." He sighed, then went on, "No, someone did him in and I am utterly convinced it wasn't one of us. God knows he's probably made enemies right and left, but how did they get in and out and have the door locked?"

"Come on, Marv, we'll go over to my house and have a sandwich, and then we should start calling dealers before one of them comes to the shop and runs into the police. Sylvie's due back late this afternoon. And hadn't you better call Helen?"

Hal put together some sandwiches, spreading ham salad on rye bread, adding a few lettuce leaves, and would have brought out pickles, but somehow felt the occasion was too somber for pickles. Marv was surprised to find he was hungry and they both ate appreciatively, but without talking. Hal had opened two Pennsylvania lagers and they drank these. After a few minutes, Marv broke the silence. He raised his bottle and said, "To Jake. The poor bastard. Never to have another beer."

"Marv," Hal cautioned.

"No, Hal, I mean that in a sincere way. I liked Jake, in spite of how he'd been lately, and I feel terribly, terribly sorry for him, for what happened. And I'll be damned if I know what happened or why."

They finished their beers in a silent tribute to Jake, then divided up the list of dealers and started making phone calls.

Hal reached Keith's mother-in-law and left a message for Keith to call, not giving her the upsetting information. Then he called Owen and spoke with Lynn, as Owen was still at the high school. He told her that Jake had been killed and it was not an accident, and the police were at the shop and would probably want to talk to everyone. Lynn's first reaction was disbelief, and then in a choked voice, promised to have Owen call as soon as he got home.

When Hal told Cora, she started to cry and wanted to know what she could do. "If you can call Grace, we'd appreciate it. The police need to know where everyone was and where everyone's keys were last night. The shop did not appear to have been broken into."

"My God, that's like saying one of us..." Cora couldn't finish the sentence.

"We don't believe that for an instant, but the police don't have any answers yet," said Hal.

He also called and left messages at his insurance office, at his home, and on his mobile phone for Richard to call.

Meanwhile Marv had reached Elaine. "Elaine," he asked, "are you sitting down?"

"What, Marv? Have you sold something of mine?"

"Terrible news, Elaine. Jake's been killed. At the shop."

"Who by?" she asked immediately. Elaine had no illusions. The possibility of an accident didn't even enter her mind.

"We don't know, but the police think it had to be someone with a key to the place, and that means us."

Elaine was chastened by this last statement. "I need a smoke," she said. Marv waited patiently. He heard the click of her cigarette lighter, then she said, "Listen, Marv, if someone shot Jake I can't be too surprised. He's always been pretty intense. I mean, he has a profound effect on anyone he's around and it's either one way or the other. But who'd kill him?"

Marv could hear her take a drag on her cigarette. Not wanting to indulge in speculation at this point, he went on, "At any rate, Elaine, the police need to talk with all of us, so if you can help out, they'll be looking for any information we can give them. In the meantime, we'll be closed. I'll get back to you as soon as I know anything else."

Marv was also successful in getting Andy and Andy sounded mystified. "Why would anyone want to go and kill him?" he asked.

Marv thought he'd better get it over with. "It isn't just that, Andy. It's the way he was killed."

"Someone shot him, you think?"

"No, worse than that. I have to tell you this: one of your antiques was used to kill him." Marv wanted Andy to be forewarned.

"One of mine? How could that be? I don't have any weapons, not like Keith. Did someone bash him over the head with a cast iron fry pan? I guess that could be fatal," Andy offered.

Marv didn't elaborate, but told him about the police wanting to talk to everyone. "We'll let you know what's happening," he promised.

He couldn't reach Clair, but spoke with her mother, who told him that Clair was on her way to see someone in New York. "She has her phone, but she doesn't like to answer it when she's driving. I'm sure she'll call us at some point. I can leave her a message if you want." Marv asked only that she call him, and then he turned his attention to Helen.

In the meantime, Hal had a call back from Owen, who wanted to know everything. Hal said, "I'm afraid there's not much the police have learned, except that he was killed at the shop and there was no sign of a forced entry. Nothing seems to have been taken, so far as we know now, and the door was locked when Ruth first came this morning."

"How was he killed or do the police know?" Owen asked.

Hal said, "It wasn't nice, Owen. The police would rather we didn't get into that yet, as they've got to do lab work on the murder weapon. All they say is that it probably happened between midnight and 2:00AM."

Owen was incredulous. "At the shop in the middle of the night? I'll be glad to talk with them, but how much do we say? I mean, everyone knows that a number of us had major beefs with Jake. That doesn't mean we'd kill him. God, I can't believe it."

"I haven't gotten ahold of Keith yet and we need to get back to the shop to meet with the police again. If you would talk to Keith?"

"I'll tell him. The damned thing is Keith may have been the last one to see him alive. God, this is melodramatic. Will it be in the news tonight? How about the papers? Will the shop be closed?" Owen had a lot of questions.

Marv had put off calling Helen till last, having dreaded her reaction to what he had to say. She was so fond of Jake and could likely be upset to the point of hysteria. How much should he tell her? But she'd want all the particulars. Would it be important for her to be here? Important for the investigation? He sighed, knowing she'd want to be here anyway. He went to a private corner and called.

After a very emotional conversation, Marv turned off his phone. As he had expected, she did get hysterical over Jake's death and almost sounded as if Marv could have prevented it somehow. She wouldn't stop crying and wanted to drive home immediately. He was able to talk her into coming tomorrow. "I hope she's calmed down somewhat by then," Marv told Hal.

"Sylvie might be able to calm Helen. She should be back," Hal looked at his watch, "in an hour or so. Who else do we need to contact?"

Marv looked at the list of dealers. "Grace and Frank aren't coming back until next week. Cora said she'd call them. If they can shed any light on what happened, I'm sure they'll call. Emmy and Charles are flying in tomorrow. In fact, I'm supposed to pick them up at the airport. That leaves Richard and Keith we haven't talked to."

"Owen said he'd talk to Keith. I think he's a little worried that Keith may have, well, I don't know," Hal finished indeterminately.

"And Clair," said Marv. "Her mother said she left for New York this afternoon. I can't imagine Clair would know anything about the murder, but they'll want to talk with her."

Hal asked for the first time, "What do you think, Marv? Could someone have stolen one of the dealers' keys? I swear they can't be duplicated. It looks sort of bad, doesn't it?" Hal reflected for a moment, then said, "When we chose the dealers for the shop..."

Marv shook his head. "We had known many of them for years, and have gotten to know them all since then. I want to feel confident; I do feel confident. But there's no point in wondering now. They'll have a lot of interviewing to do. Jake's office, his relatives, girlfriends, who knows. A few tiffs at the shop aren't motive for murder. OK, maybe there is more than that. Keith and the property deal, Laurel's husband, Jake's homophobia towards Richard. But still, murder? No, I don't believe it for a moment."

"Just how much do we tell them about those things, though?"

Marv shrugged. "I guess we'll cross that bridge when we come to it. Hal, you said you had a falling out with him over a piece of pottery, and I sure as hell did over Ruth, and then we both did when he refused to honor his commitments as a partner. I think we'll have to indicate that he rubbed people the wrong way, but on the other hand, we could mention how much all the women liked him. Except Elaine. She was wary of him."

"And Ruth," added Hal.

"And Ruth," agreed Marv. Ruth, he thought. He needed to see her, talk to her. Would she let him come over to her house tonight or was she too upset by the events of the day? He'd call her as soon as he could. They both needed to prepare for some difficult questions and it might touch on their relationship. Marv felt so clear-headed, so strong about her, that he would gladly face whatever there was to face, as long as she felt the same way about him.

Hal seemed to have sensed where Marv's mind was, because he gave Marv a moment or two before he began again. "Could it have had something to do with the shop itself? I mean, maybe there was a theft after all. We'll need to have all the dealers in, to see if any of their things have been taken."

Marv looked at his watch. "Well, partner, we're due back there now. No doubt we'll learn more this afternoon. And, by the way, I have a Bucks County corner cupboard in the back of my truck. So, we get to do a little furniture moving—something normal, thank God."

Several police cars were parked in the parking lot when Marv and Hal drove in and among them was Richard's van. "Uh, oh," Hal commented on seeing Richard's car. "Not a great way to learn about it."

"I hope he isn't getting grilled by the police. Although, on second thought, he might enjoy the drama of it. But his relationship with Jake was rocky, to say the least," Marv amended.

They opened the door to see Sergeant Garcia writing and Richard sitting on the church pew appearing utterly desolate. He looked up when they came in. "I just stopped by to leave some things and now I'm about to be arrested!" he wailed.

"Indeed, you're not, sir," said the sergeant, looking to Marv and Hal for support.

"Sorry, Richard, we tried to call you," said Marv, "but couldn't reach you anywhere. We didn't want you to learn about it this way."

"God, it's awful, isn't it? One day he's alive and making all sorts of trouble for us and the next day he's dead and making even more trouble."

"Excuse me, sir, but could you elaborate a bit on that?" the sergeant asked.

"Help me out, Marv!" Richard pleaded. "They're making a case against me!" He turned to the sergeant. "You've got the wrong person. I wouldn't shoot anyone. I don't even know how to hold a gun. Anyway, he was my client. I'd never kill a client."

"Thank you, sir," the sergeant said, obviously wanting to bring an end to what had been an emotional session. "We'll let you go on your way. We appreciate your time."

"Sergeant," Marv asked, "do you think we could bring in a piece of furniture? It's been sitting in my truck and I'd like to get it on the floor. In case we ever open the shop again."

"I'll ask Detective Willard. I'm sure it will be all right." The sergeant got up and went to find his superior.

Richard looked close to tears. "You don't know how horrible, absolutely horrible, those police people make you feel. First it was the *valkyrie* in her squad car at the entrance to the parking lot, then it was some scary person bristling with firearms and now it's insinuating questions. I feel the handcuffs closing on my wrists as we speak. I will need some recovery time."

"How about moving in a corner cupboard?" Hal asked.

"A small recompense, but it will help," said Richard. "But do you know anything? They wouldn't let on to me. I'm simply rejecting the thought that he's actually dead, you know."

"He is, Richard," Hal stated flatly. "Marv saw him. And so did Ruth and Laurel and Sally Ann."

"Sally Ann? How did she take it, seeing Jake lying there in a pool of blood?"

Marv answered, "She went outside and threw up. But there wasn't any blood. Come on, let's get the cupboard unloaded."

Detective Willard came over to them. "I'll be glad to help you," he offered. "I've had plenty of experience moving furniture."

"Your assistance is gratefully accepted," said Marv. They walked out to the parking lot and Marv asked him, "Are you interested in antiques? This piece is a real beauty, an early 19th century Bucks County corner cupboard, original red paint..."

After moving a few things around, the corner cupboard was put in place in Marv's area, and the detective asked if they could spare some time to help him. He indicated that Richard was welcome to join them, but Richard declined. "I'm going home to reflect on the uncertainties of life. Call me if you need me or if there is anything I should know."

"Before you go, sir," the detective said apologetically, "please have a look in your area to see if anything has been stolen. We want to make sure that theft was not involved."

Richard nodded and made his way to his area, to stand looking morosely around. The others followed Detective Willard to Jake's area.

"Now," the detective began, "I would like to tell you what we've been able to learn so far about the murder and maybe you can clear up one or two points."

"Any way we can help," said Marv.

"It is our belief that the victim was lying on his left side here on the couch," he pointed to the daybed, "where there were still some wrinkles and impressions on the cushion. We think he was asleep, sleeping soundly. This seems to be the case because there was no evidence of a struggle. I would guess that he never woke up and, after being stabbed, was very quickly shifted into the large chest which, when Ms. Arden first saw it this morning, was only a few inches away. We've gone over the couch. There are indications that besides the victim, another person had been with him there." The detective paused.

"The murderer?" asked Hal.

"Possibly. There were traces on the couch, as well as on the victim's clothing, and on the, ah, victim himself of a woman," both Marv and Hal winced automatically at what was obviously implied, "who had light brown hair, straight, medium length, would probably fall at about the chin. We've got DNA samples from the, ah, fluids as well."

There was an awkward pause. "In other words?" Marv asked.

"In other words, the victim had recently had sexual intercourse. It would appear to have been within an hour or less of the time he was killed. So he was what you might call 'mellowed out,' and sleeping so deeply that he was unaware of the murderer's approach. A woman could have easily killed him at that point." The detective looked at Marv and Hal, but their faces remained composed.

Marv said soberly, "Well, good for you, Jake. At least you went out happy."

Hal said sharply, "Marv!"

Marv asked, "The murderer, however, had to be fairly strong to lift the body and put it in the chest, wouldn't you say, Detective? Could a woman do that?"

"Maybe, but it's not as likely. But if it was not his, ah, encounter who killed him, she might know something or have seen something last night. Do you have any ideas about who she may have been?"

Both Hal and Marv were afraid they knew all too well who was with Jake, but Hal answered, "There seems to have been a lot of women in Jake's life. He could have arranged to meet anyone. If you're thinking it was one of our dealers..."

"I was hoping you could enlighten me on that possibility," the detective said pleasantly. "Having met Mrs. Fisher, I can rule her out." The detective added, "Her hair. It's longer and darker than the samples we found. I've been looking at the list of dealers you gave me and I wondered if anyone on it could have been here. Let's see," he perused the list, "there are seven other women listed, in addition to the ones I met this morning, although I realize we can rule out those who were not in town. But even the wives of your other dealers would have access to a key and could have used it, if they were so inclined toward the victim. Not that I am suggesting they were, but you see it could be a long and complicated and potentially embarrassing process, matching DNA and all." He stopped and smiled and Marv knew he had no alternative.

"Clair Somers. I tried to reach her, but her mother says she was off to New York this afternoon. I can't say if she met Jake here last night or not, but she may have. Her mother is sure she'll call soon, and then she'll get in touch with us. I've known her for years, Detective, ever since she was a student.

She's young, only 26. And slight, so I don't think she'd be hauling bodies around," he added.

"Well, we will be wanting to talk to her. But we can wait. I don't think we need to alarm her yet."

"Thank you, Detective. I appreciate your understanding. What else can we help you with?"

"We've taken the victim's vehicle for analysis, in case you wondered where it was. We also found something out by the back door, but that can wait too. What we really need to do now is call in all your dealers, including those we have already spoken with, to ascertain their movements on the night of the murder and also to learn the whereabouts of their shop keys on that night. We need to speak with the ones who are or were out of town too, because one of their keys could have been used."

"When would you like to do that? We can arrange to have everyone come in."

"Starting tomorrow morning? When they can make it, say, from about 9:30 on? Good. Officers will be here to take statements, as I may not be present the whole day. The victim's wife and brother will be coming tomorrow to talk with us. Also, we should be getting some results from the autopsy, although I don't think that will tell us much we don't already know."

"You don't suppose," Hal began, "I mean, he was half Italian and sometimes there is a connection."

"Organized crime? We'll be checking that too. Also, we've found a number of, ah, girlfriends as a result of the investigation. There are boyfriends and even husbands who could have been angry with the victim. But what remains is access, so we must start with the keys first. I'm sure you understand."

"Yes. We'll call everyone in."

"One more thing," the detective said. "Mr. Keating, I believe, was the victim's insurance agent? He told us an interesting thing. He said that the victim had a partnership life insurance policy which would pay, on his death, a lump sum to the partnership. You were aware of this?"

Hal looked at Marv. "I wasn't," he said, frowning.

"I didn't tell you, Hal, because Richard wanted it kept quiet. He was afraid that Jake would be upset if anyone knew. I'm sorry, partner. I should have told you. Yes, it's true, Detective. Richard said it was done as a temporary measure, until Jake got something worked out with Annette. There was a lot of animosity there. I'm not sure why. Maybe Richard can shed some light on it."

"Animosity between the victim and his wife? Also, I understand, between the victim and Mr. Keating. Were there any other quarrels going on among the dealers and the victim?"

Hal and Marv looked at each other and the detective waited patiently. Marv said, finally, "Several areas of disagreement, yes. But I am quite sure the dealers will be forthcoming and you would learn more from them. It would be in the nature of gossip from us."

"Yes, I see. Now, how about the two of you? Any quarrels? Any issues?"

Again there was an uncomfortable silence. Hal broke it this time. "Detective, Jake could be very contrary at times. He annoyed us by doing petty things, such as making unilateral decisions regarding shop arrangements, and bidding against another of our dealers, and reselling something at a much higher price, something we'd sold him in good faith. And he seemed lately to have had money concerns. He was not willing to honor the commitments we had made when we started the partnership, that is, to add more cash when necessary."

"I see," said Detective Willard. "So you took in another partner, Mrs. O'Neill?"

"Yes," Hal confirmed, "and Jake was furious with me about it."

Marv looked surprised. "I didn't know about that, Hal. What happened?"

"While you were gone, Marv. I hadn't had a chance to tell Jake myself. I guess I was remiss. Apparently he found out about our adding a new partner. I don't know how exactly. I'm afraid we had quite an argument last night. Richard and Joe were here, also Keith. They heard us shouting, I'm sure."

"What was Jake's objection?" Marv asked. "It let him off the hook, as to coming up with more money. I should have thought he'd be relieved."

"Not at all," Hal explained. "He was upset because it lessened his share of the partnership. Not that there have been any profits coming out of the business."

The detective took all this in, but did not comment. "And you, Dr. Yeager, had you argued with him too?"

Marv sighed. "We'd had words. He found out about, er, Ms. Arden and myself, and accused us of being indiscreet. Not in any moral sense because, if anything, Jake himself was amoral when it came to women. No, he was concerned that it might impact the business somehow." Marv didn't mention the word "blackmail," but he did say, "Naturally, I didn't want the nature of our relationship to be known. I suppose that looks like a motive, Detective?"

"Umm," was the detective's noncommittal reply. "But Mr. Thompson here knows." Marv nodded. "And, ah, Mrs.

Yeager?" Marv shook his head. "No. No one else? I imagine not. Well, we'll keep it to ourselves."

Marv said, "That would be most appreciated."

"I guess, as far as a motive goes, one could point to the insurance settlement," suggested Hal. "How much was it?"

"$250,000," Marv supplied. "I hadn't even thought about it. Not that we could ever accept it. That money has blood on it."

"Except," the detective interjected, "there is another factor. Mr. Keating told us that the victim had let his premiums lapse, so in the matter of a settlement, it's moot."

"I'm just as glad," said Hal. "Profiting by his death is a very distasteful thought."

The detective went on, "We have yet to get at his personal papers, his will, if any, and so forth. We have his computer and will attempt to find out what arrangements he had made. I understand he was a lawyer."

"He had a law degree, but had not practiced. I'm sure he had all sorts of deals going; he was a very active dealer. Please keep us informed on this," Marv requested again. "The disposition of all of these antiques, for example," and Marv indicated the furniture and other things in Jake's area, "need to be accounted for."

The detective nodded, looked at his notes and then his watch. "I'll let you two lock up now. We are finished here. I think we've gotten as much as we can from the premises. But if we can use the shop tomorrow for interviewing, it would make a much more comfortable situation for your dealers. If you don't mind staying closed for another day? We'll try to keep it out of the news for a little while longer. Thank you again, gentlemen. You have been very helpful." He shook hands with both of them, then added, "It's a beautiful shop."

The police were gone and Marv and Hal went around turning off lights, putting things to rights. They also checked their sales and their own areas, making sure nothing had gone missing. Hal listened to the phone messages; there wasn't anything that had to be responded to, and he went outside to call home. As Marv was about to leave, the shop phone began to ring. He picked it up before the recording started.

"Cider Run Antiques," he said wearily.

"Marv," said Ruth.

"An angel's voice couldn't be more welcome," sighed Marv.

"I've had a chance to get groceries and, if you like, I'll make dinner for us."

"Even more welcome. You are an angel." It was so wonderful to have a woman like that, thought Marv. What have I done to deserve it? He said aloud, "What have I done to deserve someone as wonderful as you?"

She answered lightly, "I'll tell you when I see you."

Hal was waiting for Marv in the parking lot. The perfect spring day that had started out with so much promise was drawing to a close, the golden light of late afternoon just touching the trees on the ridgeline.

"Sylvie is back. I'm going home, but I'll call the dealers."

"Take half. I'll take the other half, bottom of the list. Hal?"

"Yes, Marv?"

"You're the best partner anyone could have. Thanks for hanging in there with me."

They shook hands, as it seemed the most appropriate way of conveying their mutual appreciation.

"Same to you," said Hal. "I assume you'll be at Ruth's if I need you?"

"Tonight, yes. After that, I don't know."

"County jail, perhaps?"

"See you on the witness stand."

"Sylvie will bake a cake with a file in it."

"Or if it's you who lands in jail, I'll tunnel in."

"Tomorrow morning, then."

"Tomorrow morning."

Chapter 32

It was the first time he had been alone all day, this long, seemingly never-ending day, since he had gotten out of his truck in the parking lot this morning. Now, as he drove home, Marv had a sudden flash, a sudden picture in his mind of Jake lying motionless, his life ended, all that energy and intensity, all that talent and sexuality, gone forever. Marv felt uncontrollable tears and gave in to them.

He knew what it was. It was the sadness of a too-young death, the sadness of a life cut short before its possibilities could be realized. Whatever Jake would have been or could have done, whatever happiness he had to give or to receive, it was no longer to be. He had lived his life; it was over. Marv mourned, not only for Jake's sake, but for the whole world, for all the unrealized and unfulfilled lives. And it hit Marv that he was among those whose lives held an emptiness at the core. How long did he have? How long do any of us have?

But he was home and weary. He poured himself a beer and sat down by the answering machine. Clair's mother: Clair had not called yet. Helen: where are you, Marv? I need to speak to you. Sally Ann: I hope I'll get a chance to talk to you, because I'm worried about something. Helen again: What have you been doing? This is really unbearable. I'll be driving over tomorrow. Will you please call when you get home? You've turned your phone off and it's very annoying.

Marv deleted all the messages and went to get a shower. When he got out he felt more refreshed and, shaving, thought about what he wanted to do. He never had that chance to talk to Jake, to help him out, as he had planned. He was too late for that. But it wasn't too late for his own life. Marv wasn't sure what his course of action would be, but there would be a course of action. "I owe it to you, Jake, old buddy," he said out loud.

Marv made his phone calls to the dealers, asking them to come in to the shop sometime during the day tomorrow to let the police know where they and their keys had been on Tuesday night, giving any information he could to those who asked and leaving messages for those who weren't home. He couldn't reach anyone at Clair's, but left a message asking for her to call as soon as possible. Then he called Helen. He listened to a barrage of self-pity, which turned maudlin when she got onto the subject of Jake. Marv told her she didn't have to be here and, by the way, did she have her shop key with her on her key ring? "Of course, Marv, you know I always have it with me. Why do you ask?"

"The police need to find out where all the keys were last night. I told you, I thought, whoever killed Jake did not break in."

There was a moment's pause. "This is hard enough on me, Marv, without you being unpleasant."

"It hasn't been a pleasant day, Helen," said Marv in a tired voice or what he hoped sounded tired. Then he remembered his resolve. He had been covering up, telling fibs and lies for so long. Pretending, too, that things were fine when they weren't, to keep the peace with Helen. Well, first he needed to get through the investigation of Jake's murder. Then he would, he swore to himself he would, have that long-overdue

394

talk with Helen and, God willing, he and Ruth could have a talk about the future, about their lives together. "I have to meet with some of the dealers tonight. I'll see you tomorrow. We'll probably be at the shop. Drive carefully."

He went out into the fading daylight, shaking off the not-uncommon bitter taste from speaking with Helen. It would be dark soon and he felt that although a day of his life had gone by in almost total absorption, it was a day that would change his life, had already changed his perceptions of life. He got into his truck and before he started the engine, he said, "I won't forget, Jake. I'll do it for you and for me. Something good will come out of this, I promise."

When Marv arrived at Ruth's house he saw Sally Ann's white Mercedes parked in the driveway, as always slantwise, and he laughed, the first letting-go of the sadness of the day. Sally Ann, he thought, you've made an honest man of me in what I told Helen. He parked in front and went up to the door, still with a smile.

Ruth smiled back at him when she opened the door and he thought how welcome that smile was, how immediately warmed it made him feel. He said, "Sally Ann called and left me a message. Does she still want to talk to me?"

"I told her you'd be here," Ruth replied. "I've invited her to have dinner with us and she's in the kitchen helping. You know, Marv, I really like her. She's a good head."

"And a partner too. Here, before I go in, I have to tell you something."

"Yes?" asked Ruth a little anxiously, fearful of more bad news.

"You, Ruth, I'm in love with you." He took her hand and gave it a quick kiss and went back to the kitchen.

Irrepressibly romantic, she thought happily, but she did believe him. She had also believed him when he told her he hadn't gone back to the shop last night to see Jake. Jake. She'd thought of Jake all day, how mean he'd been to her, how uppity she'd been to him, how it counted for nothing now, and how bad she felt for what happened to him. But Sally Ann wanted to talk, and Ruth followed Marv into the kitchen.

Marv opened a bottle of white wine and Sally Ann held out her glass. "I didn't know until Richard told me," she was saying as Marv poured. She took a gulp of wine. "He said it was just awful."

"Hal did let on that it was quite a shouting match. But I wouldn't worry about it, Sally Ann. Jake was bound to find out and in his state of mind, whatever that was lately, he would be upset."

"But it's all my fault! Richard said when Hal came out he was really mad!" She stopped with her glass halfway to her lips. "Oh, no, Marv! You don't think Hal killed him because Jake made him so mad, do you?" Sally Ann looked genuinely distraught.

Marv, filling Ruth's glass, said quite seriously, "Some might do that, but not Hal. Hal looks tough because he's one large hombre. But he's really a big teddy bear. And the best friend I've ever had," he finished with sincerity.

"To Hal," said Ruth, raising her glass.

"And to Jake," added Marv, raising his.

"Well," chimed in Sally Ann, who had finally figured out the reason for the changes she'd seen in Ruth, "here's to you and Ruth. Now, that's all I'll say," and she winked. They drank the toasts and then got supper on the table.

Ruth had put together a shrimp salad with feta cheese and roasted red peppers, dressed with lemon and olive oil on arugula and baby spinach. Sally Ann took fresh sourdough rolls out of the oven and Marv poured more wine. There was a plate of strawberries for dessert with sweetened, heavy cream to splash on. It was a spring feast and all three of them agreed it was in honor of Jake. But then their talk turned to what would happen next and when the shop would open again.

"I feel bad about that, not being open," said Marv. "All the dealers are losing sales."

"But when the news gets out, ghastly as it is, people will flock to the shop. You know people," Ruth pointed out.

"But will they buy?" asked Marv. "Maybe they'll only come to gawk and ask about the murder with ghoulish curiosity. Or maybe we're finished. Maybe they'll avoid us as if we were contaminated."

"I don't think it will be that way at all!" Sally Ann protested. "Our customers will still want antiques and now there's even more history associated with Cider Run," she said, the five-syllable word rolling out with ease. Being a partner, thought Sally Ann, is making a difference.

"A good point and well made," Marv observed, acknowledging the new, improved version of Sally Ann, "if not the happiest history. Cider Run has had a checkered past and the trend apparently continues. Well, we'll see what happens tomorrow. I've been thinking..." he started to say.

Ruth and Sally Ann had gotten up to clear the table and stood where they were.

"Wait, let's have some coffee and I'll tell you what's on my mind," Marv proposed.

They took their coffee outside on the patio. The night was still and an almost full moon was rising in the east. Ruth remembered the last time she and Marv had sat out there drinking coffee, only a little over a week ago, as the moon, not yet in its first quarter, set in the western sky, and then she had gotten so angry! And after that they had made love. She looked at Marv and away quickly, lest she make Sally Ann uncomfortable.

Marv began again. "What I was thinking is that we should, all of us, get together at the shop and talk. Just talk and remember everything we can about Jake and the last two years. Who said what and who did what and how things seemed. We'll get somewhere, I know we will. There's a lot the police can find out, about his accounts and phone records and so on, but the fact that he was killed at the shop, and I know damn well it wasn't one of us, the fact that he was at the shop is the crucial point. We'll get to it. I'm willing to try. What do you say?"

"Well, we are, most of us, talkers, that's for sure," Sally Ann stated. "Even Andy in his own way."

"But Jake was the one with the gift of gab," Ruth admitted, "among his many gifts. And he had that beautiful tenor voice."

"He sang to me once," recalled Sally Ann, slightly misty-eyed.

"What do you say, folks?" Marv asked again. "Shall we all get together? Bring in pizza?"

"With a bottle of wine to prime the pump," Ruth suggested.

"Honey, a *jug* of wine!" Sally Ann declared.

"Now you're talking," said Marv brightly.

Sally Ann took her leave shortly afterwards and Ruth gave her a goodbye hug at the door. When she had gone, Marv pulled his truck into the garage. Where it belongs, he thought, next to Ruth's car.

They finished the coffee out on the patio, the moon climbing higher. Marv said, "Helen is coming back tomorrow. She's all upset, she really doted on Jake." He turned to Ruth, "I'm sorry, Ruth. I couldn't talk her out of it."

"I expected she would once she knew. It can't be helped. But we have tonight."

"The very words I wanted to hear," he replied, then looked anxiously at her. "There's something else I'd give anything to hear." Very soberly he asked, "Do you think you could love me, Ruth?" He reached for her hand. "We mean more to each other than just an affair. I know I love you, and I mean to go on loving you. We'll find a way to be together, somehow."

Should she admit she loved him? She knew quite clearly that she did love Marv, his humor, his enthusiasm, his sheer persistence. It wouldn't be fair to hold back, in spite of the difficulties of their situation. "I do love you, Marv," she confessed. "And I don't know what to do about it. Run away?" She gave him a wistful little smile and in answer he kissed her, the first kiss since very early that morning.

"Please don't run away, unless you take me with you," he implored. "Come. Let's go in."

Upstairs in Ruth's bedroom the shade at the southeast-facing window had not been pulled down and moonlight was flooding in. Marv stood at the window and looked at the moon. She loves me, he was thinking, and in a matter of seconds I will turn to her and we will make love. Then, without warning, a sudden awareness of Jake came unbidden into his mind. He hadn't expected it, yet felt a need not to banish the thought, but to see why Jake had intruded himself into his consciousness at a time like this. The slightest of sighs escaped him and Ruth came to his side.

"Jake?" she asked.

"Yes. I feel so unbearably sorry for him, for what happened. I don't understand, I guess, why there is this feeling that I was spared and he was not."

Ruth took his hand. "You know, I have always felt, in spite of things, that you two were really very much alike."

"Jake and I alike?" He was startled by her statement.

"There were more similarities than you'd think. Your love of opera, and going after antiques with the same kind of zest and single-mindedness. Even your sense of humor; you and he could be equally outrageous. You were not that different in your looks either—blond, tall, nice-looking."

He said, "*Was* blond. But I'm glad you think I'm nice-looking."

She didn't want to tell him her final point; it would be presuming too much. As she hesitated, he said, "You don't have to go on. I know what else we shared. A failed marriage. Although I thought in his case it was a symptom of something in his past that kept him from being able to stay committed. He once told me he had 'paid his dues' long ago and was out to enjoy himself." Marv paused, then said, "My marriage, well, was more of a mistake that kept going on long after it should have ended. What is so tragic is that I can do something about my life, I see that now, but he can't anymore."

Then he realized there was one other thing he and Jake had in common. Last night, perhaps at the very same moment, they were both in the fullness of making love, both wrapped around a woman, wrapped up in her, giving themselves, taking the sweetest of pleasures. He looked at Ruth in the moonlight, so lovely and yielding. He said, "Jake's life is over, but ours has just begun, and there is nothing more life-affirming than love. This is what counts. To have you to love, to know you love me."

The moon shone full across the bed. There was silver light and there were dark shadows, a room closed off from rest of the world but letting in the sky, someone who loved and wanted him. When he took Ruth in his arms, it was as if his mind had cleared of everything but a deep and profound need to express love, to express life. He knew that Jake, in dying, had given them this moment and he was thankful.

He fell asleep so soundly and exhaustedly that she didn't have the heart to rouse him, but let him sleep. At 7:30 she woke up and quietly got out of bed, took a shower and got dressed. She left a towel and washcloth out for him and went down to start breakfast.

Marv awoke to the aroma of coffee and had an instant of panic before he realized where he was, and then everything about yesterday came flooding back to him, the horror, the tediousness and then the perfection of last night. He was here, with her still and, best of all, she loved him. He found the towel she had put out for him, took a shower and felt happiness flowing over him. He came down to see Ruth stirring up eggs in a milk glass bowl.

"I wanted to let you sleep," she said smiling. "How does a cheese scramble sound? There's orange juice, and I've sliced a few strawberries and..."

She was stopped when he put his arms around her, nuzzled her ear and whispered, "Tell me again, Ruth."

"Scrambled eggs. With jack. Or do you want cheddar?"

"That you love me. Tell me again."

"Marv, I love you." How easy it was to say it to him.

"Am I being a pest? Just let me know if I'm being a pest and I'll go right out to the patio and shoot myself."

"Have breakfast first," she commanded sweetly.

They sat at her kitchen table and Marv wished he could always be with her for breakfast. They had a bagel after the eggs, then Marv poured more coffee for them. "I never had a chance to tell you what happened yesterday after you left," he said. He started out by going over what the detective had said, how death had been instantaneous, that Jake had been asleep and hadn't awakened.

"Thank God for that," was Ruth's comment.

Then he said, "Not only was Jake asleep, he had, a very short time before he was killed, been making love with someone and that could have been why he was sleeping so soundly."

Ruth put her hand over his. "My dear, like you," she said.

Marv saw that Ruth was smiling at him. "Lord, yes, like me." Another bond with Jake. "But, Ruth, it was who he was making love with that has me worried. The forensic evidence pointed to someone with straight, chin length, light brown hair and they have a DNA sample, of course."

Ruth suddenly remembered. "Marv," she said in a hushed voice. "I found one of Clair's museum guidebooks on the floor under the daybed in Jake's area yesterday morning. I put it in my bag and forgot about it. Clair?"

"Just so," Marv nodded. "Apparently Clair left for New York yesterday afternoon and hasn't called her parents back yet. Detective Willard, that nice, understanding, sad-looking man, does not think she did it or dumped him in the chest, pardon us, Jake, for being so cavalier with your person. But the police do want to talk to her and very much so."

"I can see why they would. But she probably doesn't know anything and then to have to be told that Jake," Ruth stopped here for an instant, then went on, "had been killed, perhaps almost immediately after she left him. This will be a terrible thing for her to deal with." Ruth, so recently in the same position, making love with someone warm and alive, could feel the anguish Clair would have. "Let me try to reach her, Marv. I'd like to be the one to break it to her, if you don't mind."

"Please do. I'd feel much better if it were you, as kindly as the detective might be."

"By the way, Sally Ann is quite impressed by our detective. She thinks he has the saddest eyes she's ever seen."

"Sally Ann seems to know about us. Is it a guess or did you say something?"

"I think she's guessed. It's the way we look at each other." I know I can hardly help myself, Ruth thought, and it will be even harder now not to give myself away.

"In that case, she may not be the only one who has guessed. Ruth, I must go home and change, and get to the shop. Come over when you can. I'm so sorry we won't be alone, but we will be again, soon. So help me."

Chapter 33

On Wednesday, shortly after the murder was discovered at the shop, Clair had come to a decision. She wrote a note to her parents, packed a bag, got into her car and left Martensdale.

Clair drove east, not on the Interstate, but on the older roads that followed the valleys between ridges of the Appalachians. She crossed the Susquehanna and skirted Pottsville, Allentown and Bethlehem. But at the Delaware River she turned north, as if reluctant to leave Pennsylvania.

She was heading to New York to see a friend at the museum, but she was in no hurry, as she was still wrestling with herself about what she had decided to do. In the car was her camera with the photos she had taken last night, the ones she'd downloaded earlier and had studied for a long time. The Caravaggio, the Raphael, the others. The artifacts from the Hermitage. Also in the car were her lists of artwork registered as missing.

She knew what she had to do. But how could she? Without warning Jake, how could she, essentially, destroy him? What had he done to her to deserve such a betrayal? Never mind what he had done in terms of betraying the world by keeping these treasures for himself, by siding with deceit and dishonor, and by engaging in criminal activities. What had he done to her, to Clair? He had made love to her, that's what he had done. He had made her feel so desired and wanted. And in return, she'd turn him in. For being unrepentant. That's why.

Clair, you little worm, you sanctimonious prig, she assailed herself. You enjoyed him, you let yourself thrill to him. And this is how you are paying him back? Well, that's one thrill you'll never have again. How about all the help he gave you when you were starting out at the shop? And what about Cider Run? You'll be out of there so fast, it will make your head spin. He is a partner in the business. How will the other partners, how will Dr. Yeager feel about you? Clair stopped the car at one of the river's overlooks and got out. The sun was low in the west, but it was still light, still warm. She could hear the water's gentle rushing sound, the spring songs of birds in the marsh grass, feel the breeze and smell the sharp, riparian scent of river. They'd put him in prison. How long would he be locked up? He wouldn't see sunlight on a river or hear bird songs. Clair felt miserable; she felt sick.

At Millford near the New York border she stopped at an inn for supper, one of the big, old rambling places that had started as a stage stop in the early1800s and continued to host travelers to the Poconos for another century. It was getting dark and she was tired and hungry. She took a room for the night and then went down to the restaurant.

Since the evening was warm, they were serving on the porch. Tables, laid with heavy damask tablecloths, were interspersed between big pots of newly-planted geraniums. White painted columns held up the porch roof and beyond the porch railing, Clair could make out the pale blossoms of flowering fruit trees. And in the midst of all this beauty, I feel like the basest of traitors, she thought. She studied the menu, ordered a glass of wine and the fresh fish special. The food and wine were excellent. Coffee, a small fruit tart, and she had stopped punishing herself and was much calmer.

The moon had come up and it was nearly full. So different from the downpour of last night. So different from last night when she was full of despair, sitting in the car and crying. And then today, so full of righteous indignation. Two young men at the next table had noticed her, particularly when she had taken a museum guide out of her bag to occupy herself while she ate. One of them now got up and came over to her table. He was, he said, aware that he might be intruding, but would she like to join him and his friend for an after dinner drink? He and his partner, he said it casually, and she smiled and accepted graciously.

It was remarkable, she thought, how much she had needed this welcome break from thinking about Jake. They went in to the bar, but brought their drinks back outside and talked for almost two hours about art, antiques, theatre, and travel. When she said goodnight and went upstairs she thought, not about Jake, but about Noel. She would accept his invitation to visit him in England this summer. She'd been somewhere for much too long, somewhere dark and disturbing. She'd gotten away from the lightness that was her nature, that went with her name, and delved into a world troubled and frightening. And compelling, yes, and it was done with her full cooperation. Jake had wanted something from her; she had wanted him. It had been agreed upon openly, but she would not consent to be implicated in the art thefts any further.

The next morning she had a leisurely breakfast and looked at the map. She traced a route back to Martensdale which she knew had some out-of-the-way antiques shops. She'd do a little shopping and then go home. No heroics for her. Jake would have to sort it out himself. She wouldn't interfere with the decisions he'd already made about his life. Besides, there wasn't anything she could do for him anyway, not in the matter of authenticating his art or trying to redeem him. She should probably call her parents. They'd left a message for her to call, but it had been too late last night to call them back. She knew they'd be at work now and she'd be home soon enough anyway.

As Clair drove southwest, zigzagging through the hills towards Martensdale, she was in a much more optimistic frame of mind. The person she really wanted to see was Ruth. She thought Ruth would understand and give good advice. Ruth was the sort she could talk to, talk things out with, before she had to face Jake again. Ruth must have been in a few predicaments herself. I could learn a lot from her, Clair thought. I hope I'll get a chance to talk with her about Jake.

Keith had started his new position at the university, a position both interesting and enjoyable, but was spending long days learning the job. When he had gone in to see Jake Tuesday night, he had not only been dog-tired, he had felt it was a hopeless cause, although he thought there was a remote possibility that Jake might have been beaten down by Joe and be more willing to negotiate regarding the property. It also occurred to Keith that the opposite could be true and Jake might be in a fighting mood after Joe. When he got back to Cider Run after tactfully withdrawing to let Joe air his grievances, he was almost ready to postpone seeing Jake. But Joe had left and Keith unlocked the door, locking it again behind him.

Jake was somewhere in the back, either in the office or kitchen. Where did he want to have this conversation? Would they end up physically going at it? He was not as big as Jake and his knee was unpredictable. Nevertheless, he was willing to take him on if it came to that, in which case it was better to go into the back of the shop. Keith headed that way. He noted that the music was still on and he thought he heard some activity. When Keith pushed open the door to the kitchen there was a sudden silence and then Jake appeared from the direction of the office.

Keith was surprised at how haggard Jake appeared. Had Joe such an effect on him, Keith wondered? But then Keith was fatigued too. Two rather weary-looking people facing each other, Keith thought.

"Et tu, Keith?" said Jake. "Is everyone ganging up on me tonight?"

"If so, you've brought it on yourself," was Keith's answer.

"I suppose you're going to start in on the property deal," Jake said in a bored voice.

"You know I want to buy that property. You don't want it. Why the hell are you doing this?"

Jake spread his hands in a deprecating manner. "I need the money," he said.

"Do you need to be hauled up before the Board of Ethics too? That's not going to help your position and that is exactly what will happen if you persist. My realtor..."

"Your realtor be damned. I don't see where ethics is involved. It's a matter of money. Either I sell it to you or I sell it to someone else. What will it be?"

Why did Keith think he was bluffing? He did, but he couldn't say why. Maybe it was because Jake looked so bad. Keith said, almost in a conciliatory way, because he realized he felt some empathy for Jake, "Look, just sell it to me for the original price, take your damned commission, and I won't take you to the Board. I'm tired. You're tired. It's late. Let's end this and get the hell out of here."

To Keith's surprise, Jake replied, "I'll think about it, OK? I've got a lot on my mind right now, so if you would get off my back, I'll think about it." And he turned on his heel and went back to the office.

"Fine, you son of a bitch," muttered Keith under his breath and he left.

The next day, Keith got a message to call Hal and another one from Lynn to call Owen. Hal wasn't there when he called but Owen was, and what he learned from Owen almost knocked him over.

The call Joe took at Cider Run from the hospital on Tuesday night had been about an elderly patient who needed his attention. Joe had thought this would be a good night to talk to Jake because he was finally angry enough, having learned about the vasectomy. The duplicity outraged him almost as much as the innuendoes. But he needed to get back to the hospital. I could just punch him out, it would be so rewarding, he thought. Then Jake came into the shop area and, seeing Joe, said, "If you're looking for Laurel, I don't know where she is."

The first thing Joe thought was that this was someone who was not well. Jake had dark circles under his eyes and his face was lined. He seemed drawn and spent. Joe automatically looked for more symptoms before he stopped himself and remembered why he was there.

And the second thing he thought was that, in spite of Jake's appearance, he was unforgivably handsome, more so than Joe remembered. He could see why Laurel had been attracted to him. She had admitted this to Joe and he had understood her loneliness that winter. She told him that Jake had kissed her one night and, in her words, she had "fled into the snow." Joe vowed to her that he would never be absent so much again.

He eyed Jake with distaste. "I know where Laurel is, thank you," Joe returned sharply. "It's you I want to see. I think you know why."

"Hey, man, I don't like to discuss the women I've accommodated and particularly not other men's wives."

"Then keep that in mind the next time you slander my wife."

Jake gave a little shrug. "I can't help it if women are attracted to me. It's been happening all my life and will no doubt go on. But this is the first time someone has accused me of slander. I've never said anything to anyone about how Laurel threw herself at me."

Joe took a step nearer and felt himself shaking with anger. "That's crap and you know it," he said with vehemence.

"You might ask Laurel. But don't torture yourself. These things happen. It's over now, if that's any consolation."

The insufferable bastard, Joe thought. "Go to hell," he said. "I have patients to take care of. And if I were you, I'd see a doctor. But not me." And he walked out.

When Laurel called Joe at the hospital the next day to tell him about Jake, she had begun by saying, "Jake is dead."

Joe's reply was, "No! He must have been even more ill than I thought. Do they know what the cause was yet?"

410

Chapter 34

When Hal drove up Cider Run Road shortly after 9:00 on Thursday morning and looked towards the shop as he always did, he could have sworn he saw someone on the roof. *Now* what are the police looking for, he wondered. He got closer and the figure became clearer. There was definitely a person on the roof, but it didn't look like a policeman. It was someone wearing the unmistakable straw hat, blue shirt and black one-shoulder-strap overalls that could only be an Amishman. Then he saw two more Amishmen on the roof and, as he got to the parking lot, sighted the truck with *Glick's Roofing and Repairs* in large letters on the side parked prominently in front of the shop. "Hell's bells!" he swore.

"Good morning, Mr. Thompson. Lovely day, isn't it?" Hal, getting out of his car, was greeted by the large, cheery, non-Amish driver of the vehicle, who also acted as the crew's scheduler. Hal had spoken with him what now seemed like years ago. "We're lucky to have such a bee-you-tee-full day, aren't we? Well, we won't get in your way, so you can just open the shop as usual and don't mind us. With the weather like this, we'll have that new roof on in, oh, another day if nothing goes wrong. Not that I think anything will. But sometimes, you never can tell with these older buildings." His eyes had been on the sky, on the roof, and now wandered off toward the orchard, never once resting on Hal.

Hal realized it was hopeless to halt the progress of the roofing crew. They were already well underway removing the old shingles. "We won't be opening the shop today, as it turns out," Hal explained. "There was an accident here yesterday and the police will be coming. Just to let you know, so you and your crew don't get alarmed."

"An accident? What happened?"

Hal was evasive. "The police aren't sure. But you go ahead, the weather can't hold like this forever." He unlocked the door and locked it again behind him. As he had expected, he could hear sounds of ripping and tearing, of banging, prying and knocking reverberating down from the roof and through the chimney. Might as well, thought Hal, might as well tear the whole damn place down after what happened.

But he didn't want their shop to be gone. He just wanted Jake not to have been killed. Sylvie and the girls had cried when he told them about Jake. Sylvie had been fond of him and Hal hadn't unloaded his grievances about Jake on her. Maybe he should have, but it wouldn't do now. Sylvie said that Jake had sung lieder to her. Her memories of him were all of his charm and appeal, in spite of the tile incident. If she had seen another side of him, it may have been different. But Hal wouldn't disillusion her, not after this.

The noises from the roof continued as Hal turned on lights and got the computer up. Dealers would need to have a look at their sales to make sure nothing had been stolen. He listened to the answering machine: Helen trying to reach Marv. Some customers wanting to know why the shop wasn't open. Hal made a new message for the answering machine, stating that the shop would be closed while repairs were being made, but would be open again in a few days. He knew that Marv would agree. Maybe the roofers being there now was for the best after all.

Marv. God, I hope he doesn't screw up his life, Hal thought. He knew things weren't good between Marv and Helen. She hadn't let him near her in, must be, over eight years. But what can you do? Have an affair? But Marv seemed to be more involved with Ruth than merely an affair, like that last time, and if Ruth felt the same way, then what? Well, he'd stick by Marv. Marv was his friend, a better friend than he'd ever had, and the affinity between them had grown stronger over the last two years. And he liked and admired Ruth. She was sensitive, bright and good- natured and he could tell how much she appreciated Marv.

And Keith. He'd stick by Keith too. Keith had called last night and told him about his confrontation Tuesday night with Jake. I just hope the police believe him, Hal thought.

Two years, Hal mused, and as Cider Run benefitted and grew because of the dealers, their lives were impacted and changed by being part of the shop. Andy, coming out of his shyness and blossoming in his new interests. Owen and Keith, getting to be such good companions. Richard, able to be his funny, bright self and appreciated. Elaine, well, she's the same outspoken lady, maybe more so, but the customers' favorite. Ruth, another one who is blossoming, but that's in large part because of Marv, he realized now. Then there's Laurel, who couldn't be happier, Cider Run notwithstanding. And Cora and Grace, helpful and cheerful, expressing their considerable talents and creativity. Emmy, with her encyclopedic knowledge and all those travel experiences. She adds class and culture and she's always got so much information to share, when she's allowed to get it out. Sally Ann, how confident and self-assured she has become, and what a generous soul. His own dear Sylvie, enjoying being at the shop so much. Helen, she was the only one who seemed to have become disillusioned, but was it the shop or her marriage? Marv, he had found Ruth because of Cider Run, and his new happiness was bubbling over. And Hal himself? He had gotten close to all these people and it took the stiffness out of him, so Sylvie said. And I do appreciate them all, but particularly Marv. Then, I mustn't leave out Jake, what had the shop done for him? Put an end to his marriage, put an end to his life? He shied away from thinking about Jake. Now, who was he forgetting? Clair. Where the hell was she?

Two police officers, male and female, arrived and Hal let them in. They were polite, discreet, and arranged some areas for interviewing the dealers. Hal offered to make a pot of coffee for them, but they said if he'd show them where the coffee maker was, they would be glad to do it. They seemed completely unaffected by the work in progress on the roof, and brought a mug of coffee out to Hal when it was made. Perhaps this day won't be so bad, he thought hopefully.

Then Keith came in. He and Hal shook hands and Hal clapped him fondly on the shoulder, before introducing the officers. And we're off, thought Hal.

Marv's truck pulled in next as Hal stood in the doorway, drinking his coffee and listening to the clamor on the roof. He automatically checked his watch, 9:45, and wondered what kind of night Marv had. Nightmares, possibly, after seeing Jake lying there? Hal certainly hadn't slept well. But the expression on Marv's face was far from distressed. Sublime, Hal said to himself, the most accurate word he could think of to describe that look.

"Nice going, Hal," Marv observed, as he pointed up to the roof. "Your timing was perfect. How do you manage these things? It must take a special kind of talent." His smile was so tranquil, his whole demeanor so relaxed.

"Maybe I'll be lucky and you'll get felled by a flying shingle," Hal shot back. Then he told Marv that Keith had called last night, and what he'd said about his meeting with Jake. "He's being interviewed now, and I'm pretty sure he'll do all right."

"We can only hope. He's probably their number one suspect, what with the property thing and his knowledge of weapons and all. But you and I know Keith couldn't do anything like that. They didn't have any new information to share on the murder, did they?"

"Not that they said," Hal replied, "but these cops seem to be OK. They even made coffee. Do you want some?"

Marv said with a smile, "Would it be as good as Ruth's this morning?" He couldn't *not* say that; it just came out and he saw Hal's quick grin, which had the effect of encouraging him, and he went on, but more seriously, "Hal, I think my life is going to come together. If we can get through this, first of all. But then, I'm going to do my damnedest to work things out. I've been muddling through with Helen too long. She's not happy, we're not happy together, as you know. Something to do with Jake's dying has really affected me. It's as though the old course of life has been irrevocably altered and change must follow."

"For your sake, Marv, I wish it. But getting through this murder investigation is the priority now," said Hal.

"I've been thinking about what we could do and I talked this over with Ruth and Sally Ann last night. Yes, Sally Ann was at Ruth's for dinner." He told Hal about the idea of a talk session, of letting things lead where they would.

Hal heartily embraced the idea. "That sounds exactly like what we all need. It could let people get their feelings out and help us deal with the whole thing better." Then he added, "I suppose Detective Willard & Company will want to be present. Do you think there would be any objections?"

"I truly believe our dealers have nothing to hide. Also, the sooner, the better. What do you say we all meet at 7:00 this evening? We could spring for pizza, beer, a jug or two of wine, anything that could help."

"Let's go for it. I'll let everyone I see know." A particularly loud crash came from the direction of the roof. "Oh, and I've changed the message on the phone, to say we're closed for a few days for repairs."

"Good. Thanks, Hal."

"But you won't like one of the messages left last night. Helen..."

"Facing the police will be nothing as compared to facing Helen," Marv sighed.

Throughout the day the Cider Run dealers came to the shop, checked their areas and sales, gave their statements about keys and whereabouts and stayed to talk. While the talk was subdued and not marked by the high spirits they usually had when gathered around the front counter, there wasn't any morbidity. The clatter and bang on the roof was a welcome if noisy distraction.

Everyone agreed with the idea of having a discussion in the evening, coming together to remember Jake and see if they could get insights on what happened.

"But pizza?" asked Richard. "It would taste like ashes."

"Ashes would do you good," said Elaine. "Ashes teach humility."

"From which you are exempt, it would seem," Richard retorted.

"I think pizza is just what we need and something to drink, too," said Cora, who had come to make both her and Grace's statements.

"A little like a wake," was Laurel's quiet comment.

Owen dashed in between classes. He had coaching duties and had to get back to the high school. There was a swollen black and blue area under his left eye which, he explained to Marv and Hal, was the price one paid for wanting to have a winning baseball team. But his concern was all for Keith. "Has he been in? How did it go? How did he look?"

Hal answered, "They let him drive off, so it would seem to have been all right."

Owen confessed he'd worried all night. Owen would, thought Hal, he's really grown to care about Keith.

Sally Ann arrived in the afternoon, dressed spectacularly in the deepest of black, a frilly black blouse under a black linen jacket, with a flowing black skirt and black pumps, the whole completed by an antique necklace of jet beads and dangling Victorian jet earrings. Her face, only modestly made up, registered disappointment when she found that Detective Willard was not there yet, but she quickly composed an expression to complement the mourning outfit and marched back to meet with the officers.

"Richard will go ga-ga when he sees her tonight," Marv predicted. "What would this place be like without Sally Ann?"

"There wouldn't be anyone working on the roof right now for one thing," said Hal. "Does Sally Ann know about Jake's last, um, actions and who was with him?"

"No, but Ruth does, though. I'd like to keep knowledge of the nature of Clair's relationship with Jake on the level of just 'meeting' with him." Richard and Elaine had told both

417

Marv and Hal that Jake had asked Clair to stay after the
shop closed on Monday, the day that the three of them had
worked together. Marv said, "What that was about, however,
we won't know until we see Clair. And I sure as hell hope it
will be soon." Marv had left it in Ruth's hands about Clair,
but what if Clair didn't make contact? Ruth had promised to
be at the shop for the evening session, but would wait until
the last minute, hoping Clair would call her.

Andy came in, shook his head in a worried fashion at
Marv and Hal. He couldn't get it out of his mind that one
of his antiques had been a murder weapon. As he went back
to talk to the officers, Marv observed to Hal, "I imagine that
joining Cider Run has brought a little more excitement into
Andy's life than he bargained for."

"Could we say the same about you, Marv?" Hal offered
with a touch of impishness.

"And about time too," Marv agreed. "It hasn't hurt you
either, Hal. You're far less staid."

"Staid, me?" Hal protested. "I've never been staid."

"I suppose it has to do with being an engineer," Marv
pursued. "It's a hallmark of the profession, a drawback
that goes along with the territory, characterized by rigidity,
stodginess, a plodding way of thinking."

"Now, see here, Marv! Just because you've spent most
of your life in an ivy-covered tower up on college hill, head
in the clouds, completely out of touch with the rest of the
world, looking down your nose at anyone who does anything
practical, necessary and worthwhile..."

In the midst of this enjoyable and diverting conversation,
Detective Willard arrived, his sergeant a pace behind him.
"Gentlemen," the detective greeted them, "can we find a
private place to talk?"

They went back to the kitchen and as they passed by Sally Ann, getting up after her interview with the police officers, Marv saw Detective Willard, caught off guard for a second, register frank appreciation at the sight of her, then quickly revert to his usual impenetrable expression. But the look was not lost on Sally Ann.

Marv asked, "Sally Ann, can you stay and keep an eye on the front?"

"I'll be here for as long as you need me," she purred, glancing at the detective.

There's something about this place, thought Marv, not for the first time.

They settled themselves around the table. "I want to get you caught up on what we've learned so far and see where we can go from there." Detective Willard took out some notes, looked at them, then laid them on the table. "We have spent most of the morning with the victim's wife and brother. She is quite definitely not in mourning for her late husband. In fact," he paused, "she came with her boyfriend. She's pregnant."

Marv exclaimed, "Hoo, boy!", as apt a comment as any.

"No kidding?" said Hal.

"But," the detective went on, "their alibis for the night of the murder are pretty tight: cars never left parking garage, check with rental cars got nowhere, and as far as a key..."

"She turned that in when she left us," Hal confirmed.

"Right, so although she was what you might call highly motivated, unless she hired a very talented lock-picking assassin, we can't pin this on her. She and the victim's brother were in a bitter argument for most of the time they were together. We've had a look at the victim's will, which leaves his estate almost entirely to the brother, most of it being family property. He'd cut her out completely. In fact, the only things that don't go to the brother are the antiques in his home and here at the shop." The detective paused again to look at Marv and Hal. "These go to Cider Run, Inc."

Marv raised his eyebrows. Hal frowned. "Annette must have been fuming," he said.

"Not that there was all that much in the way of antiques that we found in his house. Furniture, rugs, a painting or two. The brother was fine with that, by the way. He said you were welcome to them, and he'll be contacting you soon. Also, the victim's investment in the partnership reverts to the surviving partners."

"Probably done to thwart Annette as well," Hal commented.

"What about the funeral arrangements?" Marv asked.

"In Pittsburgh. The full treatment. Mass, but private, only for the family. We'll be releasing the body. The postmortem didn't tell us what we didn't already know, except for one thing we missed. There was some bruising we'd overlooked on the knuckles of the victim's right hand."

"As if he'd thrown a punch?" Marv asked.

"And connected," Hal added.

"Yes, on something hard," the detective agreed. "Like someone's jaw."

Marv and Hal were silent, considering this information.

"Now," the detective went on, "have all your dealers been in to talk to my officers? I need to read the statements, then I'm sure I'll have some questions for you."

"We're still missing a few dealers," Marv said. Please, Clair, he thought, call in! "I have to leave at 5:00 to run out to the airport to pick up Emmy Greene and her husband.

Do you need to talk to her right away? They'll be coming in after a flight from London and will probably be jet-lagged."

"I would, but if it isn't possible, find out for me," the detective ticked off on his fingers, "where her shop key has been and, if it has been home while they were gone, who has access to their house, and when you take them home, have them make sure it is still where she left it. And that the house hasn't been disturbed."

"Got it," Marv nodded. "Anything else from your end?"

The detective consulted his notes. "The victim's phone records, credit card activity, bank accounts and the like are going to take some time to go through. We're a small operation here in Martensdale and we need help with some things. Right now, everything seems related either to his real estate business, buying and selling property, or buying and selling antiques. It hasn't led us very far. We've gone through his briefcase and we've only found papers relating to realty transactions. One was interesting, but we'll get back to that later. No, that's about all." He looked up. "We have to concentrate on Cider Run, I'm afraid."

"In that case," said Marv, "we have a proposition. The dealers have all agreed to meet here tonight at 7:00. We will be bringing in pizza and something to wet the whistle, and we're going to sit around and hash over the last two years and try to remember everything we can about Jake."

The detective was suddenly alert and interested. Sergeant Garcia wrote furiously.

Marv continued, "They see this as therapeutic for them, but also think it may lead somewhere. No one had any objection to your being present at this session which, I would say, speaks well for them."

"I will most happily attend, and my sergeant too, if he may."

"Now, a request, Detective, concerning the relationship between Jake and Clair Somers. I think we can be pretty sure she was the woman with Jake the night he was killed. You'll learn, if you haven't already, that on the previous night she had agreed to meet with him here about something. Two dealers were present when he asked her to meet him. But, so far, Clair hasn't turned up and we don't know what that meeting was about. We think it had to do with Clair's museum experience. At any rate, I'm asking that we keep her relationship with Jake at the 'meeting' level, as far as public knowledge goes, and not mention the other aspect."

"I understand completely. But if she doesn't make contact today, we are going to have to issue a bulletin."

"Yes. I realize that, and it's terribly distressing. She's young, she's just, well, so trusting and I know her parents," Marv finished, trailing off.

"We'll give her until tonight, but then we really must make a concerted effort to locate her. Are her parents worried? Her life could be in danger, remember, because of what she may have inadvertently witnessed."

"And that scares us silly. I haven't said anything to her parents about the murder, so they aren't worried from that perspective. I'll find out what I can for you, Detective," Marv promised. "And now I must go to the airport."

"Don't you go off anywhere while you're at the airport, Dr. Yeager," the detective said with a sad-eyed smile.

Hal put in quickly, "Oh, didn't you know, Detective? Dr. Yeager is leaving this afternoon for Argentina." There. That ought to settle the score, thought Hal.

"Yes, and Hal has our tickets. Are you packed and ready to go, Hal?"

The sergeant had started to write this down, but looked up, pencil arrested in hand and a slow smile spread across his face. The detective grunted. People do need to break the tension, he thought.

Marv hoped he'd get a chance to call Ruth, but when he looked at the time, he realized he was already late, so left for the airport. As he drove, his thoughts were on what would happen that evening and if they could make any progress in solving the murder. He decided to check in with Jacob, just on the off-chance.

"Jacob," said Marv, "I don't suppose you know what happened."

"Aye, Marv. I know what happened. Man got hisself killed is what happened."

"I don't suppose you know *how* it happened?" Marv asked.

"Happened with that there thing you think is old. Ice pick. We didn't have none of those that I recall."

"Jacob," asked Marv and, although he began to wonder if he might be getting close to losing his grip on reality in these conversations, persevered nonetheless, "I don't suppose you know *who* did it?"

"Now, Marv, I weren't there when it happened. You know that."

Hal made a list of what they'd need for drinks, then went out into the parking lot and viewed the roof. The roofers had left for the day. The roof was covered with a tarp and it looked as if they were ready to put the new one on tomorrow, Friday. Then, Saturday, we could open the shop again, Hal thought.

Would it be in the newspaper, on the TV news by then? What would they say? Would they interview the dealers? He shuddered. That was another topic they'd have to discuss tonight. Hal thought tonight might be very interesting. As he stood there, Sylvie pulled into the parking lot. He walked across to her and she opened the car window.

"Helen's home," she said to Hal. "I talked to her on the phone and she's on her way over. Is Marv here?"

"No, left to get Emmy and Charles."

"Lucked out again. Helen is almost inconsolable." Sylvie got out of the car and Hal put his arm around her and they walked across the parking lot. "I'm afraid," she warned, "this is one time Marv may not have much success in dealing with her."

"Sylvie," said Hal, feeling this might be the opportunity to break it to her, "he may no longer want to try."

She looked up at Hal. "I guess I'm not surprised," Sylvie admitted, as they went into the shop.

Detective Willard was introduced to Sylvie, and she told the officers taking statements that her key had been with her while she was gone. Was there anything she could tell them, they asked, that might have a bearing on the murder? Sylvie shook her head, no, only that Jake had upset some people and probably made some men envious, but was utterly charming when he wanted to be and she, for one, was going to miss him awfully.

"Thank you, Mrs. Thompson," said Detective Willard. "I want you to know how cooperative everyone has been, and also to mention that I think Cider Run is a beautiful shop."

Sylvie beamed at that. She could see why this detective had Hal's confidence.

"When this is all over," the detective went on, "I'd like to have someone show me around the shop, around the antiques, I mean." His eyes flickered for an instant on Sally Ann, now busy on the phone.

Sylvie followed his glance. "I'm sure Sally Ann would be more than happy to, Detective."

"When this is all over," the detective repeated.

"When this is all over," Sylvie affirmed.

Hal left to get the beverages for the evening and it was while he was gone that Helen arrived at the shop. Her eyes were puffy and red from crying. Sylvie met her at the door, trying to look more saddened than she really felt. Sylvie was genuinely sad at Jake's death, but she had more on her mind. Who had done it? Where was Clair? What did this mean for the shop? Helen, on the other hand, was giving in to something more personal.

"Oh, Sylvie," Helen began, and started crying afresh. "I feel as if the bottom has dropped out of my world. He always made me feel so, so..." Words seemed to have failed her and she turned away. Her glance fell on Sally Ann, just hanging up the phone after ordering pizza, Sally Ann in her smashing black outfit, making the most of the occasion. Helen made a disapproving face and turned back to Sylvie. "Well, what am I supposed to do? Talk to some policemen? Do I tell them how incredibly wonderful he was and how much I'll miss him?"

"Something like that, Helen. I'll introduce you to the detective in charge and you can make a statement." Sylvie realized Helen hadn't once asked about Marv. It reinforced the meaning behind Hal's carefully worded remark in the parking lot.

When Helen was through with the police officers, she stood in Jake's area, looking at his things. Sylvie decided to leave her alone to grieve, if that was what she was doing. But Helen was grieving for herself. This is it, this is more than I can bear, were her thoughts. Without Jake this place doesn't have any appeal for me. Oh, it did when we started out, but all the life and sparkle has gone with Jake. And why couldn't Marv have prevented it? In fact, it seems to me he hadn't even been all that cordial to Jake lately. I wonder if Marv knows who killed him? I wonder if Marv...she was not thinking rationally, she knew, but that is what happens when you're in mourning for someone, someone who was so...exciting, she admitted to herself. What in the world does Sally Ann think she's doing in that black get-up? She looks completely overdone. You'd think she had a personal reason to mourn for Jake. Where is Marv anyway? He should be here. He's probably off at a sale with Hal, buying another ridiculously large piece of furniture. His behavior over the last year has become increasingly impulsive, as if he's reverting to some adolescent state. Well, when I tell him my news, it will sober him up. But that's too bad. It's too late. I've made up my mind. And she went into the restroom to repair her face.

Last to come in was Joe Fisher. Detective Willard immediately rose from where he had been sitting with his officers going over the statements, and he and Joe went back into the kitchen to talk. They stayed for what seemed to Sylvie a long time, but were both smiling and talking amiably when they came out. As Joe reached Sylvie and Sally Ann at the front counter, he gave them the thumbs up sign.

Chapter 35

I t was nearing 5:30 and Ruth decided to try calling once more. Although she had been concerned about Clair all day, the happiness from last night and the unexpected pleasure of breakfast with Marv had given her a feeling of such optimism that it seemed to embrace Clair as well, a new-found energy which could bring Clair within reach. The phone rang three times, then Clair's mother answered.

"Ruth, I see her pulling into the driveway right now. And it looks like a bench or something in the back, so I guess she's been antiques shopping." Clair's mother did not sound worried. I'm so grateful Marv spared her that, thought Ruth.

Ruth explained, "There's a meeting and pizza at Cider Run tonight, and I know Clair will want to be there. But I really need to talk to her about something first. Do you think you can get her to come over to my house? As soon as she can? I can help her unload her things at the shop, if she wants," and Ruth added, "and I could use her help in unloading some things of mine." Clair was so considerate, that should provide incentive, even if she was tired from her trip.

Ruth immediately called the shop to tell Marv, but the phone was busy and stayed busy, and she didn't get a chance to call again until almost 7:00. By that time, Ruth and Clair had spent an hour together and had formed, out of the tragedy of Jake's death, a bond of understanding and mutual trust.

When Clair arrived Ruth took her into the living room and sat by her on the sofa, looked into her eyes and said, calmly and gently, "Clair, it's about Jake." She let Clair have a second, but then quickly went on, "He's been killed. He was murdered, stabbed, no one knows by whom."

Clair opened her mouth to speak, or to scream, but nothing came out. She sat looking at Ruth, and Ruth took her hand. Ruth told her, quietly and evenly, the facts of Jake's death. Where he was, and how he had been killed, when it had probably happened, what the police had learned so far. Clair did not interrupt, but was sitting so taut that Ruth was afraid for her. When Ruth started to explain that she had found Clair's book on the floor under the daybed, her own carefully controlled demeanor dissolved and the tears came freely, releasing Clair as well. They cried wordlessly, and Ruth put her arm around Clair.

When she was able to talk, Clair kept repeating, "No, no," then slowly began to accept the knowledge of what had happened and, leaning on Ruth for support, started to talk about Jake. All her thoughts of the last few days came out in a rush. She told Ruth about her fears for him, what he had told her, the pain he had carried for his childhood friend, what she had almost done about the artwork, that they had made love and about the last night they were together. Between sobs, everything, everything that she had been holding inside came out, and Ruth listened, feeling Clair shaking underneath her arm. Finally, Clair was talked out. "Why?" she asked over and over, and Ruth had no answer.

"I don't think any of us really knew very much about Jake," was all Ruth could offer.

Clair had known about him, perhaps more than anyone, but her shock and grief pushed everything aside. There was nothing to be done now, she thought achingly. Something had taken place beyond her control, beyond her involvement with him. Ruth went to the kitchen and brought back a carafe of water and two glasses, and they drank silently, getting their bearings back.

Ruth then told Clair about the other dealers' concern and their all wanting to work together to help find answers. Clair wiped her eyes and felt some strength returning. The others needed her now. She turned to Ruth. "I'm glad you were the one to tell me."

"I'm glad I was able to be the one."

"I've been wanting to talk to you, thinking maybe you could help me figure things out about Jake. I only wish it hadn't taken this," she faltered, "this, to get us talking." Then, before Ruth could answer, she went on, "I hope you won't mind my saying this, but you and Dr. Yeager, I mean Marv, are fond of each other, aren't you?"

Ruth nodded. "Very much so," she admitted.

"I've known something was there. I've seen it for a long time. When you are around he's just incandescent. That's the best description I can think of." Then she looked sad again, "But, oh, Ruth, what will you do?"

"See what happens? I don't know. Sometimes, that's all you can do. And are you ready to be with everyone? Shall we go to Cider Run?" Am *I* ready, Ruth wondered. How can I look Helen in the face?

"I think I'm ready," Clair replied. "I want to help in any way I can. But I'm thankful we're going together."

Ruth confessed, "I'll need you as much as you need me, walking in and seeing Helen after...after..."

Clair gave Ruth's hand a little squeeze and went off to the bathroom.

While Clair was gone, Ruth got ahold of Sally Ann at the shop. "Sally Ann, please tell Marv: Clair is with me and we'll be there as soon as we can."

The hour between 6:00 and 7:00 was not a lull. In fact, it was, in its own way, as sociable as ever. Dealers arrived and stood talking. It was as if they had collectively realized that together they could tackle a very difficult subject, one which would be overwhelming if tackled alone. The exception was Helen, who sat at the front counter, withdrawn from everyone. Sylvie tried to console her, but was waved away. When Hal came back with the beverages, people helped carry things out to the kitchen and the drinks were started.

Detective Willard had dismissed his officers, but he and his sergeant stayed. As dealers came in, he made it a point to meet each one, if he had not already done so earlier, and talk briefly to each, while his sergeant unobtrusively took notes. He looked closely at Owen's bruises, but said nothing. He also observed the dealers in their interactions, partly to see if he could sense any suspicions they might harbor toward one another and partly to gauge the extent of their mood. As for the first observation, he saw no traces of doubt manifested among them. As for the second, his reason was that he had something to say to them which might be very upsetting, namely a description of the murder itself, and he hoped they could deal with it. He was glad to see they were chatting normally.

Marv returned from taking Emmy and Charles home, but before he had a chance to talk with Helen, Detective Willard drew him into a conversation about procedure for the evening. "I'd like to address the group first, if you have no objection," the detective said, "and inform everyone on what we have learned in our investigation. Omitting the very sensitive angles, of course."

Marv breathed a low, "Thank you, Detective."

"And perhaps some more of our questions can be answered. Then, I'll leave it up to you, and we'll go sit on the sidelines and try to stay invisible. I don't want anyone to be inhibited by our presence. If you think that may be the case, we'll go."

"Knowing our outspoken group I would say not, but I'll ask them anyway. Now, where would be the best place to gather? I'm afraid it's always been Jake's area we've used for socializing in the past." And how long ago that seems, thought Marv.

Hal, having gotten the drinks organized, joined them. Marv turned to him. "Shall we set up in Jake's area? Or would that discourage people, do you think?"

"I think," Hal pondered, "that although it may be the 'scene of the crime,' we will be living with it for a long time. Maybe it would be a good idea to try to expunge the horror associated with the area now and start the process of reclamation."

"Gosh, Hal!" Marv exclaimed, "I never knew engineers could be so articulate!"

"Go to hell, Marv," said Hal cheerily.

"I'll help bring up chairs," the detective offered, noting again the easy way these people had with each other.

Marv knew he had to get it over with and, while chairs were being assembled and people were busy getting their drinks, he went to the front where Helen sat by herself. He had thought of a dozen different ways to initiate a conversation with her but none seemed right, not right for the way he wanted to begin the rest of his life. But before he could even greet her, she said petulantly, "Where have you been? Do I have to face this alone?"

The only thing that seemed appropriate to say was, "Face what?" as he wasn't sure what she was referring to.

"Jake's death. Have you no feelings at all?"

"Helen," he said patiently, "that's why we're all here, all of us. We're going to face it together and you can be part of that."

"Not willingly. You arranged this; I didn't. Do any of them really care? I doubt it. I know you didn't care for Jake, particularly lately. I don't know why, but it seems that he annoyed you, you and Hal both."

"He more than annoyed us, but not enough to be killed over. You'll feel better if you participate, I'm sure." He knew he must sound patronizing, but at least he wasn't being untruthful.

"We'll see," was all she said, and walked slowly towards the group.

Cora came bringing the picture she had done of Jake sitting in the Morris chair. She had cropped the *Winter Reading* caption and had matted and framed the sketch. She had initially thought she'd frame it in black ebony, then felt black might be too austere, and instead put the picture in a warm-toned oak frame which had an Arts and Crafts look to it. The mantelpiece was empty and she placed the picture in the center. It was a focal point and had the effect of putting Jake even more into everyone's consciousness. Helen stood in front of it for a long time, then abruptly turned away. Marv went to look at it and complimented Cora, not only on the sketch itself but on the choice of frame. "It's unreal, though," he remarked. "He looks like someone from the far past, as if he died a long time ago."

"The history professor talking," said Cora.

Laurel saw the sketch when she crossed the shop on her way to the kitchen. She stopped, looked at it, but said nothing and went on. Richard raised one eyebrow when he saw it, then followed Laurel to the kitchen for drinks.

Detective Willard noticed the picture and studied it for a while. His thoughts ran along the lines of, I wonder how many hearts he broke? Then Keith came up and the detective said, "Mr. Mackinnon, may I have a private word with you?" They were gone into Keith's area for some time and Owen looked anxious. Keith returned, and he and Owen stood talking earnestly together. "No fooling?!" Marv heard Owen remark.

When Andy arrived, the detective asked him if he would be so kind as to help in making an identification. They stepped to one side and Marv saw Andy nod his head over something in a plastic bag, then look away quickly. Marv knew exactly what it was: a wooden grip inscribed with *Martensdale Ice and Coal Co. Tel 842*, into which was inserted a slim steel spike, about 5 inches long, ending in a sharp point. But the way the detective smiled at Andy, and spoke in a low voice to him, Marv was sure Andy was dealing with it all right. When the detective moved on, Marv immediately went over to Andy. "I'm sorry, I couldn't tell you before," he apologized.

"It's OK, Marv, really," a white-faced Andy answered. "The detective wondered if I'd like it back. I said I never wanted to see it again." He took a breath, then went on, "He said they'd pay me the $35 I had on the tag." Andy shook his head. "I said I couldn't take any money for it."

"Gruesome, isn't it?" said Marv. "But you know it was just happenstance." Marv knew that Andy's family, going back for generations, were Quakers and subscribed to the doctrine of non-violence, except for one notable period from 1861 to 1865.

"Marv, how could anyone do such a thing?" Andy asked. "No one here could, I'm sure of it." Andy looked around at his fellow dealers, the people who had been to his farm for the Labor Day picnic and who were his friends and helped him get started at the shop.

"And so am I," agreed Marv. "Maybe we'll get some ideas tonight."

Emmy, looking unfazed by an eight hour flight across the Atlantic and the five hour time difference came in bearing several bottles of wine from the duty free shop in Heathrow. "I thought we'd drink some toasts to Jake," she proposed.

"Mrs. Greene," Detective Willard introduced himself. "Dr. Yeager tells me your key was undisturbed when you returned."

"It was where I left it, yes. I never take anything not absolutely necessary when I travel. One time when we were in Budapest..."

"Emmy?" Elaine, wanting to spare the detective a long, although doubtless interesting discourse, interrupted, asking, "Did you get your new car?"

"It's being shipped from Brussels. Then they'll truck it from Wilmington. They prefer Delaware, because there are so many damage claims on cars unloaded in New York. We didn't have it shipped from England because Charles absolutely refuses to drive in the UK and when I do, I almost invariably break off a side view mirror. We couldn't bear the thought of ruining a brand new car, driving on the wrong side of the road. Noel met us in Bruges, well, Ostend, really, as that's the closest airport, and we had a day or two in London after that."

This gave the detective a chance to slip away and move on.

Once more the door opened and it was Grace who came in, followed by a rumpled-looking Frank. "I couldn't stay away when Cora told me," she explained to everyone. "Frank drove like a maniac, but we made it." It was well known that Frank drove the same way as he bid at auctions, rapidly and recklessly.

Detective Willard was introduced to them. "Of course, always within the speed limit," Grace corrected herself, giving the detective a guilty smile.

At 6:45 pizza was delivered and was taken back to the kitchen. Sally Ann, who had done the ordering, was roundly complimented on the choice and quantity and everyone helped themselves. She made a point of bringing a plate out to Sergeant Garcia, who accepted gratefully. Then she turned to Detective Willard and asked him if she could bring him a drink and slice or two of pizza, or would he like to help himself? There was plenty of pizza and he might like to see which kind appealed to him. Her big blue eyes, the startling black outfit, and her choice of the word "appeal" had the effect of leaving him momentarily speechless.

"Yes, please," he answered finally and Sally Ann didn't know whether it was in response to the first or the second question. But she did know she had made an impression on this sad-eyed, lovely man.

Sitting or standing, with food and drink, people gathered in Jake's area, not awkwardly or with squeamishness, but as if it were the natural place to be. Marv caught Hal's eye and

Hal gave him a nod. Good, so far, thought Marv. Except for the two that were missing. Where were they? Why hadn't Ruth, at least, shown up? He was getting more anxious by the minute, when Sally Ann came over to give him Ruth's phone message.

"Thanks, partner," said an infinitely relieved Marv.

Partner, he called me partner, Sally Ann thought to herself. She felt wonderful.

After most everyone had had their second helpings and seated themselves with another drink, Marv stood up, back to the fireplace. With Cora's sketch on the mantelpiece behind him, it almost seemed that Jake was looking over Marv's shoulder, as if he were a participant. The juxtaposition was slightly eerie and everyone was suddenly quiet.

Marv glanced in the direction of the picture and said, all unplanned, "Jake, I don't know what happened or why, but we're here to talk about you and see if we can find any answers." Then his eyes and a few others' got a little damp and there was a pause. "But, before we get started," he continued, "Detective Willard would like to tell us what they have turned up so far. You can ask him any questions and he might have a few for us. If we want, he says we can kick him out."

"No" and "That's all right" came from several of the dealers.

"Detective?" said Marv, and he sat down on the daybed next to Sally Ann.

Detective Willard stood up and he too looked at Jake's picture for a moment, then turned his attention to the dealers. It was a different experience for him, he reflected. They all looked comfortable among themselves; he was the one who felt uncomfortable. Sally Ann smiled at him and his discomfort was made bearable.

"First, let me thank you, from my sergeant and myself, for our supper. It was very welcome and greatly appreciated. Second, I thank you all for being so cooperative in this investigation. You have been more than willing to come in, to answer our questions and give us information. Such is not always the case. And third, thank you for letting me be here with you tonight. As Dr. Yeager said, you can ask us to leave at any time, if you think it will inhibit your free flow of ideas.

"Now, I'd like to fill you in on what we've learned so far. If you have comments or questions, corrections or anything else to add, please interrupt me. I'd like to start with Tuesday morning." Here the detective took out some notes.

Tuesday morning, thought Marv, in Bucks County, loading the corner cupboard into the truck before driving home, thinking about Ruth and resolving to talk to Jake.

Tuesday morning, thought Hal, getting here early to let the cleaning service in, wondering when the rain would start and how the roof would do. Such simple concerns.

Tuesday morning, thought Sally Ann, I hadn't met him yet.

"Mr. Thompson arrived prior to 9:00 AM and unlocked the door. The cleaners came at 9:00 and were finished shortly before 10:00, when Mrs. Lehman came and the shop was opened for business. Please stop me if this isn't accurate."

Hal and Cora nodded and the detective continued. "Nothing untoward happened during the day. The customers were either known to you or did nothing to arouse any suspicions. I am sorry," he added, "that your surveillance monitor only projects an image and doesn't record. However, someone was at the front at all times, I understand. No one, you had reason to believe, slipped in and secreted himself or herself on the premises during the day. That is, everyone who came in went out again, as far as you two can remember. And several dealers came in for varying periods of time on Tuesday who essentially said the same thing.

"You locked up at 6:00 and made a round of the shop and the back rooms, as is the procedure, making sure the back door was secure. When the two of you left, you locked the front door behind you.

"Now, between that time and approximately 9:00 PM, no one says they came to the shop. At 9:00 Mr. Thompson arrived to talk with the, ah, victim over a business matter. The appointment had been made earlier. I believe, Mr. Thompson, that you said Mr. Gennari was already here. You also said you had told Mr. Mackinnon that Mr. Gennari would be at the shop. Was there anyone else you told?" the detective asked Hal.

"I mentioned it to Richard, didn't I, Richard? I told Keith because he had been trying to talk with Jake and had been unsuccessful."

"Yes, right," Detective Willard corroborated. "So, you went back into the office. There was a quarrel about the partnership, and the conversation ended at approximately 9:20..." Sally Ann hung her head and looked sorrowful. "... and you came out into the shop area to find Mr. Mackinnon, Mr. Keating and Dr. Fisher, all waiting to talk to Mr. Gennari. Dr. Fisher told us that he stopped by, not knowing if Mr. Gennari would be here, and stayed when he found out he was indeed here."

"And I left," Richard declared, "without talking to Jake."

"Right," the detective agreed. "But you had overheard the quarrel and told the others."

Richard pouted. "Everybody tells everyone else everything around here! Well, most everything. It's the way things work!"

"No, that's good. I meant," the detective tried to make amends, as Sally Ann continued to look miserable, "I meant that it wasn't kept a secret, it wasn't anything so unusual, people at odds with Mr. Gennari. In fact, after you left, first Dr. Fisher and then Mr. Mackinnon had strong words with him. Mr. Mackinnon left about 9:45, locking the door behind him. From that point on, we have to extrapolate."

Detective Willard paused and had a drink from the water Sally Ann had brought him. "We think Mr. Gennari was killed here," he pointed vaguely in the direction of the daybed, "sometime between about midnight and 2:00AM. Who came in? And who locked the door afterwards? We have reason to believe that one of the dealers did meet with him here after Mr. Mackinnon had gone." He paused and looked hopefully at the dealers.

There was a short silence, then Elaine broke it. "Clair," she said shaking her head. "And I tried to warn her about him. Well, you've seen him, Detective, not in the best of circumstances, granted, but he was extremely attractive to women."

Laurel looked at her feet.

"We think she may have been here, yes," the detective agreed, "but we don't have any reason to believe she killed him."

"Oh, dear," sighed Emmy, and that was all.

"No, sweet little Clair definitely did not kill anyone," Elaine stated emphatically, "but I wish she weren't in New York so she could tell us herself."

Marv spoke up. "I'm sorry, I forgot to tell you all. She's back and with Ruth and they'll be here as soon as they can.

Ruth had to tell her about Jake. I imagine it was exceedingly traumatic for Clair."

At these words, Helen's face took on an expression that Marv, in all the years he'd known her, couldn't decipher. It was as if she were astounded at what he'd just said. Was it hearing about Clair or was it hearing about Ruth, Marv wondered, that had provoked the look on her face? His guilty conscience suggested it was the mention of Ruth, but his reason argued that it had something to do with Clair and Jake being together.

Detective Willard continued speaking. "Until they get here, however, we can move along somewhat. When we were first on the scene we were impressed with the fact that there was nothing disturbed, everything seemed to be in its place, things had not been ransacked, nothing was damaged. And no one has reported anything missing. But we did find one thing and that was out by the back door, although not near the victim's vehicle. Sergeant?"

Sergeant Garcia, slightly red faced, produced a plastic bag, from which he took a pale blue adult-sized disposable incontinence diaper, which he unfolded, looking more embarrassed by the minute. It didn't help that there was some tittering among the dealers.

The detective frowned slightly at the reaction. "This was found on one side under the roof at the back. We didn't know if it had blown in or..." The laughter became more widespread. "Perhaps one of you can enlighten us?" he asked with a perplexed look, turning to Marv.

Wonderful for breaking the solemnity, thought Marv. "Detective," he said, trying to keep the amusement out of his voice, "those are used to wrap china, glassware, lamps, pictures, candlesticks—anything and everything. We all use them." This brought more laughter from the dealers. "I mean, we all wrap stuff in them."

"Thank you, Dr. Yeager. Then it has some significance?"

"I would think Jake might have unloaded something which was wrapped and one of the wrappers came off."

Sally Ann looked around Jake's area and a concerned expression crossed her face, as if there were something she was trying to figure out.

"You can put it away, Sergeant," said Detective Willard, but with a smile. "Now, I will briefly take us through the rest. The victim was killed with this ice pick," he held up the plastic bag, "taken from one of the dealers' areas, which was used with great force and precision while the victim was asleep on his side. Death was immediate; there was no struggle. His body was put in a large chest which was nearby and the lid was closed. That was how he was found by Mrs. O'Neill when she opened the chest yesterday morning at approximately 10:15."

Detective Willard glanced at Sally Ann to make sure she was not adversely affected by his last statement, then he went on, "The victim may have, in fact, unlocked the door during the evening to the murderer. However, we found his shop key, still in his pocket. And the door was locked when Ms. Arden arrived at 9:30 AM and no one, I repeat, no one could have been hiding in the shop all night, or our very thorough search would have turned up evidence of the person. So, we have the problem of the keys. You all have accounted for your whereabouts and your keys, even one, I understand, buried in the mud at the bottom of Martens Lake," here Owen grimaced, "so unless a duplicate somehow slipped by us, we are back to the same question. Who came in, committed the murder and left, locking the door afterwards?"

If this question were meant to arouse suspicions and cause people to glance furtively at one another, it did not have that effect. The dealers, if anything, looked sadly mystified. It was time to let them talk it out, Detective Willard decided, and he moved over and indicated this to Marv.

Marv stood up and, reverting unconsciously to his former professorial role, asked the group, "Are there any questions," adding, "Class?"

It helped and people smiled again. Hal offered, "Maybe we'll have some questions later, Detective, so don't go away. But thank you for telling us, horrible as it was to have to hear it."

There were murmured thanks and the detective went to sit with his sergeant, well out of the way on the side. He was beginning to think that the lock-picking assassin theory was the only possibility.

Marv, grateful that the detective had not gone into "who profits by this murder" and the other details about money, jealousy, annulment and crimes of passion, thanked him heartily and suggested that glasses be refilled and any other business taken care of, because they were here to stay, by God, until, well, until the mystery got solved or everyone gave up.

In the break that followed, people stretched, milled around, spoke to the detective, made phone calls. The various chairs and seats were moved to form a sort of loose circle. The drinks were brought in from the kitchen and everyone settled down to the task before them. As Marv got up to speak, the front door opened and Ruth came in, her arm linked with Clair's, and they quietly slid into two seats next to Laurel.

Ah, Detective Willard thought on seeing Clair. The light brown hair, straight, cut chin length, a perfect match. And very pretty. No doubt the victim found her perfect, too, for... um. But small, slender, and certainly not strong enough to lift a body. Right. Just as they said she was. So, who killed him?

Chapter 36

Who killed him? And could they by talking it out, by remembering things about him, by bringing whatever knowledge they had into the light, could they find a way that might lead to an answer? Marv, standing by the fireplace, looked at each of the dealers, now so familiar to him, and thought it might, it just might be possible. So he began.

"We're antiques dealers, not sleuths. But tonight we're going to try our hand at sleuthing, because a murder has been committed here and the evidence points to someone who had a key. And that, as we are painfully aware, points to us.

"How could it be? We all know each other, know about each other. For two years, and some of us for longer than that, we've worked together, socialized together and enjoyed each other's company, trusted each other and shared our thoughts. And cooperated, beautifully, and as a result Cider Run is the best antiques shop in the area, in the state..."

"On the East Coast," someone piped up.

"You bet!" Marv affirmed enthusiastically. "And since we have developed rapport and a habit of communication, we're going to bring everything to bear on untangling this mystery of why one of us was killed here and how it could have happened. We'll just talk, no holds barred, and give it all we've got. Because," he added, "if we don't, Cider Run Antiques may be done for." And he sat back down.

There was only the shortest of pauses and then people began to speak, one at a time, as if they had been waiting for the chance, wanting to get things out, wanting to give expression to their feelings where everyone could hear and everyone could comment. It started out with reminiscences.

"The first time we met Jake, do you remember, Hal," Sylvie said, "was when he came here to show us the place because the realtor we had made an appointment with didn't show up. It was cold and snowy and he drove up in a flourish. That's how I think about him. Whatever he did, it was with a flourish."

"Particularly when he sang. What a voice he had," Grace added.

Sally Ann said, "He sang 'Peggy O'Neill' to me, but he made it 'Sally O'Neill.' It was lovely and I'm not even Irish."

"And now that voice is silenced," Cora stated sadly, "forever." There were groans from some of the dealers. "I don't mean to be melodramatic," she quickly put in, "but it's true. He did so many things so well and it's terribly sad to think they're all lost now."

Emmy offered, "He even had a low handicap in golf. He and Charles used to play together. They were pretty evenly matched. Then, when Charles was lining up a putt, Jake would tell one of his lawyer or economist jokes and crack Charles up so he'd flub the shot. You know, the kind like, 'If all the economists in the world were laid end to end, they still couldn't reach a conclusion.' Charles figures that if Jake had been killed on the golf course it would have been more understandable." Emmy realized the levity of the remark may have been inappropriate, but it brought smiles.

"I didn't know he played golf," Richard remarked. "It makes him seem human, willing to accept failure. Not the way he acted around here."

"He and Annette played foursome with us, but she wasn't a golfer at all. I think it must have been pretty frustrating to Jake. He was a perfectionist. I mean, look at his things." Emmy gestured around Jake's area.

"He did have excellent taste," Marv agreed. "He knew that whole genre of Arts and Crafts so well and he researched everything. I know, Hal, he got the better of you and Sylvie with that pottery piece, but that was his nature. When it came to antiques, he had integrity as well as style. He added so much solid antiques savvy to this place and I think we sometimes took it for granted."

"It's OK, Marv, I've gotten over the tile thing," Hal said with a wry smile. "And, also, we mustn't forget that it was Jake who thought up the layout of the shop. He was the one responsible for how well it flows."

"He helped me get started," said Clair in a quiet voice. "He was so kind and encouraging." It was all she could do not to start crying again.

"Honey, anyone would for you," Sally Ann said gently.

"Remember the contest?" asked Elaine. "The one where Andy won on strangest place to acquire antiques and Jake won on Worst Sale Ever?"

Sally Ann said, "Do you think he made that up, the Dead Cow Auction, or do you suppose it really happened?"

"I had the feeling his honor was involved in that contest, although there were other times when he loved to elaborate and embellish. And he could be devious," Marv remarked.

"Very," Keith added dryly.

"And make innuendoes," said Elaine, "very pointed, very unfair innuendoes." She looked at Laurel, not meaning to, but automatically.

"That's all right, Elaine," Laurel hastened to say. "Everyone knows he insinuated that he had something to do with Ben. No, Ben is one hundred percent Joe," Laurel colored slightly, "well, fifty percent anyway. But not only were we never lovers, the strange thing is that Jake had a vasectomy five years ago. I couldn't figure out what his reason was for making remarks about Ben looking more like him with his blonde hair. And anyway, both Joe and I were blonde as children."

"People often start out with light hair," Sally Ann pronounced. "I was the blondest little kid. My hair didn't begin to get dark until I was in fifth grade, and in my high school graduation picture I'm practically a brunette."

Everyone was silent, looking at Sally Ann's defiantly blond curls.

"That was then, this is now," she said serenely.

Laurel continued, "I'm sorry, I didn't mean to reveal Jake's personal medical history, but Joe found out and that was what made him finally mad enough to want to tell Jake off."

Sylvie said, with a puzzled look, "But Jake didn't dislike children. He talked about his nieces and nephews and I know he went to visit them frequently."

Emmy was frowning. "A vasectomy? Annette desperately wanted to start a family. It was very important to her."

"That might have been what ultimately drove her to leave Jake," Marv observed. "I suppose I won't be out of line if I tell everyone that Annette and her new boyfriend are expecting?"

"Expecting? Oh, good grief!" Elaine exclaimed. "If that isn't a motive for murder I don't know what is. All that insistence on an annulment, which was chancy at best, and how convenient now."

Keith gave a short laugh, "And I thought I had a good reason to strangle him!"

"But she had no key," Hal protested.

"And she and her boyfriend have already been investigated as far as Tuesday night goes," Marv added.

Owen looked thoughtful. "She could have hired someone, someone who could have picked the lock or duplicated a key. Hired killers know how to do these things."

"What have you been reading, Owen?" asked Cora.

"And when you think of how he was killed, I mean, it does look professional, don't you think so, Detective?" asked Owen. "Where was the ice pick, uh, used?"

"You don't want to know," said Marv.

Detective Willard spoke up. "We did think it might be the work of a professional. The instrument was expertly used to kill instantaneously, without any blood. Someone with medical knowledge or skill, someone around a hospital, for example, might have this knowledge as well."

Richard saw Elaine looking at him. It drew the detective's eye to him. Richard said evenly, "Trevor? Yes, he works in a hospital, in Baltimore, and that's where he was Tuesday night. No, he hasn't taught me assassination techniques."

"All you have to do is watch television, any number of shows," said Grace, "and you can pick up the know-how."

"Actually doing the thing would not be easy, though. You'd need practice," Elaine stated.

"Where did you say the ice pick, uh, went in?" Owen asked again.

Detective Willard glanced at Marv. Marv gave the briefest of nods. The detective said, "Straight through the ear drum."

Helen barely stifled a scream and started to sob.

"Oh," said Owen in a sober voice. "Sorry I asked." He looked slightly ill.

People seemed to need a little time to recover from this information. Helen continued to cry quietly and Ruth felt sorry for her. Ruth, who had been so still and knew so much more than Helen about Jake, about the night he was killed, about Marv.

"Could it have been Annette, then?" asked Hal. "What do you think, Detective?"

"She could have hired someone," the detective answered. "We have already had that thought and have made preliminary inquiries."

"That's the only thing that makes any sense," emphasized Elaine. Several other dealers voiced the same opinion.

Richard cleared his throat and stated categorically, "It won't wash, folks."

"Why not, Richard?" Marv asked.

"Because Annette is a very, and I mean very, devout Catholic. She wouldn't even settle for a divorce. She gets herself pregnant by someone else while she is separated from her husband and is holding out for an annulment because that's the only sanctioned course for her. No, if she is unwilling to jeopardize her immortal soul over a divorce, she certainly isn't going to put it in far more serious jeopardy by collaborating to commit murder."

There was a moment of reflection after this, and then Marv said, "So, it's back to where we started. But the fact remains, someone wanted him dead. Maybe if we knew why, we could figure out who."

"All those girlfriends he had—Keith and I would see him at auctions with different women," Owen pointed out. "There must have been a lot of jealous boyfriends."

"It's true. He did charm the ladies," Grace agreed.

"He was a charmer all right," said Cora. "Full of blarney, but a charmer."

Elaine said, "He was like a snake charmer. He had them mesmerized."

"More like the snake," Keith muttered.

"Don Giovanni," stated Emmy.

"Who?" Sally Ann asked.

"You know, Mozart. The opera. *Don Giovanni*. The guy's got it coming, he's seduced women all his life and left them to weep. But when he dies, you're really sorry. I mean, he's *loved* all of them. And he goes unrepentant to the end. You can't help but like him. I always did. Of course, his part is the baritone, not the tenor."

"Did Jake deserve to die?" someone asked.

"A rhetorical question, that," observed Marv.

Helen spoke up for the first time, "Can you answer it, Marv?" she asked, an edge to her voice. "Did Jake deserve to die in your opinion?"

Everyone looked uncomfortable. Poor Marv, thought Ruth. Helen has put him on the spot. How unfair.

Marv rose to the occasion. "In my opinion, no. In someone's opinion, apparently yes. My opinion isn't the important one. It's the other one we need to get at."

Well said, Marv, thought Ruth.

"Did we establish that theft wasn't involved, Detective?" asked Marv, more to avoid another challenge from Helen than anything else.

"It would seem that nothing was taken. As I said, Mr. Gennari was asleep and fairly heavily so. He was killed before he had a chance to wake up. Which, in itself, was a mercy. There wasn't anything disturbed, nothing missing, nothing out of place, so you all have told me."

Clair whispered to Ruth, and Ruth nodded. In a voice unsteady at first, Clair asked, "Could he, could Jake, I mean, Mr. Gennari, could he have fallen back to sleep, I mean, after..."

"Ms. Somers?" the detective pursued.

"I was with him Tuesday night. He asked me to come in and look at some of his paintings and artwork. He seemed very tired. When I left, he was asleep. I just wondered if..."

Laurel said, more to Clair, "That's what Joe told me. He thought Jake was not well when he saw him earlier. The next day, when I told him Jake was dead, Joe thought he had died of some kind of illness."

"He told me he was under a lot of stress," Keith added. "He did look bad, all right."

"Poor Jake," said Helen softly. She started to cry again and it must have been contagious, because first Cora and then Sally Ann began to cry.

"Wondered if what, Ms. Somers?" Detective Willard persisted, his tone growing more urgent.

"If he had time to do anything, and then went back to sleep. Like put away the paintings and things."

"What paintings?" the detective asked, rising to his feet.

"The artwork he'd brought in for me to see. They had been in the oak chest where, I understand, he was...he was..." This was too much for Clair. Ruth put her arm around Clair's shoulders and Laurel put her arm around Clair's waist on the other side, and, supported, Clair began quietly to cry.

Sally Ann, still weeping, fumbled in a pocket of her black jacket for a tissue and came up empty handed. She reached into the other pocket and brought out one of her 1950s hankies. This one read "Flags of Many Nations" and there were banners printed in bright colors on it. She started to wipe her eyes, then stared at the hankie and her brow wrinkled.

"Ms. Somers? Can you tell me more about the artwork? We didn't find any paintings or other artwork near the victim or anywhere else in his area." He tried to make his voice sound calm, but he was becoming increasingly excited.

Sally Ann was still staring at the hankie. She asked no one in particular, "Who was that guy, that art dealer, who used to come in to see Jake? The one who always kissed your hand?"

"You mean Sergi?" asked Elaine.

Laurel spoke up, "He came in late once to see Jake when I was here. I had the feeling that they met after hours sometimes." Laurel stopped there, remembering other things about that snowy evening, remembering how thankful she was later for Sergi.

"Who is he? What is his full name?" Sergeant Garcia asked, on his feet now too.

Elaine said, "Sergi Lupescu. I never forget a name. Or a face. He was Romanian."

"No," said Emmy, with a thoughtful look, "I don't think he was Romanian, although Lupescu is a Romanian surname. I think he may have been Russian. He told everyone he was from Romania, though."

"That's right, I remember," Elaine agreed, "you spoke in Romanian to him and he answered. But what makes you think he was Russian?"

"I asked him if he was from Bucharest. That's a standard conversation starter. When we were in Eastern Europe," she paused, expecting to be interrupted, but no one said a word, "I learned enough Romanian to get by. Noel is the one who's fluent."

"And Sergi?" The detective was getting anxious.

"He answered, '*Da*,' for 'yes,' then said that he vowed he would only speak English in the US. But it was the way he said '*da*.' It means 'yes' in both Romanian and Russian, but Romanians pronounce it 'daa,' like a sheep would 'baa' and Russians say it like 'dah,' as they used to say, 'Dahling, how divine!' Anyhow, I was pretty sure he wasn't Romanian."

The detective took this in, then tried again, "Ms. Somers, please tell us, what paintings?"

Clair swallowed. "A half a dozen Renaissance-era paintings by famous artists stolen from European museums and artifacts from the Hermitage."

"Great God Almighty!" Richard exclaimed. "No wonder Jake was broke!"

The detective had his phone out. Sergeant Garcia had his pen poised above his notebook. "This Sergi," the sergeant asked of everyone, "a description! Height? Weight?"

"Not as tall as Jake. Maybe five feet ten."

"If that. I'd say shorter, more like five nine."

"And no more than 150 pounds."

"You think? Closer to 140, I'd say."

"Build?"

"Wiry, slim."

"But fit, very fit."

"Athletic."

"Sort of a European build," said Emmy.

"A what?" asked Sally Ann.

"They don't eat as much as we do."

"The Germans eat pretty well."

"Hair color?"

"Brown."

"Light? Dark?"

"In between."

"Wavy, I thought."

"Color of eyes?"

"I think he had a mustache."

"No, no mustache. You must be thinking of another of Jake's foreign dealers. There was that one the first Christmas we were open."

"No, it was Sergi who had the mustache. I remember it tickled when he kissed my hand."

"Eye color?" Sergeant Garcia asked again.

"I distinctly remember he did not have a mustache when I met him. I don't like mustaches. Except the sergeant's here. His mustache is very becoming," Elaine relented.

"Well, he had a mustache when I met him," said Sally Ann firmly.

"Keith, didn't you used to have a mustache?" asked Sylvie. "Why did you shave it off? You looked very handsome. I mean, you still are, but the mustache was rather dashing, I thought."

The sergeant tried once more. "Eyes?" he asked.

"Two."

"Owen!!!"

"Very light," said Elaine. "A very pale blue."

"Approximate age?"

"Maybe early forties. What do you think, Elaine?"

"He'd had a lot of sun, wrinkles around the eyes. He could have been in his late thirties."

454

"Facial features?"

"He wasn't at all bad-looking. I thought he was really quite good-looking."

"Is that a facial feature?" asked Grace.

"Cora could do a sketch of him, couldn't you, Cora?"

Cora shook her head. "I never met him," she said unhappily. "I was never here when he came in."

"Darn!"

Unbelievable, the ability of these people to get diverted, thought the detective and he turned to make his call. Emmy raised her voice. "Romanians usually fly Tarom. But you might try Lufthansa; that connects through Frankfurt and you can get a flight to Bucharest from there. Or anywhere else," she added. "That's what we flew."

The detective looked at her in amazement.

Emmy wasn't quite finished yet. "And 'Lupescu' means 'Wolf,' so I would imagine he might use some variant of that name on his passport, or passports. He would most likely have more than one. In the EU ..."

"Emmy, I'm breathless! How do you know these things?" asked Sylvie.

Elaine said, not unkindly, "If you emerged from your workshop more often, Sylvie dear, you'd find there's a whole world out there."

The detective went quickly to the front of the shop and got on his phone. Everyone started talking at once and remembered they needed to refill their glasses. In the mild hubbub, Clair turned to Laurel.

"Oh, Laurel," she said, "I can see how you, how one could..."

Laurel looked fondly at Clair. "He kissed me once, that's all, and I ran away." But would I have? She thought, if it hadn't been for Sergi, would I have?

Clair, dropping her eyes, said, "I didn't run away. I came back for more." She looked up. "And it got him killed."

Ruth said sternly, "No, it wasn't you. You had nothing to do with it. If anything, you delayed it happening and," she lowered her voice, "you gave him happiness, the very last thing."

Clair looked stricken. "I left him and he was killed."

"Clair, Clair, you might have been killed yourself if you hadn't left!" Ruth implored her.

Clair looked wide-eyed and realized Ruth could be right.

"That's why we were so worried about you," Ruth explained.

Clair gulped and said, "Thanks, Ruth. Thanks, Laurel. I'll be OK. When should I talk to the detective?"

Sally Ann came over to them and gave Clair a hug. "That's for being so brave," she said.

Marv came up. "These people could use some food. What do you say, Clair? Ruth? A slice of reheated pizza?"

"I think I could manage that," admitted Clair, a little smile returning to her tear-stained face.

"I'll get it for us," Ruth volunteered, knowing she was leaving Clair in good company.

Ruth went through the swinging door and into the relative quiet of the kitchen, lighter in spirits as if an onerous weight had been lifted. Progress had been made and someone, not one of the dealers, thank heavens, someone else was the focus of suspicion and it looked like he could be responsible. She remembered having seen this Sergi, remembered her hand being kissed. Then she thought about Marv kissing her hand that first night and how his lips had felt, and she told herself to get off it, right now. Someone was coming through the door.

Owen came in. "Ruth!" he said happily. "Do you feel as relieved as I do? Boy, was I worried! You know sometimes they go ahead and make an arrest, whether they really think the person is guilty or not."

"But not one of our crowd," Ruth smiled at him. She cut two slices of pizza for Clair and put them on a paper plate, which she popped into the microwave.

Owen rattled around in the refrigerator, getting ice. "No, I couldn't imagine any of us either."

The door opened again and Emmy came in, followed by Keith. Emmy was saying, "I am so proud of Lee. He has a natural talent when it comes to the piano. Don't take all the ice, Owen."

"Thanks, Emmy," Keith said, "I'll tell Lee. He really likes it. He even likes practicing."

"Ruth!" Emmy exclaimed on sighting her. "How was your trip? Did you get to do some buying?"

Ruth had to laugh. Emmy could go from one thing to another so easily. "Yes, and my car is still loaded."

"We'll help you unload," Keith offered immediately. "That way, we get first dibs on your stuff."

Owen was still concentrating on the murder. "Do you think he did it?" he asked.

"Who? Did what?" asked Emmy, momentarily succumbing to the effects of jet lag.

"The Russian guy. Killed Jake."

Emmy had a thoughtful look on her face after this last statement. "I'm beginning to think maybe he wasn't Russian either," she said. "I wish Noel had heard him. He would know the accent. Oh! I need to talk to Clair!" she remembered suddenly and would have left, but Helen was coming through the door, with Sally Ann right behind her.

Seeing Sally Ann, Ruth thought, What a peach you are! You weren't sure who was here and you didn't want me to have to be alone with Helen.

"Is that Clair's pizza?" Sally Ann asked, as Ruth took it from the microwave. "Do you want me to take it out to her?"

"Yes, that would be great," Ruth replied, "and I can fix some for myself." Now that she knows I'm not alone, thought Ruth, and she gave Sally Ann a thankful smile.

Ruth cut herself a slice of pizza and put it in to heat. Why was Helen in the kitchen, she wondered? I hope not to talk to me. While the pizza slice was heating, Ruth directed her attention to checking the mailboxes.

The individual pigeonholes were used by some dealers as general catchalls, others kept theirs quite tidy. Elaine, for example, had a whole arsenal of supplies in hers—blank price tags, marking pens in various colors, a roll of tape, scratch pads. Ruth checked her own box. Only her name tag was in it. But in Clair's box she saw a little pamphlet, folded to fit in. She took it out, so she could give it to Clair. It was like the one she had found on the floor and given back to her earlier in the evening, a museum guidebook. This one was *Treasures of the Hermitage*. Ruth opened it and there was Clair's name neatly printed by her on the inside of the cover. But beneath it, written in scrawling letters with a red marking pen, were two words: *Che bella!* An immediate shot of adrenalin coursed through Ruth and her knees went weak.

Helen was saying, "Why are they coddling Clair? Ruth, you were with her. Why is everyone making such a fuss over her?"

Ruth, her mouth dry from the shock, managed, "It's that we were so worried about her." The timer on the microwave sounded and Ruth, almost mechanically, went to remove her pizza.

The swinging door opened again and Marv came in. He said, "So this is where everyone is. Food and drink as usual."

Helen frowned at him. "Ruth says you were worried about Clair. Why should anyone be worried about Clair?"

"She was probably the last one to see him alive. Except for the murderer," Marv explained.

"I still can't think what that accent was," persevered Emmy, looking puzzled again. "I mean, he had the Russian way of saying '*da*,' but it could be because he learned Romanian in another country and not necessarily Russia. When he spoke English it was highly accented, but not really a Russian accent."

In a very quiet voice, Ruth asked, "Could he have had Italian as his native language?"

"That's it!" Emmy exclaimed, snapping her fingers. "Italian is so close to Romanian. I mean, they're both Latin-based and it would be hard to separate out some of the sounds. For example, when..." Here she interrupted her discourse on the nuances of pronunciation to say, "And Jake knew Italian. I wonder."

But Helen had another agenda. "Am I the only one who feels the loss? Marv, do you realize that Jake was almost the same age, that our son would have been almost the same age..." and she started sobbing.

Marv had little choice. He put his arm around her, while the others stood with sympathetic expressions. Ruth, hardly knowing what she was doing, made for the kitchen door with her pizza and the guidebook.

She had simply not been prepared for the scene of conjugal solicitude and, in a sort of miserable fog, went back to her chair. Clair had gone to talk with the detective, Laurel was talking with Cora. Ruth put the guidebook into her bag and sat down. She was hungry and ate her pizza, then poured herself a ginger ale and downed it. I'm all right, she told herself. Sally Ann came over with the wine and Ruth held out her empty glass.

"How did it go, honey?" Sally Ann asked.

Ruth decided to be candid. "Not so good. Helen has pulled out her trump card."

"I take it we're talking about the baby who died something like thirty-seven years ago?"

Ruth took a hearty drink and nodded.

"Well, she'll use that once too often," said Sally Ann.

"No, Marv responded as expected." What right have I to him anyway? Even if he feels about me as he says, he owes her his loyalty and his attention.

"Look," Sally Ann counseled, "don't do anything rash. Just wait it out."

"I guess I have no other options." Ruth smiled at Sally Ann. "You're a dear, do you know that?"

"And so are you. Here comes Clair, and she's looking much better."

In the kitchen, Helen had stopped her crying and everyone had murmured kind things. Marv felt entirely inadequate to the situation and was glad the others were there. But when Emmy suggested that the way to honor Jake's memory was by making Cider Run the best antiques business possible, Helen shook her head.

"No," she said bitterly, "I'm through. Our daughter is going back to work. I have three grandchildren to take care of and that's where I belong. She needs me and I need them."

Marv protested, "Why are you telling us now, Helen? We can talk about it later, when you aren't so upset." Leave it to Helen to make a momentous pronouncement like this in front of others, he thought.

"No, Marv, I've already made up my mind. Shirley and I have decided and this is what I want to do. I feel like I have lost another son; I know you don't feel that way. Anyhow, you'll need someone else to keep the accounts." She blew her nose and walked over to the sink to refill her glass.

Marv started after her, but Keith put out a restraining arm. "Marv," he said, "I can take care of the books. After all, I just completed a degree in business and accounting." He looked towards Helen. "That should take the pressure off."

Helen said, her back still turned, "It isn't pressure. I'm simply going to where I really want to be." She took a drink of water and turned around. "And that isn't here."

The door opened once more and Hal came in. "The detective has asked that we all assemble again," he announced.

Chapter 37

People had moved themselves around and Sally Ann was now sitting in the seat next to Ruth. Clair, appearing much more composed since her talk with the detective, sat down on Ruth's other side. "I didn't know the police could be so nice," she commented.

"He is nice, isn't he?" said Sally Ann in a dreamy voice.

Clair looked questioningly at Ruth and Ruth winked back. Despite how I feel, Ruth thought, life goes on and I am going to be part of it. No hiding out for me. She said, "We may be seeing more of Detective Paul Willard and I don't mean in an official capacity."

"Honey," Sally Ann purred, "I would commit murder myself to, well, no, of course not, but I sure hope he doesn't wrap this case up too fast. I mean, I do, but not so he goes away and never comes back."

"But, Sally Ann," Clair said worriedly, "you don't know anything about him. Suppose he's married?" As Clair said this, she remembered Ruth's situation and didn't know whether to apologize or keep silent about it. "Oh, Ruth, darn, I'm sorry," she whispered.

Ruth smiled and shook her head. "I got myself entangled. Sometimes you just do. But, returning to why we're here: your information was what the detective was looking for?"

"Yes, and I also gave him the memory card from my camera with the photos I took. What he wants to do now is reconstruct the crime, since he knows more about the timing and how it could have been done."

Ruth saw the kitchen door open and people coming out and, as Marv came over to them, she tried to appear normal, not as if something heartrending had occurred, which was the way she felt. Marv, however, looked his cheerful self. Had he realized he still cared about Helen and was settled in his mind about his life? Or did his face reflect being happily relieved by the results of their evening's work? His smile seemed just as warm, but it took in everyone, Ruth noted.

Marv paused by Sally Ann and, his eyes bright with humor, said, "All evening I've been meaning to ask you: what did Richard say when he first caught sight of you in that outfit?"

"You didn't see him? He stopped in his tracks, stared, then went down on one knee and asked me to marry him. Everyone was looking. I told him I was flattered by his proposal, but my head had been turned by someone else."

"Perfectly Richard! We'd expect nothing less. That someone else, now, is he wanting our attention?" Marv glanced in the direction of Detective Willard, who was arranging furniture in Jake's area. "I'd better see if he needs my help."

Ruth, deciding not to be left out of the conversation, said to Marv, "Clair says we're going to have a reenactment."

"Um, just how much of one, Clair?" Marv asked.

"The murder, Dr. Yeager," Clair answered in all seriousness.

He hasn't spoken to me, Ruth thought. Why does he look so happy? I'm not happy, far from it. She said, "And he needs a victim. Are you going to volunteer?" You're mean, Ruth, she told herself.

Marv gave her a questioning look, but before he could reply, the detective rapped on a glass and asked for quiet.

"If you could indulge me for a few more minutes," he began, "my sergeant and I would like to go through the sequence of events pertaining to the murder. We now have a better idea of what happened and we want to see if it can be accomplished in the manner and in the amount of time we have theorized. It may be unpleasant, so if any of you would rather not stay, you may certainly leave." He looked around at the dealers, but no one budged.

"Ms. Somers, can you show us how the furniture was arranged when you last saw Mr. Gennari?"

Clair got up and went to where the daybed had been placed. She considered it and then had it moved to a different angle.

"Good," said the detective. "The chest is gone, but we'll use this recliner here to take its place." He brought up the Morris chair and put the backrest down as far as it would go. Then he moved it a little ways from the daybed. "Is that about right?"

Clair nodded. Ruth could see she was beginning to wilt and would have gone to her, but didn't want to hover.

"I will need someone to be the victim, preferably someone about the height and weight of Mr. Gennari. Mr. Keating?"

"Oh, what a perfect choice," said Elaine.

"Why me?" Richard groaned, but he went willingly to where the detective indicated.

"Fine. Now if you will just lie down on the couch. No, on your side. The other side. Yes. The left side. Is that correct, Ms. Somers?"

Clair nodded again and this time turned away.

"I can't tell you how much I appreciate your cooperation. All right, I shall play the part of the murderer and Sergeant Garcia will time the action.

"I think we can assume that Mr. Gennari had made an appointment with the murderer and that he opened the door for him when he arrived. It may have been early or late, but he was definitely on the premises before Ms. Somers got here and let herself in with her key. He was probably back in the office. My guess is that because of the noise of the rain and also the music playing, he could have easily moved around unheard.

"Ms. Somers, you have met with Mr. Gennari and discussed the artwork. Now, will you please walk away, as if you were going to the restroom before leaving the shop. All the way to the restroom door. Right. You can come back and sit down, please. I am going in the same direction to here, where the murderer has been hiding, in the area where the ice pick came from. And, now! Start timing."

Everyone watched in fascination as Detective Willard came from Andy's area, looking back a few times at the restroom door, then reached the daybed and stood over Richard. With a sudden movement, he simulated the thrusting of the ice pick, Richard involuntarily letting out a little shriek. He then moved the Morris chair up to the daybed and leaning over, managed to shift Richard, who had started to giggle, to the Morris chair.

"Richard, shut up and be dead," snapped Elaine.

The detective then simulated closing the lid on the chest and shoved the daybed back slightly from the Morris chair.

"How long?" he asked his sergeant.

"Less than five minutes, sir."

"Good. Ms. Somers is still in the restroom, but because it is raining so hard she can't hear sounds in the shop. However, she might come out any minute. Will she return to the victim? If she does, he will not be where she saw him last. She will think he went elsewhere in the shop and she might search for him. If so, I may have to silence her too. Ms. Somers says she was in the restroom for probably another five minutes. Please start timing again, Sergeant. Now!"

Detective Willard reached down to the floor near the Morris chair and simulated picking up some of the paintings which Clair told him had been leaning against the chest. Then he quickly went out to the kitchen. He returned and did the same thing again. "Tell me when five minutes are up," he asked his sergeant.

"About now, sir."

"Fine. Ms. Somers comes out of the restroom but she goes straight to the front door. I can now take my time, about 15 minutes more, is that correct, Ms. Somers?"

"I think so, yes," Clair murmured.

"Sergeant? Start timing, please."

The detective went to the front counter. "I deactivate the back door alarm," and he did so. Then he walked back to the kitchen, calling out, "and I unlock the back door and stack all the paintings and things, which have been so neatly wrapped for me by Ms. Somers, outside under the roof overhang in back, where it is dry and I can come around later and get them. Then I relock the back door." He returned to the shop area and walked to the front. "I reset the security alarm and look around to see if everything is tidy. No, there are two coffee cups and since I don't want to incriminate that innocent girl, I take them back to the kitchen," and he went out to the kitchen again. The sound of water running was heard. He returned, smiled and said, "And off I go, out the front door. How many minutes, Sergeant?"

"Twelve minutes, sir."

"Wait!" Owen interrupted. "You can't lock the door after you!"

Clair looked so distressed that Ruth put her arm around her again.

The detective said, "I apologize, Ms. Somers, I really do, but please don't blame yourself. You did exactly the right thing. You sat in your car, too upset to drive, so you waited until you calmed down. It was pouring, the rain pounding on the car and all the windows steamed up. You couldn't see the murderer leaving the shop. When you realized you had forgotten to lock the front door and went back and did so, he was already gone."

There was an audible gasp from the dealers and Ruth tightened her hold on Clair.

"Good God, Clair," Elaine exclaimed. "You could have been killed yourself!"

"Can I get up now?" asked Richard.

"Thank you, everyone. Now, we think..." The detective's phone rang, and he went to the front of the shop to take the call

The dealers all began to talk excitedly. Clair turned to Ruth and in a whisper charged with horror said, "Ruth, he must have been watching us! He must have been watching us the whole time! When I walked to the restroom..." Her face was crimson as she remembered what she had on or, more accurately, didn't have on when she got up from kneeling by Jake's side. Had she pulled on anything at all? Had she even put her shirt around her shoulders, the shirt that Jake had so expertly undone and taken off her? No, she had just thrown her clothes and everything into her bag and all she had on was a pair of clogs, and she had walked right by Andy's area! "Oh, God," moaned Clair.

Ruth knew that Clair was, without a doubt, correct in her assumption. He had definitely been watching. Ruth could not give her the guidebook now, not with that inscription, written so impetuously, so passionately, out of pure appreciation. *Che bella!* How beautiful! Yes, he was Italian, all right, Ruth said to herself.

They sat together in silence for a bit, then Sally Ann said, with a thoughtful air, "I didn't think the wrapping material they found out back came from anything Jake had just brought. He didn't have anything new in his area that would have been wrapped. Do you think it really happened like that? It must have."

"I guess so," said Clair with a sigh.

"And there wasn't anything any of us could have done about it," Ruth emphasized.

"And I did try, Ruth. I tried to get him to give up the paintings, but he wouldn't. He said he didn't want to." She gulped. "It was the last thing...the last thing he said."

"Maybe Emmy's comparison to Don Giovanni wasn't so far off," Ruth observed.

"That's the way I had been thinking about him, that he was unrepentant. Is he damned?" Clair asked, her clear hazel eyes earnest.

"Don Giovanni killed an innocent man. Jake just wanted to be surrounded by fine art," Ruth said.

The detective came back and everyone hushed. "Not much to report. Tarom and other flights to Bucharest did not have anyone listed under that name. We're checking on passengers to Frankfurt, probably with a connection to...

where would you say?" He looked at Emmy, acknowledging her as a thoroughly credible resource.

"You might check flights to Rome or Milan, maybe through London or Paris. We're pretty sure now that he's Italian, in which case he might go by Sergio and an Italian equivalent of wolf—*Lupo* maybe. There was something in his accent that didn't sound Russian, even though the '*da*' was diagnostic."

"Right," said the detective and got on his phone again.

"Emmy," Marv asked, "how do you do it?"

"It wasn't me. It was Ruth," said Emmy.

Detective Willard made his call and returned almost immediately, picking up where he had left off when the phone called him away the first time. "Now," he said, "we think the murderer either wore gloves or wiped off his fingerprints. The murder weapon, for instance, was clean. There are so many smears of prints on the doors and such that we didn't get anything there either. I wish we had a set of fingerprints, in case we are successful in apprehending him. If it is him. We know, now, how the murder was committed and we know why. But no one saw him, so we still don't know if it is Sergi, or Sergio, or whomever."

Ruth knew where there might be some fingerprints. She would wait to tell the detective, though, and not put Clair through more embarrassment and agony.

The detective continued, "Ms. Somers had taken photos of the stolen artwork and these will be sent on. At this point, however, things will probably be taken out of our hands and go to Interpol and other international authorities if he has left the country, and it would seem highly likely. I think there is nothing more to be done tonight and I want to say that I can't thank you enough for your part in helping to solve this crime. I'd like to do something for you." He turned to Marv and Hal. "When are you planning to open the shop again?"

Hal said, "The roofers should finish tomorrow. We thought we would open, quietly, on Saturday. It's the media you're thinking of, isn't it?"

"I'm going to have to break this story, but I'll try to shield you as much as possible, keep the main focus away from Cider Run. Nonetheless, you will get reporters and a television crew showing up. You'll have to decide how you want to handle it."

"Well, you know what they say," Marv observed. "There's no such thing as bad publicity."

"I'll come over tomorrow to let you know what is happening. Someone will be here?" the detective asked.

"Hal and I will be here, one or both of us, all day, and I'm sure some of the others as well," Marv assured him.

"Good. Thank you again, everybody. I wish I had people like you to work with all the time."

"And we would like to thank you, Detective," Marv said, "for being so considerate and understanding."

First one, then another, then all the dealers began to clap, rose to their feet and gave the detective a round of applause. Then Owen whistled and they all cheered. Detective Willard blushed and made for the door.

Ruth quickly went to where the sergeant was still gathering his notes and spoke to him. He followed her to the kitchen, where he carefully put the red marking pen from Elaine's mailbox into a plastic bag and the guidebook into another.

When Ruth got back to her seat again, Hal was talking. "What do you think we should say to the reporters? Do we need to coordinate our stories?"

"I do think we should be consistent," Marv agreed. "The media will be looking for sensational stuff and we had better decide how we want to present ourselves. Sometimes they ask very leading questions."

"What should we say if they ask about Jake's love life?" asked Grace.

"Or about the guy who did it? We don't even know if it was Sergi," said Elaine.

Marv instructed, "Concentrate on the shop. What would make us look the best? I think when they ask about Jake, we should tell them what an exceptional antiques dealer he was and what good taste he had and how he appreciated art, even though it got him into trouble. But he was an asset to the shop and we'll miss him."

Hal added, "And that we are referring all detailed questions about the murder to Detective Willard."

"Right," Marv seconded. "We don't have to be totally non-committal, but at the same time, we don't have to answer everything they ask. I think if we say positive things, it will put us in a good light. And if we refer other questions to the police, it says that we are cooperative with them, that we respect them, and that also puts Detective Willard in a good light."

Sally Ann immediately started planning what she'd wear for the television news.

"And if we come off sounding like dedicated, knowledgeable antiques dealers, murder or no murder, the shop benefits," said Ruth. I need to stay in the picture, she thought to herself.

"Exactly," agreed Marv, smiling at Ruth.

Don't smile at me, thought Ruth, or I'll melt.

"So," Hal went on, "we open again on Saturday, with our new roof. Tomorrow we'll do a little rearranging and right now, folks, let's tidy up and congratulate ourselves on a job well done," he looked at his watch, "and go home and get some sleep."

People got up and stretched. It had been quite an evening. A murder recreated, a murder apparently solved, and the business was still intact.

"We can't let that pizza get old and tired. How about it, Andy? Another slice or two?" Grace offered.

"Sounds good to me," said Andy and followed her into the kitchen, where several other dealers were going, all with the same idea.

Emmy came over to talk to Clair, and Ruth heard her saying that Noel really hoped Clair could come to England after the term ended in August and spend a few weeks with him. "He wanted me to ask you again, Clair," said Emmy.

Clair replied shyly, "I'd love to see Noel. I do think I'll go." She smiled at Emmy and got up from her chair to continue the conversation.

Ruth was pleased that Clair had something positive to help ease her out of her experiences with Jake. As for me, Ruth thought, there is no one except myself to do any easing. She got up and reached for her bag, ready to go. Out of the corner of her eye she saw Marv in conversation with Hal, but Helen was nowhere in sight. Could she talk to him? What was there to say? As she stood hesitating, Keith came up to her with Owen beside him.

"We're ready to unload you," Keith announced. "We get first dibs, remember."

Owen said, "And we'll help unpack things for you too. Then we get to unload Clair's stuff." He rubbed his hands together in anticipation.

Ruth was instantly warmed by the friendliness of her fellow dealers and the good feeling she had being part of Cider Run. Right now, she thought, she'd take that for consolation, and the three of them headed out to the parking lot.

Marv had settled times for tomorrow with Hal. "I've got to show up at my office for a few hours," Hal had said. "There aren't any big projects that need me at the moment, but I am supposed to give at least nominal attention to the firm."

"I think things are pretty well under control here now," Marv replied. "Actually, things are better than I had hoped."

"What? The investigation?"

"That too," said Marv.

"Well, it's not put to bed yet," Hal observed. "Until this guy gets caught, or at least until they find out who the person was who took the artwork, we can't be sure. But I do think the heat's off us, at least for now." Hal noticed Marv's look of suppressed excitement which he had come to know so well. He fixed a curious eye on Marv. "What did you mean, 'That too?' Has something else happened? You haven't had a chance to talk to Helen?"

"No, but she took the opportunity to talk to me, in the kitchen and, in front of Emmy, Owen and Keith, declared that she was leaving me, Cider Run and the whole shebang, and taking over while Shirley goes back to work. Can you beat it?"

"She said this here, tonight? Does she know about you and Ruth then?"

"Apparently not. This was a decision she'd made over a week ago with our daughter. I wasn't to be consulted, just told. This came after she had made a big scene in the kitchen about Jake being like a son to her and I had to comfort her.

473

Unfortunately, Ruth was a witness to that and fled. I'm afraid Ruth might have misinterpreted what she saw and she wasn't around when Helen announced her latest intentions. Does everything always have to happen at once? Why is it you lead such a quiet life, Hal? I've got to talk to Ruth," Marv looked around to find her and saw her going out the door with Keith and Owen.

"Marv, hadn't you better talk with Helen? She can't be serious."

"Oh, but she is. We'll talk, I'm sure, but it's always at her convenience and it doesn't matter if other people are around. Particularly if other people are there. Then it can seem as if they're on her side. No, as I told you, Hal, my priorities have been rearranged by Jake's death. It was a wake-up call." He looked towards Jake's picture on the mantel and they both were silent for a moment.

"Just one thing, Marv," Hal persisted. "Are you using Ruth, or...?"

"No, Hal, I love her. And I've told her so."

"And Ruth? I guess I have no right to ask, but I care about you, both of you."

"I have reason to believe she's OK with me," Marv answered with a grin.

Hal sighed. Marv was irrepressible. "All right, I'm with you, partner," said Hal, and they shook hands, as they'd so often done. He had a lot to tell Sylvie, Hal thought, unless, of course, the Cider Run grapevine had already sprung into action, which it usually did. He went to find her, and Marv went to find Ruth.

Outside in the parking lot the night was still and the air held the scent of apple blossoms from the orchard. The moon had risen and, though not as bright as in the darkness of Ruth's bedroom the night before, it shone above the hills, bringing a lump to Marv's throat. His mind went back to last night, to the silver moonlight on Ruth's smooth skin, as they lay on her bed, their arms around each other. He thought of the way her skin had felt under his hand as he traced the curve of her back, then down along her hip. In this mood and filled with a certainty of her from last night, he started to walk over to where he could see her. She was with Keith and Owen, just shutting the back of her car, the three of them with chairs and a small table.

"Ruth!" he called, his voice not entirely free from the emotions the moonlight had summoned.

But Keith answered. "Stay away, Marv!" he warned. "This stuff is ours."

Owen chimed in, "Yeah, Marv. We got here first!"

"I just need to talk to Ruth," Marv explained.

"Sorry, old pal, she promised us first dibs. You'll have to wait your turn."

Marv had reached the group, now approaching the front door of the shop, laden with things from Ruth's car. "Ruth," he said, "can we talk?"

Ruth stopped and looked into his face, her need for him fighting with her dignity. There was a lump in her throat too. Such a short time ago she was so full of optimism and happiness. They had seemed so close, of one mind. Now she was afraid of what he wanted to talk about, afraid to know what he was going to say.

But Owen rescued her, or so she assumed. "We've got another trip to make before we're unloaded, so buzz off," he said authoritatively.

Ruth summoned her strength. "Can we talk tomorrow? I've promised to help Clair with her things too." She saw the disappointed look on Marv's face, and she hurried to the door, feeling anguish, but knowing only that she had to protect herself.

Marv easily guessed what was happening with Ruth, that she had been hurt and confused by the scene in the kitchen. But with people around, there was nothing he could do, nothing but vow to make it up to her as soon as possible. The shop "culture," as his colleagues in the sociology department would call it, the give-and-take, the camaraderie, the spirited atmosphere of banter and friendship which he had been so pleased about, which he was so proud of: it was thwarting him now! And if Ruth heard from Keith and Owen or Emmy about Helen's leaving? All right, then Ruth would know what he had been so eager to tell her. Everybody tells everyone everything around here, Richard had said. Although he'd rather Ruth heard it from him first. Damn, he said to himself, I've made her suffer again. Ruth, he said silently to her, I'll set this straight. And I'll more than make up for tonight.

But neither Keith nor Owen nor anyone else within hearing of Ruth got into a discussion about Marv and Helen. Talk reverted to antiques and then to speculation about the media. At one point Ruth heard Keith tell Owen that he was looking forward to having a go at the books, but she didn't have any idea what books he was referring to. When she left, she hadn't seen Marv again.

Ruth drove home in a far different state than when she had come. In regard to the murder, it was now possible to see how it was accomplished and the door locked when she got there the next morning. She also realized that it was Clair who had held the critical pieces of the puzzle, although several things still remained to be put in place.

Perhaps a whole answer would never be forthcoming, but the main parameters were there. Someone, someone who wrote impassioned words in Italian, had been present and the artwork was gone.

Then, almost home, she could no longer hold back thinking of Marv. He wanted me to love him and I did, and I do. Now what? Was it all over? She felt tears start and they were oddly comforting, because they were an affirmation, an acknowledgement of what they'd had together.

"Oh, Jake," she said out loud, thinking of him for the first time with a feeling of affection, "You knew all along I could be in for something like this, didn't you?"

Chapter 38

The weather held, and the next morning Marv arrived at Cider Run at 9:00 to see the crew swarming over the roof, nailing down the new shingles. As he was putting his key in the door, the large and amiable driver of the roofing crew came over and said apologetically, "Had to run some people off when we got here this morning. I knewed they wasn't customers, because they was here too early. I said you-uns would be closed on account of the roofing. I hope that was all right?" He looked up in the direction of the roof, not at Marv.

The press, already, thought Marv. "That was exactly the right thing to say," he answered. "Some of us will be here today, but we'll be keeping the door locked. Just knock if you or your crew need to come in, use the restroom or whatever."

"What? Oh, no, there's a nice orchard out back here. That's fine for us." He looked skyward. "Weather's going to be changing soon. We'll get the new roof on before that happens, though. So, did everything about the accident turn out all right, what Mr. Thompson was saying yesterday?" He looked vaguely in the direction of the hills.

Marv guessed what Hal had said by way of explanation. "Well, we've lost one of our dealers, but we'll go ahead and open again tomorrow. If anyone asks, customers or more of those pesky reporters, and there may even be a TV truck showing up, feel free to tell them we'll reopen on Saturday and send them on their way."

The driver looked pleased to be given a role to play in such an interesting drama and Marv was hopeful they wouldn't be bothered by the media quite yet.

Marv unlocked the door and went in. He was glad of the chance to be alone for a little while. Last night after he had gotten home things had come to a head. Helen had not wanted to talk about her decision or anything else, but he did and, uncharacteristically, had insisted they have it out, then and there. Her habit all these years had been to decide things and tell him, at the time and place of her choosing, and his role had been to listen and comply. This time it was different. She was tired, he knew that, and it worked to his advantage. He had a feeling this might be the only occasion he would have and he needed to get things said.

She had begun by stating that her decision was made and there was no point in talking about it. He said, to her surprise, that he did not want to talk about it; instead, he accepted it. Whether she thought he would try to talk her out of it or beg her not to go, he did not care, and that was obvious.

"Then why are you keeping me here, saying you need to talk? I've driven all the way from Bucks County this morning. It's late and I'm tired. Surely you can see that, Marv, and have a little sensitivity."

"What I can see," he said, "is the end of our marriage." It was blunt, but there it was. "Are you ready for that? Because even if you aren't, I am."

She looked at him wearily. "Our marriage? Didn't you call it quits years ago when you had that...that affair?" The word was spit out.

479

"No, it was an unforgivable thing for me to do and it was done out of desperation. But neither of us wanted our marriage to end then, if you recall. We agreed to try to pick up the pieces after that and I thought we had. Tried, at any rate."

"Pick up the pieces? How could we?" Helen said in a disgusted tone.

Marv continued with his train of thought. "I guess I was deluding myself, thinking you could still be happy with me. You weren't and you aren't. We tried; we failed. Even my taking early retirement, as you urged me to do, and starting the shop didn't help."

She said nothing and he went on, "It was Jake's death that brought home to me how little time any of us might have for happiness. If being with Shirley and the children will bring you happiness, then you must do what you want."

"Thank you, I will," she stated emphatically.

"Then I will do what I want, and that is to be free to find someone to love and who will love me."

"Love?" Helen said, almost scornfully. "Love is what I feel for my grandchildren. I am well beyond feeling any other kind of love."

"And have been for a long time," he added, a little cruelly perhaps. Was it dishonest of him not to mention Ruth, to admit he had already found someone? Maybe, but it would be a gratuitously vengeful thing to say at this point and might hurt Ruth too.

Still not convinced that her actions could be construed as precipitous, Helen returned, "So you are planning to throw away all our years together?" He had always gone along with whatever she decided. Why should this be any different?

Marv wondered, did she really believe that by planning to live away from him, she wasn't letting their marriage and all those years go? He said, "That time is over. We only have tomorrow." Trite, he conceded to himself, but nonetheless true. "I don't want my tomorrows to be a continuation of the same thing."

Helen countered, "What about all that reverence for the past you've always spouted? The sacredness of history? Just tossing it out?"

"The past isn't changed because I want my life to be different now."

Helen smothered a yawn. "What are you saying then, Marv? I need to get some sleep. I have a lot to do tomorrow and it doesn't involve philosophical speculation."

Marv said succinctly, "I want out. If you are leaving me, I am leaving you."

"And you have, I take it, thought about all our friends, all the people at Cider Run, when they hear you and I have gone our separate ways and then, as you threaten, you take up with someone else?" At least, she thought, I won't have to be around this time.

"Helen, you have already told them you are leaving. Have you forgotten what you said in the kitchen, when Emmy, Owen and Keith were there? It's probably gotten to everyone at the shop by now. I assumed you did it that way on purpose. Truly, Helen, you've left me no option. It's time. We'll have to work things out with the house and everything, but it's time. You've started the ball rolling and it's fine with me."

There were more things said, Marv recalled. He had been very calm. There had been few recriminations and no real loss of temper on either of their parts. That should indicate the level of passion or, really, the lack of passion in their marriage, he thought. And so they had agreed: they would separate and would deal with the details later. The Flow Blue china they had accumulated over the years, for example, was to go to Shirley ultimately anyway. Helen had said, "She may as well start enjoying them now," and Marv realized that he no longer felt the need to hold onto them. He went to bed in a mood both relieved and apprehensive, but at peace with himself.

Now, at the shop, he wondered. Would he have been so bold, so sure, so detached in ending a thirty-eight year marriage if he didn't have Ruth? Perhaps he would have, given the rearrangement of his thinking caused by Jake's death. And if Jake had not been killed? Would he have gone on with Helen, unhappy, both of them? Here is the lesson of history, he thought. Both those things did happen. Ruth happened and Jake's murder happened, and they were turning points for him. By the same token, Helen had made her own decision about her life. That was another catalyst. It was meaningless to speculate what he would have done if they hadn't happened. History, he mused, everything hinges on history.

What he must do now is talk to Ruth and tell her, first of all, that he loved her and, second, that he and Helen were going their separate ways. He looked at his watch. 9:15. Yesterday had been long and arduous. Let her sleep a little longer, if she were sleeping, or give her some time to relax today. He could picture her as he saw her yesterday morning, in her blue and white kitchen, with a cup of coffee and the morning paper. The paper! Yike! He'd better think about what they were going to say if his stalwart roofing crew driver could not stave off the press. He went back to the office and started writing some ideas for a statement, to the accompaniment of tapping and banging on the roof.

Ruth felt surer and stronger with the morning. While she did not even try to put Marv out of her mind, she decided to keep busy and get things done. Market, first, then get the tomatoes and sweet peppers planted and the other vegetables she hadn't had an opportunity to put in yet. There was plenty to do and she would go over to the shop in the afternoon, but not until then. Not until late. The things that Keith and Owen had helped her unload still needed to be organized in her area, tagged and priced, and that would keep her occupied well into the evening. She would not be idle.

Had she jumped to conclusions last night? Now she was thinking in a more rational fashion. He is the one who has extenuating circumstances and needs to work things out. Will he be able to? Will he want to? Yes, I do believe in him. But he has to go easy, go carefully. I know he doesn't really want to hurt Helen. I am the one who must be patient. I must tell him, let him know I understand. And then she thought, that first night, when I could see where we might be heading, I had said, "I have less to lose than you." I knew I was taking a chance, letting myself care about someone who wasn't free. It's his call now. But whatever happens, I do not regret loving him.

By early afternoon there was a lull in the activity at Cider Run. It had been a busy place most of the morning. The telephone answering machine had been changed to say they'd be open as usual on Saturday, but Marv had still taken any number of calls from customers, and had explained that repairs would be finished by tomorrow. Those who had heard there had been an accident were told that, yes, it was true and the police had asked they not talk about it. Some of the dealers had come in to ready their areas and find out what was happening. They all helped put the shop back in order after last night's marathon session, the rug vacuumed, and the cups and plates gathered up, if not all washed. For the time being they left Jake's furniture in place in his area, but Marv removed the price tags and put them carefully in Jake's mailbox. As if he might come in and retrieve the tags, thought Marv, saddened again and still feeling remorse that he hadn't spoken to him as he had planned to do.

Sally Ann arrived, dressed in a dark blue suit straight out of the Forties, complete with handkerchief folded in the top pocket. It was chosen expressly for a TV interview, but seeing no media truck and finding Marv there, Sally Ann went out again and came back with some lunch for him.

"Sally Ann, what a blessing you are!" he exclaimed, as he gratefully accepted the sandwich she offered.

"I've heard about what Helen is planning to do, what she told you last night when Emmy and Keith and Owen were there," she said, eyeing Marv to see if this were an acceptable subject and, getting no indication to the contrary, went on, "Does Ruth know?"

Marv had a startled jolt, suddenly remembering he hadn't called her. "I don't know! I must call her. Sally Ann, what should I do to make up for last night, when she saw me in the kitchen with Helen?"

Sally Ann interjected, "I know all about that too. Ruth was very downhearted when she came out." She wanted Marv to know.

"I was afraid of that, that I'd hurt her. I need to do something really nice, something really special."

"Take her somewhere," Sally Ann suggested boldly.

"And I know just the place," Marv responded, his happy look restored.

He couldn't reach her when he called her at home, but he left four words on her answering machine: "I love you, Ruth." Then he got on the travel websites.

Hal came in and he and Marv went over what they would say to the media when it became unavoidable. They included Sally Ann in this discussion, as neither Marv nor Hal had any desire to be interviewed on TV and were happy to give her the job.

"Are you ready to be an un-silent partner?" Marv asked her.

Sally Ann, her blue eyes looking thoughtful, said, "I think so. No one will hate me, will they, because I'm not, well, I haven't gone to college and don't know how to write policy statements and things like you do."

She would have said more, but Marv understood her concerns. "You don't have to do anything you don't want to do or anything you don't feel comfortable doing. You know the business and you're one great dealer. I think you represent the shop very well. We have confidence in you, Sally Ann."

Sally Ann raised her chin at this and looked every bit the TV personality. "Tell me what to say," she replied smoothly.

Marv and Hal had another conversation, privately. Hal had begun by asking Marv if he and Helen had reached an understanding last night. "Not that it's any of my business, but I want to know if there are changes in the, er, partnership."

"Hal, it is your business and, yes, there are changes. Helen and I have agreed, as amicably as possible, to separate. She is no longer interested in being a partner in Cider Run and, as far as that goes, being a partner with me."

Hal nodded. "I see. Is this final then or do you foresee some thawing, I mean in your relationship?" Hal didn't know how to put it. "I mean, if you and Ruth..."

"Ruth doesn't know yet. No, Hal, it's as much Helen's decision as mine. She told me to go ahead and contact our lawyer."

"But how do you feel, Marv? All those years being married and then, bang, it's through."

"I feel as though I can finally breathe, Hal. I am taking in great gulps of air and it is sweet, I can't tell you how sweet. Maybe I'll regret some things; one is bound to. But not now. I only feel I can start to live again, as if I've been given a second chance at life."

Hal looked at his friend and thought, yes, I can see it's true. And I wish him the best. He said, in his somewhat formal way, "I hope everything works out for you, Marv." Then he realized how he had sounded and went on, "I think you're plucky and courageous, in spite of being a little quirky, more than a little quirky, but that's all right with me."

"Thanks, Hal," said Marv. "You're not so bad yourself." And looking towards the front entrance, he murmured, "Uh, oh, the Law," as Sally Ann came through, Detective Willard by her side.

"Good afternoon, gentlemen," Detective Willard greeted them. He looked quite relaxed and seemed pleased with everything, Marv thought, but perhaps Sally Ann's presence had something to do with his pleasant mood. "Could we have a conversation? Mrs. O'Neill, would you join us?" They went into Jake's area once again and seated themselves.

"I see your roof is almost finished and was told by a large person in overalls guarding your door out there that you will open tomorrow. I'm glad to hear it. I'm sorry you had to be closed at all, but I think we had no choice. The, uh, large person was insistent that no one was to come into the shop unless they had a key and belonged here." He paused and smiled at Sally Ann. "If Mrs. O'Neill had not been close to the front and rescued me, I might still be out there arguing with him."

Sally Ann blushed prettily and Marv said, "Sorry, Detective, we were feeling a bit media-shy and weren't ready to face them yet, so I enlisted outside help. But what can we do for you, now that you've made it into the inner sanctum?"

Hal asked, "Have you learned anything more, Detective?"

"Quite a lot, in fact." The pleased look was even more pronounced. "It is amazing, when I think back on it, how, when we were here last night talking, everything started to fall into place. The motive, the murderer, the means by which he got away and the door still locked."

"It was you who pulled it all together, Detective," said Hal.

"No, until you started coming up with things, we were pretty nearly empty-handed. Then you began to give us pieces, piece by piece, and some very telling pieces they were. Particularly the last one, which Ms. Arden gave my sergeant. That was the clincher."

"Ruth gave your sergeant something? What?" Marv asked. "I hadn't heard about that."

"Oh?" Detective Willard glanced at Sally Ann and quickly away. "Perhaps I'd better leave that till last and start at the point where I left you all."

"That would be most accommodating of you, Detective. If you don't enlighten us PDQ another murder might take place," Marv said cheerfully.

"Yes, well," the detective began, "in the first place, you were right about Sergi. He left on a flight Wednesday night from Philadelphia using a French passport with the name Serge Loup, landing in Paris on Thursday morning."

"He was really French?" asked Sally Ann.

"No, not French, just covering his tracks. It wasn't until Thursday night, last night, you remember, that we got on to the international authorities. By that time it was early Friday morning in Paris. We'd missed his arrival by a day. But for some reason he didn't get a flight out of Charles de Gaulle until Friday, a flight to Rome, as Mrs. Greene had suggested. So he was in the airport when the French police went into action. They missed him by minutes, apparently."

"Oh, no, too bad!" said Hal frowning

"Or so they claimed, and that seemed very strange to us. They did, however, get the two large bags that he had checked through to Paris, bags containing the paintings and artifacts that Ms. Somers had photographed, and which were still wrapped in the, er, blue packing material."

"What?!" Marv cried.

"It seems they had not gotten rechecked to Rome and were in unclaimed baggage."

"This is fantastic!" exclaimed Marv. "You mean he deliberately left the goods?"

"Yes, that is exactly what he did. He did it because at that point his job was done."

"His job?" Sally Ann asked in bewilderment.

"His job," the detective nodded. "He passed himself off as a dealer in order to gain Jake's trust and find out about his artwork. But when we sent the fingerprints we had, we got back an interesting statement from Interpol. Sergi, whose real name we will never know, is a member of a group that calls itself *Societa della Arte Perduta*, Society of Lost Art. It's a brotherhood of sorts, based in Italy. Its purpose is to locate and recover works of art that have been stolen or disappeared and while they usually negotiate, they have been known to use other means. It's almost medieval, knights-errant with a crusader zeal, who are quite successful and also quite ruthless. They have been accorded singular respect in Europe, as well as protection. That's why Sergi slipped through the hands of the police. These people have an understanding with the governments of most European countries."

"But Sergi had killed someone!" Sally Ann protested.

"Yes, and it probably wasn't the first time either. We heard that he was one of their most skilled—and lethal—agents. As for his escaping, we were told it was 'regrettable,' but it isn't surprising. One American versus a country's cultural heritage, priceless works of art which are national treasures? It's just a different point of view. That he did it, by the way, there can be no doubt, thanks to Ms. Arden's find."

"What did Ruth find?" Marv asked again.

"Also," the detective went on, ignoring Marv's question, "Interpol was kind enough to tell us that Sergi, when sighted in the Rome airport before he vanished again, had a nasty-looking bruise on his jaw, nasty enough to have put him out for a while. He may have been extremely angry at Mr. Gennari, as well as needing to complete his task."

"And connected," said Hal in a quiet voice, looking up at the picture of Jake on the mantel.

"And connected," echoed Marv respectfully. "I guess that's why Jake could go ahead and entertain Clair without worrying about being interrupted."

"Entertain Clair?" asked Sally Ann. "Oh, you mean they were...Oh!"

Detective Willard looked at the floor and said, "We didn't want that to get around, but they were, uh..." He looked at Sally Ann and then looked at the floor again.

"Well, we all sort of guessed," she admitted. "But don't worry, we won't embarrass her."

The detective looked at Sally Ann, a grateful look, because if anyone was easily embarrassed, it was he, and Sally Ann knew it. And he knew she understood and his regard for her increased ten-fold.

Marv broke in upon this touching vignette. "So Sergi has melted into the Italian landscape and won't resurface, at least not in his former guise?" he asked.

"Essentially, yes," the detective replied. "The Italian authorities have taken full responsibility for failing to apprehend him and the case is closed as far as they are concerned. And as far as we are concerned as well." Detective Willard rose and gazed for a moment around the shop. "I want you to know again how much I appreciate your help, all of you. I hope you'll allow me to come back, when you are open, of course, and have a closer look at the things in your shop. You've probably guessed that I am quite fond of antiques and my wife loved them."

He shook hands with Marv and Hal and Sally Ann, and as he went towards the front door, Marv accompanying him, Sally Ann whispered to Hal, "Did he say his wife 'loves' or 'loved' antiques?"

"He said 'loved,' past tense," Hal assured her.

In the late afternoon the roofers had finished and cleaned up. Marv and Hal stood in the parking lot looking at the new roof. Hal said, "I don't know about you, but I feel a hundred percent better knowing we have a decent roof on the place."

"Spoken exactly like an engineer. We've had someone murdered here, all been suspects, had the most harrowing two days, my marriage has ended and I can't get ahold of Ruth, and what do you care about? A damned roof!"

"Yes, and I also care about dinner tonight. Some of us have to look at reality, whereas you go along, feet never touching the ground and someone always rescues you in midair."

"I say, Hal, ain't that a mixed metaphor?"

Hal was preparing his retort when Emmy drove up, still in the old Volvo. "Emmy!" Marv called as she got out. "The very person!"

Hal smiled to himself. It was good to be returning to normal, good to be opening again, and then he saw the TV truck pull into the parking lot.

Marv was deep in conversation with Emmy. "Somewhere really special, intimate, romantic. A small hotel. Four-star."

"I know just the place. But you don't think Helen would really...?"

"Oh, no, not Helen. I'm taking Ruth." The world may as well know, he thought.

Emmy, who had instantaneously readjusted her thinking, exclaimed, "Ruth! Perfect! Ruth will love it. It has a garden where they serve *petit-déjeuner* in the morning. It's in the Seventh, on the Left Bank. I'll give you the website." They went inside and headed back to the office.

Hal came into the shop, carefully locking the door behind him. He could see the TV crew unpacking their things in the parking lot. "Sally Ann!" he called. "You're on!"

They did a little updating on their statement in view of Detective Willard's latest information and went out into the parking lot. They had decided earlier to do interviews outside, in front of the shop, not inside where the murder had taken place. Cider Run would remain what it was, an antiques shop, not a curiosity. That someone had been killed in it was tragic, but accidental, and did not reflect in any way on the shop's integrity. Nor would they let it detract from the outstanding quality of both antiques and dealers.

On this the partners were resolved. As the TV crew approached, Hal looked at Sally Ann and saw that she was composed and collected and poised. She'll do splendidly, he thought.

Later on, after the TV people had gone and everyone else, Marv tried Ruth again. There was still no answer. Perhaps she didn't want to talk to him. Perhaps she had given up on him. He'd just have to go ahead and camp on her doorstep. He decided not to leave another message right away and was turning off lights, shutting things down, when he saw her car come into the parking lot and his whole being was flooded with happiness. He watched as she got out of her car, a huge bunch of flowers from her garden filling her arms, lilacs and tulips and iris to celebrate the reopening of the shop. So like her, he thought. He went out to where she stood trying to close the car door with her elbow, and when she looked up he began, "Ruth, I have so much to tell you!"

She forestalled him with, "No, don't say a thing, Marv. I have been thinking all day and I realize I have no right to come between you and Helen. You've had a whole life together and family and you barely know me. I can't expect you to...to love me exclusively." She was beginning to falter, but had to get it out.

This time he put his hand to her lips and said, simply, "Shhh."

They went back to the kitchen and got the flowers arranged, the noise of water running making conversation impossible. When the flowers were done, he took her hand and they sat down at the table. He looked into her face, the face he had been longing to see, and was so glad just to have her there that he couldn't speak.

Ruth started again about not wanting to put any pressure on him. "I have been so selfish, Marv. I have been so happy, but selfish."

He found his voice. "And so have I and intend to continue. Is your passport up to date?"

"What?" she asked incredulously, partly withdrawing her hand.

"Your passport. Because if not, you'll have to get it renewed and expedite the renewal. I've already made reservations: June 26th through July 3rd, returning on the 4th, which is a good travel day, fare-wise. Emmy knows these things."

"What?" she said again, this time with a smile beginning.

"Our hotel is in the Seventh, near the Quai d'Orsay. There's a garden. You will come with me, won't you?"

"Marv, did you...?"

"I did," he nodded. "Did quite a few things actually. I said I had a lot to tell you? I do. Will you come with me? Is it a deal?"

Ruth shook her head in disbelief at this wonderful man. "Marv," she said putting her hand over his, "I can't imagine a better deal."

"It's the least I can do, Ruth, give you Paris."

Chapter 39

Saturday morning. By 7:00 AM the *Martensdale Times* had been delivered to thousands of homes in the area. It was stacked in newspaper dispensers in front of restaurants, stores and buildings along Main Street and in the lobbies of local hotels and motels. Delivery vans took the paper out Martensdale Pike and other roads leading away from town, dropping bundles in locations throughout the county where it was put on porches and stoops and in the newspaper racks of businesses, the front page prominently displayed.

LOCAL REALTOR SLAYING LINKED TO INTERNATIONAL ART THEFTS

Italian Police Fail to Capture Suspect in Rome Airport

Marv, up at 7:00, had a shower and went down to put on coffee. He and Helen had only spoken briefly. She had started packing the day before and seemed uninterested in his doings. He had volunteered a conversation about the shop. "Are you going to come in today? We've been putting the shop back in order. Ruth brought in several bouquets of lilacs and tulips and the place looks quite nice." Had she heard anything about Ruth and him? Would she react? Fortunately, no.

Helen didn't even glance up from sorting toiletry items. "You are going to have to get used to my not being there. You may as well start today."

He disregarded this and continued, "Detective Willard came by and told us what has been happening. It seems that Sergi was our man, all right. He made it to Rome and disappeared."

Helen said, "I'll read about it in the paper. It's really too upsetting to think about Jake now," and she turned her back. "I've got a million things to do before I leave for Bucks County this afternoon."

So be it, thought Marv.

With the coffee started, Marv went out to the front porch and picked up the newspaper. He looked at the sky, saw soft blue with only a few white puffy clouds, heard the birds singing, and filled his lungs with the fresh air of spring. And told himself: no matter how garbled and inaccurate the story I am about to read will be, life is good. Then he went back to the kitchen and unfolded the paper.

MARTENSDALE – *Police here have released information on the slaying of local realtor and art dealer Jake Gennari, who was found in his place of business on Wednesday morning, having been stabbed to death late Tuesday night.*

Ruth woke up at 7:15 and smiled luxuriously. They would be together, they would be in Paris! And there might be a future for them after all. Last night Marv told her of Helen's decision and their conversation. He also talked about his past involvement and the emptiness of his marriage, the refusal of Helen to give or receive affection. Ruth was relieved to know she wasn't, somehow, the sole cause of breaking up a happy marriage. It was far from a happy marriage; it was far from a marriage, at least the kind that Marv wanted, and he had gone looking for love before.

She checked the bedside clock and realized with a start that with all they had to say to each other last night, very little had gotten done in her area and she needed to have it ready today. She quickly got her shower and went downstairs, starting the water for coffee. Then, while the kettle heated, she went to bring in her newspaper.

> *Detective Paul Willard of the Martensdale Police Dept. explained that the circumstances surrounding the murder required them not to disclose any information prematurely. "When you deal with Interpol, they stress an absolute news blackout until they are in command of the situation. In this case, we had given them fingerprints and they were able to identify the murderer, although not apprehend him in time."*

Cora, just off to be early at the Saturday yard sales, got the newspaper on her way out the door. She had a look at the headline and took it back into the house, handing it to Bob with a warning, "Don't destroy the paper until I get a chance to read it!"

After Grace read the article, she said to Frank, "I think they're going to need me at the shop today. I have a feeling it's going to be a zoo. You'll have to go to the auction without me. Can I trust you not to buy up everything you see?"

Rosie called Sally Ann at 8:00 Saturday morning. "Mom!" she exclaimed. "I saw you on the Eleven O'clock News last night. You looked gorgeous! When did you get that suit?"

A Pittsburgh native, Gennari, 39, was a lawyer and antiques collector and had bought several paintings for his collection on trips to Europe, not realizing they were stolen. Police say he was murdered for the paintings, which were then taken by the suspect, believed to be an Italian citizen traveling under an alias with a falsified passport, on a flight from Philadelphia to Paris. While the suspect himself escaped to Italy, police in the Paris airport were able to recover the artwork. Detective Willard had sent on photographs of the collection, which aided the international authorities. "The paintings and other artifacts will now go back to the museums from which they were stolen," Willard added.

Hal thought, what an all-around good person is this Paul Willard! He said to Sylvie, "If Detective Willard and our Sally Ann start up a relationship, they have my approval."

"As if they needed your approval, Hal," Sylvie laughed.

Gennari was a respected realtor and partner in the firm of Cider Run, Inc. A graduate of the University of Pittsburgh and the University of Pennsylvania Law School, he also studied voice at Curtis Institute in Philadelphia and sang lead tenor roles in several productions.

Keith snorted, "Respected realtor!" when he read the article. As it turned out, though, Jake had dropped his option to buy up the CCC camp property. This information was among the papers that the detective had found in Jake's briefcase and he had told Keith about it on Thursday night. What made Jake relent, Keith didn't know and would never know, but the bad feelings about Jake had started to dissipate, and he and Owen were on their way to owning the property.

Emmy, reading the newspaper before her first piano lesson of the day, thought to herself, so much misinformation! And so much left out! Jake should have gone on with his music, she sighed. Then this never would have happened.

Humph, thought Elaine, over a cup of coffee and her first cigarette of the day. It makes it sound as if Cider Run were a real estate office. And Sergi or no Sergi, I still think someone's insanely jealous boyfriend did it.

He leaves a wife, Annette Durand, of Washington, D.C. and a brother, Brian Gennari, and his wife of Pittsburgh and five nieces and nephews. A private funeral and Mass for the family will take place at St. Katherine's Catholic Church in Pittsburgh, the Most Reverend...

Laurel, feeding little pieces of mashed fruit to Ben as he sat on her lap, listened while Joe read the paper aloud to her. Nieces and nephews, she thought. Jake was such a contradiction! He had been, she believed, genuinely taken with Ben and yet, there was the vasectomy. Had something happened, something traumatic, which scared him off of having children himself?

The article had a picture of Jake, most likely supplied by the realty company. Clair, at the kitchen table, looked at it, tried to swallow her breakfast cereal, but could not. It will take a while, she thought, it's going to take a while to put this into perspective, get him out of the front of my mind—that face, those arms, those hands. Her eyes full of tears, she put down the paper and left the kitchen.

Richard, getting ready to go to Cider Run for the day, looked at the photo too. And thought, once again, thank heavens for Trevor.

Andy, heading out to an auction, saw the headline and shook his head sadly.

And Owen frowned as he read the article. Lynn asked, "What is it?"

"The guy got away," said Owen darkly.

Marv finished reading and thought, Good, at least they didn't mention Johnny Appleseed this time, and he fixed himself some more toast.

Hal had said two days ago, "We'll open, quietly, on Saturday." After the morning paper's story and yesterday's newscasts on television, "quietly" proved impossible. When Marv got to Cider Run shortly after 9:00, a TV crew was already filming the exterior of the shop and someone was wandering around in the orchard. Hal pulled in a few minutes later and was closely followed by two more cars, each with newspaper reporters. Sally Ann, guessing that she would be called upon again, drove in and emerged from her white Mercedes in a similarly white ensemble, an authentic Dior, pencil slim skirt, bolero jacket, 1954 vintage. The scent of White Shoulders surrounded her. The TV crew converged upon her as moths to a flame.

Marv made an announcement as best he could, while cars kept arriving. "We'll be opening the shop at 10:00 and you are all welcome to come in then. In the meantime, if you want to speak with us, we would rather it were outside."

This seemed to be acceptable for the reporters, and the previously thought-out, thoughtful-sounding replies were made about Jake, his outstanding taste, and the sadness they all felt. When the reporters had been temporarily satisfied, Hal and Marv escaped into the shop, leaving Sally Ann to carry on.

"Do you think it's all right for her to have to face them alone again?" Hal asked, as they got in the door.

Marv looked out through the glass, as Sally Ann, gesturing towards the orchard for the camera, was saying something to the interviewer. "She's the ideal advertisement for the shop, all we could hope for. As long as she remembers who really planted the trees."

Ruth arrived next, saw Sally Ann leading the TV crew into the orchard and, while they were otherwise diverted, slipped into the shop unnoticed. Richard drove up immediately after her and was not so lucky. He paused for a moment to see what Sally Ann was up to in the orchard and was roped in by a reporter, then persuaded by the TV crew to join Sally Ann in an interview. The parking lot began to fill up: dealers, customers, friends and the merely curious.

Once inside, Ruth stopped near the door, watching the commotion outside. Hal came to her side and said, "I guess we're not going to be opening quietly after all."

Ruth laughed, "Far from it. Things may never be quiet again."

Hal caught the double meaning and glanced at Ruth. She clearly had the look of a happy woman, he thought. He wanted to say something to her, let her know how he felt. "Ruth, I just want you to know, I, uh, that is, Marv has told me about you two, and I told him that I thought it was good, I mean, fine for him." He realized, seeing Ruth's amused expression that he needed to add, "I mean, for you as well. I hope it is. It is, isn't it?"

"Hal, thank you," she said and gave him a smile of appreciation. "Marv says you're the best friend he's ever had and I can see why."

Hal was supremely pleased by the compliment.

Ruth went back to the kitchen, as she had brought one more bunch of flowers, this time lilies of the valley. She found Marv by himself in the kitchen, hands in a sink full of soapy water, washing cups and plates. Turning, he saw it was Ruth and, stopping what he was doing, said, "This may be my only chance today, Ruth Arden, to tell you I love you. I would take you into the office and lock the door, but the TV crew would doubtless somehow find their way in."

Ruth glanced behind her and, seeing no one, went up to Marv and gave him a quick, soft kiss. "You're so appealing when you do dishes," she said.

"Also helpless to your advances," he returned. "I shall do the dishes from now on and always in a mood of the most hopeful anticipation."

The kitchen door swung open and Grace came in. "Hal says we're getting a coffee service set up. Here, let me help."

Marv relinquished the sink to Grace and brought down a large tray. He explained, "We thought we'd use Jake's area, take in the coffee pot and all the cups we can find, sugar, milk. Sylvie is bringing doughnuts."

"Then, this afternoon," Grace added, "we'll switch to cookies, if I can get away to bake a batch or two."

"A very nice idea," Ruth approved. Not only nice, but one of those things that made Cider Run so special, so appreciated by customers. Someone would bring in goodies, someone would always be thoughtful. She looked at the flowers she was still holding and quickly put them in a glass of water, then went out to find a vase. Not just any vase, she knew, but a Grueby vase, small with a soft green matte finish, art pottery from 1905 she had seen in Jake's area. She transferred the flowers into it. The mantel was still bare except for the picture of Jake. Ruth put the bouquet near the

501

picture and, looking at the sketch of Jake, thought, Jake, I'm glad I knew you. I'm sorry I couldn't be your friend, but I will only think of you with fondness. Then she went to get her area ready.

By the time the shop opened many of the dealers were there and then dozens of people were in and out. The TV crew was allowed to film in some of the areas, focusing on the antiques. Many of Jake's regular customers came and there was always a gathering of people in his area, talking about him and expressing sadness, people shaking their heads in disbelief at the death of someone so young, so talented. Marv never dreamed he would hear himself saying such kind words about Jake, but he did, say them and mean them. Several people wanted to buy Jake's things, but it had been decided that until the will and other legal aspects were sorted out, they would not sell anything of his. And so the morning went. Hal arranged for deli salads and sandwiches to be brought in at lunchtime and a buffet for the dealers was laid out in the kitchen.

In the early afternoon Ruth was doing some rearranging in Clair's area after customers had bought several of her things. All of a sudden she heard Richard, who was standing nearby, do a quick intake of breath and a hushed, very hushed for Richard, "Holy Toledo!!"

Surprised, she looked up and thought wildly for a second, No, it can't be. It's Jake! But of course it wasn't Jake. An older version of Jake, as handsome, but his hair starting to gray a little at the temples. More distinguished-looking perhaps, dressed in a navy blazer, not what Jake would have worn on a Saturday at the shop. She must have been staring, as had Richard, because Brian Gennari smiled at them, the same beautiful smile as Jake's, and came over to them.

Clair hadn't gone to the shop. Her summer theater obligations had begun and she needed to finish costume designs for the next play. It was interesting work and fun and she was content to switch off from antiques for a bit. Also, she knew how distressing it might be to hear about Jake all day at the shop. She missed seeing her fellow dealers though and had called, talking to Ruth, who agreed that it was pretty intense and still only morning.

"Maybe I'll come in later," she told Ruth.

"Do. We'll be glad to see you. By the way, several of your hats have sold and I've heard a lot of compliments about your area."

"Thanks, Ruth. Can I ask? You and Dr., uh, Marv?"

"Much to tell. Things I hadn't thought possible, good things."

"I'm so glad! I'll talk to you soon."

In spite of the fact that Clair had known Marv and Helen for a long time, she had never felt they had a good marriage. It was, she thought, that Helen and Marv were two very different types. He was so spirited, playful and fun; she was so disapproving and impatient with him and, Clair had to admit, rather humorless. They were ill-matched; that was all there was to it. Ruth was so much better as a companion for Marv and you could tell they made each other happy. Clair had seen that for some time.

Would she herself ever find her match? It certainly couldn't have been Jake. He was an episode, an experience. It was as if she had been invited to participate in a grown-up world for which she was almost, but not quite, ready. To be taken for a brief, breathless ride and given unbelievably sweet treats to enjoy, but not to keep. All of him, yes, but only for a few moments. One must never care too much. She had almost, almost, come close to caring too much, after he had told her about himself, after she had a glimpse into the pain he carried. Jake. His picture in the paper this morning and she couldn't eat. She looked at her watch: almost 2:00. Her lack of breakfast made itself felt, and she headed downstairs to the kitchen.

She could see her parents through the patio door, outside this spring day, working in the garden, and from the dishes in the sink knew they had already had lunch. Clair got out sandwich makings, fixed herself some lunch, and settled down at the table. The mail had come and there was a letter addressed to her. She ate her sandwich, looked at the postmark: Pittsburgh. Not until she was through eating, she told herself.

Hey, pretty girl, Sheree had written.

I would have emailed, but didn't get back to my office computer and we fly to Anguilla tomorrow. One last fling before the heavy summer practice season starts and the guys can't think of anything except football. And they're much too tired to do anything. You get my drift.

So I wanted to let you know what I learned before I go off for two weeks. I found the obit. Just as you thought, it was 27 years ago. All it said was that a Mass of Christian Burial would be held for the boy, 12 years old, and who his relatives were and where he had gone to school and church. Also, that he loved baseball and was in the choir at St. Katherine's.

But you said it was a suicide and they don't allow Mass in those cases, so I did some more checking. The enclosed article was in the paper a day after the obit and I thought I'd send a copy to you. I wasn't sure what to make of it. I can only guess he did what he thought he should do. When you talk to him next, maybe you'll find out more, but probably not. It's a wonder he was able to talk about it at all.

But don't let your love life suffer! We'll have to get together when I get back—it's been much too long!

Love ya' forever,
Sheree

Enclosed in the envelope was a copy of a newspaper article dated 27 years ago. Clair unfolded it and read the headline and laid it down on the table. She couldn't trust her hand to hold it steady.

FOUL PLAY IN BOY'S DEATH

PITTSBURGH – An investigation into the death by strangulation of a 12-year-old Pittsburgh boy was undertaken following the admission by one of the child's playmates that he had accidentally caused his friend's demise. The youngster, also 12, said they had been playing and "messing with a rope," which was found around the victim's neck...

"Oh, no, oh, God!" Clair said aloud.

...and which had caused the child to strangle. Although the boy confessed his part in the tragedy, he was not able to give police many details. No action will be taken against the young playmate who, police say, was greatly shaken by the incident.

Clair sat still, thinking about Jake and what this meant. It was impossible to get back to her work now. She needed to deal with this information, put it into place somehow. Ruth. She'd go find Ruth and they would talk it out. If they got a chance. Ruth had said it was busy at the shop. Ruth also said customers had been there, buying her things. Clair thought, I do need to be in today, I'm part of Cider Run. She decided to wear a skirt and maybe a nicer top, and went upstairs to change.

Marv and Hal had taken Jake's brother back to the office to discuss some of the legal issues associated with Jake's death. They had mostly finished talking about the terms of Jake's will that impacted Cider Run and Brian was giving them information on his own concerns. Even though there had been a pre-nuptial agreement, in which family property remained in the Gennari family, Annette was putting up a fight. "It's not Cider Run's problem, but it might cause bad feelings if any of you here were friendly with her," he cautioned.

"Don't worry. She left us without a backward glance," Marv assured him. "Antiques were of little consequence to her, or so we gathered. How anyone could feel that way baffles me."

Brian smiled at Marv. "And now that I've met you and have been in the shop, I am even more satisfied that Jake wanted Cider Run to have his antiques and his share in the partnership transferred to the two of you."

Hal ventured, "It may have been done only to cut Annette out, but we are very pleased he did so. His taste was superior and all of his things were, and are, of the highest quality."

"Maybe a little too high, in the case of stolen museum treasures," Brian said with a rueful smile. "I'll be coming back next weekend and we'll arrange for Cider Run to get the antiques still in his house. And please know that what you choose to do with them is entirely up to you."

Marv looked at Hal. "We have talked about that and think we may leave his furniture where it is and use his area as a gathering place. He always let us do that in the past, and it would be appreciated by dealers and customers alike."

They had risen and Hal added, "We have coffee set up there now. Would you like to stay a bit longer and meet some more of our dealers?"

It was a friendly and relaxed gathering, with both Sylvie and Ruth joining them. Grace had managed several batches of cookies and the coffee was fresh. Although people did a double-take on seeing Brian for the first time, his personality, if not his appearance, was unlike Jake's and his manner was calm and pleasant, in spite of the turmoil and sadness of Jake's death. But even more endearing, Marv thought, was that his frank appreciation for his brother's favorite endeavor was obvious.

"Jake kept saying I should come see the shop," Brian commented, looking around. "He was inordinately proud of it. High praise from someone who was so fastidious about details."

Ruth thought this last particularly true and it reinforced Jake's concern with the integrity of Cider Run, why he had taken her to task the way he had, worrying about indiscreet behavior on her and Marv's part. His words, "repercussions on the business," came back to her. Her thoughts must have been shared by Marv because he said, although lightly and with good humor, "But you can't believe how much grief he gave us!"

In answer, Brian laughed, and his laugh sounded just the same as Jake's. He warmly seconded Marv's observation,

"Even though I was four years older, he managed to take it upon himself to instruct and correct me on everything from A to Z! He was always the perfectionist."

Clair had just walked in the door and at this moment was almost to Jake's area when Brian laughed. He was sitting in the Morris chair, his back to the entrance, but Ruth, facing the front door saw Clair come in, walk halfway back then stop, hearing Brian's laughter. Clair braced herself for support on a dresser and her face drained of color. Ruth immediately went to her. "It's all right," she said. "It's his brother."

Chapter 40

Brian rose to shake hands with Clair. She was still unable to speak and shook hands wordlessly, looking at his face, those same blue-grey eyes. Trying to ease the awkwardness and by way of introduction, Ruth explained, "Jake asked Clair to examine his artwork, since she has had museum experience. She, more than anybody, helped the police. I am afraid she was the last one to talk with him." Clair took Ruth's chair and sat perched on the edge, Ruth standing next to her.

Brian sat back down, smiled at Clair and said, "Yes, the police told me," then, seeing Clair's deep blush and knowing the reason for it, went on hastily, "Jake had mentioned to me a few weeks ago that there was an art expert at Cider Run whom he was going to consult. I'm very pleased to meet you."

Clair found her voice at last. "I'm sorry to be so tongue-tied. You look so much like him." She dropped her eyes; she had been staring at him. This wasn't what she meant to say, she thought, annoyed with herself. "I mean..."

Ruth, still standing by Clair, gave Marv a glance, then looked in Clair's direction. Marv got up quickly and said, "Brian, don't go without saying goodbye. Hal, Sylvie, come on, we need to mingle with the customers."

Clair seemed unaware of the others leaving. "I mean," she continued, turning to look at Cora's sketch of Jake on the mantel, "he was very much like you, but, but..." And, disconcertingly, she felt her eyes fill with tears. "Oh, I'm sorry," she apologized again. Could I please, please get control of myself, she thought desperately.

Brian leaned closer and said softly, "But troubled, is that it?"

Clair looked up at him and nodded. "I hardly knew him, that is, I only knew him for a little while. But he told me about some things that had happened, things I'm still trying to work out in my mind." It was now or never, she told herself. "About the boy who committed suicide when they were twelve years old." Brian gazed at her steadily and she continued, "I have a friend on the *Gazette*. She just sent me this," and she took the copy of the article out of her bag and handed it to Brian. She went on, stronger now, "It wasn't that I didn't believe him when he told me. I could see how painful it still was for him. But I wanted to find out for myself and now I've read this, which he hadn't told me about. So I wondered..." She couldn't say it, but she thought it. That Jake had, as Sheree suggested, done what he felt he must do, that at one time he had made a completely unselfish, redeeming sacrifice for someone else.

Brian, sitting in the Morris chair, looked so like Jake the night he was telling her about himself that Clair was almost holding her breath. But Brian was fully in the present and clearly understanding of and sympathetic with Clair's emotional state, knowing how like Jake he must appear to her. He also realized how her intimacy with Jake must have affected her. He said, "You are one of only a very few people who have any knowledge about it. I think you should know the whole story."

He handed the article back to her and said, "It's true. The boy did kill himself, hanged himself. He was Jake's best

510

friend and Jake had gone over there that afternoon. About ten minutes later he came running home terror-stricken and showed me the note the boy had written to him. Jake was terribly upset, not only with what he'd seen, but with the fact that his friend had committed suicide. It would cause such anguish to his family, so many questions, so much guilt as well as grief. They wouldn't be able to hold a funeral Mass, Jake insisted; they wouldn't be able to bury him in consecrated ground." Brian gave Clair a sad smile. "He was a very sensitive and insightful person even then, at twelve years old, my little brother."

Clair thought, insightful and sensitive to others, like his brother is now. But somewhere along the way, Jake must have lost much of that latter aspect. Did he feel it no longer served him? And yet, he had been sensitive to her, and so gentle with her. Oh, no, thought Clair, I mustn't let myself think of that while someone who looks so much like him is sitting here.

Brian went on, "Jake's idea was to somehow make it seem accidental and he was determined to do so, even if it meant lying to the police. I couldn't talk him out of it, so he went ahead and did what you read in the article—put the blame on himself. The only thing I insisted he do was go to Confession. That was the hardest part for him, because he was afraid the priest might be the same one who had molested his friend. We went to another church finally, but Jake never got over it. And he gave up on the Church because of it.

"Unfortunately, without ever thinking about it, we had participated in the covering up of child molestation. One didn't expose those things then. It has only been recently that the Church has begun to take responsibility for its part. Jake and I hadn't talked about it for almost two decades.

Then, when the cover-ups in the Church began to surface, he questioned our actions all those years ago. Should we do anything about it now? We agreed that it was best not to, in order to spare the boy's family, but it still tormented Jake. And me as well, for his sake." Brian looked at Clair and considered, then said, "Jake decided to have a vasectomy, even though he was very fond of my own children. I couldn't talk him out of that either."

"Yes, he told me he had. I thought there might have been some reason that went beyond his only wanting to lessen any ties with Annette."

"He said children were just so vulnerable, that they couldn't always be protected."

Brian had spoken calmly, but he did not hide from Clair the sorrow he was feeling. She thought, how despairing he must have felt for Jake. She said to him, "Thank you. Thank you for telling me, although it must be terribly difficult for you to bring it all up again. But I feel so much better knowing about it; I understand Jake so much better." Maybe Jake had been capable of love after all, she thought. Maybe he wanted me to help him deal with his past. Could I have? Not without losing myself in the process. He would have been all-consuming. She gave a little sigh of sadness.

Clair's expressive face registered her emotions and Brian felt he knew the reason for the sigh. He said gently, "You're right. It is sad and bitter to recall, but I was proud of my little brother; I guess I always will be. And I could understand why he spent years compensating, the way he threw himself wholly into things, trying to ease the pain he carried with him. His serious study of music, and the almost obsessive pursuit and acquiring of antiques, and then there were always..." Brian realized what he almost said to her, this lovely and grieving young woman who, only minutes before Jake was killed—the detective had been quite candid and Brian knew his brother's techniques with women—had without a doubt been tenderly and thoroughly made love to by him. Had also, if he knew Jake, given him measure for measure, young as she was. Jake had a way of eliciting the responses he wanted from women.

Brian quickly revised what he was going to say. "That he told you about himself means he thought very highly of you. Not many people were allowed into his past like that. Not Annette. I think maybe it's only you and I."

"I'll never forget him," she said, lowering her eyes again so the tears wouldn't show.

Brian looked at his watch. "I must be going soon, but I wonder if I can ask for your assistance."

She looked up again. "Yes. Of course." Clair was only too happy to help him. He had given her some needed resolution, the answers she was seeking, and had helped her begin to cope with her feelings.

"Did Jake show you the Canaletto?"

"No, but he told me about it. I guessed he hadn't brought in everything that night."

"There are two other paintings in his house, American landscapes, and I remember when Jake bought them. But the Canaletto was recently acquired, in the last two years. Can you research it for me, find out if it was stolen and from where and return it? If there's a reward, you should have it."

"I would be glad, very glad to, but if there is a reward, I want it to go to Cider Run." She paused, then went on, "You should know, I was going to force Jake to do the right thing, make him return the artwork, but I couldn't go through with it. It was too late anyway, by then." She looked distressed for a moment.

Brian said, "Thank you, Clair, for caring about Jake. Can we talk more? Jake and I were very close, and I think it would help me if I could talk with you about him. I'll be over here next weekend and bring the painting in. I hope to see you again?" He got up and so did Clair.

"Yes, please do. I mean, I would like to talk more too," she said. It's not like a door I want to slam shut. Not that I could slam it shut, she thought, and she held out her hand, automatically, to shake hands. And when he took it and they very properly shook hands, she looked at his hand clasping hers and thought again, those arms, those hands.

It was getting close to 5:00 and the activity at the shop had finally wound down. A few customers were still there, being helped by Richard and Sylvie. Sally Ann was entering a sale into the computer at the front counter and Hal, Marv and Ruth were clearing up the coffee things and taking them out to the kitchen.

"Shall I help you two wash up or do you want to be alone?" said Hal, unconscious of the heretofore presumption of his statement.

Marv stopped in mid-action of opening the kitchen door, raised his eyebrows in mock horror and said, "Hal Thompson, I am shocked, shocked and dismayed. I am scandalized, that you should be thinking such thoughts! Why, if I didn't know you better, I'd say you had given up engineering and gone into marketing."

"Oh, Marv, come on," Hal started to say, then grinned. "Nothing's going to be the same again, is it? And, you know what? I'm glad!" He put his load of dishes down by the sink and went out the kitchen door. In another second he was back. "Except for you and me. We'll be the same as ever."

Hal came out of the kitchen the second time, chuckling to himself, and was on his way up to Sally Ann when the front door opened and Detective Willard came hesitatingly through. Ah, thought Hal, I knew it!

Detective Willard caught sight of Hal and said, "Mr. Thompson, as you can see, I can't stay away."

"Have you come to give us more information on the case, Detective?" Hal asked.

"No, this time it isn't business. The case is closed as far as our department goes."

Hal thought, he has seen the white Mercedes parked outside, he knows she's here. Aloud he said, "Then you are making good on your promise to visit us as an antiques lover?"

Hal realized, too late, that this last word would set the detective off into an agony of embarrassment and he was right. Detective Willard colored, looked at the floor, looked up again, saw Sally Ann coming out from the front counter and said to Hal, "It was my wish, and I hope it is not too late, that someone could show me around the shop and we could talk about some of the pieces here. I have been admiring one or two pieces." Then, having stumbled into another potential semantic embarrassment, he tried to steer himself back to course by saying, "One or two antiques."

He stopped speaking as Sally Ann came up to them, gave the detective an enchanting smile and said sweetly, "May I be of assistance?"

Hal melted away to the front counter.

Sylvie reported to Hal and Richard later that she had overheard the following conversation.

Sally Ann: "Where would you like to start, Detective?"

Detective Willard: "I would be honored if you would call me Paul."

Sally Ann: "Paul is a lovely name! I'd be happy to call you Paul. Where should we start?"

"Could we start with dinner tonight, Mrs. O'Neill?"

"Only if you call me Sally Ann."

Before they left, and left together, Detective Willard took Ruth aside and handed her an envelope. "We don't need this anymore," he told her. "Perhaps it should go back to its owner. I leave that to your discretion." He knew Ruth was protective of Clair. "Thank you, again, for your help. I'm very grateful to all of you."

Ruth nodded. "Thank you, Detective. We'll be seeing you again, it seems?" She smiled at him.

Letting his guard down at last, he breathed a fervent, "I sure hope so!"

Ruth went into the kitchen, opened the envelope and took out Clair's guidebook from the Hermitage. She looked at the inscription, *Che bella!* A scrawl in red ink. She thought, it nailed the identification, but he got away. Where was he now? Was he feeling remorse at what he'd done? Did he still think of Clair? She put the guidebook into her bag. Someday, she thought, but not yet, she'd give it back to Clair.

She was about to leave when Marv came out of the office. He said, "Did I hear that our worthy constable was on the premises? Is he still? I have one unanswered question."

"He has left and taken Sally Ann with him. They are, prepare yourself, Marv, on a first name basis."

"Splendid! We couldn't have scripted it out better ourselves. So, if things go well, we'll see him hanging around quite frequently, would you say?"

"In his very words, 'I sure hope so!'" Ruth quoted. "But what unanswered question were you going to ask him?"

"It was about you, actually," Marv said sheepishly.

"Me?" Ruth asked in surprise.

"Thursday night when we had our talk session, Emmy said it was you who figured out that Sergi was really Italian. And the detective, may he charm our Sally Ann tonight, said you had given his sergeant something that clinched the whole identification. What, Ruth? What was it? I can't believe I haven't asked you before now. Is there some secret life you've been leading? Have you been, all along, an espionage agent?"

"Alas, Marv, you've found me out," Ruth confessed.

She reached into her bag and took out the museum guide. She opened it to the inscription and Marv exclaimed, "Good Lord! He gave it all away! He totally gave himself away! He couldn't resist; he had to tell her. What did he write with?"

"One of Elaine's marking pens. He even put it back into her mailbox."

"With his fingerprints on it." Marv shook his head. "Does Clair know?"

"She knows he must have been watching her and Jake together, and she knows that when she walked back to the restroom afterwards, with nothing at all on, we fear, she went right by him."

"Poor kid. She did make an impression, though."

"I think she'd rather she hadn't. But sometime I'll give her the guide back, when I feel she'll be able to handle the emotion. It did identify Jake's killer."

"*Che bella*," said Marv. "A tribute to her beauty." He shook his head again. "How did you come by it, anyway? It wasn't the one you found on the floor Wednesday morning?"

"No. Sergi must have found this one and put it in Clair's box. I fetched it out, thinking I'd take it to her. When I opened it, I saw what was written and the adrenalin hit me like a shot. It was when Helen was there and..."

"And then you saw us and, I love you for this even more, you bolted."

"Yes, with an aching heart, Marv. And you were so blithe all the rest of the evening."

"Will you come to Paris with me next month? We can talk about it there."

Ruth smiled at him.

"Good, that's settled," said Marv.

Andy came into the shop at 6:00 as Hal and Sylvie were closing out the sales and Marv and Ruth were turning off lights.

"You've missed all the action," said Sylvie. "Jake's brother was here and he looks just like Jake."

"Wow!" Andy exclaimed. "Imagine another guy like Jake."

"And Detective Willard has come in and taken Sally Ann out to dinner," said Hal.

"No kidding? Going out together? That's great!"

"Where have you been?" Hal added, as if he couldn't tell, seeing Andy loaded down as he was with tin ware, two wooden buckets and a piece of picket fence.

"Sale at a farm. Wait till you see what's still in the truck. Help me carry the stuff in? There's a really neat Victorian screen door, painted white with scrolls and beading, and a porch swing and some shutters and..." Andy had definitely become an antiques dealer.

At last it was only Marv and Ruth. As they stepped outside and Marv locked the door behind them, Ruth looked across at the hills. The angle of the late afternoon sun, shining clear and golden on the ridgeline, gave the illusion of shortening the distance, each tree seeming to stand out, as if the hills were almost close enough to touch. "The end of the day," Ruth observed. It was usually a thought with overtones of melancholy, but not at this moment, not when she was so happy, being with Marv.

"Or the beginning of the evening," said Marv. "And the night? Yet to be determined." But he knew what the night held for them, and the thought of it was still miraculous to him. Not wishing to appear to Ruth quite as absurdly sentimental over her as he felt, he brought himself back to the moment. "Now, however, about this evening: I'm thinking something cold to drink and then dinner."

"Sounds delightful," Ruth agreed. "But don't you have to go home, do something with Helen? Surely she expects you to be there. She didn't come in at all today."

"She has already left for Bucks County. Nor did she feel it necessary to say goodbye to anyone." He said it matter-of-factly, without emotion, but felt again the lack of involvement he'd always had in Helen's decisions. Then he brightened. "I'll go home, but only to make myself presentable for my date tonight."

Ruth, hearing the resignation in his voice when he made the first two statements, saw in a flash what his life had been like and felt even stronger that his life should no longer be like that, not if she could help it. She smiled up at him. "Am I to expect you at my door then, chocolates and flowers in hand?"

"Or anything else you could wish. You've only to ask or, if you don't ask, I'll anticipate it."

"Like Paris?"

"Like Paris."

"Lucky, lucky me." Ruth sighed. "I have come to the right place at the right time."

His voice full of the wonder he felt, he said, "Ah, Ruth, I'm the one who is lucky. And, you know, I never thought I had any luck at all. Then you happened, and my luck changed."

They were quiet a moment, lingering outside in the golden light, not wishing to part just yet, even for less than an hour until they would be together again. Marv looked into the sky, then down at the gravel they stood on.

"And after Paris, Ruth, there's something I want to do, want to ask you. I probably shouldn't say this now, but I feel I must anyway." He paused, took her hand in his and looked imploringly at her. "Will you let me pave the parking lot? I know it's a big step. You don't have to answer right away. Think it over, take your time. I want you to be absolutely sure about it."

Ruth said without hesitation, "I have been thinking about it, Marv, and my answer is 'yes,' but it all rests on one thing."

"And that is?"

"You won't mind having pie for breakfast."

"There I draw the line!" he exclaimed, giving her one of his shocked looks.

She said pleasantly, "Apple pie. Heated. With a slice of cheddar on top. Off of blue and white transferware. Autumn morning. Coffee."

"On second thought—blue and white, you say?"

"But you won't have it only to please me?"

"I will do anything to please you." He put his arms around her, held her close, suddenly serious. "Just love me, Ruth. That's all I want, you loving me."

"And I do, and I will," she promised.

He kissed her lightly and stood back. "Even if I pave the parking lot?"

"Even so."

"I'm looking forward to those autumn mornings."

Epilogue

The letter came the second week in June, addressed to Clair at the shop and postmarked Athens. Someone had put it in her mailbox. Dealers often got postcards and letters from customers or other dealers addressed to them at Cider Run, so it didn't seem particularly unusual. Clair found it there when she came in to work, wondered briefly who was vacationing in Greece and, in the quiet of the morning, opened it, then sat down at the kitchen table.

Bella Signorina,

I write to tell you my regret for what I had to do and am sorry I have given you loss. I would not have done if I could have avoided, but I did not have the choice. Please believe me.

Your friend was not willing to make deal with us and I could not convince him of otherwise. You know he was a quite strong man, and when he hit me with full force because of being angry, I was blacked out. I had not doubt he would come back and finish the job, so I must be sure it did not happen.

The back door I locked so as not to make easy anyone coming by to steal antiquities, but the front door, she could not be locked when I left.

I make apology also for writing in your book, but I was overcome. Ever since I am not able to get you out of my mind, but please be assure, Signorina, I shall not contact you again nor will you ever see me in your country. This I swear.

I hope your life is well. I pray for your happiness always, as I also pray for the soul of your friend.

Addio